STRANDS

STRANDS

S. Elise Peeples

To Marilyn & George,
Thanks for being such
warm & wonderful people
& for being such good neighbors!
Love,
Elise

Eshu House
Publishing
Berkeley, CA

Eshu House

Publishing
Berkeley, CA

This book is fiction. The characters, incidents, and dialogue are drawn from the author's imagination and are not meant to be the true account of anyone living or dead.

Library of Congress Control Number: 2009942139

ISBN: 978-0-9656576-3-1

To my grandmother Harriet for her perseverance in the face of obstacles that would have defeated most people and her patience with me for over twenty years as I wrote this book, and later, for her insistence that I finish. May her life not have been lived in vain and may her outspoken chant in dedication to the voices of women forever resound.

AND

To my mother Ruth, the inspiration for Emma—a character with the flexibility and resilience to take one small step at a time into the unknown, facing her fear and transforming herself—for her generosity in allowing me to use some of the facts of her life as a vehicle for healing Motherliness everywhere. And for her love and support my whole life.

ACKNOWLEDGMENTS

First, I want to thank my husband Adam David Miller for being my first creative writing teacher; for his patience with the many versions of this book; for his unwavering support for my projects, his editing help, and his love.

I am grateful to Donna Wood who provided mentorship and invaluable help with my trip to Ireland and Veronica and Padraig Walsh who rented me an apartment in their house in Spiddal, Ireland where I wrote the first full draft of the book.

Thanks to Mary Berg who was a stalwart supporter from the beginning, Connie Carlson who inspired me from the start and always, and Adrianne Aron, my writing buddy, was a reader of early drafts who helped me shape and hone the project. I thank my dream group (Valerie Kay and Judy Mueller), and the Spiralettes (Viviane, Brigid and Lucy) who gave me encouragement to continue.

My writing group gave me much needed critique and praise: Donna Brenneis, Alicia Orozco, Gail Betty, Susie Dodd and I thank them.

Thank you to the teachers along the way who included Adam David Miller, Kate Braverman and Gail Sher as writing teachers and from the spiritual angle: Elenna Rubin Goodman (founder of the Bay Area Daré), Deena Metzger and Michael Ortiz Hill (who brought the Daré from Africa), Mandaza Kandemwa, (Zimbabwean Elder and Traditional Healer), Dr. Elena Loboda (wisdom keeper of the Veddik tradition in Siberia), James Baraz (Buddhist teacher), and Silvia Nakkach (singer, sound healer and teacher).

For their comments on drafts, I thank: Mary Berg, Meg Withers, Constance Hester, Sue Peeples, Lucy Colvin, Cynthia Waters, Elenna Rubin Goodman, Meredith Stout, Pamela Clarke, and Ruth Peeples.

Without a place to get away from home at various points, I could not have written this book. I thank Linda Cohen, Sue Peeples and Marguerite Pike, Peter Barnes of the Mesa Refuge, and Nicole Milner for the donation of writing space at critical times in the process.

I doubt if I would have taken this book out of the drawer yet, if it were not for Owlsnake (Robbie Wilson), who heard Harriet's pleas from the land of the ancestors and gave me the wake up call to finish the work.

The one evening of a Women's Wisdom Council conceived by Elenna Rubin Goodman that gave me the courage to be present while my mother read this book and that helped turn the looming distraction of a health crisis into an opportunity to deepen us all: Elenna, Pamela, Juli, Siddika, Laura, Alexis, Lacey, Dipti, Karen, Lucy, Brigid, Joya, Elenna, Cynthia, Owlsnake, Katie.

I reserve a special place in my heart for copy editor, Lorri Ungaretti, who took the manuscript of a person she had never met before and engaged with it beyond just the professional into the realm of dedication to the spirit of the book.

Cover design collaboration: Cynthia Waters and Peggy Ho with help from Sarah Kerr.

My grandmother and great-grandmother who came to me on the wind and the rain.

Grandmothers' Council

We are the butterflies around you. We are the ones without words who are transformed and who transform the world. We take the flour, the flowers, the baking soda, the yeast, the air, the water, the earth and fire them up. The world is our kitchen.

We are the grandmothers seeing now with Mother Earth's eyes— our own regrets run like a fast-moving river, but there is no time to drown in it. We can help make you healers and peacemakers if only you will stop and listen.

We want so much for you to experience, for instance, the joy of a luscious apple pie. You have a lovely apple but your vision is so limited, your blinders so severe that you cannot see the poison surrounding it—that it is out of season, shipped from far, far away using petrochemicals to get here, that near-slave labor was used to grow it and pick it and ship it. That the only reason it looks perfect is that it was sprayed with pesticides. Eating the apple is not the sin, but seeing only the flash and dash of face value, is.

We know about face value. Our own faces became wrinkled and dry in our old age and our wisdom in life was dismissed as senility, our heads patted, we were put in old age homes, left to rot.

Squint your eyes now, and pay attention to the edges of your vision. Don't believe so literally in what your deceiving eyes see. Look again, see the invisibles, see us, your ancestors, see the elementals. And above all, listen, listen, listen.

Listen to the stories of the earth, the soil, the water, the air, the farmers, the indigenous ones, the ancient ones. Let yourselves become empty vessels, instruments of peace and healing that the wind plays cosmic music through. Play and listen, play and listen—it is not so hard—you do not have to be right. It is not about you.

And you are all such lovely instruments—we can hear that even when you cannot.

No matter what your face or body looks like—, how old, young, fat, thin, white, colored, male, female, queer, straight, healthy, ill, disabled, able, mentally well, mentally ill—you have been fashioned by your life to be an instrument in the orchestra of the spheres. Do not hide your disabilities, non-conformities, and deformities. They are the very stuff that disqualifies you from the small game, the one we can no longer afford to play, and blesses you with vision to see beyond face value. Come out, come out, wherever you are.

If you think you can run away from us, re-think. Whether your grandmothers came from sea or from land, from Africa, Europe, China, or wherever—or even if you always lived here—we will find you because we are woven into the strands of your DNA.

You imagine yourselves as individuals, making decisions, thinking for yourselves, creating a life. But one thing you have never been is just one thing. You have always been a collaboration among ancestors—from cranky to saintly—a weaving of buried histories, unrequited longings and unfinished stories.

The warp of your lives, the foundation upon which you weave, is a present from the past that only we can know from the inside; only we contain the clues to its textures and tensions—the fear of small spaces or tidal waves, a déjà vu feeling about the particular shape and feel of a hanging valley, the way you laugh when you bounce on the trampoline, or cry when you are angry, the disgust you feel as your teeth grind against shredded coconut in a cookie.

Whatever weft you add now, whatever patterns,

colors and textures you choose—your smiles, frowns, intelligence, kindness, intimidation, or bravado—all of it is warped. The dreams, the songs and stories, the very bloodlines that run through your bodies inform your fingers how to work your particular warp, keeping it free of tangles and tears.

It is time to weave your way. Run away if you want. Just remember: how far you get depends on the strands running through you. Perhaps, instead, you will choose to weave slowly between the elusive strands of past and future, in a spiraling path where the moment is all that matters and all that matters is not you.

THE CARTOON

Cartoon: A drawing or design of a planned tapestry. It may be placed under the warp, used only as a reference during weaving, or traced onto the warp strands. Sometimes the cartoon is only an image in the mind of the weaver.

PART ONE

PATTERNS

Looking at one pattern will often inspire new ideas and variations. The weaver may wish to use only a section of the pattern draft or weft for the design or build upon the one given. It's important to beat the weft evenly so that the pattern will not vary in size throughout the fabric. This will also occur if the tension is not even. Often a different pattern will emerge on the underside.

Chapter 1—The Glimmering: Emma

Some people say that when you're seventy, your life is pretty much over.

August 12, 1996

As I sink into my weaving reverie, my mind goes where it has gone so often in the last two weeks, back to my surprise seventieth birthday party. I finger the threads, drinking in orange and morning sky blue, sending the shuttle rhythmically across and back, across and back.

My mind recreates the conversation at the party with my neighbor Judy and my cousin Diana. "Who's Hallie?" Judy asked me casually, as if I could answer nonchalantly without a buzzing in my head. I could utter no response but my eyes were wide open, frozen.

Diana who had brought the subject up in the first place was quick to reply for me, "Why, she's Emma's biological mother, my aunt. Hasn't she ever told you? It's a fascinating story."

We were standing eating chips and dip at the party. Judy's violet eyes looked from Diana to me and back again, questioning. How many people in these sixty-four years since I had been adopted did I neglect to tell? I barely told my own children and then only after they were teenagers and began asking questions.

Judy looked as though she had just walked into a familiar house where someone had rearranged the furniture and she didn't know where to sit anymore. It's not as if I hide the circumstances of my birth and subsequent life—it's more that I don't think of myself as adopted, don't define myself that way. Hallie was always a stranger to me, a mentally ill stranger, and I wanted as little to do with her as possible. No, I never mentioned it to Judy who has been my best friend since Ralph and I moved to Cedar Hills about seven years ago. There was no reason to mention it.

It's Wednesday morning, more than two weeks since my first-ever surprise party. The party shocked me and seems to have shifted everything. Time has arranged itself to Before Party (BP) or After Party (AP). Strange, I'm doing the same things I've always done—gardening, cooking, cleaning, weaving, a perpetual motion machine. But my life feels wobbly, like a table with uneven legs.

More than once lately, I have found myself sitting empty-handed, shaking my head. The other day, Ralph walked in on me in one of those moments, a worried look on his face and said, "What's wrong with you these days, anyway?" I shrugged, unable to answer him.

When I am planning a weaving—picking out colors and warping the loom—the possibilities seem endless. Hard to say where I go during those times, but I'm not thinking about next week's bake sale, the menus for the week or shopping lists. I engage a side of myself I rarely find useful in other parts of my life. Now I pick out a thick wool for the warp to ground the weaving. Even though it won't be seen when I'm through, its quiet strength informs everything that follows.

At some point in the weaving process, I surrender to forces larger than myself that really control the weaving: the result is always a surprise, and not always pleasing. Inevitably, the finished product startles me.

My life so far, on the other hand, has been predictable. That's the way I like it. But I keep recalling where something seemed to start—the day of the party. As I opened the door to the church hall, all I could see were pinks and reds, open mouths yelling, "Happy Birthday, Emma!" In order to keep myself from turning and running right back out of the door, I focused on the green and yellow crepe paper fluttering frantically from the draft behind us.

My three grown children surrounded me like bodyguards, giggling from having kept the secret too long. As our daughter Lucy pulled me into the room, our oldest Mick furiously snapped pictures. In self-defense, I took a quick inventory of my appearance: pale green pants and shirt that I made myself, with matching tiny globe earrings. Ralph and I had bought them on our Australian vacation five years ago. Our three grandkids seemed to be everywhere, as their parents, Adam and Mary, attempted to quiet them. Ralph grinned like a kid who'd pulled off a string of naughty deeds without getting caught and was now able to confess.

Since I couldn't escape, I just wanted to retreat to a corner somewhere. I had always been sure that hardly anyone would come to a party just for me. But here they all were, 150 of them from all over the country—the world, in fact. My cousin Diana had come all the way from Ireland.

At one point during the party, my daughter Lucy cornered me, "You're always throwing parties for Dad or one of us. We thought it was high time we threw a party for you." Lucy towered over me by a good six inches. She must have gotten that height from my biological father, though since I never met my biological father, I am not sure how tall he was. He died before I was born.

I would much rather the party had been one I arranged on Ralph's behalf. Everybody loves Ralph.

Darn, I'm pulling these strands too tight and the fabric is getting lumpy. Obviously I'm out of the reverie; now I just feel anxious. As I weigh possible changes, I start to breathe faster and my hands feel clammy. I'll have to re-do the last couple of rows.

It is already hot in this room, even though it is only 9:00 in the morning. This Ohio summer has been nothing but humidity—no rain, just muggy days and nights.

After Diana told the world that I had been adopted, Lucy noticed my discomfort and grabbed both Judy's and Diana's hands and pulled them over to the world map hanging on the other end of the hall. "Diana, show us exactly where you live in Ireland. You've come so far!" she said, looking over her shoulder at me and winking. Then the three of them huddled together talking excitedly yet quietly, and I couldn't hear what they were saying.

Both Diana and Lucy seem to be suddenly obsessed with talking about my "real" mother.

Lucy has taken an interest in the family tree, particularly the branch that was practically severed and certainly atrophied after I was adopted. She has shown me pictures and writings from my biological family that she unearthed in her research. At first, her interest simply irritated me—why should she have more interest in it than I have? I wanted her to follow my example and bury it, but Lucy is on the lookout for "meaningful" stories. Sometimes I wish she'd seek social significance in libraries or legislatures and leave my history alone.

And then there was Diana at the party. Every time she saw me she would nudge me and point at the women taking the plates into the kitchen and slip something in like, "If Hallie were here, she would probably insist that the men do the cleaning up of the hall and the women be in the foreground. She shook things up wherever she went." Right, and I never do that and never have, so we've nothing in common, really.

I usually don't think about having been adopted at age six—it's had little to do with the life I've created. From age six until I was in my sixties, I got along just fine without any relationship with Hallie (that's what I called her—never Mom). When Hallie was in her early nineties, she came to live in a convalescent hospital near Ralph and me. But by then her mind was all but gone. She had spotty memory and didn't seem to care about the past or the future. Anyway, she was never a mother to me after I was adopted—just a strange old woman who didn't remember who I was half of the time. Mercifully, she finally died, just shy of her 100th birthday.

"Did you see the picture we made for you, Mom?" Lucy asked, her eyes alive, flashing their green as she pointed to the picture on the wall. "You at six and you now—both in the wicker chair. You're so adorable in both."

I stared at the photos. Taking up the majority of the space in the frame was a recent picture Mick took of me seated in a wicker chair. In the lower right hand corner was a small picture of my six-year-old-self in the same pose, also in a wicker chair. I looked back and forth between the two photographs trying to see similarities. The same person? I wondered. Where is that girl?

"I remember when that early one was taken," I said, thinking out loud. "My sixth birthday—I'm pretty sure I'd just been officially adopted by the Parkers. I was...not exactly happy." I stopped, wondering if I even knew what I was talking about. So many years had gone by. But I remember my stomach hurting and I remember that they promised me butter pecan ice cream if I smiled.

All of a sudden, the white walls of the church hall seemed to glare at me and I smelled dry grass and gasoline. I got so lightheaded I had to sink into the nearest chair. I wrapped my arms around myself remembering how on that day I had started my life over—I was my adopted parents' blank page. Even my last name would be filled in by them.

"A blank page, a blank page..." I must have said it out loud because Lucy bent her head toward me and asked, "What'd you say, Mom?" Then she whispered conspiratorially, "We got your favorite butter pecan ice cream for today."

Lucy's voice reverberated in my head—or had it been another voice from the past?—talking about ice cream. I tried to focus on the party, not on the picture, but the faces there melted together in an unrecognizable blur. I remember blinking and trying to focus several times. Luckily, just then, I glimpsed Adam and Mary helping their children fill their plates at the table. I smiled and waved at them. They're such anchors for me, the perfect family, following in our footsteps. I had always thought having three children was the perfect number, two to replace Ralph and me and one for re-population. Now, after becoming aware of over-population, I think it would have been wiser to have one or two. Lucy and Mick don't seem worried about replacing themselves at all, but I think that's a shame—they would miss out on so much joy. I concentrated on Adam and Mary for a while to get my bearings.

Ralph was holding forth in the corner, rallying his old friends. "All seriousness aside," he proclaimed, his favorite way to introduce a subject.

For more than thirty-five years Ralph had been a minister in the United Church of Christ, a liberal Protestant Church, until he retired just a couple years ago. During those years he had developed a certain charisma—or did he have it before he ever got a platform? I can't remember that far back. He was handsome then, but now he's a magnet, especially for laughter. Sure, now he has lost some of his good looks—his hair is thinning, his body thickening—but he still has those mischievous, laughing eyes that see the humor in everything.

Remembering the party makes my stomach queasy. I need something cold to drink so I jump up to get myself some iced tea. As I pass the kitchen window, I notice plants that are coming early to the end of their season, except, that is, for the dogged dandelions whose determination verges on predetermination. I am too antsy to return to weaving just now and figure I can use this energy in the garden to pick the green beans. I put on sunscreen, my hat and gloves, and head out.

My favorite plants this year are the climber green beans that bloom a bright shade of orange in the spring. Now a moth or beetle is eating them way up high, killing off the top ones. About six feet up they show brown leaves with big ragged holes. Well, we have enough beans to eat, more than enough.

The beans like to hide until they get so big they're inedible. Maybe it's a survival thing. When I discover those overly curved, bulging ones, I leave them on the vine until they turn yellow and then brown, and save them for next year's seeds.

Of course, the choices for beans are few—saved to be a parent, devoured, or left to rot. I can't exactly say I chose to be a mother. It's more that I didn't decide not to. Now my three children are grown and gone, living all over the country. I can't imagine what my life would have been without them.

The sun burns its presence into my back; my straw hat and long-sleeved muslin shirt cannot keep it from penetrating. For many years, I've been wearing my naturally curly hair short. Now it's all gray and getting whiter all the time.

I work quickly to finish the chores, gather my weeding tools and head back up to the house.

For the last couple of years, Lucy has been corresponding with me; she is working on a book about her biological grandmother and she wants my help. Lucy believes that though Hallie was locked up in a mental hospital for thirty-seven years, she never was crazy, but a radical feminist and socialist before her time. I really don't know that much about Hallie except what I was told by people here and there, mostly quite negative things about her immorality and how disagreeable she was all the time. I visited her a few times while she was in the psychiatric hospital and after she got out and was living in a little apartment in Detroit and being semi-cared for by her brother, Danny, and his wife, Claudia. She seemed crazy to me then, and all I felt was distance. I was happy to keep it that way.

And it wouldn't bother me that much, Lucy asking questions about Hallie, but lately she keeps slipping in questions about me, too. Last time she visited, she asked me how I felt about my adopted parents. I remember saying, "They did the best they could; I'm grateful to them."

Lucy had replied, "Yeah, well, I remember the last words Grandma said to me before she died, as I held her hand and leaned in towards her to hear. She pulled her hand back and said coldly, 'Your hands are sweaty.'"

I had said to Lucy in Mother's defense, "Sure she was critical at times, but she was dying and not in her right mind. She could be harsh, but she's the one who gave me what I needed. More than I can say about Hallie. Besides, what's this got to do with Hallie's story?"

I found out then that Lucy's story was not just about Hallie but has expanded to cover four generations of women in our family, starting with Lucy and ending with her great-grandmother, Alice. Quite frankly, my part of it is not all that fascinating. The other kids don't seem to be interested; I can't help wishing Lucy were more like them—willing to leave well enough alone. If you have built a good loamy topsoil, one that holds enough water and drains well, who cares what's under it?

Particularly in the winter and spring, when I approach our house, I can hear the sound of the Grand River, a designated wild river that runs at the bottom of a steep incline right behind our house. Now, with the drought and all of the leaves still on the deciduous trees on the hill, I can't hear the river. Nonetheless, I always listen, just in case. The sound is soothing to my sense of being in the right place.

This house was built with love, I think, standing in the circular driveway looking at the Crab orchard stone house. Ralph's parents built it over a period of five years on the weekends after their children were grown and on their own. They scrimped enough money to buy a piece of land an hour away from their apartment above a bakery on a busy street in Cleveland. In those days, an hour away was thoroughly country. On Fridays, after working all week, they would drive out in their 1940 white Ford sedan and put in whatever work they could, sleeping in the car, or in a tent when weather permitted, and then on Sunday night they'd drive back to the city.

They loved the old cedars and elms and took care to leave all of them standing. The driveway curves around them, making it difficult to clear the snow in the winter but worth the extra trouble. We have to give the paperboy a big tip to get him to deliver the paper to our door. I wouldn't even have a sunny space for a garden if it hadn't been for Dutch Elm disease that spread through one of the groves and left nothing standing. Though we hated to lose the trees, I am thankful that I did not have to decide between cutting them down and having a garden.

Since for most of Ralph's career we lived in parsonages owned by the church, we had to figure out where we would live when he retired. About seven years ago, this Cedar Hill church pulpit came open and we saw it as a perfect opportunity to move into the house that Ralph's parents left us when they died. After he served as the minister here for five years, Ralph retired; by that time, we were already well-settled in the town. Most of the neighborhood has become suburban, but this house stands far back from the road, surrounded by tall cedars, elms and oak, making us feel we are in the wild. And no one can build behind us, not with that steep hill and designated wild river below us.

Every few steps I bend at the knees to grab a weed that has bullied its way through the stones. My neighbors often remark that they're in their forties and can't bend that low. Hallie could bend at the knees and pick something up right up until she broke her hip at age ninety-four. There must be some good things about those genes...

Since the party, the first thing I see as I enter the hallway leading into the living room is that picture of the two me's. "It's OK, Mom," Adam had said, "we can hang it where there is a nail, and I'll adjust it down lower when I get a minute." The picture remains unnaturally high. Since Ralph tends to be a little unsteady on his feet, Adam usually helps us with that kind of thing. But between saving the last remaining old growth forests or some such thing and spending quality time with his three children, Adam doesn't have much time left.

I can't get used to seeing the picture there. It causes my stomach to churn with unwanted emotions. As I approach the picture, I feel myself returning to age six again. The corners of my mouth turn up in empathy with that girl. It was as if that very smile had ruptured something in me, something as delicate as a membrane that connected my inner and my outer. I learned then that a smile could be worn just as deliberately as the pink hair ribbon my new mother had struggled to tie just right. I could be frightened to death and still smile. And the deal I made with myself was that from then on, I would look right and be good. The butter pecan ice cream would be mine, the people around me happy, and I would not be abandoned again.

As I lean closer to the picture, I can almost hear my six-year-old self saying, "OK, here's the deal: you be good and I'll keep you safe." That little dealer! But if she's the dealer, then surely I, at seventy, am the dealt. A good title for the picture: "The Dealer and the Dealt."

Well, then, my whole life has been the fulfillment of the terms of that deal. I've certainly done what was expected: I married, took care of my husband, birthed and raised kids, did volunteer work, was faithful to God, participated in church activities.

But meanwhile where was the dealer? After so many years of virtual silence, all of a sudden she seems to be speaking to me, and butter pecan ice cream won't shut her up. What'll it take this time?

It's hot even in the usually cool living room so I switch on the overhead fan. We don't have air-conditioning, but with the trees and the system of fans we installed, it's usually quite comfortable even in the worst heat. Slipping off my shoes, I sit down in my favorite rocking chair, prop up my callused bare feet on the wooden rocking footstool that Ralph made, and begin sorting yesterday's mail.

A bill from Presbyterian Life Insurance reminds me of Sam who was an associate minister in the Presbyterian Church in the last town we lived in. One day, he left his wife and his job to go and find himself. Back then, I was the first to scoff—as if leaving his family would give him answers. We lost track of him long ago, never knowing if he'd found his answers. I shake my head in disgust at a man who could do such a thing to his family.

No matter how hard I try to finish the mail, I can't seem to stay awake. Maybe I'll just let my eyelids shut out the light. I can't stop thinking about deal, dealer, duty... and wondering whatever happened to Sam. I drift off to sleep to the sound of the fan making a hypnotic whoop, whoop, whoop sound.

I am at my birthday party. When I speak, no one can hear me and they look away. For a while I smile and listen, but the people are talking about things that don't interest me, like baseball scores and television shows. When I try to change topics, I am ignored. Gradually people begin speaking a different language, one I've never heard before with hard gs and guttural rs I can't understand a word.

Frightened, I run out into the wilds and feel cold; I look down and see that I am naked. My bare feet slip into a large puddle and I get drenched. The more I run, the more certain I am of my destination. I stop running at a cabin situated just at the edge of a field that goes up and down rockily to the ocean.

Inside is a huge loom, even larger than my largest one housed in our garage. I look at the wool set up on the loom, all shades of green, blue and gray coming together at odd angles to make a landscape. I sit down and begin to weave; the rhythm of the treadles is a language I understand.

The rhythm joins with the sound of the fan, and eventually I realize I am awake.

My first thought as I awaken is of my cousin Diana's offer. At my party Diana said, "Hey, lady, there's a weaving class that might interest you in October in the West of Ireland, near Galway. It's run by an international group called the Peace Weavers; they teach weaving and conflict resolution skills. Sounded like it would be right up your alley."

Diana continued, "Come on the money Father gave you when he died. He'd approve—always loved the way you saved your pennies for travel, a real Kaufmann trait." Diana's father, Danny, was Hallie's brother, my uncle. He and his wife, Claudia, had been kind to me for as long as I could remember. He was very successful in the stock market and when he died, I'd received some money from him. I have to admit that even though I wanted to bury the past, there was a part of me that hoped for a larger inheritance—we had always been poor in comparison to him. Was I related to him or not? Or just the perpetuation of a bad seed? In a way this token money left me in doubt. I was an afterthought, a mistake that would never be fully forgotten nor fully claimed—somewhere in between where dreams and reality cannot be pried apart.

Uncle Danny, having grown up with Hallie, was one of the few people who really knew her. Lucy told me that when she interviewed him, he had started to cry, shaking his head regretfully and saying, "She was brilliant. I loved her dearly and looked up to her. But she threatened to kill our mother—we *had* to take that seriously."

Diana had added, "Treat me nice and I'll even give you an introduction to Irish lore and help you find decent accommodations."

I replied noncommittally, saying, "I'll let you know." I haven't mentioned it to Ralph because I've never really given it a second thought. For one thing, I can't imagine what Ralph would do there all that time. In the dream, I was alone in that Irish landscape.

I remember traveling to Ireland with the kids when they were teenagers. I was determined to have six weeks in the British Isles and Europe, but Ralph could get only four weeks off for vacation. So, for the first two weeks in England and Ireland, we were without Ralph. I wondered if I could manage alone. We had to camp; there was no other way on our budget, and even then we could eat out only once a week.

I must have had *some* gumption back then. We had rented a car, hopped in and I began driving on the left side of the road. I can't imagine how I had the courage to do that without Ralph. The memory is embarrassing. Who did I think I was? I feel heat flooding my cheeks to dare think of going far away alone. Still there is an attraction, a thrill to the memory of having done it before—a feeling of self-reliance.

The doorbell's sharp suddenly dissonant chimes startle the wits out of me. My first unguarded thought is that it is Hallie at the door. I must be going out of my mind—Hallie's been dead for years now. Still, my heart is pounding and all I can think about is what my adopted mother used say, "Try that again, you willful child, and I'll send you back to Hallie." I'm seventy years old, for crying out loud—these memories cannot still hurt me. And yet here I sit trembling, afraid to answer the door.

But I have to answer the door. What will this visitor think if I don't? I am a friendly person who always welcomes guests. I force myself to get up and answer the door.

I am so relieved to see Judy there. Normal-looking, reasonably-acting Judy, my neighbor who's been the church secretary for the last twenty years. We became fairly close when she worked with Ralph before he retired. She knows the gossip of the church and often gave us the heads up to problems that may have been brewing.

Judy barely looks at me, glancing beyond me into the house. "Oh, I hoped I'd catch the reverend. I've got a question about his part in the service on Sunday." Though Ralph retired two years ago, Judy still calls him "the reverend" or "Reverend Ralph."

Then she finally looks at me and says, "Oh, honey, what's wrong with you? You look like you've seen the devil himself!" She puts her arm around me and leads me back to my chair. I sit down, put my feet up and begin to breathe normally again.

"I'm just feeling unsettled these days, like I've got to get out of here for a while."

Judy looks puzzled. "What do you mean 'out of here'? We could take a walk if that's what you want."

"No," I insist, "out of this life." That's it, I think. I've been living a lie."

"Can I get you something to drink? You're not sounding very well. Do we need to call the doctor or something?"

I sigh. "No, no, I'm fine. You caught me at a bad time. I just need a minute to rearrange my thoughts."

I hear myself continue, "Well, I haven't mentioned this to Ralph so..."

She pats my leg, then puts her hand over her mouth and says, "Mum's the word."

I hesitate, worrying—I haven't thought it out yet. In fact, it feels rushed, as if it is being forced out prematurely.

Finally, I manage to slow it a little. "Listen, do you want some tea or coffee?"

She shakes her head. "Can't stay that long—got to finish the bulletin. But now I'm curious."

I take a deep breath and, looking away from Judy, out towards the garden, I begin, "When Diana was here—you know, my cousin from Ireland—she mentioned a month-long weaving class in Ireland. Sounded interesting but I couldn't figure out what Ralph would do there, so I put it out of my head. Wouldn't dream of going somewhere without Ralph..." I catch myself on that phrase and am somewhat startled by it. Then I add, "Actually, I *did* just dream it." I look far away out the window and beyond the horizon, not at anything in particular, trying to make out the details of some future I can barely imagine.

When I finally look at Judy, she is leaning forward in her chair studying me. "Sounds like a great opportunity to me. Ralph'll be fine right here, playing pool every day." Ralph and his men friends in the community, many of whom are retired, meet every weekday afternoon in the basement of the church where there is a pool table. It makes them feel like bad boys—as if they are doing something immoral, hanging out down at the pool hall, telling men-only jokes. Judy continues, "How long did you say you'd be there?"

"A month," I wince at the sound of an eternity. "That's a long time, isn't it?"

Judy chuckles. "Look, at our age a month goes by in less time than it takes a cat to nap. Come to think of it, sometimes I do nap that long. Ask Ralph. See what he thinks."

I hesitate. "Actually I wanted to have it thought out first so I could tell him—not ask him. I'm sure he'd rather I stay put."

"Hmm," Judy says, thinking it over. "Well, maybe he'd come along—never know."

Judy isn't getting the picture. "But he doesn't get along with Diana. And what would he do while I'm in class? Besides..."

"Besides what?" Judy asks, looking at me intensely, eyes widening to take all this in. Again, I can't hold her gaze.

"Oh, now I get it; you *want* to go alone, right?" She leans forward again, wanting to hear the rest of the story.

I busily pick the shriveled flowers and yellowing leaves off of the African violet sitting on the end table beside me. "Remember, I told you about the time I took the kids to Ireland without Ralph? Don't get me wrong, I was scared, but something happened then. I've treasured that time...being without him, I mean, having to be the responsible one and succeeding at it."

I stop myself. Judy's husband was killed in a car accident four years ago. She surprises me, "I know just what you mean. It's called independence—being your own person. Since Ted died, I've been able to listen to music I want to hear, cook food I want to eat and clean up when I'm tired of the dirt." She leans back in the chair and looks up at the ceiling. "It's been a relief at times."

I can feel tears starting in my eyes and I look up at her tentatively, "But Ralph's not dead. His feelings would be hurt."

Judy's usually white and relaxed face starts to pinken and get tense. "Why should you have to wait 'til somebody kicks off before you can start to live? It's not fair. Women waste years living for other people. Don't pass this up. Ralph will be here when you get back."

Judy shifts back to upright and bounces out of the chair, "Got to run. Let me know if I can do anything—see you in church." She hugs me tightly, forcing the air out of me and then leaves behind a cloud of gardenia perfume. I gasp, barely able to get enough oxygen back into my lungs. Oblivious to my distress, Judy makes her way out the door throwing a reassuring look over her shoulder.

Ralph is still over at Dave's, probably watching a game on the big screen TV. He'll be home for lunch, but it's only about 11:00 now. I slip back into my weaving room to think things through. The weave on this sampler I've been working on is just too tight. I'll start over, this time using greens, blues and grays, like the shades in the dream.

As I work, I find myself wanting to call Lucy. I wonder if I could catch her before she goes to work. It's three hours earlier in California. I'm sure she'll be supportive of my trip. I could use some of that right now.

Chapter 2—The Between: Lucy

Nature or nurture? What if there is simply no way to ever separate them and say here is one and here is the other? The answer lies in the place where nature and nurture overlap.

August 12, 1996

Just as I am getting ready to leave for work, my mother calls."Hey, Mom, how are you—everything OK?" I say in my sunniest voice that belies all that is going on with me. I woke up with a blaring headache, one of many I've had lately.

Before I can catch up with her, she is off on a tale of a trip she may take to Ireland without Dad. Oh, my God. All I can think is that she is going to ruin her marriage after all these years. My bad luck with relationships is contagious. I must have contaminated her through the mail with those damned letters. She's always been so strong. A rock, really.

I shudder, feeling suddenly nauseated. "Mom, wait a minute, have you thought this out? Does this have anything to do with my research and the letters?" I pause for a breath, unable to think straight. There is silence on the other end. Tentatively I say, "All that must be unsettling, right?"

Not the response she is looking for. "You sound like I expect your father will—I am finally acting independently, can't you recognize that?"

I reply, "Maybe you should think it over some more, before you decide anything drastic?"

"I've been thinking, that's mostly what I do. Now I feel like taking action." She abruptly hangs up the phone.

I rub my forehead hard until it turns red; I know there are acupressure points here somewhere that could help this pain. I wobble through the bedroom to the bathroom to get some aspirin. She hasn't told Dad yet, so maybe it's not too late for her to forget about the whole thing.

I know I have to call my mother back, be supportive, but who am I to say a word about marriage or how to keep a relationship? My only marriage to Kent, a perfectly lovely man, though deeply damaged by Vietnam, ended in divorce after three years. I wasn't ready for a divorce; we hadn't fought or tried to work it out. Kent just said he couldn't go on letting a woman take care of him so that he could continue to avoid dealing with the fallout from Vietnam. He could never talk to me about it—couldn't talk to anyone who hadn't been there or so he said. So when he took off, I was left with a lot of love and nowhere to put it.

After a period of dating men whose flaws always outweighed their virtues, I fell in love with a woman. I believed all of my worries about relationships had ended. Terry was perfect for me. I felt almost as though I had fallen in love with all things female, including myself. I had never been happier. So I think, oh, I'm gay, that's why none of the other relationships have turned out right. I'm thirty-seven years old—you'd think I would have this worked out by now. But I don't.

My cat Mancha comes over to be petted and that can only mean one thing—I almost forgot to give him his breakfast. He is so black sometimes he looks maroon. I got him after the divorce. He knows what he is here for—to receive my love, but also to make sure I don't get hurt again. He is very protective. In general he does not tolerate men at all, won't give them the time of day. He let me down with this Terry thing, though, since he liked her just fine. Oh, God, so did I.

I just can't seem to stop crying over this break-up and my headache rears up again and bites me behind the eyes. I'll put some ice on it. And I have to call my mother back and get it right.

She's going to Ireland for what reason? Did I hear her say she wants to find herself? I stirred this up by asking her a lot of questions about her past. It was so hard at first to get anything out of her because she would just say she didn't remember. I can't imagine how one could forget so much of one's own life. I mean, where was she? What was she thinking about? I have to say, though, I am fascinated by my grandmother Hallie's story. I found out recently in some of my research that she was probably either a lesbian or bisexual. That was after I fell in love with Terry. I just hope I don't turn out to be schizophrenic like Hallie, though I highly doubt that's what she was, just because they diagnosed her as such. What did they know then about a woman as unconventional as she was? For that matter, what do they know now?

A weaving workshop my mother said. That part sounds good. And something about learning conflict resolution through art. I have been a mediator myself for a number of years now, learned it as a counter-balance to working in law firms as a paralegal. I couldn't stomach the contentiousness. As a philosopher, I am interested in how consciousness changes. Can we help it along, become agents of evolution, or do we have to just wait and wait and be sorry and regretful when thousands more die needlessly in wars?

My mother and I are drawn to many of the same subjects, though we come at them from much different places. Religion is a big stickler between us. She is set on Christianity and I have turned away from most of its dogmas. I adopted many of the important values that my parents taught me, incorporated them into my life—minus the myth that seems to me, well, like myth. To give them credit, they have been in a very liberal branch of the Christian church. I just can't get over what is done in Christ's name nor can I ignore the patriarchal nature of Christianity.

For a number of years I considered myself a humanist but I wasn't all that happy with that philosophy either. The people often seemed a bloodless lot believing that reason was supreme. For me humanism was too much like Western philosophy, lacking in the acknowledgment of the great mystery. Something basic to humanity seemed to be missing. While working on my Master's degree in philosophy a while back, I came across the idea that in Western philosophy reason is linked with men. Men, mind, rationality were all in one half, the top half of a dualism that defined itself against the other half: women, body and emotions. In my Master's thesis I theorized that love, creativity, resolutions to conflicts, medicine and many other essentials all exist in a place I named The Between.

When I explained this philosophy to my mother, she said, "you talk of mind and body, but where's the spirit?" I would answer that spirit is in our connections. It's the feeling I have when I'm in the forest and looking at the trees and birds and feeling a part of it all, my skin connecting me as well as separating me. That is, for me, a spiritual experience.

In some ways that philosophy has become my religion, looking for and accessing the Between. If there is a God in this schema, then connection is it.

Speaking of religion, I wonder how my mother will fare in a Catholic country, especially with the disdain she feels for the worship of the Virgin Mary. She has some vendetta against Mary—well not against her per se, but against giving her too much credit for being the bearer of Christ. A while back, I was reading my journal from when I was thirteen and I found a description of a conversation with my mother who ranted about "those Catholics." "She was just a woman," my mother said. I thought she hated women and that included both of us. It was quite confusing.

Though I have embraced feminism in the past, I'm not sure I got it emotionally, or this affair with Terry wouldn't have hit me so hard. I must have been unconsciously holding onto a disdain for women, including myself, that my mother passed along and through a means as emotional as falling in love I headed entirely the other way. I don't know where this is all leading, if I am a lesbian or not, but I certainly want to find a way to give women our due. Women's voices have been silenced for many centuries and this silence is still not questioned with any regularity or in the revolutionary way required to actually change things.

All those male philosophers for centuries piled one mistake on top of another to reach the untenable place we are in now. "I think, therefore I am." What? How about, I was born of woman, therefore I am—you old male joker! Ever think of that? Andrea Nye, an Australian philosopher I have a lot of respect for, asserted that all of those amazing systems of logic in Western philosophy were designed to keep emotion out of rational thought; but at their core, they are based on one major human emotion, fear!

Thank goodness I don't get a lot of morning sun in this little apartment to worsen this headache. Afternoon sun, yes, and hopefully by afternoon I'll be better able to handle brightness. It's not easy to find an affordable one-bedroom apartment in Berkeley, especially this close to BART. It's a perfect location. The owners of the house turned their upstairs into three small apartments. Mine is the one farthest from the street, with a Japanese garden on one side and the backyard on the other. It was hand-delivered to me by the former tenant, a friend of mine. I love the smell of the night-blooming jasmine that hugs the stairway railing.

When the aspirin and ice begin to calm the headache, I call work and tell them I'll be late and then call my mother to retract my initial negativity.

She says, "Maybe you can come along with me to Ireland, Lucy?"

"No, Mom, I can't run away from my life just now. I'm working on two books now, one fiction and one nonfiction. And that's in addition to my job at the court. No, it's not a good time for a vacation." I don't mention my screwed up social life to her. Maybe some other day I'll tell her about that.

At work later in the morning, I am feeling better. My eyes are still puffy and red from all the crying I've been doing; it's beginning to seem that this is just the way I look. I must be allergic to tears because when I cry, my eyes become electric green, and the whites as well as the skin around my eyes turn red. I look like Christmas in meltdown.

Our office is in the basement of the courthouse, so there are no windows; the limited space is divided into cubicles with four-feet walls that attempt to give us privacy but, frankly, we can hear just about everything that's said in the office. Our job is to protect the rights of old people who are being put under conservatorship where someone else will be in charge of certain parts of their lives. Our office arrangement is not the best, but we figure it directly reflects how much respect is held for the work we do. We should feel blessed, though, I guess, because most states don't even have such an office in place to protect old peoples' rights.

My best friend in the office, Amy, comes into my cubicle. "You don't look too good. How's the head?"

"Fine, I'm fine." My eyes start to water again as I look at Amy's compassionate face. She knows all about what I've been through and offers me a dear and solid shoulder to lean on.

"How about we talk business—get your mind off other things, yes?"

I nod, taking a deep breath to steady myself.

"I've got this case, Mattie Meyer. She is fighting conservatorship by her daughter who lives up in Santa Rosa."

Court investigators make sure people know their rights because, once in place, a conservatorship of the person takes away their rights to decide where to live, how to handle personal needs, and often what medical decisions to make. Conservatorships of the estate take away people's rights to control their own assets. If, in our report to the Court, we say that the proposed conservatee opposes the conservatorship, legal counsel is appointed.

Amy shifts her considerable weight around in the chair to find comfort. "My knees are killing me again."

Amy has tried every diet known to womankind to get rid of her excess weight. But even if they worked, the fix was only temporary. She has stopped trying since the yo-yo part of dieting is supposed to be worse for your health than the weight alone.

I look at her sympathetically and ask, "Anything I can do?"

She shakes her head helplessly, shaking off the suggestion that there is anything anyone can do and continues, "Like I was saying—one, Mattie doesn't feel she needs conservatorship and two, she doesn't want her daughter to do it. Seems they have religious differences. Mattie is a Wiccan of the first order— the daughter alleges that she has full moon ceremonies at her house and other out-of-the-mainstream sorts of things. Mattie has also supposedly changed her will to leave all her worldly goods to Greenpeace. Seems she loves whales. This, of course, is royally pissing off the daughter, as you might imagine."

We both chuckle, knowing how often the controlling factor in these cases is not what is best for the old person but what is going to happen to the estate.

One good thing about being a court investigator is that we have the opportunity to learn all sorts of esoteric and varied information because people themselves are so diverse in their interests and lives.

"What do you know about the Wiccan religion that might help?" Amy asks me.

I think for a moment. "It's goddess worship, the goddess being the earth herself, the womb from which all things grow. The goddess has the power of life and death, right? She is the body and the body is considered sacred."

When Amy and I talk about subjects such as this one, we don't argue, we just throw in what we know or suspect to be true and follow where that leads us. Our discussion ranges from the mundane to the sacred, from the philosophical to the scientific to the spiritual. For now, we talk about the worship of nature and the seasons, how the full moon ceremony is one of the rituals marking time passages along with the solstices and the equinoxes, as well as May Day and Halloween.

I had read Starhawk and various other authors in this vein when I was writing my book. Now it occurs to me that goddess worship might be just what I was doing with Terry. Maybe it wasn't about Terry at all, but about the larger context of learning to value the female and the body. If I could believe that spin on it, maybe I could move on from Terry and instead feel the larger implications.

Now I'm curious about the case. "We do have freedom of religion in this country, even if one is old. Isn't that so?"

Amy narrows her eyes conspiratorially. This was just the bait she needed to get me interested in the case. "Want to go with me to see her? You could pick me up at the top of the stairs so I don't have to walk that long hall to the garage."

We arrive at Mattie's house a few minutes after our appointment time of 11:00 a.m. The house sits atop a series of stairs in the Berkeley hills. It looks as if she has lived there for decades; the stairs are in bad repair, as is the house. I can see that someone interesting lives here just by her choice of color for the door—a fire-engine red with trim painted with white stars and moons.

Amy takes one look at the stairs and hands the case to me. "I'll wait in the car. You can swap me a case—any one you want. I'll owe you one."

When I first knock, I hear no movement and wonder if she is still asleep. But presently I see her pull the curtain aside, decide I am OK, and begin to open a series of locks.

She is a bent-over 85 year old with long white hair laced with yellowing hues pulled into a ponytail. After introductions, she leads me through the house, which is neat enough, though it looks as if a thorough cleaning might be in order. It smells musty with a touch of vanilla, as if she were just burning a scented candle.

On the patio in back, Mattie has every kind of plant imaginable. The smells out there are so varied, I can't make out a distinct one. As I brush by some mint, the smell emerges from the crowd to greet me. She tells me she has been an herbalist for fifty years and points out the medicinal herbs of sage, mugwort, echinacea, borage, calendula and comfrey.

"In fact, I was in the middle of a conversation with rosemary when you arrived."

I saw no one when we came through the house. On the patio there are nothing but plants. "Who's Rosemary?"

"There in the corner." She points to a flourishing rosemary plant with lots of small blue flowers. "She was telling me to burn some when you came. You need some help with ancestral memory. Isn't that so?" Mattie folds her hands over her chest and looks at me authoritatively.

"Well," I say, surprised. "I am not even the investigator assigned to your case. That would be my friend who is sitting in the car because she has bad knees and can't make the stairs."

"That's not rosemary's problem—*you're* here, aren't you? And you *do* have ancestral issues?" The way she said issues sounded more like "isus" with an "s" instead of the usual "sh" sound.

I look intently at her, noticing her yellowish cat eyes. "I like to keep my personal issues out of the interviews. I'm here to interview you, Mattie."

Mattie rolled her eyes and looked conspiratorially at the rosemary. "Look here, have you ever heard of the saying 'healer, heal thyself'? Of course, you have," she says, moving on without taking a breath. "Well, I'm not talking about that. I'm saying that it may look like I am the one who needs help around here, and that you are here to help me but as a healer myself, I have found that some of my best healing for others heals me as well. Know what I mean?"

She's making a lot of sense to me, and I can feel my resistance melting. I say, "Oh, you mean that the healer and the healed are not separable—that one becomes the other and they hand it off back and forth?"

"That's just right, isn't it rosemary?" She says as she picks some dead branches off the rosemary, presumably so that it can hear better.

I turn to the plant, half-expecting an answer, then quickly recover. "I'm actually writing a book just now on that very subject—well, not exactly that, but it is a good example of my philosophy applied to medicine."

Mattie's eyes light up. "Oh, you're a philosopher! I don't think I've ever met a woman philosopher before. So what is your philosophy?

I pause, wondering if I should get into this with her now. I usually keep myself out of the picture when I do my interviews. Maybe a little explanation wouldn't hurt since she does seem interested.

"I call it the philosophy of the Between. Healing could be an example. Picture two side-by-side circles that overlap in the middle. Then imagine one of the circles is the healer and the other is the wounded. The place where the circles overlap is what I call the Between."

I take my notes and draw the two circles so that she can follow me. "So from my perspective, this overlapping space, this Between, is where healing actually happens. And if you think of mind and body this way, too, you'll see that they are inextricably linked and have great mutual influence. Healing takes place there." I point to the Between.

Mattie traces the circles with her gnarled finger, disfigured by arthritis. "So you're saying the healing is in the connection between healer and healed, between mind and body, right?"

I smile and nod. "That's it. In most Western medicine, there is no recognition of a connection, and doctors are put in a superior position over the patient. The way it would look in the Between model is that healer and healed would be peers with energy and information moving both ways in that place where they are connected, a kind of healing flow, more liquid than solid."

"And that's where the power of healing lives," Mattie adds, practically whispering. "But Western medicine pretends this space does not exist and therefore doesn't have access to that kind of healing. That would explain a lot." She pauses, reflecting. "But you are not just talking about medicine, are you?"

"No, but unfortunately I can't get into all of that today. Maybe we can talk another day. Or I'll bring you something I've written."

As Mattie and I talk, I feel is as if I have stepped outside of time to find a kindred soul on that patio in the Berkeley hills. We finally return to the question the rosemary raised as Mattie turns to me and very gently asks, "Would you mind if I burned some rosemary now, just in case it is you who needs it?"

What can I do? I have obviously lost all objectivity in this interview anyway and, in my philosophy, which does not coincide with the court's, there is no such thing as objectivity. I acquiesce to her suggestion.

The rosemary gives off a pungent bitter smell, not unpleasant. She takes a feather and wafts the smoke in my direction. This is not going in my report, I think to myself.

Mattie says, "What's that you say?" I have not spoken. She is talking to the rosemary again. "Oh, she needs to take some home and burn it daily for a while." She turns back to me, "I'll give you a cutting."

"No, really, I am not allowed to take anything from an interviewee—*that* could get me in real trouble. My landlord has some rosemary growing in the yard. Will that do?"

She nods excitedly. "I suggest you burn it before you sleep and then maybe sleep with some under your pillow. That way your dreams can help put you in touch with these ancestors wishing to connect."

Though I would love to stay and discuss my book, I know Amy is waiting in the car. I ask Mattie the orientation questions, which she answers correctly. She opposes the conservatorship. She won't move into a home with no land, no plants and no memories.

However, her grasp of finances and math is tenuous at best and on the kitchen table I notice several envelopes stamped in red with LAST NOTICE. This time, as I walk through the house, I can smell a kind of sour smell, somewhat akin to rotting vegetables. I see in the corner that she is drying some of her herbs and wonder if that is the source of the smell.

I ask Mattie to walk me to the car to make sure she is able to handle the stairs. She practically skips down them, and I deliberately watch her go back up. She manages the forty-seven steps without once resting. I'll have to study the accounting to see if the repair work on the steps and the house can be done without taking drastic measures—like removing her from the house. She is someone I would like to see die in her sleep, in her own bed, in the house of her rosemary and her memories.

I get into the car chuckling and shaking my head. "Couldn't have worked out better. It's mother/daughter stuff at its best. Right up my alley." Amy just smiles, not remarking on my change in demeanor since I walked into the office this morning.

In spite of my interest, I don't need another case to work on, especially one that may be complicated. I'm giving a talk at the court investigator's conference up in Grass Valley next weekend and I still have research to do. Amy and I plan to do some sightseeing on the way up. We need every opportunity to supplement our seriously-draining jobs with the lighter side of life. On the way home that evening, I note that I have gone the whole day without crying.

When I get home, the message light on my answering machine is blinking. It is Ann. "Just wanted to see how you are doing. Maybe you could call me back?"

Ann had been one of my best friends and I hers. We met when we were both paralegals working in the same law firm. She still works in a law firm and puts in more overtime than any other person I know. But she also gathers comp time and whenever she can, adds it to her vacation and travels somewhere exotic. She just returned from a sailing trip that began as an around-the-world trip but she got tired after a while and came home early.

When Ann left on her sailing trip, she and Terry were lovers. After introducing me to Terry and before she left, Ann said, "Take care of Terry for me, OK? She's going to need a friend, especially after I break up with her after the trip. She's just too butch for me." Ann was very much in the closet at her job and in other arenas as well. And since we all thought I was straight, it wasn't supposed to get complicated.

I walk over to the stereo and, in spite of my resolve not to, I put on the "Best of Emilou Harris" and begin thinking of Terry's slight build, dishwater blond hair and big hazel eyes. Her sense of humor made it easy to get along with her. If only we had just stayed friends. But I look back and wonder who I was with her. She liked golf so I started golfing, hardly my first choice of a sport. But I had no real talent for golf and, of course, it would have required real effort and practice for me to get better. But what I really wanted was to practice being with Terry, so I did whatever it took to be near her. Is that love? No, it was probably infatuation, but it felt as big as anything I've encountered in my life. It took me over and inhabited my every moment.

My biggest regret is that conversation we had one evening over drinks after hitting a bucket of balls. This was after we had made love several times. In that conversation, she said the fatal line, "I think I'm falling in love with you."

If she hadn't said that, I wouldn't have let myself fall so far in love or in infatuation or wherever the hell I fell. The whole thing would have gone differently if that one simple line should never have been uttered. But as it was, I let my guard down, let my soft inner self out. I even told Amy in the middle of this summer of love that I knew I was running toward a cliff and I just continued to run. Damned if I didn't jump over without any armor.

When Ann hit land, she was in San Diego. She called and asked Terry to meet her there. Terry reassured me, "It's over between us, but I'll meet her this one last time for old times' sake. I stayed home and bit my fingernails, though I was confident that Terry would tell Ann she was in love with me and come home to me, and then Ann and I would resume our friendship. Three weeks ago today, I got a fateful call from Ann, not from Terry.

"Thanks for taking good care of my sweetee, Lucy. We're back together and will be coming home this weekend." Had Terry even mentioned me at all? Of course she had and that's why Ann was calling. Terry couldn't do it. I don't remember what I said. I was in shock.

"Making believe that she still loves me…" is blaring out from the stereo. Yes, and I am still making believe. I'm mad at Ann, not Terry. I wish I could get mad at Terry, the little chicken. So again Ann is leaving me a message. Well, I'm not here.

At least I have enough wherewithal to go out and cut some rosemary, put it in an ashtray and burn it. I watch the smoke drift out the window that is always open enough for Mancha to get in and out. The smoke seeks the spaciousness of the outdoors. Suddenly, the apartment seems too small for me and, in fact, this skin seems too small for this strange energy I feel jumping erratically through my body. I hope I haven't picked up some strange illness—it's not a good time to get sick. I fix myself some chamomile tea and finally fall asleep.

Chapter 3— Migration: Emma

How do birds know it's time to get out of Dodge? You think it's in their DNA strands, encoded there for thousands of years. Instinct you call it. But maybe birds are guided by their ancestors. Maybe their ancestors are still speaking and they are still listening. In the DNA or in chirps from the hereafter? Who can say?

August 12, 1996

Talking to Lucy a few minutes ago disturbed me more than it helped. She seems to feel responsible for my sudden changes and regrets starting an avalanche. I've noticed sometimes catalyst people are like that—they start a chain reaction or a series of events that mostly affect other people and then they panic at the result. But I don't view Lucy as a catalyst this time. I see her more as a witness. I claim full responsibility. It's not as if I am asking for a divorce or even a separation. It's a vacation—that's it—a working vacation at that. Modern married people take separate vacations all the time.

When Lucy called back and tried to smother the doubts that had sprouted in our first conversation, I was reminded of those lawyer shows on TV where the lawyer blurts out his theory of the case without substantiation and the other lawyer objects. While the blurting is not allowed on the record, it is certainly in the heads of the jurors. So, now I'm supposed to disregard that first conversation.

I see myself in her—bad reaction to shocking news but later we come around. Odd to think of Lucy as similar to me even in minor ways. It seems to me as if Lucy should have been born to someone else. When she was growing up, she spent most of her time with her older brother Mick. Sometimes I can't even remember raising her. She always had big ideas about what she wanted to accomplish and she has, for the most part, become what she aspired to be.

My dreams were nebulous. It's certainly easier to say what Lucy is than to say what I am—non-practicing social worker? minister's wife? cook and bottle washer? mother? who knows?

It's lunchtime, and Ralph will be here soon. I have decided to follow Lucy's advice and wait a day or two to tell Ralph. The dream of Ireland keeps coming back to me. I had felt so misunderstood until I got to the cabin with the loom in it. I don't believe in dreams as predictors or advice-givers—not like Lucy—but I am giving Ireland some serious thought.

As the heat penetrates the house, I put lots of ice into the glasses before pouring in the last of the iced tea. Automatically, I start a new batch, a never-ending summertime task. The table on the screened-in porch off the kitchen is surrounded on three sides by cedars, oaks and elms. It's a little more work to carry things out there, but to eat in that glorious place is worth every extra step. This outdoor smell of life is one of the reasons I like camping so much. It's hard to describe the scent, but it smells like my original home, although I don't know what I mean by that. Many of my friends can't imagine why I love camping so much and I can't explain that, either.

I slice wet, pulpy orange tomatoes and burpless cucumber from the garden, set out the baby Swiss cheese, ham, fresh homemade whole wheat bread, peanut butter, and applesauce.

"You got a letter from Lucy and I got nothing but junk," says Ralph as he comes in for lunch, tossing the mail on the kitchen table.

"Good, I'll read it later," I say, trying to suppress my desire to grab the letter and run out of the room with it. Though I'm scared by what Lucy might uncover about my biological family, I have to admit that the project intrigues me. Maybe Lucy will find out something that makes her happy instead of restless. If she would just marry and have children herself, maybe she would lose that angst. But to Lucy such a life is too mundane. Whenever I get a letter, I am ambivalent about opening it. Maybe Lucy has uncovered something ugly; maybe she discovered something that will make her old mom's life seem more exotic.

I direct Ralph to the lunch waiting out on the porch, and he plops his 210 pounds down in his usual spot. He pauses for a long, deep drink of iced tea.

"Talked to Phyllis this morning," Ralph says reaching for the cheese.

"Phyllis Stuart?" I cringe at the subject but try to project a positive, unbiased interest. Her name never fails to get a rise out of me. "It's been a while—what's she up to?"

"Do we have any catsup? Be good on the cheese." I go to the fridge to retrieve the catsup, a condiment I find distasteful. I often forget to put it out on the table even though I know Ralph will ask for it—a bit of rebellion on my part. Some rebellion! *I* am still the one who ends up making the extra trip to the fridge.

Ralph looks at the food on the table as if it is prey that he needs to hunt. He gets a kind of lustful look on his face, afraid if he chooses one thing, he might have to forgo another. He wants it all.

"She lost her job at the halfway house," Ralph says, his mouth half full of crackers. "That means she's got no place to live—that was a live-in job. Funds got cut. Somebody believed having people like Phyllis around spoiled the inmates. It's the get-tough-on-crime thing." Ralph pats the bottom of the catsup bottle over his ham, cheese and tomato sandwich.

"Did she say what she'll do?" I ask warily. This woman follows Ralph around like a puppy dog. She never seems to have any other friends. She is probably in love with Ralph, not that he has any feelings for her other than whatever he gets out of her flattery. When we moved here to Northeastern Ohio, Phyllis was a two-hour's drive away, and I thought that would be the end of that.

I take a bite of tomato. "Oh, that's sour. Maybe I left it on the vine too long."

Ralph ignores me and continues talking about Phyllis. "No, it just happened—she hasn't thought what to do yet."

"I'll bet she's thinking of moving here, isn't she?" I say with an irresistible sarcasm that I swore I wouldn't give in to.

Ralph gulps his sandwich. "Well, yeah, she has half a mind to. She's been lonely since we left. Boy, I was hungry! Dave had nothing to eat over there today."

"I figured it was just a matter of time before she followed us." I crunch down hard on a slice of cucumber. "Why can't she get a life of her own?"

I've never liked the way Phyllis could wheedle in on someone else's life, and everyone is supposed to feel sorry for her. She is forty years old and was married once very briefly—just until the groom found out that he didn't have full access to her trust fund. Certainly her adoration of Ralph is an ego boost for him, but to me it is a nuisance—not really a threat because she is so ineffectual, but it is enough to upset the balance of our relationship.

Ralph's words cut into my thoughts. "You know, she relies on me. She's like a daughter—but one who asks my advice—unlike my real daughter."

Ever since Lucy went to graduate school in philosophy, Ralph has found fault with everything she does. He feels she rejected religion and thus stepped outside her role in the family. He wanted her to follow in his footsteps and become a minister; instead, she got what he calls a Master's in Atheism. I think he's exaggerating the whole thing.

Ralph continues, "Well, it's true. When's the last time Lucy came to me for fatherly advice? Maybe when she was four. Where'd she learn that independence?"

"Not from me? Is what you mean?" Suddenly my cheeks blush for the second time today. I feel a sense of foreboding, as if I have suddenly become someone Ralph doesn't know. The real problem is that I don't know me, either. I am haunted by the little me in the wicker chair who seems to be rocking everything.

Ralph looks at me strangely, and I wonder if my cheeks are noticeably on fire. Then he says, "No, you and I are partners—we do things together. Sure, you could be independent if you had to. Besides," he paused, blinking rapidly, as if his vision were suddenly impaired, "we're talking about Phyllis."

My blush has reached my brain. "Maybe I need to—for a while."

"What?" Ralph says as the conversation leaves him behind.

"Be independent." My face is on fire.

Ralph looks as if he would give the world to back up, take a more familiar road. "What on earth are you talking about? Independent of what?"

I feel my stomach fluttering. Yes, that's it. It's coming together. Aloud I say clearly, "Here's the deal: I'm going to Ireland for a month to study weaving starting in late September, and Phyllis can move in here and take care of you. She'd love that."

The words fly out of my mouth before I can censor them, as if they were perched there like birds waiting for the exact conditions to pick up and migrate from inner to outer. True, I had made a decision to wait, but the time to act arrived without my blessing and in spite of my best intentions.

Ralph's head jerks backward and then he looks at me hard, his brow wrinkled in puzzlement. "Move into our house? What for?"

I try to slow down, catching up with my words. "I said, I want her to take care of you. That way I wouldn't have to worry about leaving you alone. It could work."

Ralph looks anguished. "You've completely lost me."

I can't help but feel sorry for him—it's all happening so fast. I try to catch him up. "Diana suggested it when she was here. She knows a great school for weaving in a small town in Ireland. There's a course starting October second and running for about a month. She's offered to help me find a place to rent for the month and teach me local customs. They teach tapestries like that blue and gold iris I attempted last year—the one you liked so much."

"Well, that's just crazy," says Ralph shaking his head and setting the rest of his sandwich on the plate. "That's not how we do things. Surely Diana meant for me to come, too."

"Well, I ..."

"When d'you dream this up?" He pauses, his face blanches. "A separation—is that what you want?"

Now why is he jumping to that conclusion? "Oh, no, I wouldn't call it that."

"What would you call it then, a honeymoon?" He snaps.

"In a way—a honeymoon with myself. It's got little to do with you. I mean..." I take a minute to collect myself. "It's more to do with me. I'm surprised, too, but it seems right. Do you realize that I've never lived alone—never in my whole life? I went from living with the Parkers to living with a roommate. Then at college I always had roommates and then we got married."

Ralph seems lost by this discussion. "The whole point of moving here was that we would be spending our golden years together. You said you liked living here with me."

"I do. I do like it." I take a deep breath. "At the risk of sounding like run-away Sam, I feel as if I need some space to find myself."

Ralph rolls his eyes. "You are seventy years old, dear. He was—what, thirty five when he left his family in search of some abstract idea of happiness? If you don't know who you are by now, give it up. Besides how will you recognize 'you' when you see it? *I* know you. There *is* no other you."

"How would you know there's no other me?" For a moment I actually think he has some hard evidence to clear up this whole mess.

He sighs. "Pass the peanut butter, please. The knife, too, if it's not too much to ask."

"Sorry, here..." I say, my mind grasping for an anchor. "I haven't even decided and, of course, we'd have to talk to Phyllis."

Ralph spins the knife around on the table, an arrow of chance. He watches it carefully as if it will stop at the right answer and he'll know what to do. "Phyllis can't cook—not like you anyway." He pouts.

Again the words come gushing out like blood, "Now all of a sudden you want my cooking after all your complaints about not enough meat or sweets. She'll cook whatever you want and if you want chili every night, fine. Go out to eat—go out for steak if you want to." I stop myself just before I say, "I'm not your mother."

Ralph stares at me as if he's never seen me before. "I hear words... Just one thing wrong—they're not yours. What about the garden?"

I sigh, staring out the window at the subtle movement of the trees. "By October, the garden is pretty well self sufficient—a little weeding and, of course, picking things. Surely Phyllis can handle that. I'll be back before you know it."

"And what if I don't want you back—what then?"

"What, and I suppose you'd choose Phyllis over me? Go ahead and take her and good luck—you'll need it." I stop and take a breath. Calmer, I continue, "Can't you just play out your father/daughter thing—she be the daughter you always wanted, and you the loving father she never had?"

"I have a daughter, don't forget—what I haven't ever had is a mistress."

I pause for a second and stare at this man that I have lived with for forty seven years. I'm not going to take that bait, perched fat and juicy on the trap of my own insecurities. I refuse to demean myself and snap back. "Try one of these no-fat cookies. They're actually pretty good, considering," I say forcefully.

"No, no cookie!" He pushes his chair back away from the table. To refuse a cookie! Now I know he's deeply upset. It flashes through my head that he'll get a cookie or maybe some apple pie from a sympathetic wife of one of his friends later in the afternoon. But I imagine that's all it will be—something sweet to eat. All I say is, "Suit yourself."

For a while there is silence. The porch seems to be getting hotter. Finally, Ralph goes into the living room to take his daily nap in his Lazy Boy recliner.

I sit surrounded by lunch scraps for a long while, unable to move. The tomato seeds begin to dry out and stick to the plates. Maybe I am crazy. Am I ready to jeopardize my marriage? Doubts threaten to sink my passage to Ireland.

Finally, pushing those voices aside, I go into the bedroom to call Phyllis. She seems surprised, even thrilled by the idea. No, she hasn't found anything yet and yes, she would love to put off finding something. I hang up feeling vindicated.

Diana is surprised to hear from me as well and assures me she will register me for the weaving classes right away and start looking into places to stay. She suggests I come the fourth week of September and then by the time the workshop starts in October, we will have something suitable lined up.

After his nap, Ralph left for his afternoon pool game. When he returns at five o'clock, I have already reserved my flight to Ireland. Ralph plops down in his chair, puts his feet up and flicks on the TV with the remote control. Remote, remote. Certainly descriptive—brings the TV closer and makes me remote.

"Oh, no, lost again, those Indians—by just one lousy run. Been that way all season. Remember the last game when..."

When he launches into a lecture on the team of the moment, I usually tune him out and just smile and nod my head. Because usually, no, I don't remember the last game when...but I also don't want to admit it because then he'll have to explain that one again, too.

"I've booked my flight for the twenty-ninth of September, Ralph," I say loudly to overcome the blare of the Budweiser commercial. "My flight is out of Cleveland. Hear me?"

"I heard," he says without taking his eyes from the screen.

"And are you OK?" I ask, stepping into his line of vision, searching his face for clues.

Craning his neck to see around me to the commercial, he says, "Fine. My wife decides that she needs to leave me—out of the blue. Tells me one minute and goes the next. Oh, yes, fine."

My stomach is once again in turmoil. "Nothing to do with you, really. It's about me." I repeat.

"Yeah, that's what you said," Ralph murmurs half humming along with the jingle for some life insurance company.

"What? Could you mute that thing? I can't hear."

"I said—you said it, I didn't."

"And you don't believe it?" I push the power switch to turn off the TV. The insanity of its intrusion makes me want to gut it and force-feed it to itself, the way it tries to force-feed me its ideas of a happy life.

Ralph continues to stare at the blank screen. "Could you for one minute put yourself in my shoes?"

I pace back and forth in front of the television. "Of course—how many years have I been doing just that?" I can just picture his shoes walking over a variety of surfaces as I judge whether this path or that in the woods would work for him. Meanwhile, I am not even looking around at the scenery myself. I suddenly have the feeling that my whole life has passed me by. I sit down like a rag doll in the chair across from him and when I recover enough I say softly, "Don't—you— see? The problem is not *your* shoes—it's mine. I don't even know what color they are, let alone what they feel like. Do you? The question is 'Can you put yourself in my shoes?'"

Silence follows while Ralph picks up the sports page as if to read it—anything but look at me then he says, "Lucy's the one who stirred you up. I knew this whole correspondence thing was trouble. You and she are different. You don't want the same things. She used to fit into this family fine, but lately she wants to take us over— 'enlighten' us. She's twenty five years younger than you. Do you think she knows something you don't?"

"Let's not argue about Lucy. This is about me." I honestly don't know if he has heard a word I said. Has he *ever* heard a word I said, in our entire marriage?

We eat dinner in silence then Ralph goes off to the bedroom TV to watch yet another baseball game. I wonder whether if I learned how to do a play-by-play like a sports announcer, he would listen to me then? He seems to remember who was on first in the second inning better than anything I've ever said to him.

As I stretch myself awake the next morning, my arm brushes Ralph's bare shoulder where it emerges from his undershirt. It's more familiar to me than my own. I remember the day Ralph proposed to me—the same day that he had been accepted to seminary. "The next few years will be hard," he had said. "I'm not sure how we'll make it financially. but I am sure I need you."

I had promised to support him, thinking that maybe there'd be time after that to pursue something of my own, maybe get a Master's in Social Work or music. After the kids were grown, I finally did get a Master's in social work. But being a minister's wife turned into an unpaid career in itself.

Ralph is still murmuring dreamily. When he stirs, he reaches over for his usual good morning squeeze. "Strange dreams," he mumbles, stretching and yawning loudly. "Did I dream about your going to Ireland without me?"

"No, dear, but we have six weeks together before that."

Ralph grunts and turns over to begin getting up. Because of a genetic disability in Ralph's family—Charcot, Marie, Tooth, a neuromuscular disorder, named for the doctors who discovered it, Ralph has always had difficulty with his feet and his balance. Lucy and Mick inherited it as well. It became noticeable as they moved into their teen years as certain nerves did not function well and the muscles they served became weak. The strong muscles then overcompensate, causing a high arch and hammer toes..

Ralph has a particularly bad case of it. In addition he had polio when he was a teenager. These ailments have given him foot infections and terrible pain since he was young. When he was forty-four his left foot was amputated, and then just a few years ago, the other one had to go as well. Each time, he was much better off without the painful foot. Though he has two prostheses, he walks easily and for the most part painlessly over smooth surfaces. He has trouble with rough surfaces where he needs to use a cane. I worry about whether Phyllis will be able to care for him properly. But it's not as if I have to do things for him on a daily basis. He is capable of meeting his own needs. I watch as he puts on his prostheses and walks to the bathroom. Those legs are second nature to him now.

As the days pass, I stop thinking about "whether or not" I will go and concentrate on what to take with me. Some eventualities I can not plan for—the "what ifs," such as what if I get sick, or am cheated because I can't do the money math, or can't find a place to live, or have to rent a car and drive on the wrong side of the road and have an accident, and so on. Sometimes when I start thinking that way, I remember the birthday party and the possibility of a deeper, larger plan.

Chapter 4—Evolution: Lucy

In Yoruba myth, there is Eshu, a god of chaos, confusion and creativity. Say god embodies the modern scientific concept of chaos, mixes together with evolution, and voila!, the kind of creativity necessary to form this complex and dazzling world emerges. Chaos didn't stop when the universe was formed—it is the rule of life.

August 21, 1996

Amy loves to drive fast. Maybe because she has to walk slowly, she gets her power behind the wheel. It's 7:30 am and we've got snacks, money in our pockets, an Emilou Harris tape that we will not play and no plans until 6:00 this evening when the conference officially starts. In no time, we are in the foothills of the Sierras. In Auburn, an old gold mining town, hardly anything is open, but we find a tavern called Making Tracks that has model trains running constantly around the upper edges of the walls. We order iced tea—it's hot already this far inland, and we're not used to it.

We ask the waitress, a spindly middle-aged woman teetering on high heels so early in the day, what she recommends seeing in this town.

"You'all been in the gold mine yet?" she asks through the smacking of her gum.

"No, we can't even remember if we've ever been here before so treat us like aliens." Amy says she can't remember half the things she's done in her fifty-five years, though some of it must have been pretty wild. Having lived through Berkeley in the sixties—occult experiences, drugs, violence, sexual freedom all around—nothing shocks her. She had two kids during that time and was scared out of her wits much of the time with the out-of-control nature of the place.

The waitress slaps her order book on the table and says seriously, "Don't joke about that, now. My husband was abducted by aliens last year and has never been the same. So I'll kick your butts right out of this place…" For a moment we are both quiet, not knowing what to say and then she breaks out laughing and we join her.

Since the gold mine is the place to go but doesn't open for another hour, Amy and I talk. If we were marooned on a desert island, we probably wouldn't run out of things to say to each other for fifteen years or more. If it's not great philosophical conversations, then it's talk of the absurdities of love lost—or found, for that matter. Now there's someone you want to be marooned with.

The gold mine is in a preserved park area and we have to walk a little ways to get to the entrance. Amy is hesitant to walk in but decides she needs to experience it. On the way, we pass people setting up for a fancy affair.

At the mine entrance, there is information about the mine which we read briefly and then head into the descent.

We don't get very far, Amy because of her knees and me because I suddenly feel claustrophobic and remember that being trapped in a mine is a recurring nightmare of mine. I feel again as I did when burning the rosemary the other night, a feeling that I am not big enough for the energies running through me. And this space certainly can't hold those energies either.

We retreat quickly and sit for a while in the display area.

"Me and the dark side—I don't like it," I say trembling. "How can anyone ask us to enter such a place where at any minute our air supply could be cut off?" Hearing about mining accidents has always chilled me to the bone.

Amy rubs her knee. "People still do it, too, all over the world. I guess being a court investigator is not such a bad job, if you compare it to mining."

"Let's head on down the road and get settled in," I say standing up abruptly and starting to move away from that place.

Just before we round the corner to where the event was being set up we hear haunting flute music. We keep walking until we can see that the event is a wedding ceremony and the music is being played by seven flutes. We stay on the perimeter but can hear some of the exchange of vows. The sun filters down through the redwood trees and spotlights the flutes.

We stand and listen for quite a while and then head toward the parking lot. The last thing I hear is, "From this day forward…" and I think, yes, that's what I need to do, think about the present and the future. But that thought doesn't help since what I am really thinking is that from this day forward I will be without Terry.

Amy looks over at me and says, "Oh, no, you're crying again."

"It's weddings. They do it to everyone, don't they?"

"It's Terry again, isn't it?" says Amy as we get back into her car.

"I'm sorry, I just can't stop thinking about my pathetic life and how my relationships never last. This one makes me feel so sucker-punched. Why didn't I listen to you and not let it get this far?"

"Because you know I always err on the side of caution. That's why

I've been celibate for fifteen years now. I cut it off way before I get hurt. All I see are people's faults and before it even has a chance to start, I just know we'll never make it. Sure, it saves some hurt, but I miss out on good times, too. And you had good times with Terry. It was great to watch."

"Yeah, I did it for you—someone had to live so you could enjoy yourself vicariously."

Amy looks hurt by my sarcasm, but she seems to understand that I am lashing out at her just because she is there. "Yeah," she says without defending herself, "what I know is that you gave yourself away generously and in good faith."

Her kindness breaks my heart open even wider and I feel vulnerable to everything and everyone. I didn't realize how much a broken heart is like a broken record, playing the same pain over and over. As we pull out of the parking lot, I say, "I wish I hadn't agreed to do this talk tomorrow. I'm going to look like hell, especially if I see any more horrors like mines and weddings."

The car zooms onto the highway. "We'll keep it on the light side from now on, OK, if I can just figure out where that is," says Amy pushing the lock button on her door.

The conference site began as an old sawmill that had been preserved and refurbished with hopes that it would help revive an area devastated by unemployment, industry after industry boomed and busted—gold, timber, paper mills. They were banking on an international market that would be attracted to its natural setting but have all the amenities of Western civilization. The court investigators got a good deal on the conference site because the investigator in the county, Craig Natingger, was one of the prime movers in the effort to get it built.

Craig is out near the office telling people where to park and how to check in. Posted signs welcome us and direct us—obviously he has more staff than our office does.

"Hey, ladies," Craig says sticking his head in our window. "Want to make sure you have everything you need." He winks, "Know what I mean?"

"Yeah, well, big boy," Amy says in her inimitably flirtatious manner, "if we get a hankering for something that's not around, we'll be sure to come looking for you. Where you staying?" She winks back.

Craig's freckled skin blushes. If he expected demur, he must have forgotten to whom he was talking. Now he can't think of a thing to say and shuffles through his papers. When this job was first created, it drew mostly men, often retired cops. But now women are becoming the majority as with most public sector jobs. "Looks like you two'll be staying in Moonlight Lodge." He points directly ahead of us to the large stone building. "First floor, as you requested."

We settle ourselves and go looking for the pool. Swimming is good for Amy's knees and since, because my neuro-muscular disorder makes walking more of an effort for me than for most people, my preferred exercise involves water. For me it is more effort to stand on land than to spend hours just hanging out in water even where I cannot touch the bottom. I'm comfortable there.

The pool is too small to swim serious laps. so Amy and I just fool around doing the breast stroke and talking. We gossip about Craig and how he's never been married and is perhaps gay but with none of the telltale signs. Amy has been somewhat attracted to him over the years but probably just as someone she can't possibly have. She and Craig have bantered back and forth endlessly at these conferences but it has never led anywhere.

Ron and Sheila, investigators from San Francisco, join us at the pool. Neither is dressed to swim but they take seats in pool-side recliners in the shade. I am glad to see Ron. He often doesn't make it to the conferences, and I have always liked him. I wonder if he and Sheila are an item.

"You come up together?" I ask them.

Sheila nods and replies, "It was supposed to be the three of us, Ron, Mark and me but Mark got sick at the last minute. He's going to kick himself for missing this one. It's the best location we've had since I've been working here—what ten years now?" I notice a wedding ring on Sheila's beautifully manicured finger and still nothing on Ron's.

"Don't know how many will actually show up for the lectures," Ron says, "with the exception, of course, of yours, Lucy." I detect his dark Latin eyes twinkling just slightly.

I laugh modestly and he continues, "No, really, yours is the one I came to hear—the issue of medical powers, who gets to decide when someone has had enough life. That comes up over and over, and we never quite know what to do with it. So hearing about what is legally allowed will be helpful. As I understand it, you're also going to suggest ways to handle it up front, right? Unlike what we do now, which is to ignore it and hope someone does the right thing."

"Yeah," I say, turning to do the sidestroke so I can see him better. "I've used mediation with doctors, nurses, the family and the conservatee. It's hard for people but they end up appreciating it. It's strange. We ask doctors to make decisions that are not medical but essentially are about quality of life; the conservatee and her family are far more expert there."

Sheila cuts in. "No more shop talk now—this is our free time!"

"Sorry, Sheila. Ron, you and I can talk later, OK?"

Ron nods. "You still seeing that Tad guy, or Tom—what was his name?"

"Ted? Ancient history. I was already broken up with him by last year's conference, but you weren't here for that one, right?"

"Mostly I steer clear of these things. Find them boring. This one seems better than most." Ron is a small wiry Cuban, about four inches shorter than I. He seems to need lots of physical activity to keep him engaged. Conferences where people sit around all day and listen do not generally appeal to him.

Amy pipes up, "You could try giving one of the talks on something important to you, you know." Amy is on the committee that puts the conferences together, and they have a difficult time finding speakers.

Sheila begins talking to Amy about a subject she would like to present at the next conference and when we get out of the pool, Amy and Sheila walk off together discussing her idea.

I can't help but notice that Ron looks away as we get out of the pool to dry off. Thank goodness, he's not one of those gawker-types. I wonder if he would like to look but is just polite or if he has no interest in what I look like in a bathing suit.

At dinner, Amy and I sit with Ron, Sheila and several investigators from San Mateo County. We get into story mode—telling about strange cases we've encountered and how they turned out. This part of the conference is actually the most enlightening part for me. There are plenty of commonalities, like the lesson I learned early on that the biggest abusers of old people are their families. When conservatorships first started, the court only required non-family conservators to be bonded, but this was soon discovered to be a big mistake. Family and money are a bad combination. So often kids think their parents' money is theirs and it's just a technicality that the parents are still using it.

Amy says, "Remember that deposition of one of the conservators—what was her name?" She scratches her head but comes up with nothing. "The one where the lawyer's first language was not English and she tried to pin down the conservator about his lack of credentials. When the conservator said he had gone to the school of hard knocks, she wanted to know where it was, if it was accredited, and how many years it had been there!

I add, chuckling, "Yeah, she went on and on until finally someone was able to stop her and pull her aside and explain her mistake."

Investigators encounter all kinds of freaky things, seeing behind doors that are usually closed and observing people's intensely idiosyncratic ways of living. Rich or poor, doesn't matter. The intersections of religion, family background, sibling order, physical and mental anomalies, culture and finances create unpredictable dynamics. Before this job, I imagined that other people's lives were similar to mine, and I might take a guess at what was behind a closed door. Now I don't dare assume a thing.

My talk is the second one of the day, and I am pleased with the response. After a while, I cut off discussion and say, "I'm happy to discuss the subject further in our free time."

Afterwards I feel antsy and don't want to stay for the rest of the morning's business. I skip out to take a walk in the woods. There are several trails. I choose a three-mile loop that leads to a waterfall. I have worn various kinds of leg braces on and off over the years. Some are designed to help me walk and some are designed to reverse the deformity of my feet. Now I have on a pair of the latter. They are not as comfortable but they do seem to be helping the shape of my feet over the long term. And I do all right—I can walk as far as five or six miles with no worries except that I might get more tired than my counterpart would. This path is quite strenuous. It is relentlessly uphill.

I meet no one on the path. It is gloriously hot and the sweat runs down between my breasts and into the waistband of my jeans. Shorts would have been better but the braces reach almost to my knees and I look ridiculous in shorts or skirts.

The swimming hole in front of the waterfall is too tempting to resist. I strip off everything. It feels especially good to get out of the braces. I put my feet in first and revel in how the cold feels on my recently freed feet, then slide my whole self in slowly. The coldness feels at once harsh and delicious. Once I am in, I paddle over to let my head be battered by the falling water. No separation between me and the rest of the world. I float with my breasts pointing toward the sky, nipples exposed and erect in the gentle breeze. When I am just too cold to stay any longer, I pull myself out onto the rocks and let the wind and sun dry me. That's when I hear a rustling and footsteps on the path. I grab my tee shirt to cover as much of myself as I can. I could have used at least ten more minutes in this place alone.

At first Ron doesn't see me and starts to strip down to get into the water. I wish I were more hidden and could just watch this next part, but he'll look up and see me any minute, so I gently let him know I am there by causing some stones to roll toward the water. He freezes, staring at me, not the polite behavior of yesterday. Recovering himself, he turns away and says, "I had no idea…sorry. I'll go." He grabs his shirt to put it back on and starts to go.

"Wait, Ron. It's not fair. I've already been in so if you'll just stay turned a minute, I'll dress and get out of your way." But I am still too wet to get dressed and my clothes don't cooperate in going back on. "On second thought, Ron, how about if we just act like grownups and swim or sunbathe or do whatever. I won't gawk if you won't gawk."

He hesitates.

"You at least have the option of leaving your shorts on. But I've got to get a little drier before I can dress."

He takes off his shorts and his underwear and proceeds to jump in screaming, kicking and splashing and threatening to undo the dry I have already achieved. But I lie back, determined not to fixate on the glimpse of his sinewy tan body that I can't erase from my mind's eye.

A few minutes later he says, dog paddling in the center of the pool, "You aren't going to let me swim alone here, are you? More fun with company."

Adults, I say to myself as I jump in—we are both adults. But the minute I hit the water we are kids, laughing and splashing, a playfulness that seems inherent in water and snow. Our height difference doesn't matter at all in the water. I go to the lovely rock ledge right under the waterfall and sit there letting the water blind me. A few moments later, Ron nestles in beside me and when I look at him, we share a kiss. Oh, it isn't such a naughty thing, two kids kissing in the falls. I recover a bit of my senses and say, "Someone is going to come…"

Then with a kindled look he says, "Oh, I hope to God it will be you!"

I gasp. It is such an unexpected thing to hear that I turn all warm and slippery. The next kiss we share is not so innocent and the one after that is downright not at all. The kisses are mutual exploration, not conquest, just the way I like it. The oneness feeling comes over me again even as I try to get control of the situation. Can't be done. I give myself over to Ron's ministrations of pleasures. During the kissing and touching part and through my climax, I am thinking of Terry. When I recover myself, I notice that Ron is serious about wanting me to enjoy myself; he seems not to have considered his own pleasure all, and when I think he will move in for his pleasure, he starts to move away.

I grab him back and with my eyes open pull him into me. Now Terry's face can go to hell. He is more than willing once he gets there to enjoy himself. I want to know if this kind of sex still work for me. "Yes, yes," I croon.

At lunch I can't find Amy, so I sit at an empty table. My thoughts are a jumble. Mostly, I am whipping myself mentally that I let that happen. It wasn't about Ron; I used that poor man, though when I left him he appeared satisfied. But the thing he doesn't know is that it can't go on. This is such a classic rebound situation. I don't even know Ron.

On cue, Ron approaches my table and asks if he can sit with me.

"Please, not now, OK? I can't talk about it."

He rests his tray on the table but does not sit down. "We don't have to talk about it; I just wanted you to know nothing like that has ever…"

I cut him off. "Not now," I say in as mean a tone as I can muster. "Forget it happened…please." I feel like an idiot for complicating my life this way. I can feel myself drawn to him again, and I push those feelings away, knowing that I am not capable right now of feeling anything but confusion.

"What happened?" Amy asks innocently as she sits down. "Sit down, Ron. Whatcha waiting for, an engraved invitation?"

He shrugs, his feelings obviously hurt. "Just a little civility would suit me, but I promised I'd meet Sheila—oh, I see her over there. See you."

I huddle with Amy and tell her a brief version of what happened, sparing her the personal details. When I finish, she is obviously shocked. "Talk about a roller coaster, from the gold mine to the waterfalls and crashing back down again."

"More down than up."

"Tell me you weren't up at that waterfall. It was good, wasn't it?"

"It was stupid."

"No, it was natural, biological and maybe even evolutionary."

I look away from her, my head spinning with contradictory thoughts. "You can't mean evolutionary. Evolution in the right direction would maybe make us sterile so we'd end up with fewer humans. Oh, my God, Amy, I went off the pill when I started seeing Terry…She was shooting with blanks, so to speak." I say, not making much sense even to myself. Then I add, "But, really, that was best part of being with a woman—she wasn't shooting at all."

Chapter 5—Fight for Flight: Emma

What if a running away from your life is really a turning toward?

September 16, 1996

In the middle of September, when Phyllis comes with all of her worldly possessions, the three of us settle into an awkward balance. Completely unacquainted with most of her body, Phyllis walks like a clumsy marionette whose strings have been over-stretched. She is a romantic with a rich fantasy life, which probably includes marrying Ralph and living happily ever after.

Naively I thought that in addition to training Phyllis, Ralph and I would use this time to make sure our foundation is strong. But I notice Ralph seems to be practicing doing without me; he has started treating me as Phyllis does, as if I am invisible. He asks no questions about my plans and instead deliberately makes plans with Phyllis while I am still here.

As I coach Phyllis, she tries to be friendly, but usually, in spite of herself, says something to hurt my feelings. It's clear Phyllis's friend in the family is Ralph, not I. He can do no wrong, and I do not even exist. Her fantasy cannot accommodate a real-life wife.

About a week before my flight, I panic. Ralph is distant—not including me in his activities or asking for my advice. I am on the edge of a cliff. and before I even make the leap, the rocks are crumbling beneath my feet. Where is the leverage for take-off?

One morning when I wake up crying, Ralph notices my sniffling and asks what's wrong.

I breathe in big hiccup gulps, trying to get enough air. "I feel like I'm losing you."

Ralph looks nonchalant, as if he wants to punish me. He says coolly, "What do you mean? Aren't I the same as always?"

"It's as if you see our time together as your duty or something."

He knits his eyebrows together. "How so? I'm not doing anything differently." Blowing my nose, I say, "It's a feeling. It used to be you and me against the world and now I'm on 'the world' side. I don't mean for it to be that way."

Ralph thinks a minute, then says softly so that I have to strain to hear him, "I'll be here when you get back. That doesn't mean it's easy..."

"Thanks," I choke out, trying to contain myself.

After that, we are kinder to each other but I don't get the close bonding I want and Ralph doesn't completely disconnect.

On the morning of my departure, Phyllis rises early to surprise us with breakfast. The table is set, and pancakes are burning on the stove.

'You didn't have to do this," I say, glancing at the mess in the kitchen.

Phyllis gives me a big smile. "I thought I'd give you a send-off, Emma. Excuse me, they're burning." She runs to the stove and grabs the iron skillet, burning her hand. As I put her hand under cold water, she says, shaking her head, "Never have gotten the hang of electric stoves—always turn them up too high."

As the smoke alarm screeches, I take a white dish towel and wave it in the air to move the smoke into the other room.

We leave in plenty of time to catch my 5:30 pm flight because the last time we'd gone to Ireland had been such a harrowing affair. We'd been all ready to check in at the ticket counter with time to spare before the flight when I realized that instead of Lucy's passport, I had brought Ralph's and he wasn't leaving until two weeks later. I almost threw up with dread.

We called our good friends who lived near us, a good hour from the airport, and asked them to break into the house, grab the passport and drive like crazy. Our trip hung in the balance.

The whole family was stationed like a relay throughout the airport with the fastest runner, Adam, the farthest away. When he saw them coming, he was to run until he could signal Mick, and so on down the line until Ralph, who was at the gate, could plead with the attendant to hold the plane. Seconds after the pilot called to close the gate, word came down that our angels had arrived. The flight attendant held the doors open and we got on.

Thinking about that time makes my palms sticky with sweat. I distract myself by calculating the time we need to leave. If the heaviness in my stomach is any indication of durability, the pancakes should get us through to a late lunch near the airport. Though I had planned to have the time alone with Ralph, I invite Phyllis to come along so that she can keep Ralph company on the way back.

No airport dramas this time, at least nothing visible. No, this drama is a soliloquy. Waiting for boarding, I see several older couples obviously traveling together. Second thoughts spontaneously combust in my head: why didn't I just bring Ralph along—he loves to travel; it would be so much easier. I should have tried shorter trips first; strange people, a strange land—and Diana is strange as well. My legs feel rubbery, as if they won't hold me when the time comes to board.

Finally, when my row is called, I first hug Phyllis and then Ralph, quickly. I hand the attendant my boarding pass, turn and walk through the exit door and down the ramp toward the plane. I look back once. Phyllis is grinning, almost leering, and Ralph looks stunned. I don't look again; tears begin to take salty bites out of my eyes. Five weeks stretch out endlessly in front of me, an ocean at the end of this gangplank. I can think of no good reason to go forward; yet somehow I continue to walk toward the plane.

I settle in, focusing on mundane things: seat belts, pillows, things that have never been known to provoke tears. I hide my red puffy eyes. Each time I think of Ralph or look out again at Cleveland, I begin crying again. Never have I felt so sentimentally attached to Cleveland, but it was here that I met Ralph in all of his gawky handsomeness that somehow put others at ease. He has made my life so easy, paving the way. I rely on that charm. Where is the ground under my feet?

Just before liftoff, a very small, very old woman takes the aisle seat next to me. There is no room in the compartment over our heads, so she struggles to place her stained gray canvas bag—that looks as if it has been through a war—into a bin just behind us. She can barely reach the compartment, let alone lift up a bag, so I leap up to help her. I manage easily; my strength surprising me. The woman thanks me, and I smile at her as warmly as I can through my tears.

Her words startle me. "Excuse me, please, I believe you are sitting on my seat belt?"

"Sorry." I shift in my seat to let her get to her seatbelt. "I'm a little nervous. Do you live in Ireland or are you just going to visit?"

"I'm Irish-born through and through," she says and now I can hear the brogue. "My name is Brigid, after the Saint."

As the plane begins to move away from the gate, Brigid turns to me and asks, "You need my help?"

Puzzled, I reply, "I don't know what I need. What kind of help are you offering?"

She squints at me as if she cannot quite make out the features on my face. "You are familiar with Ireland?"

I perk up, glad to be having a normal conversation with someone. "Not really," I say, "I've been there only once before, many years ago."

She nods and says, "Where will ya be staying?"

I am beginning to breathe normally and the tears have stopped. I explain that at first I'll be with my cousin who lives in Dublin and then I have to find a place to stay near Galway where I'll be attending a weaving course. It sounds so matter of fact, like people do it all the time.

She nods again and smiles knowingly, "Ah, Connemara, yes, you have relatives there."

I don't know what she's getting at with that kind of statement; her words have taken on a quality of fortune telling. I say, "Well, no, I don't think so. I mean, my cousin is in Dublin. Ah, she used to live in Killybegs in the Northwest."

She says confidently, "Yes, relatives will be there, but you aren't expecting them. They are not on this plane."

I let that remark go by without comment, getting the picture that Brigid is a little senile. Not wanting to exert the effort to understand her brogue and her riddles, I lean back against the seat and stare for a while at the maroon and navy wave designs on the rugs covering the front panels of the plane's interior. They are intended to be restful, but to me they exaggerate the unreality of air travel—it's so three-dimensional and changeable. Train tracks or the road limit you to two dimensions, and that suits me better. Now Brigid is mumbling repetitively. Sounds like a chant. Maybe she's praying.

In my mind, religion is a puzzle. Logic and continuums are unable to contain it. Catholicism is the most superstitious of all the Christian religions, the way it glorifies Mary—as if she were important in comparison with Christ and the Holy Spirit.

Even Diana who was raised Protestant seems to be into this Mary thing. Diana gave me a Waterford crystal piece of the Madonna and Child for my seventieth birthday. To spend all that money on such a thing! Diana was never a mother herself and must still have illusions about the divinity of motherhood. Some have said that labor was a punishment for original sin. I don't know if I'd go that far, but it certainly isn't spiritual, that much I know. I make a note to myself to keep my feelings private on these subjects so I won't fall into hot water with the locals.

The movie shown during the flight is a drama about tornadoes. There is no way I am going to get a headset and watch something frightening. Every time I open my eyes, I see images of the world twisting out of shape. The people in the movie aren't running away from the tornado as any normal person would, but they are actually chasing it. Most of the passengers seem mesmerized by the images. Brigid, though, is sound asleep.

After a while, I fall asleep and wake to flight attendants passing out breakfast, which I eat hungrily. I fall back to sleep again and the next thing I know, the pilot is announcing our descent into Shannon airport. My stomach lurches and I reach for the airsick bag, just in case. Brigid advises me to try deep breathing. Once I begin to breathe deeply, my stomach stops twisting.

"It's not so much airsickness," I say to Brigid, "as anxiety. Don't know what I've signed up for—next thing I'll be hyperventilating."

"Tis not a prison term, lass, but a good vacation fer ya. Don't be ruining it with yer doubt of yer future. The present is here. Remember, what you see with the eyes is the present moment, and in Ireland you cannot see far enough to predict what's to come. The winds are too fast for yer weak eyesight, dear. Don't strain yerself."

At least she took my mind off the landing for a minute. I am no longer straining with anxiety about the future, but now I am straining to understand her puzzles. Is she making sense and I am just dense?

The flight attendant delivers the usual message about the tray tables and seat backs. Through the shifting clouds, I can make out land formations. When I turn my attention back to the plane, Brigid has disappeared. We are all supposed to be in our seats by now. The flight attendant is hurrying to close the overhead compartments, and I alert her to Brigid's absence.

The attendant checks her seating chart and says, "There was never anyone assigned to this seat, so she may have gone back to her assigned seat. I'll double check the bathrooms just in case."

"She was a very old Irish woman wearing dark clothing, a skirt, kind of short..."

"A short skirt?"

"No, no, a short woman."

The attendant seems impatient to get back to her duties, "I don't remember such a person—not on this plane—but I'll check just the same."

I lean back, close my eyes and take a deep breath. The attendant's words "not on this plane" echo in my ears. The old woman had said that, too. It was something to do with relations of mine awaiting me in Connemara. What is Connemara anyway? It isn't on my map. Even with her puzzles, her presence was stabilizing.

As the plane lowers itself into Shannon airport, I reach for the locket with my family's picture hanging around my neck. Family. Isn't that what it's all about, finally? Well, Diana is family, too, I have to remember—actually, she is the only part of my biological past that is still alive.

When the plane breaks through the clouds, a sense of wellbeing floods me. It is as I remembered it—completely green. I can see the stone fences weaving their way through the uneven countryside.

Diana had given me the option of flying into Dublin and then driving out to Galway with her or just flying into Shannon to meet her there. Since I don't much care for cities anyway, I'm glad I opted for choice number two. Shannon may be in the middle of nowhere, but it is certainly the center of green.

Chapter 6—Resolution: Lucy

Life has no stages; the word resolution
lies. Life has questions, connections.
--from Forever Afternoon by Adam David Miller

September 29, 1996

Mattie and I are sitting on her patio on a clear, warm September morning. The herbs are cracking open their flowers after a chilly night, and they smell vaguely sweet, giving off just a tantalizing hint of who they are.

The lawyers and the judge are taking Mattie's case to adversarial extremes and it looks as if it could turn into a protracted legal battle. I called ahead and asked Mattie, "Can the two of us just sit and talk a bit—see if we can work something out?" Mattie was amenable to that and, in fact, seemed relieved.

When I first got there, she looked me over, especially staring at my stomach, as if she knew I was pregnant. I received the test results yesterday that confirmed what I already knew to be true. I think Mattie may say something about it, but thankfully she refrains.

It had been a little while since we talked and in the meantime, she has had a chance to experience this wonderful legal system of ours and is more open to seeking an alternative.

I have concluded that Mattie needs a conservator of the estate, meaning someone to help her take care of her finances but not her person, so that she can still decide where she lives and make medical decisions for herself. Her lawyer suggested that the Public Guardian take conservatorship but that office moves more slowly and is too cumbersome for someone living in her own home. In my humble opinion, it would be best if Mattie would agree to have her daughter do it.

I take a whiff of her lavender to calm my nerves before talking. Memories come to me of being carried home from somewhere, maybe church, where I had fallen asleep. My mother must have been wearing a lavender perfume. I feel cared for and protected.

Mattie picks dead leaves off what smells like oregano. I have become attached to this person and want to give her what she is asking for but I also see that she needs a little help. I have come to look up to her and maybe to rely on her mysterious advice, but that doesn't mean I think she is totally able to care for herself. I mean, who is, after all? I myself could use some help sorting out my feelings and seeing where they may lead. Is

Ron someone I can actually trust or is he just a convenience? This falling in love thing has taken all of the certainty out of me and I wish I could have some kind of interim period where nothing counts against me and I don't have to sign any contracts. I don't trust my own judgment in regard to relationships right now. Maybe I'm the one who needs someone to tell me what to do, to make my decisions for me.

I swallow my doubts. After all, Mattie's future is the subject today. "Can we talk about your daughter a minute? I know she disagrees with who's going to get your money in the end, right?"

Mattie looks defeated and old and I wonder what toll this fight is having on her health. "My daughter, Mary—can you believe I named her that? It was in my Christian days, but recently I found out that Mary was a figure in pagan life and that the Christians simply moved her over into their world." She looks off toward the bay and I feel she is somewhere else altogether.

"You were saying that Mary, what?"

"Mary wants to do what Mary thinks is right and not what I think is right." Mattie walks around the small courtyard until she finds a patch of sun to stand in. Looking over her shoulder, she says, "You know, you have kids thinking that maybe they'll take care of you when you are old. Don't count on it—they grow into their own agenda and it has little to do with yours. It's your choice, dear, just as much as it is mine now."

I hear her allusions but am determined not to discuss them with her. Instead, we air her feelings about her own situation. At the core of it is the will, the one document Mary wants to change but Mattie will not. She tells me her daughter is good with finances and comes to see her at least every month.

Mattie seems demoralized and sits with her head down. I reach out and take her hands and finally she looks at me. I ask, "Is she trustworthy, this daughter of yours?"

Mattie considers the question just briefly, looking over my shoulder as if she is getting clues from the rosemary and then she looks back at me and says, "Oh, yes, she's a Christian, after all, and she wouldn't steal from me, no."

I review with her the fact that Mary will have to account for everything she spends money on from Mattie's estate and that the court investigator's office will periodically evaluate those accountings. As conservator of the estate, she will have no extra power over Mattie's will. I think Mattie's desire to remain totally independent has kept her from hearing the details of what was being asked of her.

Mattie says with resignation, "You think I need help, don't you? This is it—all downhill from here, I guess."

My heart sinks. Yes, it's true, I think to myself. Circumstances are forcing her to let go of her independence little by little. I have no idea how that must feel to someone who has known so much freedom in her thinking and her life up until now. "Oh, Mattie, no. It is a piece of you, a small piece. You're much more than what you spend money on. You'll still be living here and making your own decisions about your day-to-day life. Your herbs will still be your daily companions. Mary will just be making sure bills are paid and overseeing the house repairs. She can't do anything outrageous without court approval.

It's as if she hears me for the first time. Mattie agrees to let her daughter be conservator of the estate and she agrees that money must be spent for necessary repairs to the house. As I am leaving, Mattie gives me a hug and says, "I like what we just did. You didn't try to convince me of anything, just brought out the facts. That's what you need for yourself, too. Don't let anybody tell you what you ought to feel or do. It's up to you."

Later, I notice a small package in the car seat. She must have put it there when I wasn't looking. It is lavender bath salts. I sit in the car for a minute, just letting the smell wash over me. I think of all the things we humans are forced to let go of over our lifetimes. No, it doesn't seem fair that when we get old we often come into so much suffering. All that letting go must be preparation for the final letting go. I think of Terry and how hard it is for me to let her go. And yet, perhaps absence is creating a space for something else to happen. And the more I hold on, the less possible it is for whatever is next to emerge.

I drive carefully down out of the hills and onto the freeway back to Oakland. From the minute I got the pregnancy test results, I knew I would have an abortion. My plan is not to have kids at all, ever. It's a question of both politics and personal choice not to pass on this disability I inherited. I'm going to let this fetus I am carrying go back where it came from, and it can just try again with someone else.

I know at least some of my friends will try to talk me out of it. It's not that they aren't pro-abortion—most of them are, but not for people they know. Those people ought to follow their destiny which inevitably means having the baby. Mattie is right; people have started acting as if they know how I feel. I don't feel as bad about the abortion as about the fact that I need it and about my actions that got me in this position. I used to counsel young girls about birth control and become very judgmental when someone said, "it just happened and I wasn't prepared…" Now I feel compassion toward them—a little late but there it is.

Am I destined to be a writer and have the life I choose or do I have to go through with something that changes everything? Say you fall in love with a womanizer and abuser, is that destiny or can you say, no, I'm not doing this to myself and move out of the state? Maybe my destiny is to gain compassion toward women who go though this. Maybe my destiny is to claim the right not to have children ever, at all and still be a perfectly fine human being and find another way to live a female life.

When I finally get to the office, I have a message from Ron. He has been calling once a week since we returned from the conference. He doesn't have my home phone number, so he calls here. He's persistent; I'll give him that.

Since I found out I'm pregnant, I've been seriously considering having an abortion and then getting out of town for a while. My mother's offer to join her in Ireland has all of a sudden become a temptation. I can't see myself just going on with business as usual afterward, or maybe I just want to be with my mother. It's perhaps not the best time to leave, but it could be a perfect opportunity to work on my writing.

Knowing I'm going away for a while gives me the courage to finally call Ron back. When he answers the phone, "Ron Sanchez, how can I help you." My heart begins beating faster. I don't know. Can he help me? I don't think so.

"It's Lucy, Ron, I…"

"Oh, my God, finally." He moves ahead quickly as if continuous talking will keep me from hanging up. "Look, before you say anything, I'm not trying to pressure you—I just want to talk, clear up any misconceptions we might have about each other." He is speaking fast and barely breathing. "And I had an AIDS test taken; I'm negative." He finally takes a breath.

"I'm pregnant," I whisper into the phone so no one else in the office can overhear.

There is silence on the other end of the phone for a moment, then, "I'm happy… I'm sorry… I'm ashamed…I'm joyful—how do you want me to feel?" He asks in a non-judgmental way.

He really is a kind person. I sigh and say, "Sorry will cover it for now."

He sighs deeply. "I *am* sorry—I usually don't have unprotected sex. I mean, I just don't." He paused as if wanting to choose his words carefully. "And I wasn't going to, but I assumed when you pulled me…"

My stomach clenches at the re-living of the moment. I was such an idiot. "It's my fault. I'm not trying to blame you—I take full responsibility.

It was a choice, a rather bad one, but a choice and now I'm making another one—you're not Catholic or a right-to-lifer or anything are you?"

"No, no, I was born Catholic but quickly turned atheist after we got to this country from Cuba when I was about three. Have you made an appointment? I'll be glad to go with you." Ron is talking fast as if he expects me to hang up at any moment.

"I appreciate the offer, Ron, but I don't even know you, really. It would be uncomfortable, I think. Amy will go with me."

"I'm happy to pay for it …"

"No," I say. "It's covered, so don't worry about it. I just thought you should know and now you do so..."

Before I could sign off, Ron says, "Wait a minute. I'm not through. You already know I want to get to know you. Making love to you there…it has, shall I say, disrupted my peace of mind. We could go out, get some coffee? I'd like to understand… why won't you speak to me about it? Is it my height or something that makes you think it's impossible between us?"

I sigh again not wanting to get into this. I want to avoid telling him that I wasn't making love to him, but to someone else, but here he is busy making up stories to fill in the blanks. "Trust me, it will be easier for both of us if we don't. It's nothing about you—I think you are an attractive, respectful and kind person." In spite of myself I begin to cry again—kindness does that to me.

"Are you crying? Look maybe I can help?"

"No, you can't. I have to get some things figured out."

"How?"

The "how" was something I had been considering every waking moment and probably in my dreams, too. "I'm planning to go visit my mother who's in Ireland for the next month. She left today." Before he can ask another question I use my favorite excuse to get off the phone. "I have another call, Ron. I'll call you later."

That didn't go badly, I think. He didn't try to convince me to have it, or offer to marry me or try to convince me that abortion was wrong or that we were fated to be together, all the scenarios I had imagined. Maybe in a year or two, I'll have the courage to see him again.

I take some steps to see if I can pull off the trip to Ireland, make a few calls to find out what it would cost, check to see that I have enough vacation time saved up. If I can just get some of these cases resolved, I can get away. It might be the best thing in the world for me to get some perspective on my life. I could go for three weeks, part of it with my mother and part of it by myself working on the four generations book. If I do go, I should spend my spare time between now and then working on getting through the rest of the Hallie's papers that I inherited when my great uncle Danny died. He knew I was working on this book, and no one else had ever shown an interest in her papers and books, so he gave them to me.

It was heartbreaking to interview him before he died and to see he was still in misery over signing the papers to have Hallie locked up. In 1932, a woman could not sign the papers to have someone committed. It had to be a man, and Danny's mother coerced him into signing. He was Mama's little boy and seemed to do her bidding until she died. But to carry that kind of guilt around with you for sixty-some years—that's rough.

Later that evening, I continue going through the box of Hallie's papers. The musty smell makes me think of things left too long uncared for and untouched. Some of the papers have become brittle and yellow, and I wonder when was the last time someone cared enough to look in this box, which is all that is left of Hallie's life—save her only child, Emma.

To me, it seems impossible that Emma isn't more interested in Hallie's things and in her life. Her yearbook from Albion College in Michigan displays a cracked brown leather cover announcing in gold lettering "Ye Albionion." For me, it proves that Hallie *was* somebody. She certainly wasn't somebody for most of my life. I didn't even know my mother was adopted until I was about twelve and, even then, Emma's biological mother remained very much a mystery.

During Hallie's senior year in college she won the Women's State Oratorical Contest with a speech, *Man-Made Morals,* which was published in the yearbook. The speech rails against the double moral standard that falls hard on women and lets men off the hook entirely. Near the end she states, "We must challenge the system which bids us open our front door, kill the fatted calf, and welcome with open arms the prodigal son, while it silently thrusts out the back door the prodigal daughter."

Thinking about Hallie, and how much trouble her untamability got her into helps keep my mind off my own problems. However, much of her material is quite painful to read—for instance, endless letters she wrote from Mannington where she was institutionalized for thirty-seven years—that's as long as I've been on this earth! The papers include draft letters to the press telling them that her daughter was taken from her illegally, letters to attorneys pleading her case and so on. I have no idea if any of these were ever mailed. In one addressed to the *Detroit News* she states, "I seem to be in a State Hospital and the hospital did not sign my release which I know it should have."

My palms and nose begin to itch from whatever is on these papers. I notice that she kept notes from the want ads announcing places to live, as if she were searching for a place should she get out of the hospital. And there are many newspaper clippings of automobile accidents and murders and tragedies reported in the newspapers. I doubt she knew the people involved—there are just too many. Maybe it's just like what I'm doing now, concentrating on someone else's tragedy to avoid thinking of her own?

There is a letter from Charlotte who must have been her longtime lover. The letter is dated 1930, after Hallie married Charles. It says:

Dear Hallie,
Seeing you on the 22nd would be fine—shall we meet at my rooms? Please bring whatever document you have regarding your arrangement with Charles. I do not want to interfere but I am, as always, wanting you here. And am as always your loyal friend,
Charlotte

I can't imagine what documents she is referring to. Then I am startled to see handwriting that looks like my brother, Adam's, small and pinched but regular. It is from Charles, before they were married.

Dear Miss Kaufmann,
Thank you for understanding my proclivities—last Saturday was most entertaining. I have never met a woman so unconventional and free. I enjoy your company very much. I do not wish to curtail your freedom in any way but I would like you to be my wife in an arrangement that will be mutually beneficial. As I have said, I will gladly take on the domestic duties of cooking, shopping and cleaning. You will be entirely free to pursue your career. Perhaps another school district will hire you. If we can agree to the details, let us move forward.
Yours affectionately,
Charles

"Proclivities," I wonder what he means by that? Was he gay, too? Were they providing cover for each other and, if so, how does Hallie end up pregnant by him? But I am living proof that these things can happen when two people are in close proximity. I can imagine that she resisted having the baby. It must have killed her to know she was pregnant—that her body was betraying her own desires. I know the feeling. I heard a theory that in pre-patriarchal days, women were so in touch with their bodies that they could keep from getting pregnant when it wasn't the right time and get pregnant when it was—*that* would be evolutionary.

When I first started working on this book, I interviewed both Hallie, who was living in Ohio at a nursing home near my parents, and her brother Danny, who was living in Detroit. My parents had tried letting Hallie live with them when living in her apartment in Detroit became untenable, even with Danny and his wife's help. But Hallie was impossible. She seemed to hate men. So she wouldn't speak directly to my father. If, at the dinner table, she wanted the butter, she would say to my mother, "Have that man pass me the butter." Then once Hallie caught Dad retrieving something that was stored in her bedroom, and she flipped out that he had dared enter. Dad couldn't stand her animosity. He was used to people liking him automatically. So they had found a place for her in a nursing home and she seemed just fine there. She got to write out rules about who could and couldn't enter and how they should approach her, and people generally followed those rules.

I'll take these pictures from the box of material with me to Ireland. Mom has not seen most of them. In fact, I don't know if she's even seen this one of Charles where you can see the dimple in his chin. And there is one of Hallie and Charlotte that I had touched up, enlarged and framed. It sits on my desk. The two of them are dressed in knickers and are standing on the steps of an old dilapidated porch with their arms interlinked. From the looks on their faces, we can see that they are at one with themselves, not posing or forcing anything, but letting their real selves shine for all to see.

I can't help but wonder what happened to Charlotte. She seems to drop off the map after Hallie was institutionalized. Hallie has draft letters to her but there are none that I can find from her. They must have had a terrible fight, or maybe Charlotte tried every way she could to get Hallie out and she couldn't. Maybe she found another lover, one who wasn't married. I guess I'll never know.

I wonder if Terry and Debby will last, if their love is fated to be the one that takes them into old age. My parents have it—at least they did before my mother took off to Ireland—but so few do these days. We've learned to keep hate going for generations, why can't we make love last?

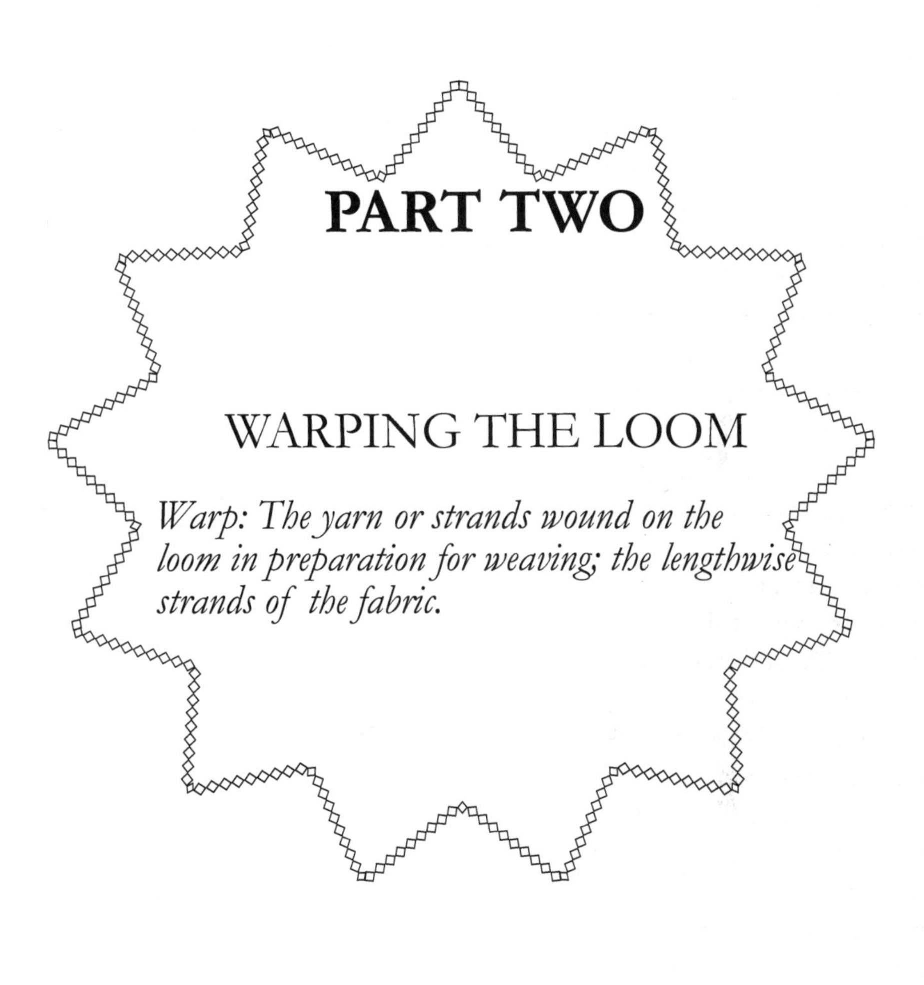

PART TWO

WARPING THE LOOM

Warp: The yarn or strands wound on the loom in preparation for weaving; the lengthwise strands of the fabric.

Chapter 7—Biochemistry

For Emma and Diana it was all about biochemistry: "bio" meaning biological family and "chemistry" meaning what happens when family elements mix: alchemy? explosions? chain reactions? chaos? feedback loops? or no bonding at all? For Emma, this experiment could not have been tried at home; Ireland had become the likely test tube. There was no control group—in fact, there was no control at all. Once the experiment was started there was no way to go back to a pre-experiment comportment. Yet, even with all of that risk, there was the chance of magnified growth, the discovery of fractals of fragile and robust beauty. Their study of biochemistry was about to begin.

September 30, 1996

Diana Kaufmann nervously ran her hands through her short, unruly hair as she awaited Emma's flight. She had left Dublin just after the bad commuter traffic died down. Even though Shannon airport was farther from her home, it was more manageable for her than the airport in Dublin. Driving the congested Dublin streets, fine on foot or by bus, took more attention to other people than she was willing to give.

All her life, she'd had plenty to do just managing her own self. The few friendships Diana had over the years were weak and often short-lived. Relationships with family were even harder; she distrusted the very idea of family, a mere mention of the word gave her tremors, bringing to mind people who never understood and always wanted to change her. Even Emma had been guilty of that at least once—years ago when Diana was still living in the States. Emma had lobbied her to quit drinking, not realizing how close Diana was to the edge. Sometimes, Diana felt, she could be so close she needed a drink just to stay alive, but Emma couldn't understand that. Diana, weary of failed explanations to others, had not tried to explain.

At age sixty-four, some niggling questions intrigued Diana, questions she thought Emma, as the eldest survivor in the family might help her answer. Emma embodied Diana's last chance, perhaps, at putting together the pieces of her own life. Years of independence and being a loner lost out to a need to know herself, to figure out why she was here on this earth. After weighing her options, the decision to invite Emma to come to Ireland had won—just barely.

When Emma's first reaction to her invitation had been lukewarm, Diana had sighed relief and quickly retraced her steps back into her fortress. But when Emma called asking, with her vulnerability up front and center, "Is the offer still open?," Diana was thrown back into doubt. Hearing Emma's excitement, she felt trapped, unable to take back the invitation.

Diana had persisted in making her father understand that sociability, marriage and children—all those things her elders wanted from her—were not what she wanted for herself. Then, suddenly, her father died a year ago. He was gone and so was the maypole of her life. She had designed her life around proving her parents wrong. Now both of them were dead and she was free. But there was a lostness about this freedom—who was she if not the opposite of what her parents had wanted her to be? One of the sides had let go in the middle of a tug-of-war, leaving her to fall hard, her breath knocked out of her. It was freedom all right, but along with it came a profound disorientation. She had spent the last year just trying to get oriented again. Now she wanted simply to move on—forget about her family, create something of her own. But loose ends seemed to dominate her landscape—ends she had left dangling when she fled to Ireland twenty years ago. Emma was one of those loose ends.

Diana wished that Danny had willed Emma a sizeable chunk of money and could have washed clean the legacy of Hallie's commitment into the hellhole Mannington. But, she mused, maybe Danny thought money had something to do with the "Kaufmann curse." This curse manifests itself in ways similar to the Midas touch. Along with great wealth comes a profound unhappiness. Such extremes seemed to permeate Diana's family. Diana's part of the Kaufmann curse was an explosive intensity from both sides of the family—from one side there was brilliance and from the other, intense compassion. With the brilliance to see the world for what it was, coupled with the ability to feel for those who are its victims, Diana often felt the world was just too narrow and the suffering too immense for her to sit comfortably on its surface. As she aged, she slowly found ways to make it livable, but just barely. She had the ability to make money, but she refrained from it deliberately, as if exercising that ability would drag her down even further.

In some mysterious way, the obligation to make sure Emma was not forgotten had been passed on from father to daughter. Now Emma was Diana's worry. They were related and yet, perhaps because of Emma's adoption, Diana and Emma had totally different temperaments. Diana imagined that perhaps Emma had the key to escaping the Kaufmann curse.

So here Diana was at Shannon airport waiting for Emma's slightly delayed flight. Waiting was her least favorite activity, next to cooking. In good physical shape from years of swimming and walking, Diana belied her age and strode about the airport, her jeans fitting more snugly around her than last year, yet she was not ready to give in to the next larger size.

To Diana, Emma seemed so normal—gracious, hospitable, kind, a wife and mother, religious. She was, in short, what most would expect of a woman. What would Hallie think of this daughter she named after Emma Goldman? Diana wondered if Emma's apparent serenity was merely heroic front.

Serene was not how Emma looked as she walked away from customs to the baggage claim area where Diana waited. Emma looked as if she hadn't slept in days, glancing around nervously. Emma managed a smile when Diana greeted her with, "Welcome, cousin, to the Emerald Isle." When they looked at each other, wariness and uncertainty were mirrored back.

Emma, preoccupied, asked, "Did you see a small Irish woman in a dark wool skirt carrying a tattered gray canvas bag?" Since Brigid's bag had been stowed behind them, Emma couldn't see if it was still there as the crowd behind her pushed to de-plane.

Diana shook her head. "No, why?"

Emma sighed, feeling shaky again. She said, "It's a long story. She was my seat mate on the plane and before we landed, she seemed to just disappear into thin air—the air is thinner a ways up, isn't it?" Emma stared off into the distance for a minute and shook her head as if to clear it.

Diana looked at Emma curiously, wondering if she would be picking up strays everywhere she went. When Diana traveled, she barely spoke to people, let alone got attached to them. "I don't suppose there's much we can do about it. Maybe she didn't check anything."

"You've got a good day to arrive, though," said Diana, trying to find something to talk about as they walked to the car. Emma looked doubtfully at the cloudy sky and considered laughing but decided against it. Diana took the weather seriously. It was the one thing she had in common with her neighbors, and since it changed constantly, it provided the fodder needed for at least a minimal relationship with those around her.

"Here's the car," Diana said indicating a small red Fiat. "Let's put your stuff in the boot with mine."

Though Emma had learned some of the British language idiosyncrasies the last time she visited, she knew it would take her a while to get them straight again.

"You'll catch on," Diana told her. "Besides, where you're going is Irish speaking territory, and you'll probably need to learn more than a few strange English phrases."

Emma asked, "What is Connemara? It's not on my map."

Diana nodded matter-of-factly, "Oh, it's the old divisions that people who've lived here awhile call it but it doesn't usually get put on the map—it's not official anymore. What I know about it is that people keep it afloat through story and lore—Connemara is famous for its crafts. I'd venture to say that the muse is alive and well there, nurtured by attention and practice. But it's a place everybody knows everybody and everyplace . People are known through their relationships to each other."

Emma looked puzzled. "What do you mean their relationships?"

Diana looked into the distance, trying to figure out how to explain this rather strange concept to Emma. "Well, you may be a writer or a potter, but you are not necessarily known by that—you are known by who your friends are, who your parents were or are, what land you take care of. I can't explain it well…but it's like you're not just an individual as you are in, say, Dublin. You're part of a network."

Emma filed that to think about later, when she had had some experience with the place.

Diana had planned to show Emma the Cliffs of Moher before heading to Galway. When Diana traveled, she simply changed her watch and adjusted to the new time. She expected Emma to be the same way.

"Ready to see some sites?" Diana asked enthusiastically.

"Will it be *very* far?" Emma asked, wondering if she would be up to sightseeing after the long flight. Maybe it wasn't so much the long flight that had exhausted her but the tilting at fears that she had been doing since she woke up that morning—or was it the morning before? All she really wanted was to escape into a world of sleep where she had no responsibility.

Diana was determined. "You can nap on the way, if you like."

Emma, looked around at the scenery that contrasted sharply with Ohio's drought landscape with its limp, exhausted looking plants and jaundiced trees. "I doubt I can nap if I'm going to miss something—my eyes simply will not stay shut. You know, I think my eyes have a mind of their own. Sometimes they cry when I've no intention of crying—like at the airport when I was leaving Ralph." Emma realized that she had no way of knowing what Ralph was doing. That thought was more foreign than the terrain she had just flown into.

Diana sat with the key in the ignition, listening to Emma rattle on, waiting for a decision. She thought, it damned well seems like Emma had enough energy to travel a bit more—that is, unless her mouth was also on a separate circuit...?

Finally, they reached a consensus to head northwest toward Ennis, stop for lunch and then decide. The road was good and the clouds began to clear, leaving the sun free to sparkle on the world around them. Emma stopped her chatter, and they quietly enjoyed the simple beauty of the place. Diana was relieved that Emma knew how to be quiet.

Finding a small, not too smoky pub to enjoy a light lunch, they caught up a bit on the details of the aftermath of the birthday party. By the time they finished, Emma had recovered and claimed she was ready for the Cliffs.

The road from Ennis to the coast was narrow and winding—Diana's kind of driving. Unlike city driving, where the obstacles were usually other cars, there in the Burren the challenge was the land itself. The only crop in this region was sheer rock rising up out of the earth. It gave them a sense of immediacy, as if the rocks had just erupted from the land moments before their arrival. A work in progress. Because of the wind and lack of soil, nothing but lichens grew. Sometimes, when the sun hit a wet spot on the hills just right, the rock glinted like a flashing mirror. Diana and Emma wove their way between rock on their right, and Galway Bay on the left.

Diana pointed left without taking her eyes off the tricky curves, "Out there are the Aran Islands; this is about as close as you can get to them without taking a boat. We may want to ferry out sometime; they rise right out of the sea. The storms come across the Atlantic with nothing to stop them and end up right in the inhabitants' laps."

When the wind was up at the Cliffs of Moher, it made Diana feel alive, as if, focusing on the drama in the outside world relieved her of her constant internal drama. Diana, in her effort to distract herself from herself, could find peace in the turmoil that was the natural world—the more drama, the better.

Emma, on the other hand, could well imagine what the waves looked like in a storm, crashing against the sheer immensity of the cliffs. What was outside of Emma tended to influence her mood. If the wind gusted uncontrollably, she felt out of control. Where wild weather brought out the adventurer, the conqueror in Diana, in Emma it brought out fear of the unknown. Perhaps Diana knew too much what dwelt in her interior;

Emma, too little. These dynamics seemed already to be shifting.

"I came out here once," Diana began, "before they had this fancy path. Oh, see that dirt path beyond the rail?" She pointed and Emma's eyes followed the trajectory. " That's where you used to have to climb. One time it was so windy I was sure I'd be blown off the path; I ended up crawling up it, clinging to the land."

Diana continued, "Now, if you look along the cliffs in a kind of straight line, on the other side of the bay is Spiddal, where the Crafts Centre is. These cliffs are what you will see across Galway Bay and a little west from your workshop." Diana pointed across the bay. It was clear enough to make out some land but not much detail.

Emma rolled the name *Spiddal* around on her tongue. "Spiddal—funny name for a town, isn't it? I keep wanting to say spittle, not too glamorous or spindle, like on a spinning wheel. But there's no n in it. Know what it means?"

Diana arched her eyebrows and cocked her head, "No idea—its Irish name sounds like An Spee Deal."

Emma smiled at the sound of the name. "That's more romantic than Spiddal, isn't it? Maybe I'll call it that—An Spideal," Emma said letting the Irish speak to her.

Looking out over Galway Bay, Emma began to relax, feeling the freedom of not having to know everything. The country drew in around her, comforting her, rocking her. She said, "We're surrounded by rock. But it doesn't feel cold and harsh—it feels protective."

"The Connemara coast," Diana said, gazing pensively across the bay. "There's magic there—it's a legendary Mecca for art. A bit barren for me—I tend to like the lush green spots better. Still, I halfway wish I were staying with you."

Emma brightened at the thought of not having to stay alone, "You're welcome, you know."

Diana considered it. A few hours ago, she had been sure that whatever time she spent with Emma, even a ride from Shannon to Galway, would be too long. Though gradually she was feeling more comfortable with Emma, she was not about to tempt fate.

"Right now I've got too much in the pot about to boil over in Dublin," she replied. "A visit, perhaps?"

Approaching Galway, Emma noticed that the terrain was much more Irish-looking with stone fences and green fields. She remembered driving near these "hedges" when she was in Ireland before. She thought she could brush up against them if the oncoming car seemed too close, which they mostly did. Then, after watching for a while, one of the kids realized that these weren't hedges, but grass and vine covered stone walls, the softness an illusion.

Galway was not the sleepy place with quiet, winding streets she remembered. The kids had joked about Galway because each street they took brought them right back where they had started. But Diana knew her way around and, after passing the square, where there were ten buses all trying to maneuver in the small streets, she drove onto a side street with shops, street musicians and people milling about. There was a contagious excitement, a holiday feeling about the place that Emma couldn't help but catch.

Diana had booked them at a bed and breakfast in lower Salthill on the far side of Galway where she had stayed once before when she needed some peace and quiet for writing. One thing Emma did not know about Diana was that in addition to being a serious writer of non-fiction, to support herself she had written upwards of twenty romance novels under an assumed name. Though the books were popular, she did not have to deal with an adoring public—or any public at all. She wanted it that way. Her privacy mattered beyond any possible praise. Not only that, but if the public had seen the real her, in her mismatched clothes bought at the used clothing store, and if they had seen the shambles that she called her house, with its piles of unread books and magazines, they might have lost interest in reading her books. This way, her mystique carried readers far above and beyond where they might otherwise have been dropped onto the hard rocks of her reality.

Colette's B & B was on a small road just inside the main one running parallel to the beach. They situated themselves in a back bedroom overlooking the garden, a quiet room as Diana had promised. Colette had set out the makings for tea with biscuits (or what Emma would call cookies).

"Suddenly I feel the need for tea," said Emma, moving toward the small white electric teapot in the corner of the room.

Diana took in several deep breaths, "Ah, yes, there it is—it's not you, lady, it's the air does it. So many people thinking about tea all at the same time, it's hard to ignore."

Diana rested on her bed, finally able to relax. This wasn't so bad, she thought—now if I can just get through the evening without a drink, I'd be quite proud of my hospitality.

Diana didn't drink regularly anymore. Occasionally she slipped a bit, as she had after Emma's birthday party when the family had stopped for lunch on the way to the airport. Those social situations required something of Diana that she never seemed to have; she had ordered a strawberry daiquiri. And when the first one didn't make a dent in her anxiety, she'd ordered another one; but it took so long to get there that she canceled the order. In the old days, she'd have marched back to the bar and demanded service.

At dinner not far from their B & B, Emma talked about her decision to come. Diana just listened, savoring the fresh fish and salad, letting Emma think out loud. She was content not saying much. With some friends, Diana was always like that; she would get them talking and not have to say anything about her own life. Other people's lives intrigued her. Luckily, most of the people she knew did not read romance novels or they may have recognized a few strikingly familiar characters and situations.

Chapter 8—Homing Devised

How do you know when you are home? Is there something different about the frequency of energy? If you live with others, it must have to do with frequencies being in harmony; when they are not, the place loses its homey feel. And if you live alone, with what frequencies do you hum? Other animals and insects inside and out, the art on the walls, the food in the kitchen, the sunlight as it makes its way through your windows?

October 1, 1996

Emma had in mind a rustic little cottage on the sea in Spiddal, something like her dream—a stand-alone cabin with all of the amenities and lots of privacy. She imagined herself enjoying being alone, feeling the freedom to choose what music she played, what food she cooked, what time she ate. But what would she do? She had considered others before herself for so much of her life. Truth was, she *wanted* to love being alone, but she had no idea how she would fare.

Her ideal place included proximity to the Crafts Centre so she didn't have to rent a car and drive on the left side of the road. To Emma, having a car felt like one more burden. And she didn't mind a lot of walking—would do her good.

Heading west along Galway Bay, Diana and Emma encountered miles of uneven, rocky shoreline. It was not a shoreline that evoked long carefree summer days of lounging on a beach. No, it looked like a gauntlet thrown down beside them. Diana and Emma drove through a couple of little towns. Just before they reached Spiddal proper, a series of white buildings sat off to the right with pathways between them—the Craft Centre. They started their inquiries there with a thin, dark-haired woman in the painting studio. The leads they got were as fragile as the woman's desire to help was robust. She suggested checking the grocery store bulletin board and, of course, the pubs—the hubs of gossip and local knowledge.

The grocery store bulletin board had little bits of paper with phone numbers, but most of the leads were for shared housing. Emma didn't think someone would want a short-term roommate; she was worried about whom she might end up with; and if she had someone else in the house, she might fall back into care-taking mode. Though she was frightened of being alone, she felt as if that was just what she needed.

After they called two of the numbers without luck, they headed for Diana's favorite place: the pub. They were greeted by two very friendly and very tipsy men sitting in dapper suits with Irish tweed caps. One called the other Daddy, though it was apparent from their ages that he was not. They were merry, likable and encouraging, but they had no concrete leads on housing. Diana decided not to mention to Emma that the couple was gay, not knowing if Emma would be comfortable with the idea. Diana chuckled, wondering how anyone could miss it.

Though they had expected to see a real estate agent's shingle, they found no such thing in Spiddal. "Used to be," said the waitress at the cafe they stopped in for lunch, "but they gave up the ghost a few years back." All the leads wound around like the roads in Ireland and ended up dead.

At one point they got into the car with no idea where to head. They looked at each other and began to giggle. As Emma laughed, she covered her mouth with her hand, just as her mother, Hallie, used to do, though Diana was more familiar with the gesture than Emma. Diana had known Hallie during the thirty-seven year lock-up in the mental institution and spent time with her later, too, after she finally got out.

Diana felt that she understood Hallie better than anyone else in the family, certainly better than Danny. He had always felt guilty about being a bad brother, right up until he died. But Diana had raged with Hallie's rage, had felt the same pain and was thankful that she had managed to stay on this side of the institution. Diana's strong connection to Hallie felt almost biological. And yet Hallie wasn't her mother; she was Emma's. Except for a few of Emma's gestures like the hand over the mouth and the way her eyelids drooped, Diana could see barely any resemblances.

Giving up on finding space in Spiddal, at least for that moment, Emma and Diana returned to Galway for the evening. After dinner, strolling on the shell-strewn beach, they spoke to each other softly, tentatively.

Diana bent down to pick up a pinkish-white shell that had the allure of perfection; but a closer look revealed it to be broken, ordinary, not something she would keep. It reminded her of the way her life felt, so much promise, so many privileges, a kind of glitter that on closer look lacked wholeness. So much was lost to the sharp winds and rough seas of secrets, scandal, and stealth.

Diana's curiosity was stronger than her tact and she wanted to bring the secrets out of the closet. She asked, "How much do you know about Hallie, Emma?"

Emma didn't answer right away. She had been half-expecting and half-dreading that Diana would ask her about Hallie.

Uncomfortable with the silence, Diana broke it, "I mean, if you ever want to know more, I can probably fill in some of the details."

Emma did not look at Diana as she spoke but stared ahead, down the beach. "I'll tell you what I told Lucy when she started asking me questions I couldn't answer: I'm just not a curious person. The past doesn't interest me the way it does other people. I look to the future."

Diana stopped in her tracks, looked around at the footprints in the sand behind them, some of them already erased by the incoming tide and contemplated, just for a moment, what it might be like only to look forward. Finally, she asked timidly, "Might you be afraid of the answers?"

Emma could honestly answer that, yes, she was afraid of what was now breathing down her neck, but she didn't want to appear vulnerable to Diana. The fact is, she didn't want to *be* that vulnerable. She'd much rather the pat answers she had given herself and others all her life would hold a little while longer—maybe until she died.

Though they had stopped walking, Emma did not make eye contact with Diana. "I don't know," she answered, trying to appear apathetic. She gazed out to sea. "It's just not important to my life."

Oblivious, then, to Emma's discomfort, Diana pushed onward, "Well, for instance, have you ever thought maybe your mother's craziness could have been passed on in the genes? Not such a farfetched idea, considering what studies of mental illness have uncovered lately."

Emma's walls of resistance flew up, readying for an attack. In her mind, she was there for a weaving workshop and maybe to try out her alone legs—nothing more.

Walking quickly ahead of Diana, Emma suddenly recalled an incident that happened several years after her adoption by the Parkers, and a few months after Mrs. Parker, on Emma's urging, had taken her on an ill-fated visit to Hallie in the institution. On that particular day, Emma refused to eat liver and onions that were dished out for her and threw a tantrum; Mrs. Parker made her sit there until she finished them. During the tantrum, Mrs. Parker yelled out, "You're willful, just like Hallie. I won't tolerate it in my house!"

It felt like a slap, though a slap would surely have been preferable. Emma got the food down through her nausea, waited until her father buried his head in the newspaper and her mother retreated to the kitchen to do dishes, and sneaked out. She got as far as the schoolyard and didn't know where to go from there. She sat in the middle of the playground, leaning up against the tether ball pole. Her father found her, hugged her, and told her everything would be all right. Mrs. Parker, not in a forgiving mood, said, "You remember that extra bed in Hallie's room, the one with the dirty blue bedspread in the corner with the spiders?—that's waiting there for you, if you ever behave like that again."

When Diana finally caught up with Emma, she apologized for being too intrusive. After they turned around to head back, Diana, unable to let the topic remain closed, asked, "But what if, just what if, knowing something about your biological roots and family is crucial to your life? What if, without it, you can only go so far?"

Irritated, Emma answered glibly, "Plenty of people never know what their roots are—they survive. And seriously, I have found out a few things from Lucy's research—like maybe Hallie wasn't schizophrenic, just brilliant and radical. Then, not only did I not get the schizophrenia gene, I also missed the brilliance gene." Her strained laugh tiptoed on the edge between self-deprecation and self-preservation.

The hot coal of a boundary penetrated even Diana's thick sole as she stepped on it. This time, she complied when Emma changed the subject to the difficulty of dealing with sand between one's toes.

At the end of the second afternoon of fruitless searching, the two women happened on an office a little west of town sporting a sign that read, "Cottages for Rent." That day, they had resolved to follow every lead no matter how tenuous.

A small gray-eyed man came out to greet them and, seeing that they were tired, without missing a beat, brought two chairs out from the back. When they were comfortable, he asked if he could be of help.

One more time, Emma went through her spiel about housing.

"So you would be just one person looking, yeah?" They both nodded. "And," he continued, looking straight at Emma, "you are the one who wants it?" Emma nodded again. "I probably can't help you," he said quietly. The price of his three-bedroom cottages was much higher than Emma could pay.

Staring out the window at the white cottages, he sighed, "Yeah, as I said, these cottages would not be fer you."

When he paused, Emma almost rose to leave but her exhaustion and a hope based on nothing, made her hold the chair a little longer.

He continued, "Now I do know a woman down in Spiddal who's a place she sometimes rents. But now I don't know if it's rented out and I don't know what her price'd be." He paused as if waiting for one of them to jump up and down and say, "How can we find out, now?" But neither moved; they looked at each other meaningfully. His slowness of manner seemed a test of their patience and thus their suitability for such a place. Were they like most of the impatient Americans with whom he dealt?

He went on, "I could call her?—that is, of course, if I can find her number." He rustled through the stacks of papers on his desk.

"We would appreciate that," said Emma in her most patient voice even while her mind was skipping and doing cartwheels. She was determined to still her crossed leg that was jumping with energy.

He finally located a number and called. No answer. When he paused again, Diana had to restrain herself from interrupting him to make him feel the urgency of this matter.

"Well, I believe if I look around I'll find her work number—she's probably there at work." He shuffled around more papers, came up with it and dialed the number.

"Yes, could I speak with Mrs. Ryan, please? But don't bring her to the phone if she's busy because I can call again later... Yes, well, as I say, don't bother her if she's busy."

Turning his attention to the two women in his office, he said, "She works in retail and if a tour bus has just come in, why, she gets overrun with business."

"Oh, yes, Valerie, my girl. Padraig Doyle here. And how are you this fine day? Yes, I won't complain. But you see, I got these two women in here who could be better. I was wondering if your rental unit is free at the moment? Uh huh. How many bedrooms is it? Three, huh." He wrote that down on his pad.

Diana and Emma exchanged glances of panic—three bedrooms meant it probably would cost too much. They held their breaths. "Well, one of these women is inquiring after renting it." The man gazed at Emma with the intensity of a probe meant to make any skeletons she might have in her closet stand up and take a bow. After a bit he said, "She looks all right to me—kind of blue-green eyes and gray hair, curly, cut short. Seems a good person to me. Think you'd like her." He paused, listening. "Why does she want it?"

He looked at the two of them and Emma said quickly, "To stay while studying weaving at the Craft Centre in An Spee deal." She had used the Irish phrase without even realizing it. His face lit up and he repeated exactly what she had said using the Irish.

"Uh huh. Now, are you sitting down there? Yeah, they were thinking of something in the neighborhood of half what I'd have to charge." He paused again listening. "But you'd meet them, huh? Be home tonight after half six? Good, I'll pass that along." With that, he hung up the phone.

Emma had a strong urge to demand to know exactly what Valerie said, but some part of her knew she must keep still.

"You know I rent these cottages out to a lot of folks from the States. Many of them come here to seek their roots. Some find them, but most have no luck—it's been too long. Why there was one gentleman here not long ago told me the sad story about his grandmother who'd left Ireland being as she was so poor. The choice was sometimes to leave or to die. So much had she grown to hate her native land that she wouldn't speak of it ever again once she reached America. Such that when he got to Ireland to search for roots, he'd so little to go on, couldn't find a thing related to him, not stone, nor tree, nor human. We're all related to the sea though, don't you think?"

Emma had not heard a word he had said since he hung up the phone. Diana, at least, followed the story, making appropriate tsk, tsking noises.

"She wants us there at, uh, six half? and meet her?" Emma blurted out.

"She means half six," corrected Diana. She looked at the man. "She's only been here a few days—hasn't picked up some of the expressions yet."

He winked at Emma, eyes twinkling. "I'd say she's got some important ones, wouldn't you?" After several more stories and discussion of the bus schedule, the man began to write down the address. Then he said, "Well, there's really no address; you just go across the street from the high school and three doors down to the west, about a mile short of An Spideal. By the way, I believe if I'm not mistaken, every room in her apartment has a view of the sea."

Emma gasped audibly and tried to remind herself not to get her hopes up.

"The name is Padraig Doyle," he said handing Emma his card. It sounded as if he said Porridge with a hard "g" on the end but whatever it was, it was sweet to Emma's ears. They both thanked him profusely and headed west toward Spiddal.

Diana was sorely tempted to stop in the pub and have a brew but she knew that tea-totaling Emma would start leaping to conclusions. They pulled over in the high school lot and sat staring for a while without speaking.

Diana felt edgy and tired. She thought about how perfect the location of the place was—only a mile from the Centre, so close to the sea and on the road to Galway. But she was sure the price would be too high and said so to Emma.

Emma wished Ralph were with her. He would be telling jokes and saying things like, "It'll all turn out for the best," and he was usually right. She tried not to snap at Diana's negativity.

While secretly coveting the simplicity of Emma's life and her unwritten philosophy that "life is a garden," Diana had, in earlier years, outwardly shown disgust toward it. More than once, she had made fun of Emma's apparent lack of guile and cynicism. Right then, Diana's own pessimism overtook her as it often did. She knew this was where faith would help her—handing it over to some super-power. But though she knew it would be a relief to hand it over, she could never surrender. She'd rather be pessimistic than disappointed. She said impatiently, "She'll want too much money. Figure out how high you are willing to go and I'll negotiate for you—I know the customs better than you. Let me do the talking." She got up and started pacing.

"Sit down. you're making me nervous," Emma said as she took out her pad and translated pounds to dollars, deciding that she could go as high as seventy-five pounds a week. "I'm sure we'll work something out; Pork wouldn't have sent us if he didn't think so."

"Padraig, it's Padraig," snapped Diana.

Emma said sweetly, "I can't get my tongue to say it."

Diana hated it when women played dumb and she hated it even more when Americans did, because they just didn't care enough to make sure they got it right. She retorted, "Just call him Paddy then. That's what most English speakers do."

Emma looked hurt and Diana continued, "Anyway, concentrate on how high you're willing to go."

After a while, Emma glanced across the street to the house and saw a slight woman wearing a patterned scarf over her head. She had expected to see a car drive up, but there was none in evidence. She motioned to Diana and they headed for the house. As they approached, Valerie stretched out to shake their hands and gestured for them to follow her downstairs. Emma had been thinking rustic, but this was modern and, just as Padraig said, each window looked out over a beautiful garden full of roses, petunias, impatiens and fruit trees to a farmer's field laced with stone fences and then the sea.

The sun was low in the sky and reflected off the sea into the windows. The sight compelled Emma to gaze out each window as soon as she entered the room. To her, what mattered was what could be seen from the room, not what was in the room. And it didn't feel lonely at all.

Valerie apologized for the state of the place, saying that she had not had a chance to clean thoroughly since the last people moved out. Emma and Diana could detect nothing that appeared "unclean." The place was furnished lovingly with twin beds in two of the rooms and a big double bed complete with comforter in the master bedroom at the end of the hall.

After the tour, they sat down in the stuffed chairs in the living room and began to talk business. Emma noticed that behind where Valerie sat was a fireplace that had been boarded up. She wondered briefly if she would stay warm enough there without a working fireplace.

Valerie began, "My husband and I both work, so we'll be gone most of the day. You wouldn't even have to put up with footsteps over your head."

Emma knew that she should continue the small talk for longer but before she could stop herself, she blurted out, "I am very interested. It's just a matter of the price, then, I guess."

Diana jumped as if she'd been burned, then recovered as Valerie, blushing slightly said, "Well, I'd have to ask sixty quid a week for it."

Emma breathed a deep sigh of relief and asked, "And I can have it just for a month?" Valerie nodded, and they finalized the deal.

Diana, amazed by Emma's good fortune considering her lack of finesse, said to Valerie, "So kind of you."

Valerie straightened up and said, "Oh, it's not out of kindness I do it. It's good for us both. I wouldn't want somebody in here always having parties or the like. I like having an artist here. Makes me feel like the place is being used well."

"An artist?" Emma questioned before she realized that Valerie was talking about her. She blushed saying, "Well, you won't have to worry about parties with me here. You'll hardly know I'm here. I'm 70 years old, after all!"

Valerie asked, "Oh, by the way, how is my cousin Padraig? He's in the right field, don't you think, dealing with people like he does?"

"You're cousins!" exclaimed Diana. "Why you'd have thought he was referring to some distant client somewhere."

"Yes, he's definitely in the right field." They laughed.

Valerie insisted on bringing them tea. "Just close the door when you leave," Valerie said as she left them to enjoy their tea and become acquainted with the place. "If you come before 2:00 tomorrow, I can let you in. If it's past that, I'll just leave the key in the door fer you."

As Valerie was leaving, Diana noticed that one of the paintings in the living room, of a pheasant in the countryside, was signed *Valerie Ryan* and she asked Valerie if she had painted it. Valerie looked uncomfortable and answered, "Yes, I did it—took an art class a while back. I'm no painter, though—it's just something to put on the wall."

Heading back to their bed and breakfast in Salthill, Diana's little red Fiat could barely contain them.

"Do you think that Padraig was real or was he a leprechaun?" asked Emma, playfully. "He wasn't as small as I'd expect one to be, but then again, he wasn't tall, either."

Diana, ready to believe anything after their luck that afternoon, replied confidently, stepping on the gas. "Oh, for sure he was. Her cousin, my ass!"

Chapter 9—Manifest Destiny

Emma's dread drifted away; she felt as if she were being led around by the hand, gently, magically. She might fall, yes, but somehow whatever held her hand would pick her back up and set her on the path again. She could not recall a time when she had felt quite this way. In her first six years, when she was still in Hallie's control, she had gone from household to household while Hallie went off doing her work. She had not been in control of her destiny then and had learned not to trust the hands that led her. But Hallie had always come back eventually, that is, until the last time.

The idea that she might have a special destiny was not something Emma allowed herself to think. In fact, if asked, she would have said there was no such thing as destiny. The closest she might come would be to believe that God was leading her. But Emma tended more toward believing that "God helps those who help themselves."

October 2, 1996

Emma awoke laughing from a dream where she was vacuuming and the spiders were talking to her. One said, "Don't kill us or you kill yourself," and they chase one another around, singing "Itsey, bitsey spider went up the water spout."

"You seem in a good mood already," Diana said sleepily, stretching her arms high above her head, grasping the brass headboard.

Emma smiled, "I dreamed about singing spiders."

"Oh, was it "Itsey, bitsey spider...?" and soon both were singing and performing the hand movements. Something in their very different childhoods matched and produced a spark.

When she was a child, Emma had been the poor cousin—poor in money as well as in luck. Though Emma went to visit the Kaufmann side of the family every summer, she had felt much more at home with the Parkers. Diana and her family looked at her strangely—maybe with them Emma would never be anything but crazy Hallie's kid. For her part,

Diana remembered Emma wearing brown or beige homemade clothing that lacked style. The family was embarrassed to be seen with her. And when they went out to eat, Emma didn't know how to behave. Once she befriended the waitress, talking more to her than to the rest of the family.

The summer visit invitations seemed fragile to Emma, as if they could be taken away as easily as they had been offered, more the fulfillment of an obligation than a certainty. The debt could be paid off any time, and she never would see them again. Though Emma enjoyed the extra privileges during those summers, she never wanted to get too comfortable or allow herself to become overly-intimate with any of those relatives. No, as children, Diana and Emma had never been friends.

Now Emma imagined what it would have been like to grow up near Diana and to have lived as cousins. In the Parker family, Emma was the only child. Most of the time, she had stayed by herself and kept quiet. Her mother, never able to tolerate noise of any kind, sometimes insisted her husband turn off the radio during one of his favorite serials. Like everyone else in Mrs. Parker's life, he always did what he was told.

Diana's job with Emma was done, and now, in a sense, she was free to go. But when Emma invited her to stay for a few more days at the apartment and explore the environs of Spiddal, Diana leapt at the chance. To familiarize themselves with how the buses worked, they took the bus out to Spiddal to register for classes that morning.

Downtown Spiddal had a church, of course, several pubs, two grocery stores (one of which doubled as a post office and petrol station) a vegetable and fruit stand and a taxi office. Before they went into the Craft Centre, they made a detour down the cement stairs to the beach where they could see across the bay to the rocky burren area they had explored a few days before. Before long, Diana had her shoes off, pant legs rolled up and was up to her knees in the ocean. She had always been a water child—loved to be near it, in it, on it. She had been an avid sailor since she was eighteen and had sailed many places, sometimes by herself. Back when she lived near Vancouver, she sailed up to Alaska alone, along the inland waterways.

Emma was timid about getting her feet wet and sandy. Ideally, she liked to plan ahead for such occasions, having towels and a change of socks on hand. But she followed Diana's lead. They splashed, laughed and dallied, sharing their rocks and shell discoveries and generally losing track of time.

When Emma called Ralph from the bus station in Galway. Phyllis answered, "How are ya'all" in her semi-southern drawl. At least it sounded that way to Emma, after all the Irish brogue she had been listening to lately. Phyllis seemed a little too comfortable, too much like the woman of the house. "Ralph's gone to get the mail. He'll be right back." Emma wondered why was he so late to get to the Post Office?

"We're getting along fine," said Phyllis. "Oh, but one thing I wanted to ask you—where do you keep the oven cleaner?" Emma had visions of overfull, orange faux-cheese casseroles burbling over into her almost-new oven. Since Valerie had offered to make her phone available for Ralph's calls, Emma gave Phyllis the number and requested that Ralph call her on Monday at 1:00 pm Ohio time. "Don't forget to tell him now," she said, "I'll be upstairs by the phone waiting."

The dynamics of that weekend provided a kind of telescoping of Emma's and Diana's lifetimes and their relationship into a few short days. Up until then, it had been highly debatable whether the two were "related" or not, depending on one's ideas about what constitutes a family.

Emma's relationship to the Kaufmanns fell somewhere between "family," as in those who raised her, and a solely biological connection. Even though Mrs. Parker was a very difficult woman, she was the one who could make life miserable or livable for Emma over the long haul—not Hallie or Alice or Danny.

Diana had a strong belief that genes contributed greatly to who she was. Emma's apparent escape from the Kaufmann curse puzzled her. How could Emma's life be so "normal," considering she was Hallie's daughter?

That night, Emma proposed that they sleep together in the double bed and have a slumber party, something she never had as a kid.

"Do we have to talk about boys and crushes and rock stars? Or maybe the curse of pimples and periods?" responded Diana quizzically.

Emma laughed, "Make that wrinkles and no more periods, and we've got a deal."

"So, lady, how about crushes?" Diana asked as soon as the lights were out.

"Crushes? I don't have any—you're the unmarried one."

"Oh, come now, what about that Padraig guy with the intense gray eyes. I saw how he looked at you."

"He was trying to see into my character, nothing more," said Emma as she covered her mouth with her hand and they laughed.

Diana had been worried that Emma would be interjecting God at every opportunity, as Diana's brother Claude always did. When Diana explained that she had put Emma in the same category as Claude, Emma gasped.

"Claude! No way!" Emma sat upright as if she needed to be higher for this conversation. She explained to Diana the difference between her faith and Protestant fundamentalists. As she summarily described it:, fundamentalists were full of hate for anyone who did not believe exactly as they did; whereas, her god was a god of love.

"What about you? What do you believe?" Emma asked, as she snuggled back down into the covers to listen.

"Religion fascinates me—but I can't get my heart into it." Diana told Emma a story about when she was recently in St. Brigid's Hospital in Dublin recuperating from minor surgery. A news flash came on the radio that someone had found the bones of Christ in a cave. Diana described how this had intrigued her because it was evidence of the validity of Christ's story, at least the part about his having been buried in a cave. Diana told one of the nurses in that very Catholic establishment about it and asked her to save the article if she came across it in the newspaper.

From the horrified look on the nurse's face, Diana realized her blunder. The nurse could never allow that the bones could be Christ's bones, because if she believed in the resurrection, she must also have believed that he walked out of that cave with his bones intact.

Diana continued, "I guess if you don't believe in your bones (excuse the pun) that Christ was resurrected, the story is just a story with interesting and verifiable—or not—facts."

Emma yawned widely and turned over. Diana, still unsure which things Emma could feel free to talk about and which were sacred to her, said, "Did I offend you, too, by telling that story?"

"No, no," Emma mumbled into the pillow. Then, deciding she couldn't let it go, she turned back toward Diana. "Without the resurrection, everything crumbles."

"Well, I think that's just too far-fetched. And while we're on this subject, another thing I can't stomach—and I think this is where Hallie always got stuck, too—is the role of women in the religion. I mean, what happened to the mother of Christ? Especially in Protestantism, she is shunted off to the side forever as some dirty creature, necessary but then disposed of handily, primarily by invisibility."

Emma's face reddened with determination. She explained her view that Mary was just the vessel used for the Word to become flesh—that she *should* be in the background. "We don't dwell on the bodily aspects, but the spiritual ones."

Diana, unable to contain herself, jumped up from the bed, turned on the lights and said, "God, I wish I had a cigarette and a drink."

Emma recoiled, shrinking further under the covers.

Diana began pacing. "Don't worry, I don't and I won't. But how can you think so poorly of mothers when you were one yourself?"

"Turn the lights out; you're breaking the slumber party rules," Emma said, knowing that she had broken her own promise to herself to stay off this Mary topic in Ireland.

Diana did as she was asked and returned to bed.

Emma began. "I try not to think too much of my body, I'll be leaving it soon enough—why bother to get so attached?"

Diana brought the topic back to home. "Maybe that's why you never ask any questions about your own mother."

Here it comes again, thought Emma. Everything seemed destined to lead to Hallie. She thought for a minute, then said unemotionally, "I never considered that, but maybe it's true—biology is just part of the worldly make-up—it's got little to do with spirituality. Better to study how to be a better person than to learn about my mother. Besides, you tell me she didn't even believe in God."

A slim moon began showing its light through the crack in the curtains. Emma lay stiffly on her back, and in the dim light Diana could just make out the tight lines on her face.

"A minister once proposed to me," Diana said mischievously as she picked lint off of the covers, "and I almost took him up on it—but never in a million years of Sundays—and that's what it would have felt like—would it have worked out." She shook her head, imagining the gossiping parishioners whispering behind her back about some damned thing or other that she would probably have done or said wrong. She continued, "His dreams included saving the sinner in me."

Emma did not hesitate, "Ralph's dreams were my dreams."

Diana found that difficult to digest. "Ever feel like changing your mind?"

"Nope. I never needed to open other doors, especially after I married Ralph."

On this issue, Diana told Emma, she was aligned with Hallie. Neither of them had been able to live lives in which they gave up the lead role. Neither of them could tolerate the behind-the-scenes prop work that seemed required to make marriages work. They had both tried relationships for a while but were simply no good at them. Every time Diana tried to behave in ways she thought were feminine, she felt like a man in drag and not a good drag at that—one easily detectable as a fraud.

It took courage for Diana to speak of those feelings that had often led her off the deep end. "Even women who start out questioning gender roles often capitulate in the end. Then they resent those who refuse to play the part. I've had more than my share of females threatened by my choices."

Over the years, Diana had found out the hard way that it was not men who were the strictest enforcers of these roles, but other women. One's own mother could be the ringleader with the whip.

Emma took a deep breath and told Diana what had been happening to her since the birthday party, about the picture of herself at six, the butter pecan ice cream bribe, and the dealer and the dealt.

Emma's face was flushed as she finished, "I wanted a chance to get to know the dealer side of me, since I've lived mostly in the dealt side. Can you understand?"

"It's crystal clear. But maybe knowing more about Hallie could help…" Diana said softly, turning on her side to start her dreaming and murmuring almost inaudibly. "After all, you both abandoned little Emma at the same time."

Chapter 10—Thermodynamics

Sometimes it seems as if each individual lives in her own world with unique rules and assumptions, unique immutable laws. Being born to a certain culture does not guarantee that a person will accept what has gone before, what she may see as illogical, irrational, or just plain unfair. So-called facts about gender are believed as firmly as the fact that the earth is not flat or that gravity exists. Even so, there are those who live their lives as if the world is full of nothing but gravity; others skip gravity, don't worry about the shape of the world and live in the humor of each moment.

The truth is, gender simply will not stay within prescribed boxes. It is more dynamic and fluid than flat, more like a waterfall than a falling brick. Perhaps gender follows a more complex law, one that takes into account heat, energy and relationship, more like the laws of thermodynamics.

October 4, 1996

The weekend had by this time begun to take on an encounter group quality. Emma and Diana were wearing down each other's defenses and at the same time reaching inside themselves to test what they knew to be true, puzzling out their pasts.

On Sunday morning Diana awoke from an intriguing dream, which she immediately told to Emma:

I am getting married. But I am standing where the groom normally stands, at the altar and everyone is looking back, wondering who is going to come down the aisle to marry me. I am looking, too, because I have no idea who it is. He is wearing a veil and when I pull it up to kiss him, I see that the man is Charles Gildebecker.

"Your biological father. He was so handsome and a great guy from what I hear," said Diana longingly.

"I don't know a thing about him." Emma said matter-of-factly, snuggling into the covers.

Diana got out of bed and started to pace. Her heart started racing and she felt oddly as if she had just been insulted. How could Emma know so little about her biological family; it was as if Emma were rejecting her, along with the rest of the Kaufmann clan, without a fair hearing.

All Diana knew about Charles was what she managed to pick up from conversations with her family and friends who knew him or had heard stories. He died before she was born.

"One thing I do know about him," Diana spoke her thoughts out loud, "was that to get Hallie to commit to her pregnancy, Charles had sworn that he would raise you himself." She gave Emma a long look to see if she had any reaction, but she lay seemingly unperturbed—not looking at Diana, but surely listening.

Diana continued, "Charles took advantage of the shifting roles of men and women in the twenties, reshaped himself a new man who could be both father and mother. I wonder how Charles got Hallie to marry him? Maybe he pestered her until she gave in, or maybe she needed a safe shelter to run to after she got herself into trouble, which she frequently did, or do you suppose she really loved this 'new man'? What do you think?"

Emma stretched her arms over her head and yawned. "I wouldn't have the slightest idea. No one's ever mentioned that part to me."

"Your lack of imagination about this blows me away! I mean, haven't you fantasized about it, at least?"

Emma sat up and shrugged. "Not really. I guess I just thought they were in love like anyone else who marries. Weren't they?"

Diana sighed, unable to believe Emma's lack of interest. "It was more complicated than that. I know that part of the bargain, from all accounts, was that he agreed to do all of the domestic chores—oh, yes, lady, a man after my heart." She thumped her chest, feigning an exaggerated heart beat.

"In your dreams..." Emma said warming up to the subject. They laughed the laugh of the well acquainted, the laugh of those who do not to have to explain anything.

Diana speculated as she pulled on her navy sweat pants, "He must have adored her—a hellcat he never succeeded in taming, not that he'd wanted to. If he lived longer, you'd have been raised by him.

"His mother was Irish—did you know that? Yes, your paternal grandmother was Marie something—Marie Collins, I think. I never met her. Maybe she died young. I don't know."

Diana pulled on a sweatshirt with a picture of a glass overflowing with white foam—the caption under the picture read Bailey's Irish Cream.

Diana said, "Everyone liked Charles. Even Dad, who did not dispense compliments lightly, called Charles a gentleman. And the rest of Hallie's brothers couldn't stir up a dislike for him, either. Grandmother

Alice met him only once, but she had little to say about him." Diana laughed. "And that's a most positive sign coming from her."

Emma nodded in agreement remembering that their mutual grandmother had been a woman of few words and those she did speak were usually harsh.

Diana went on, "Still, Hallie and Charles didn't invite anyone from her family to the wedding—no one, not even Danny, and Hallie always had a soft spot for my Dad. By then, though, I think she felt betrayed by them all and wanted nothing more to do with them.

"Kind of like you moving to Ireland, isn't it?" said Emma as a parting shot, as she strolled into the bathroom, red plaid flannel nightgown swinging with the movement from her hips.

Eating cereal with blackberries, Diana remarked, "Usually I just have a piece of bread and jam, standing at the sink."

Emma took a spoonful of cereal, crunched for a minute and then said, "That's because you have no one to fix it for you. Maybe there is a Charles for you out there somewhere."

Diana took the remark seriously for a minute and then shook her head, "I'm way too set in my ways now." Then, looking out the window, Diana changed the subject. "Look, the weather's even better than yesterday. It's unprecedented! How about a swim later? You're a swimmer, lady, aren't you?"

Emma had taken up swimming late in her life, and now she was a regular. However, she was used to swimming in a heated pool and she wouldn't go in if the temperature dipped below 80 or 81. Diana explained that the day was as warm as Ireland ever got and the water, too, after an unusually warm summer. Emma was quite sure she would not venture in. But Diana insisted that they both put on their swimsuits under their clothes, just in case they got brave.

The path to town from her place was so narrow that they were required to walk single file. At one point where the path expanded, Emma asked, "Can I say one last thing about last night's conversation?"

"Please don't let me stop you." Diana smiled slightly, thinking that maybe Emma's past was not as distant as Emma liked to think.

"You know, I never thought of Hallie as having abandoned me. Anyway, aren't you the one who always talks about the terrible 'Kaufmann curse?' It was all for the best that I was raised outside of that family. I never looked back."

Diana slowed down a little and looked Emma in the eyes, "But, you never *really* stopped thinking of her, right? Wasn't that part of the deal? You had to be what she was not—good mother, Christian, model female, totally sane and normal in every way, ad nauseam?"

The path narrowed and Emma fell behind Diana, thinking, that's not what I've done. Diana made it sound so predetermined.

When they were side by side again, Emma deliberately bumped her hip against Diana for emphasis, "But I agreed to the deal. That was a choice, wasn't it?"

"Sure, for survival. Were there any other choices? You had Hallie's imprisonment to show you what happened to 'bad girls.' You never even had a chance, I'll bet..."

Emma froze, startled by Diana's remark and did not even hear the rest of her sentence. All of a sudden, she felt like a victim of some horrible crime, or as if she had never really lived her life. Energy rushed through her body. She grabbed Diana's arm to stop her from walking, "What do you mean I never had a chance?"

"Let go. Damn, you're strong, lady. Don't get desperate on me now. All I meant was, what chance did you have to discover what *you* wanted out of life? The deal was you did what everyone else wanted, right?"

Emma regretted having opened the subject again and desperately wanted to take back what she had said about the dealer and the dealt. She said, finally letting go of Diana's arm, "Don't take it so literally."

But Diana was like a pit bull, her jaws clamped around this thing. She took Emma by the shoulders and made her look into her eyes. "No, just look at your life, at what you did. You married the next best thing to God—as close as you could get, short of being a nun. You're the one who took it literally—don't put that on me!"

Emma shook herself loose from Diana's grip and started on ahead of her. The path narrowed again, and Emma continued to speed ahead toward Spiddal. Diana caught up with her and they walked fast, side-by-side without touching. Emma's breathing was fast and furious. "Don't bring Ralph into this. I love Ralph; I have since forever. She puffed, "There's ...absolutely... nothing... altruistic... or goody-two-shoes... about that!"

Emma raced to the deserted beach. She was burning up. Before Diana could even get her shoes off, Emma had stripped and was up to her eyeballs in ocean. By the time Diana had her pants off, Emma was used to the water and swimming laps parallel to the beach.

"Nothing like waiting for me, lady!" Diana yelled into the wind.

Emma laughed at her goose bumps. "You've got to learn to plunge. It's good for the circulation."

After a while, they stopped swimming laps and the two of them stood and jumped with the waves, surprised at their unpredictability. After a while, the cold chased them back to the rocks, grabbing for the towels.

Later, sipping hot drinks in a dimly lit pub, Diana and Emma were each lost in thought. Emma felt a new, invigorating energy flowing into her. In spite of herself, she was becoming more curious about her "other" family history. Diana, on the other hand, wondered if she could take much more talking. She toyed with the idea of taking off early and getting back to her Dublin flat where life was, for the most part, predictable and certainly quiet.

Back at the apartment, though, Diana found herself settling in again. Emma persuaded her to go out for a walk. With rain jackets in hand in case the dark clouds portended a change in weather, they headed up a small road into the hills and away from the ocean, with Emma carrying a plastic bag in her pocket for collecting berries.

Near an isolated house on the hillside, they suddenly heard shouting, "Will you just shut it up?" This was followed by a slap and then quiet. Emma froze. She was catapulted back to an incident from her young motherhood. Lucy was eight or nine months old, fussing after a long trip to the Parkers' house one Thanksgiving. Mick had already learned about his grandmother's proclivities and stayed out of the way. But Lucy had no such awareness yet. From the drawer that served as a make-shift cradle in the bedroom, she awoke, became distressed over the foreignness around her and started screaming. The noise agitated Mrs. Parker, and Emma, knowing her mother's temper, ran into the bedroom to attempt to quiet Lucy. When she failed, Emma, at her wit's end, struck Lucy's face. Emma never forgave herself. She even confessed it once to Lucy who had no memory of it. The confession hadn't relieved her guilt.

Quietly troubled by the memory, Emma said to Diana, "I know Mother did the best she could in raising me. At least, she was steady and predictable. I imagine Hallie was not."

Diana chuckled and shook her head. "No, predictability was not a strong suit of Hallie's. One thing you could bet on, though, was that if there were men around, she'd fight with them on the subject of the moment—didn't matter the content—she was right, they were wrong. She broke up many a fine dinner party that way. Because of that, my mother decreed that we couldn't disagree at the table, ever. Even if we had to sit in total silence."

The road narrowed into a gravel road with grass growing in the median. There was no traffic so they meandered along, each in her own rut. Berries were growing next to a winding stone fence. The wind in the branches of a nearby tree hugged a deserted building making a creaking, ghostly sound—a good setting for bringing out the family skeletons.

"So, go on, tell how you got to be you," Emma said. "Tell me about the Kaufmann Curse. You talk, I'll pick," she said, pulling out the berry bag.

Diana spoke of her father, Danny, who ended up supporting his wife, his son's wife, and his sister Hallie—and at times even Diana. Danny's father had deserted the family, leaving his mother Alice resentful and angry. From this bitter mother, Danny heard lecture after lecture about how it is men's responsibility to look after and support women. The message got through to Danny, but he also picked up the underlying message—that women were weak and unable to care for themselves.

Emma and Diana took shelter in the doorway of an abandoned building to avoid the rain, which was drumming on the grasses and leaves, making them look like animated marionettes. In a voice barely audible over the wind, now picking up, Diana said, "I've always felt I lived in Hallie's world. We both chose to live our lives—how did Hallie put it?—'as a man,' yes, that's what she used to say. To her that meant following her pleasure, not worrying about how others saw her. That was considered mentally unstable in those days—still is, to some degree. When I was seventeen, my parents gave me the choice of going with Mother to a therapy center in the Rocky Mountains or being committed to the state hospital. I, of course went with Mother. Can't say it helped much but it kept me out of trouble for a while."

They listened to the rain and wind. Emma broke the silence when she could stand it no more. "That must have upset Danny terribly because I know from Lucy that Danny signed the papers that committed Hallie to the institution the final time. He did it for his mother who couldn't legally, as a woman, sign the papers. When Lucy interviewed Danny just before he died, he was still teary about having been the one that put his sister away for so long."

This was new information to Diana and she struggled to take it in. She felt as if her blood had stopped circulating, as if it couldn't go on as normal, now that she knew this horrible truth. Her face white, she said nothing.

Emma felt Diana's discomfort but felt she needed to continue anyway. "That's the reason Danny felt so responsible for Hallie's messed-up life."

The rain let up and, without speaking, Diana left the shelter of the doorway and began walking back to the apartment. Thoughts raced through her mind. She couldn't believe that after her father had done that to Hallie, he would have even considered it for her. Why had her father never told her that story? Perhaps he was too ashamed. Diana's heart clenched against the information.

She felt ambushed. Her own father had done this? It was all right when Diana knew more about the family than Emma, but this… She would have to think about it later—it changed everything she knew about her father. Alice must have forced him.

Finally Diana stopped and let Emma catch up to her. Wanting to feel in control again, Diana said, "I understand from my mother that Alice tried to adopt you when Hallie was committed, but for some reason, it never went through. If you thought your adopted mother was bad, can you imagine what it would have been like to have Alice as a mother?"

Emma replied quickly, "I didn't say my mother was bad. I said I'm grateful for what she did."

Diana looked at Emma incredulously. "Grateful?"

Emma did not look at Diana but started picking berries again. "What's wrong with grateful? She took me in when no one else wanted me."

"I just told you your grandmother wanted you," said Diana to Emma's bent-over back.

"I'll see if I can work on being less grateful, then," Emma answered as she stabbed herself with a thorn from the berry bush.

Back at the apartment, Emma brought out a tray of food that she prepared with some effort. Diana was in the living room with her shoes off and her feet up on the footstool. Diana had not lifted a finger to help Emma since they began staying in the apartment. Emma knew this was part of that "no domestic duties" routine, but she couldn't quite see how it worked in reality unless there was someone else around to take care of day-to-day living. Instead of confronting Diana on that issue, however, Emma decided to challenge her in another way. "What made you start drinking?" she asked.

Diana swallowed hard, took a deep breath and launched into a long job history, detailing her first few jobs where she had broken some cardinal rules about women staying in their "place" and was fired. That was the start of years of keeping her mouth shut to please the men in charge, betraying the innovations in her head. She practiced making herself smaller, repressing large parts of herself. Drinking provided a release, an outlet that she could rely on to get her through the day, the week, the job.

Diana sucked in the aroma of the vanilla bean tea and took a steadying sip. Then she said, "By the way, Emma, thanks for bringing out the tea. You know, I've never thought much about food—never cared one way or the other for it. Don't like to cook it. I usually wait till I'm famished and then just get out the cheese and bread. Something simple. And I eat out once a day—that takes care of it. Kind of bizarre, but it's the best I can do."

Emma realized that her resentment had faded. Diana had come through for her in so many ways on this trip. It hardly mattered about the chores. She replied, "Don't worry—I like doing it anyway. I like to spoil myself a little with food, and if you get some of the spillover and enjoy it, then good."

The rain started again and their attention was pulled to the pounding of the wind and rain on the windows. With this downpour, a doorway wouldn't have been nearly enough to protect them.

Emma, returning to the subject at hand, asked, "Couldn't you just trim yourself down around the edges, to fit in, just enough to get by?"

Diana snorted. "Ever cut your toe nails and gone a little too far and ended up with a bloody, sore toe? Oh, lady, that's the point I was already at when I was asked to cut just a teeny bit more. No, some people think drinking is suicidal. For me, it was a way to stave off suicide for a while. Lots of times it was seriously a choice between drinking or suicide; what gets me is that there's no word like 'alcoholic' for a person who thinks constantly about suicide. The word 'depression' just doesn't cut it. Why is that? I drank to stay on this side of death. Alcohol wasn't the disease—wanting out was."

Diana sipped her tea. "I tried over and over again to carve out a way to be a person, an individual, and a woman without a man and children. But that was the way to the same bottomless abyss that Hallie had fallen into. Sure, Hallie married and had a child. In her heart she was in non-compliance with a man and babies as central features of her identity. She kept her maiden name, the baby was going to be raised by Charles, she was still not going to do housework or cook. She thought she had figured out a way to change the way the world functioned with her words and ideas. But once Charles was no longer in the picture…

Emma sighed, seeing where this was going. "Yes, when there was just me and her, it was a steady free fall." Emma took Diana's empty tea cup and added it to the tray to take back to the kitchen.

Twilight was sinking into the world around Emma and Diana.

Shadows lengthened and colors faded, leaving behind black-and-white silhouettes to stand in for them until the sun returned.

After driving Emma up to the Centre on her way out of town, Diana parked the car near the beach, and they walked down by the water to say their good-byes. Emma flashed back on the goodbye she had said to Ralph and Phyllis at the airport—how lost she had felt and how scared. She hoped this one wouldn't involve crying.

Just then, at the same moment, they both noticed a swimmer out a ways in the surf. It reminded them of their swim and they caught each others' eye and smiled. They had to pick their way over the huge boulders to get down the beach. Diana thought of extending an invitation to Emma to come to her house in Dublin some weekend, but she was in the middle of a renovation and the place was a wreck.

"Maybe I can get back here sometime before you leave," Diana said hesitantly.

Emma replied without hesitation, "I'd love it. Thanks for all you have done. We did good, finding the place and everything and getting to know each other a little." She nudged Diana with her shoulder.

Diana kicked at the sand surfacing a shell unlike any she had seen before. It was large and spiral and white. "A souvenir," she said, placing it in Emma's outstretched hand.

As they headed back up to the road, Diana said, "Listen hard to that shell, lady, and maybe you'll hear the voice of the sea or any other voice you need to hear."

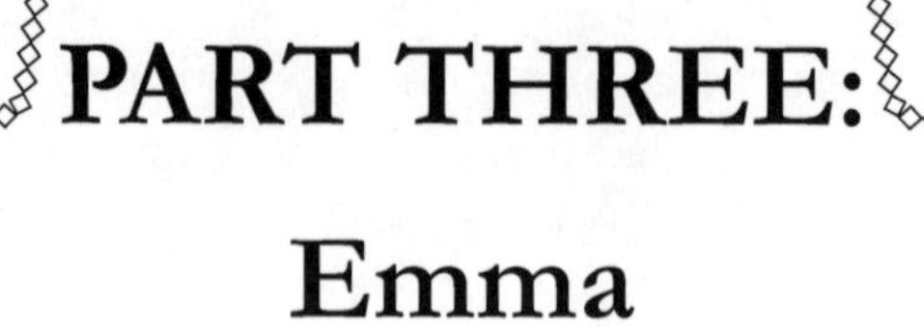

PART THREE:

Emma

BLENDED WEFTS

Several strands of weft are used together to create a wider range of colors, to weave images that seem to overlap, or to gradate an area from dark to light. The yarn bundles can be a blend of subtle or sharply contrasting colors.

Chapter 11—The Listening

You can't imagine how important listening is. Silence should be your closest ally.

October 5, 1996

I look around at the others gathered for the first day of the weaving workshop. We are all women, many of us over fifty. The few younger women in the cavernous room look a bit frightened. Scattered around the hall are looms of various sizes, from huge ones to laptops. The barn-like room should feel cold, but it is warmed by the floor-to-ceiling shelves stacked with skeins of yarns and fabrics and the woven wall hangings.

My eye catches a glint of silver metallic yarn that has been used in several of the tapestries, making them seem ancient but shining. Reminds me of my dark and silver hair, more silver than dark now.

Many of the hangings, obviously inspired by the Irish landscape, give me a déjà vu feeling of the woven images from my dream. An Irish woman who looks about my age begins to speak. She has long, long gray hair woven into a French braid and wound around her head. Her hands look strong but gnarled with arthritis; her face wears a sheen of serenity. She softly introduces herself as Rhiannon and when she speaks, all ears perk up because no one wants to miss a note of it.

"Welcome to Ceardlamm Centre. Failte an Ceardlamm," she lilts in both English and Irish. She checks to make sure everyone can speak English well enough to do without constant translation.

"The course will teach us new weaving techniques along with skills in conflict resolution," she says. My mind wanders to conflicts in my own life. Ralph and I had few conflicts in our marriage; in fact, I have to strain to remember any of significance. Then I remember a time when Ralph and I have had to get things straight about how much he could and couldn't see his parishioners for counseling, especially when they were pretty, young, just-divorced types. There had been one in particular he bonded with. To this day, I don't know how far it got. Jenny was her name and she was everything I wasn't: a virtuoso concert pianist with no children. In short, she was what I would have wanted to be if I hadn't married—if I had pursued a music major instead of switching to the more practical major of social work.

That was the only time in our marriage I can remember Ralph actually being mean. He talked about her constantly, and it seemed as if wanted me to *be* her. Each time he realized I wasn't, he got upset. As much as I explained it to him, he couldn't see that he was doing anything differently. I handled that conflict by dissolving into tears every time it came up. Then he dismissed me as emotional and irrational. And I did feel crazy. I finally got him to stop seeing her, and after a while things got back to a semblance of normalcy. For a long time after that, I felt betrayed and unable to trust him. At some point, I must have let it recess into my unconscious—that is, until now. The thought unsettles me, especially since Ralph is so far away.

I force my wandering mind and emotions to return to the room. Rhiannon is explaining about how the World Weavers began ten years ago during a particularly troubled time in Northern Ireland. From its inception, World Weavers has included Catholics, Protestants, Muslims, Jews and those of other or no denomination.

"Are there any men in the organization?" asks a forty-year-old black woman with a British accent.

Rhiannon smiles mysteriously and responds, "A few men have attended the workshops, but none are on the board of directors. Men have not pounded down our doors so we've remained primarily a women's group where men are welcome."

She speaks of other places they have conducted workshops, including Northern Ireland, the Middle East, Bosnia, South Africa, Nicaragua, El Salvador, Chile, New Zealand, the former Soviet Union, the southern United States and San Francisco, where they worked in conjunction with the AIDS quilt project. People who attend at the home base in Dublin come from all over the world and take ideas back to their communities and begin work on their own.

It is not an intellectual mastery I feel from her, but a knowing that permeates her being. She seems a creature not quite, or maybe not solely, human. In fact, when she laughs, she looks like a silver fish, sounds scaling off her as her whole body undulates; her loose blouse and long skirt, the colors of the sea, sway around her.

Instead of setting up looms, we are asked to start with a few exercises in Tai Chi. "You'll learn that weaving should not be done in a vacuum, without some grounding with the earth," she explains.

Rhiannon is graceful and slow as she narrates her movements. First, planting her feet slightly separated and then bending from the head down, she says, "Bend each vertebrae until you are as far down as possible without strain." Soon she has her hands flat on the floor. Most of the class has trouble even touching the floor, but I can do it with no problem.

She teaches us stretches for the shoulders, saying, "You'll want to remember those—that's where the weaving'll get you."

Before class is dismissed, Rhiannon assigns us homework. "Practice listening to your environment. If it's to other people talking, try to be quiet more than usual. Make sure you hear what is said. If there are no people in your life, listen to the birds or the ocean. Key in to your sense of sound."

On my way home, for the first stretch of the walk, I am able to stroll directly on the beach because the tide is about halfway out. I listen to the water lapping quietly against the shore but ideas race around in my head, taking my attention away from the sounds. Will I succeed at this workshop? I don't consider myself an artist, more a craftsperson. Others in the class are much more poised and experienced. For my tapestries in the past, I have always found a pattern to copy. Art class in grade school was the only class in which I ever cheated. The teacher made it clear to me that my work was not good, yet I wanted desperately to get a good grade. For our final, we were to draw an original piece, and I traced something to get an A. The thought of it still shames me and colors my relationship to art.

I catch myself listening only to these thoughts running around my head. That wasn't the assignment. I bring myself back to the sound of the waves.

Before long, I am turning into the Ryans' driveway, easing my way around the back toward my enclave. For a moment I smell the breezes as they come through the yard carrying odors of ocean, roses, lavender, as well as an acrid smell that I have learned is peat burning.

Peat burns much cleaner than wood, and since there is so little wood in this area, peat provides the main source of fireplace warmth. How odd to think of burning the very ground on which you stand. Maybe it's not that different from burning coal but it feels more graphic—as if people will at some point consume the whole island. What has taken centuries for nature to build takes only a few minutes for humans to burn.

Calling Ralph only makes me nostalgic for home. Though Sean and Valerie are accommodating and kind, we are strangers to each other. They allow me to call Ralph on their phone and live in the apartment that Sean built here, but it is clear they are not trying to be friends. How will I keep from getting depressed and lonely during these long evenings and nights? If Ralph were here now, he'd probably want something and I could busy myself getting it for him. I might even bake him brownies. But brownies are the last thing I want, so what now?

Once I sit down and relax in a soft chair in the living room, the one that faces the window and the sea, I relax a bit. Behind me is the boarded up fireplace with a broken chimney. I can hear the wind whispering behind the boards—it sounds almost like a human voice. I concentrate on the sounds, doing my homework. Again my mind interferes, beginning to replay conversations with Diana over the weekend. I pick up the shell she gave me, put it to my ear, listen to its windy echo. What wisdom might Hallie give me if she could speak to me?

For seventy years I've avoided thinking about such things—afraid someday I'll go crazy like she did. Oh, I need my counterbalance—maybe Ralph is all that has kept me sane all these years. I stare into the dark, listening as the whispers behind the boards slowly shift their shapes into words. They sound like "let me." *"Let me, let me, let me."* I hear, *"just let me be."*

"Let me lull you with a story, daughter, daughter, mine." I drop the shell, shattering it on the hard tile floor. These are not kidding-around, almost words. They are quite distinct.

"From a time when you were not you—swirls of nothing before, before your birth, before you came and became."

I shake my head vigorously, trying to cast out the sounds. Pressing my face against the window, I look desperately for someone who might be speaking. Nothing there. I stumble to the heat duct to see if the words are coming from upstairs. No, the sounds seem to be emerging right out of the wind itself. I hear my heart loudly beating in my ears as if trying to drown out the voice.

Where can I run to? I am mad—it has happened so fast. I heard the word "daughter," yes, I'm sure of it.

I sit stiffly in the chair, holding my breath, afraid if I move the voice will go on, afraid also that it will stop.

The voice continues in a raspy way as if speaking after a long sleep, *"My stories, so many stories, may tell who you are. To start, may we start now? Something nice, something sweet—not to scare you, blare you away with the worst. When you are ready...Breathe now, dear, breathe; it's not your time, not yet."*

She's right, I have not been breathing and when I do, I quiver almost uncontrollably on the exhale. I wrap the afghan around my shoulders, listening to the words of my mother.

"I learned to play the piano, to tickle the keys, to dream a melody, at age seven."

Her voice sounds like a piano now, rhythmic and melodious.

"Music was the one medium Alice and I both loved—music could whisk away an ordinary drudge day, make it blossom into the extraordinary. She wanted hymns;

I wanted more. That day, we played Shubert, the Trout Quintet and a new French composer, Debussy."

The wind is silent now, and I hear music. It is as if someone is playing in the next room. I relax, listening as a little girl might as her mother played just for her.

"You'll like this story, Emma, just lean on the music," the voice says as I look out the dark window, making out the shapes of a young girl sitting at a piano.

June, 1905

Twelve-year-old Hallie sits close to her mother on the piano bench playing a duet. The piece is one that a friend who was in the military just brought back from France. It is called "La Mer" by Debussy. Hallie has orchestrated this concert in the living room for extended family and friends. They moved much of the furniture out of the room to make space for folding chairs.

Hallie is the picture of health—rose in her cheeks, brown hair that shines with natural highlights, muscles in her legs from playing sports with her four brothers. You can tell that she will become something wonderful. Of course, no one can imagine her becoming a star basketball player, since there is no such thing as organized women's basketball. But a concert pianist, maybe.

Because Hallie knows it would please Alice, she let her pick the pieces they will play tonight. Alice looks at Hallie as if she has just given her the world. Perhaps tonight is the last time Hallie will ever see that look.

They play to enthusiastic applause. Maybe it is peace through concession, who knows? And maybe if Hallie could have conceded on other things, life might have given her more idyllic scenes like this one.

Danny is only two and a half and, with help from one of his three older brothers has picked roses for the occasion to give to the performers after the show. Instead of handing them the flowers, Danny flings the roses at their feet. When Alice and Hallie swoop to pick them up, they are stabbed with thorns and have to throw them back down. They make a howling show of it, tossing the roses as if to each other but missing them, dancing and bowing so Danny thinks this is the way it is supposed to be. On one thing mother and daughter agree: gem that Danny is, he deserves all of the consideration in the world.

The red of the roses fades into black as I find myself once again looking out a darkened window, wondering where I have just been.

"I have a feeling, feel like talking. Hope, do hope, you won't mind--listen with heart, leave mind behind."

I shift in my chair, my back aching from not moving. I say barely audibly, "Why didn't you come to me at home, a long, long time ago?"

"Tried to reach out on Days of the Dead—tried and re-tried—but no response, not a whisper."

Still wondering about my sanity, especially as we have a back-and-forth conversation, I say, "I don't believe in that holiday, so I'm sure I wasn't paying attention. It's related to Halloween, I suppose?"

"There are so many, many things you don't know, don't believe. But you hear me now."

I concede that on this trip I have suspended certain disbeliefs. If my mother wants to tell me her stories here, then maybe I'll listen—I have plenty of time. "I've already begun to change my mind about you, based on what Diana told me."

"Ah, Diana, ally—wish she'd had an easier, breezier time."

My stomach growls loudly and I realize it is close to eight o'clock.

Hallie laughs, a twirling whirlwind of a laugh, *"At least, very least, no worries about food anymore—always such a problem, the cooking, the politics..."*

I remember that when Hallie was in her ninties and living in a nursing home near Ralph and me, all she would eat was ice cream sandwiches and chocolate. She had been a vegetarian most of her life, which made what she ate in the nursing home fairly limited to begin with, but that latest diet had seemed ridiculous. For a while, we tried to encourage her to eat better, but when she would eat nothing else, we figured if she'd made it that far—what harm could it do?

It is amazing that Hallie lived to be ninty-nine considering what her diet had been in the institution. When Lucy first started writing the book, Hallie told her that in Mannington the cooks used food coloring to make food the proper color. She said she knew because once, when they served carrots, they made a mistake and colored them the color of fresh broccoli. Can you imagine? Since she didn't eat meat, she had to eat plenty of those pseudo-vegetables.

Hallie breezes back into words, *"Stories and such not for you to feel sorry for me. Please, won't you do something, brew something?"*

Startled, I say, "Do something, like what? I'm no writer and my memory is bad—I doubt I'll remember everything."

"Oh, you'll remember..." Her voice fades into wind again and I am brought back suddenly into my quiet little living room looking at nothing, hearing the wind resume its usual erratic gusts. Again I wonder if I am going crazy. I notice the broken shell on the floor and clean up the pieces. They feel hard and sharp in my hand, very real. The room has not changed. Everything is where it had been a few moments ago before that voice...

For this minute, I'm not going to consider it; I've got dinner to get ready. Cutting the local, organic carrots into rounds, I appreciate their bright orange color.

As the vegetables simmer, a gentle knocking comes at the door. Peeking out the curtain, I see Valerie with a basket in her hands.

"You aren't feeling lonely, are you, dear?" The compassionate way she says it makes tears fill my eyes. More crazy than lonely, I think, but I just nod.

She says sympathetically, "Time will help it, you know. Give it time. And I brought you some onions and apples from the garden. Hope they suit you."

I thank her and she bows out, saying that she doesn't want to disturb me. But her leaving disturbs me. The fact that I am alone disturbs me. My hearing voices that no one else hears disturbs me. This wouldn't be happening if Ralph were here. He'd walk me back to the bedroom, maybe give me a little love pat on my bottom and we would bump each other gently, vying for space in front of the sink to spit the spent toothpaste. I'd put my cold feet on him in the bed and he'd feign horror. That's reality. I wonder if I can get a plane out of here tomorrow. I turn out the lights. The darkness penetrates my pores—it's in me as well as out. I never knew it could get this dark.

The next day, bright sun fills up every corner of the apartment, and the discussion with Hallie seems like a conversation with galaxies that are not evident now. Maybe I dreamed it or let my imagination run wild. My worries are more mundane today, like sweatpants I have broken in over many years. How to fill my days—the workshop is only from 1:00 to 5:00. I have solutions to these problems: I'll relax, read, pick blackberries, walk along the seashore... Half of me hopes Hallie's visit was a dream and the other half just wants my mother. I can feel my body pulled like a magnet toward her presence, wanting that memory I never had.

At the seashore, journal and binoculars in hand, I am the only human. I settle into a soft, high hillock of grass towering over the sea. I can see the Aran Islands in the distance to the west and, of course, the Cliffs of Moher directly across the bay. I am thankful Diana gave me that context on my first day.

I lie on my back and let the sun heat my face and the pounding ocean iron worry-wrinkles from my mind.

"Can you hear me over ocean? I'm over the ocean, daughter, daughter, daughter." The repetition of the word "daughter" are in sync with the waves.

Startled again, but finding myself smiling into the sun, I say, "Yes, I hear you fine, oh, persistent wind."

"I've got nowhere else to be and a lifetime of stories."

The sea smells strongly of fish and old rotting seaweed. I take off my jacket and prop my head up on it, feeling strangely at ease with the idea of her talking to me. "What is it for today? Something sweet, I hope, like yesterday?"

Hallie says in a rather gruff voice that I'd yet to hear from her, *"Use up the sweet ones, sweet one, you'll be craving, raving for them later."* Then softer, she says, *"but there was my niece, Chloe, Hank's dear daughter—always had the sizzle of spit on fire!"*

Leaning away from me and pointing towards the sea, is a large shiny black rock still wet from the tide, draped with bits of seaweed. I stare at the rock, and the shapes of the seaweed slowly form into a little girl, not Hallie this time.

October, 1913

Hallie and her six-year-old niece Chloe are walking in the woods near Chloe's home where Hallie is living temporarily, just until she can earn enough money teaching school to go back to college and finish her degree. A person in Michigan can qualify to teach after just two years of college. Hallie already earned a teaching certificate at Ipsanlanti College, near Detroit.

Hallie is wearing what to Chloe is a most outrageous outfit—bloomers and what looks to Chloe like one of her father's shirts. Her burnt orange hat flops over her ears. Hallie's clothes are nothing like what Chloe's mother ever dares to wear.

Because Hallie doesn't like staying on the main path, when they come across a cow path, they venture to see where it leads. They never go the same way twice.

Chloe believes that since Hallie has no children of her own, she must not know how children should be—or at least are—treated. Chloe thinks Hallie has it backwards because she curses and yells at Chloe's father (Hallie's older brother, Hank), who is used to being treated with utmost respect by women, but she never yells at Chloe.

Suddenly, the footing becomes muddy and rough. After jumping gracefully over a particularly muddy hole, Chloe looks back at Hallie and says, "Why don't you have children? If my mother had decided such a thing, I wouldn't be here!"

Taken aback for a moment, Hallie replies with a twinkle, "If I'd had children of my own, I wouldn't be here with you now, would I?"

"Why not?" Chloe asks.

"Why, I'd be home with them right now, of course, and have no time to be here with you!" That is the end of that discussion.

Hallie hopes if she ever does have a child that she will be just like Chloe. Their relationship is so uncomplicated and seems more like one of peers than adult to child.

When they come upon an opening in the woods shaped like an ellipse, Hallie is reminded of a poem she loves by Emily Dickinson. She recites it for Chloe:

Still at the Egg-life--
Chafing the Shell
When you troubled the Ellipse
And the Bird fell.

Can the lark resume its shell?

Chloe laughs, fascinated by the rhythm. To Hallie it is a rather ominous poem, and she doubts that Chloe understands it; she has yet to fall, to be broken open and to yearn for a way to go back. Hallie wishes she could protect Chloe forever.

They walk for a while in silence until Hallie says, "Honey, soon I am going to leave you."

Chloe looks panicked. "Take me with you, please?"

"Who would take care of you and keep you out of trouble while I'm at school?"

Chloe replies confidently, "No one. I'm a big girl, and I'll wait until you get home to get into trouble." Then she laughs, the light carefree laugh of someone who is still flying.

Her laugh rolls itself back out to sea, and Hallie is gone again. I sit up, stretch and glance at my watch. It is getting late. I walk quickly toward home. Is this what it's like to be schizophrenic—thoughts and emotions out of sync? Right now, I don't feel crazy or out of control and maybe that's exactly the problem—I should feel crazy.

Perhaps it's magic, not craziness. If magic can happen anyplace, it's here on this strand where ocean and land meet and boundaries blur, between fish and mammal, between life and death, between water and soil. With the tides coming and going according to the moon and the sun shifting summer into fall, nothing is remotely solid. While I'm here I'll make like the seaweed, ride the tides, expect nothing, predict nothing. Just listen and see where I land.

Chapter 12—Roots

Did you know that roots do not just go down into the ground, but down into the prior generations and up to the future generations? And sideways, connecting us all.

October 6, 1996

"Picture an entire root system extending from your feet down deeper and deeper until you tap into the molten energy at the center of the earth."

My feet tingle with energy—I've always thought these kinds of exercises were mere metaphor, but this time I feel it.

Colleen continues, "If you can't see the ground you're standing on, you may think you're in mid-air somewhere—maybe even at the right hand of God. That's a dangerous thought." Colleen tosses her bright and unruly red hair back behind her shoulders. Some people may have thought she looked dangerous herself and maybe slightly crazy. She must have been harmed by someone who thought of himself as the right hand of God.

"So, look where you're standing, where your feet are today." She looks down at her worn leather sandals. "Today they're in Spiddal, Ireland. Now look where your roots are—where you were born and to whom. Who are your ancestors?"

My stomach flip flops. Ancestors. What is it with this ancestor thing? I've lived seventy years and have barely ever worried about where I come from. First Lucy, then Diana, then Hallie, then Colleen all talking about how important it is.

Colleen looks directly at me as if she knows something about me that I don't. "What do your stories and my stories have in common? Some stories have themes of severe oppression and victimization. Some have within them the seeds to create new stories. How do you want to see yourself? As victim or as actor? Or a little of both? For homework, think of a lifescape—that's what we call the tapestries—that represents the story you were born into. Include the landscape, perhaps and also the emotional-scape surrounding your birth. Tomorrow we'll set up the looms. Most of the weavings you do here will be small due to time constraints, but you will learn not only the techniques but also who you are."

My mind is a blank—I don't know the story of my birth. I know that people don't actually remember their births but usually we hear tales about it as we mature. I have told of my children's birth stories to them many times. But I have imagined my own in so many different ways and until now there was no one who could tell me.

After loading my backpack with carrots, cauliflower, and celery at the Spiddal vegetable and fruit stand that claims to have fresh items every day, I begin the walk back. Drawn to pay homage to the ocean again, I sit on a rock on the beach for a while, before heading back up to the road. Today the tide is low. Seaweed is strewn about on the rocks and sand as if to shuffle it for the birds and insects to play their hands to win food. Never having lived near the sea, I don't know much about tides. I did learn from Diana that tides are twelve hours and twenty-five minutes apart. I calculate: if low tide is at about 4:00 pm today, it will be at 4:50 pm tomorrow. Maybe I'll chart it. It seems crucial that the sea and I become friends in this place defined by the sea.

Maybe I was born from this sea generations and generations ago. I read a theory once that humans evolved from out of the sea. I feel a pull to come back home. Closing my eyes and listening to its language, I can almost understand it and its call to me.

After settling into my chair in the living room, I say aloud and self-consciously, (wondering what Valerie would think if she overheard me), "Hallie, I need your help." Almost immediately, the wind picks up and the room is infused with air. I know she is here again, miraculously. I feel a strange kind of power, and I smile to myself: maybe this is how babies feel when they cry and a parent comes right away. I feel warm and secure.

When I explain my assignment, I ask if she will finally help me with my homework and share the story of my birth.

Her laugh is like wind chimes just before a storm. *"Homework, yes, to work at home with you and be at home with you."* She pauses. *"But now we're past the sweet, sweet, sweetness and light-on to the lightening and thunder because, as you know, the circumstances, dire, dire, of your birth were... Let me, allow me, to deliver..."*

For a moment I hear only the sound of the wind outside and my own breath, which has suddenly become shallow with fear. Maybe Hallie is right, maybe I only want to hear the good stuff. It's as if what I am about to hear is happening now, in this room, instead of seventy years ago and an ocean away. I stare unblinkingly at the window in front of me and I begin to make out a face, a handsome man with a dimple in his chin.

July 16, 1926

Charles and Hallie are out for a drive in the country in their brand new white Ford, bought from real estate sales commissions Charles had earned. Hallie is in an unusually good mood, considering she is eight months pregnant and has been generally cranky throughout the pregnancy.

Her marriage isn't like any other—she made no deal to give up her independence in return for support. Charles and she have that all worked out. He will do the domestic labor that she despises, and he will not try to change her as so many have before. Charles represented independence from her family and from the wagging tongues that incessantly accused her of wicked ways and interfered with her ability to make a living.

She actually wasn't doing all right by herself. Powerful forces in her life assert themselves without regard for proper time and place. For one thing, she gets what she called "urges" and then she goes looking for just about anyone who talks sweet and appears gentle. Her body can not distinguish married from single, old from young, rich from poor, male from female, black from white. And that gets her into trouble with all sorts of so-called proper people. By the time Charles asks her to marry him, she has already been fired from teaching jobs, chased out of a couple of towns, and in jail once. She was considering leaving the states of Michigan and Illinois, just to get away from her reputation.

Charles keeps putting his hand on Hallie's puffed out stomach and singing, "I found a million dollar baby at the five and ten cent store." They laugh about how their child is going to make a million dollars and they'll have to hang their heads in shame around all their socialist friends.

When they run out of gas, they feel stupid about not having paid more attention to the small details of life, the ones that keep a car going. Charles insists, "You stay here. I'll be back in a hurry with the gasoline." Hallie has a bad feeling. Normally, she would go with him, but she is feeling tied down because of the pregnancy. And it is a hot, hot, muggy night—overcast, no moon and darker than the inside of a womb.

She waits and waits for Charles to return, helpless in that machine that needs to be fed to be of any use. She sometimes feels that same way—has a lot to offer but needs to be fed from time to time. She needs a mother herself, especially since she is becoming a mother. Charles has been a much better mother than her own mother has. He cooks vegetarian food for her, the way she wants it. She has had so little nurturing, so few friends.

Women are generally jealous of her, men flirt with her, preachers sear her with their eyes and then pinch her behind the scenes where no one can see. Even the prostitutes are upset because she gives it away. According to Hallie, monogamy has never been big enough for the complexity of human beings that exist in this world. If it were, why are so many willing to come with her for a while? That kind of thinking, and her actions has not made her friends of either the male or female persuasion.

The plan is to take the baby and move to their white clapboard house out in the country where the air is fresh and the neighbors so far away it will be hard for them to meddle. This baby will never know she has a grandmother named Alice.

But what happens to poor Charles has to be told to tell the birth story; Charles never comes back with the gas.

Hallie is awakened from her sleepy stupor with a clack, clack, clack of a policeman's lantern knocking on the windshield. She looks out into the light, dazed and disoriented. Why a policeman? Did I do something wrong? Maybe we parked illegally. "Just out for a drive, officer," she says calmly so as not to arouse suspicion. Then suddenly she wonders if Charles had been arrested. It wouldn't be the first time, but arrests have always been in connection with the union before.

"Hallie Gildebecker?" the policeman asks gruffly. "No, Hallie Kaufmann. I am married to Charles Gildebecker. Why do you want to know?" But by now her whole body knows that awful news is coming. The policeman can not see how pregnant she is because most of her is in the shadows. If he could, he probably wouldn't just blurt it out. He says coldly, "Your husband has had an accident. He was struck by a truck just south of Route 10. Killed instantly." Then seeing her shocked face, he adds, "I'm sorry to have to tell you this, ma'am."

She goes unconscious at that point and remembers no more until much later. She goes into shock and from there straight into labor. The policeman takes her to the nearest hospital, and soon thereafter, she begins pushing—it is as if she is trying to push the life out of herself. It is Charles' baby, she thinks, not hers. Either the baby should be dead or she should be dead, or both of them, but this way can't be right. She doesn't even want a child—the pregnancy was an accident. She'd tried to get rid of it at first—did everything from drinking potions to taking hot baths in vinegar to throwing herself down the stairs. Nothing worked. And Charles begged her to stop. He made so many promises.

He's always lived up to his word until today... And now? She is going to have to take care of that screaming baby by herself. With their combined salaries, she and Charles have barely been able to make their mortgage payments. What is she going to do with this baby? She has nothing to give, is as good as dead herself. She can still hear Charles humming, "Million dollar baby" and she wants to scream. He was the only one in this world who understood her.

When she can focus her eyes, it isn't Charles she sees but Alice. When Alice walks into Hallie's room holding Emma in her skinny arms, Hallie knows she must still be alive—a lively dread and anger have replaced the numb void. Her stomach clenches against the onslaught; her body knows even before her mind does that Alice is going to try to take Emma away.

Eyes. My eyes can't stand to look anymore. I close them tight, feeling a burning behind them. This is someone else's birthday story, not mine. This was not how I told the story to myself so many times. Sometimes I fantasized that when Charles died, Hallie held onto me for dear life because I was all she had left of Charles. Sometimes I imagined that Charles saw, held and loved me, just before he died. But not this.

I wish I could shut my ears as easily as I can shut out the world of vision. What I heard in Hallie's story will echo in my head forever—her selfishness—how my existence might ruin her precious little life. I can almost feel my armor hardening. Sarcasm is as deep a state as I am willing to enter. Yes, it was a tragedy and yes, she might actually have had to do something she didn't want to do! I tear up as I try to quiet the voice inside me that has told me for years that my existence was a burden to everyone. Here's my proof.

I get up, feeling stiff and heavy, and walk to the window to stare into the dark. How different she is from me. I think of when Mick was born and how I fell in love with him immediately. I didn't think of myself then—no, he chased out all thought of myself. I began dreaming dreams for him.

Hallie's voice sounds shaky, *"Emma, my innocent dear, are you there? Are you breathing?"*

I can't tell Hallie how I feel, not yet—but I need to hear the rest. I'll try for now to pretend it was someone else's birth. I simply say, "I'm still with you, Hallie." I certainly can't even bring myself to call her Mother or Mom, not after hearing all that. Besides, if she is just "Hallie," she could be anyone's mother or no one's.

"Is this enough, enough to weave a birth story? Oh, the landscape—rural, rolling Michigan hills, farm country—little towns scattered among the farm land. The hospital in Creekside, Michigan."

"Thanks for the story," I say softly, trying to appear nonchalant. "Can't be fun to re-live it that way." My voice comes out in staccato as if even the words are not connected to one another.

"No, even though it's long distant—it is the tumultuous horizon far behind us, where you and I met--isn't easy, not for you, either—not some warm, fuzzy story about snug laps and being cherished. If I could change, rearrange..."

The idea of her changing things makes my head spin. What would she have changed—the fact that I was born? I stand up abruptly. "I'm fixing dinner now. Enough stories."

The silence is deafening without even the sound of the wind. And I can't stop humming that Million Dollar Baby song. The song and everything it represents nauseate me.

The next morning, I awaken with a start as if I have been falling and just hit the ground. The image I remember from my dream is that of a white eggshell broken open on a background of total darkness. It is empty. There is something stark and disturbing about the image. I push it away. But the egg is a symbol of birth, and I begin to weigh the possibility of using it for the tapestry. Considering this image has only two colors, it wouldn't be hard to set up. I detach myself from the feeling of being the broken egg by reciting the nursery rhyme "Humpty Dumpty sat on a wall, Humpty Dumpty had a great fall. All the king's horses and all the king's men couldn't put Humpty together again."

I think cynically, oh, no matter, the king's dead anyway. He certainly won't be of any help to his little girl. Suddenly, a great sadness overcomes me and I want my Daddy. If I go any further into that place of sadness, I'm afraid I won't come back. I feel a kind of panic rising, so I push the emotions away and walk unsteadily up to the Centre. My feet feel like rocks themselves, hard and inflexible, so I stumble as I go. Since I am early to class, I cross over to the ocean where the tide is high. I sit curled up in the fetal position, head tucked into my knees on a large flat rock surrounded on three sides by ocean. I can feel the pull of the waves on my body. I picture being in the womb, about to be born, head pushing into the birth canal, yet still surrounded on three sides by water, helpless in the face of larger forces, pushing, pushing. They are relentless, these waves, these breaths. Why have I lasted this long anyway, fatherless, motherless? All that trouble I caused, and for what?

For a while, I resist letting the water and wind push me back toward the Centre. But soon I sigh, stand up straight and walk as confidently as I can across the street. Now, I reassure myself, is not the time to give up the ghost. I can even chuckle a little at my own joke.

By the time class starts, I am strangely calm. We have several days to finish our first project with access to the studio between 7:00 am and 9:00 pm. Usually someone will be around to answer questions. At the loom beside me is Margaret from New Zealand. She is short and stocky with straight but unusually thick white hair. Her bangs are long for an old lady, I think, and I notice she can make them move with her breath. This is her first experience with tapestries. She wears light bland colors, the dullness broken only by a bright hand-woven scarf worn loosely around her neck. I see she is having trouble tying the knots because of arthritis in her hands.

"Let me show you a trick I've learned," I say, as I pull out a crochet hook I have used to get me through many a tough knot situation.

Margaret watches, then smiles and says, "That right there is worth the price I paid for this workshop. Bless you, guardian angel."

I return her smile, admitting that I have done one useful and good thing today to redeem my sorry self.

Next to Margaret, Lea from Philadelphia is working, her brown skin glowing and her eyes bright. She has chosen to use the four primary colors; it is going to take her a while to finish. She insists that she has nothing better to do and will work on it whenever she can. She is young and can manage more hours in front of the loom than either Margaret or I can. I glance at Lea's sketch and see a kind of wholeness there that is not present in mine. I am jealous, wishing I could weave something loving and sweet. I dismiss the thought. After all, the point of the assignment is to get to know my own roots, not to make up a beautiful sounding, but false, myth. I've done that long enough. Already I want to disown my newly discovered past, change it back into fantasy. There is certainly one good thing about not knowing about your past: you can make up something that suits you.

I go back to my own loom and after choosing the fibers I want—none of them soft—I set up the loom and then begin to sink into my weaving reverie. Ah, I have missed this since I left home. I haven't had a chance to just weave and be dreamy. Never having worked much with black before, I find it restful to my eyes and I work for a few hours. But when the white enters the picture, the contrast jars me. Suddenly I realize that I need to talk to Hallie before I can continue.

Without waiting, I start talking to Hallie on the walk home, careful to make sure no one is near enough to eavesdrop. "Why didn't you just let Alice have me if she wanted me so much, Hallie? She couldn't have been that bad."

Hallie comes roaring in loud and clear. *"You want Alice stories? I can fill you up rotten with Alice until all you can do is regurgitate! But too soon it is too soon too soon."*

Her voice follows me into the apartment. While opening a can of chili, I tell her that, though it sounds boring, I was happy being a girl, getting married and having children. "I even like to cook," I say, as I stir the chili. "These are important things to me—not something to sneer at. There are plenty of times when we're called on to sacrifice ourselves for something larger."

"Don't oppose that. But when the sacrifice is not what you do *but who you* are, *I blow lines in the sand then—don't cross them. You never rebelled, put in a new bell, one that toned a different tune?"*

In spite of myself, I think of the Dealer and the Dealt from the pictures in the wicker chair of me at six and me at seventy. All those years after the deal—did I know then who I was—do I now? I don't know where the lines are, or the cracks... The kid's rhyme comes into my head—step on a crack, break your mother's back. What was that message? Don't skip along having fun because a misstep could be the very one that breaks your mother's back? Or pay attention and don't be so self-absorbed that you harm your mother?

I'll think about that later, when Hallie is gone. I finish eating, and settle into my regular seat. Now I am familiar with how this works. I concentrate on the vague reflections in the dark window and let my eyes unfocus, until once again shapes begin to form, a footstool, an angry face.

⌛

May 12, 1907

A fourteen-year-old Hallie is sitting in the living room, feet propped up on a footstool covered in dark richly embroidered patterns made by her maternal grandmother, Susan. This is one of the few things they have of hers; she died when Alice was being born. Hallie is reading Emerson's Essays and studying for a test she has the next day. And she is concentrating on it hard when she hears Alice from the kitchen demand, "Put down the book and get in here and help me."

Hallie has always loved reading. She has escaped lots of things since she learned to read, but Alice doesn't like her reading. Sometimes Hank or Andy smuggle her books from the library, the more adventurous the stories, the better she likes them. She often wonders if there is such a thing as a girl's heart and a boy's heart—because if there is, Hallie definitely has a boy's heart. She is the subject of these books and not the hero's reward.

But no one else can see it. They expect her to be cute, wear dresses, be quiet and defer to others and above all, to serve. She doesn't want to be a woman; she wants to have someone to support her and give her credit for doing things well, someone who will wait for her to come home victorious or follow her, no matter how outlandish her plans. She wants, and that is enough to get a girl into trouble.

When Alice calls her, Hallie is engrossed in Emerson, not just for the test, but because Emerson' musings makes her think. Hallie doesn't budge from her position and yells to Alice, "There are four able-bodied people out here, any one of whom could help you, Mother. Besides, Mother's Day is over."

They had a big laugh about Mother's Day, the newly instituted holiday that just passed the week before. Alice had wondered what she needed a day for but when Henry and Danny relieved her of cooking on that day, she was quite pleased with the idea.

"Of whom, of whom," mutters Alice. She hated it when Hallie used grammar she had never learned how to use. She begins to beg, "Please, Hallie, you're my only girl—the boys are of no use in the kitchen."

"That's not logical, Mother. They can learn as well as I."

"Don't sass," she says, leaning out the kitchen door. "No test in school is more important than learning to cook. You're only in school to learn how to be a better wife. No other reason."

When her mother returns to the kitchen, Hallie appeals to her father. At that moment, he is a little drunk from whiskey he started drinking the minute he came home. He is half-asleep and simply says, "Hallie, do as your mother asks."

Hallie's face is red. "You're the one who told me I was smarter than my brothers. Can't you tell her how important school is for me?"

After a hard day at work, Henry did not want to be bothered. "Just make peace," he says as he leans back and closes his eyes.

From the living room, everyone could hear Alice muttering, "Wouldn't kill you to help out. To think I was happy I finally had a girl. Hah, girl's more trouble than all them boys put together. Nothing but trouble. Doesn't help that my own husband tells her how smart she is—better to tell her how pretty she looks."

Loudly, Hallie announces, "I'm going to my room to study. I don't care for dinner tonight." As she stomped up the stairs, she called out, "I'll do my fair share but no more than the boys. You'll have to tie me up first."

Alice starts after her, then stops and at her departing back yells, "I'm taking you out of school tomorrow, young lady!" She returns to the kitchen and throws her knife into the sink, punctuating her rage.

The clanging shatters my concentration and I lose the picture. "Alice took you out of school?" I ask.

"That's a long story for another time, a time when you understand more. Emma, you're thinking what a stubborn child I was—oh, and I was, 'tis true. Once started, I just couldn't back down, back out, put it into reverse, go around, no. My life, my life, my life depended on it. Maybe too much I understood so young. Can't remember when I simply did what I was told. If it didn't make sense, I wouldn't do it. Can you imagine, imagine that?"

I smile, feeling a softening edge of understanding taking shape in my mind. "I'm sure glad you weren't my daughter. I'd have been tempted to slap you silly."

The next day, Valerie brings a letter from Ralph. Word from home stabilizes me. Ralph says he is getting along with Phyllis. Says they'd gone to a play at the playhouse and are re-organizing his workshop. That's good. He might as well make use of Phyllis. She's a pair of hands, anyway, and it makes me worry less that he'll try to do something he shouldn't by himself and lose his balance.

I'll write back something breezy about the class and the ocean. Not a word gets out about Hallie or they'll come in white coats and drag me away. No, that I won't tell lightly, though it would be nice if there were someone here I could trust with the information. I wish Diana were here, but I won't tell her in a letter or on the telephone.

I haven't changed my mind about Hallie. In all her stories to date, I relate better to Alice than to her, even though she is making a concerted effort to be understood. To me, she seems selfish and heartless.

When I arrive at the class, Margaret is already huddled over her loom, working away. She doesn't look up when I greet her, and the way she is leaning forward, her bangs cover her eyes. She answers, "Yes, good to see you again." Though she hasn't seen me. Then, without looking up, she says, "I think I've got it." I look over her shoulder at her weaving and she has created a small boat tipped almost sideways on a rough sea. When she finally turns around to face me, her eyes light up with warmth. "Colleen came in last night after you left and helped. Are you feeling all right? You left in a rush last night, didn't you?"

I sit at the chair in front of my loom, "I guess I let the subject matter get the best of me. My birth was no cause for celebration."

The look in Margaret's eyes turns to sympathy. "I thought—but I didn't want to say anything to offend you—but looking at your motif and colors—I thought maybe your mother died in childbirth as mine did."

I tell her a bit of the story. She looks up at me with tears glinting in her eyes and says, "Black and white, it is, then—not much brightness in that story."

"'Tis unusual," says Colleen as she looks over my weaving, just before she dismisses class for the weekend. "I like it. You might try loosening it a bit near the edges—they tend to roll inward right there," she says as she points. Colleen tells me that she lives between my place and Galway and offers to give me a ride home whenever I need it. She also offers to be available if there is anything I need to talk about.

"Thanks a million," I tell her, forcing myself to sound normal with the Irish colloquialism I find myself using a lot. "I may take you up on that when it's raining, though generally, the walk does me good."

"You know, previous students have found it a wee bit lonely on the weekend, especially if they didn't go in for the pub scene. Here's me telephone number should you need it."

"That's kind of you, but I have plans to explore the area tomorrow, and I'm perfectly content to read instead of going to pubs. I like the quiet." Yes, I think to myself, if only it were quiet!

As she leaves the building, Colleen calls out, "I mean it, Emma, about the chat, OK?" I nod my head, wondering if I am fooling anyone. How fragile do I look?

Carefully I cross over the street, especially busy with weekend traffic. The woman Diana and I saw is here swimming alone again. There is a chill in the air and even through several layers of clothes, I am barely comfortable. I marvel at how this woman can strip and plunge herself into icy water. But I smile watching her. She seems tentative at first, and then she begins to play with the water until she is wet and can begin to kick and swim and just let the ocean support her like a good friend.

I am at the end of the beach when the woman gets out and jogs towards me. "Are you going in then?" she asks.

"Oh, no, not me—I'm not that brave! I admire your courage."

"Can't you swim, then?" she asks, shaking the water out of her hair and rubbing her head with a towel.

"No, no," I say, "it's not that. I swim fine in a heated pool, indoors without a current or waves. Here it's hard to predict..."

"Oh, that I like. Ireland has that same unpredictability, too. Must be, because there's no way out but through the water, you know?"

Chapter 13—Context

The Irish have a way of incorporating the past into the present by leaving old buildings in various states of disarray, using them in practical ways—as storage or utility sheds. The little buildings look as if they have grown out of the ground itself, not hard to imagine considering all the stone still mired in the ground in the fields. The fences and stone buildings create a mosaic of nature mixed with human endeavor, and it's not always clear which is which.

October 9, 1996

Friday night is quiet—no wind, no rain and no Hallie. Seeing the woman swimmer today reminded me of how much fun it had been when Diana talked me into going into the water. Lucy would love it. I write her a casual letter and invite her again to come. She's the one who should hear these stories. I also write to Ralph and neighbor Judy. It feels as though by imagining a conversation with these people, I bring them here.

On my Saturday off, I pack a lunch of cheese and cucumber sandwiches, tomatoes, Irish apples, popcorn, water, and a couple of cookies. I head off into the hills and the road passes some old abandoned stone buildings. One has plants growing out of it and no roof; another has a replaced roof put on some time ago, and a tree has draped itself over it so that the tiny house and the tree look like lovers.

As I pass each little cluster of houses and out buildings, I create a stir from the animals of the house. None seem too ferocious, and I just keep walking. In front of one of the last houses on the road, there is a small dog, white with black patches over each eye, sitting next to a black cat with its back turned, seated next to a rooster. They almost look as if they're waiting in line for something. Reminds me of the first line of a joke: a rooster, a cat and a dog were all sitting around in a bar, and the rooster says...

Soon there is nothing to see but stone fences and berry bushes and a little cemetery. I find a tombstone with what looks like the date of 1729, and I wonder what my ancestors were doing then. I muse about the shifting sands of chance meetings, travel, moves, deaths, firings, failing crops, health problems, religious persecution, and such that place people next to each other and make possible the particulars of the descendants who come later. It's all just a roll of the dice.

In many other cultures, knowing one's ancestry was highly critical both to one's own identity and to the choice of a spouse. If I had lived in a culture of arranged marriages, I would likely never have been marriageable material with a crazy mother.

I find a likely lunch spot by a scrawny tree growing soft grass under it that looks as if it's been flattened out by cows taking a nap. A huge tombstone also rests under the tree, and I lean a moment against it, feeling its cool solidness.

The wind gusts beyond my sheltered spot, making the small trees bow. This time, the clouds pass rapidly, clearing the way for blue, and I relax again, listening to the whispering winds until the gusts turn into words.

"Emma, my brave daughter, all alone on the edge of the world. I am proud of you—you who face all your unknowns, face them down, dare them to change you. I left you alone for a bit. May I visit now?"

Feeling proud of myself as well, I say without hesitation, "I'm ready for another story, and this time, I'll try to keep an open mind."

"This story in all its glory, will upset, distress you. It was hushed up, shushed up but good. You'll see the reason the family won't speak of it. But maybe you will step towards understanding me, maybe. A bit risky for me—you could fall and maybe on your grandmother Alice's side."

I am doubtful, too, and wonder if I will ever understand how she felt. "Tell you what, I will listen and then say nothing until I've had a chance to mull it over, OK? I'm not very accurate with first reactions, at least that's what my kids tell me."

"Fair. Ask questions, be curious if you can, though. Remember compassion."

Hallie speaks as though she is re-living every moment of this scene. I lean back on my rock, staring across the path to a shiny new black tombstone that reads, "Mary Ann Gallagher 1982-1996." A picture of a fourteen-year-old girl begins to emerge. A shiver runs through me as I concentrate on the unfolding scene.

January 11, 1908

Hallie is fourteen. On this cold twilight in December in Detroit, the Kaufmans have again run out of coal for the furnace and wood for the fireplace. The shrill wind blowing off the lake makes the walls seem like tracing paper. Henry's arthritis hurts him if he gets cold and Hallie, always protective of her father, often scavenges for fuel after school. She has to go to isolated, out of the way places, like down by the railroad tracks where, now and again, she finds coal that has bounced out of a car and rolled away; or she goes to the old saw mill, or Jesse's Furniture Workshop, after hours. Sometimes she runs across branches of wood downed by storms, so she always carries a hunting knife in the side compartment of her schoolbook bag, to help cut away branches that aren't quite all the way off the tree. The knife was a Christmas present from Henry—one her mother disapproved of, of course. Alice would rather Hallie have a kitchen knife for chopping vegetables.

Today Hallie is checking one of her usual spots, the sawmill. Sometimes during loading or unloading, pieces of wood fall down the stairway leading to the basement. She descends into the dark.

When she reaches the bottom of the stairs, just before her eyes adjust to the dark from the bright sunset above, she feels a hand spread across her mouth, clamping so tight she can make no noise. The more she struggles, the tighter the hand gets; the other hand begins to tear at her clothes. Her book bag is still hanging across her body, slung from her left shoulder, across her chest and down beside her right hip, making it difficult to get her clothing off. She grabs hold of the book bag, holding onto it for dear life as if its presence will shield her.

She is pushed down onto her face, her legs flailing uselessly behind her, failing to make contact with anything vital. This person, or animal, is pushing up her dress and grabbing hold of her undergarments to rip them off. The thick sawdust mixed with dirt of the place gets into her throat and lungs as she inhales frantically and snorts to get air. Adrenaline is shooting madly throughout her body like electricity, charging her up.

The creature finds the tops of her woollies and yanks them down around her knees, then sits on her, keeping her helpless as he fumbles with his own clothes. She feels the cold draft blowing across her exposed skin. Then he is pushing on her with something hard—hard, poking glances that kept missing their mark. She thinks of the time her push broom handle fell off and she had to find just the right angle to get it back in. She wants to stay calm, to gather her energy for the right moment to resist.

The man, breathing heavily, becomes frustrated as he shifts and grunts, but cannot get the right position. She holds herself tight against entry. Finally, in desperation, he turns her over and wedges his knees between her legs.

She almost does not recognize Tom Nestor's twisted, sweating face. He is a boy from her neighborhood. As soon as he realizes that he has been recognized, he becomes more brutal and says, "This'll teach you a lesson, girlie. You're not as smart as you think you are." Now he has everything to lose—if she lives she can report the rape; and if he doesn't get inside her, he will be humiliated.

His left hand moves from Hallie's right hand to around her throat and his weight shifts just enough that Hallie can maneuver her right hand into the outside side pocket of the bag and feel the reassuring firm leather skin of the handle of the hunting knife that seems to jump into her hand. Tom has almost completely cut off her air supply. She draws the knife out quickly, up over his back and she brings it down hard, ramming into him. He lets go of her throat and tries to stop her arm, but pinned like a mounted butterfly as the rest of her is, all of her energy and rage is pouring into that one free arm. That arm full of adrenaline is invincible, unstoppable. She rages at him for all the times she's felt pinned down before, all the times she's felt helpless and slams the knife into him not once, but over and over, past when he has stopped struggling, until she is spent under his weight that grows heavier by the minute. As blood spurts then drips steadily from his body, she is unable to find the strength to move away from its sticky dripping. Finally, she musters all of her energy and pushes him off. His body moves like a rolled up woolen rug that has been left in the rain and hits the floor with a dull thud.

Is she screaming? Is there absolute silence? She doesn't know if she has gone deaf or if, in fact, she still has the capacity to sense anything. She feels nothing; it could be any time, anyplace—maybe it is midnight at the North Pole. She lies there for what feels like all of winter. Finally, she hears her brothers, Danny and Andy, calling her name.

When she did not returned home at suppertime, Alice got worried and sent Danny and Andy to find her. Danny knew all of the places she usually went to look for wood because, on the weekends, he often accompanies her. By the time they got to the sawmill, it is very dark and increasingly colder. Andy curses himself for not helping Hallie gather the firewood. He always seems to have something better to do.

Danny points to the stairwell where he has often gone with Hallie, but always in the daylight. Even then, it was scary enough. "There," he says, "she usually looks down in there."

"Hallie, are you down there?" Danny's high-pitched voice screeches from a safe distance away. They can hear nothing but the echoes of horse hooves on the nearby street. Hallie hears the familiar voices and tries to answer, but her throat is seared by the cold air and the words freeze before she can fully form them. When nothing comes out of her mouth, she pries her sticky fingers off the knife and throws it across the room where it clangs to a stop. Danny and Andy are just about to leave when they hear that noise and call again.

"I heard something, did you?" asks Andy.

"Yeah, but if it's her, why doesn't she answer? I have to go to the privy, Andy."

"Hold onto it, will you? I'm going down first," says Andy. "Are you coming? She might be hurt or something." Andy speaks confidently for Danny's sake. "Maybe it's just a rat down there. You follow me and be careful."

They take one step at a time, trying to get used to the darkness. As Andy nears the bottom, his foot steps on something large and corporeal and he recoils into Danny who is breathing down his neck. "Aaah! Get back!" He jerks his foot back up to the last step.

With that, Danny lets his urine loose. "What, what's wrong, Andy? What's going on?"

Andy pushes tentatively back into the thing with his toe, getting no response.

"I don't know, Danny," Andy says impatiently. "Just a minute..." Andy's fear is creeping up his throat. "Danny, go back up and get help. There's some kind of trouble here. I don't think you should be here. Go up and get the pol..."

Just then Hallie moans. "Hallie, is that you?" cries Andy trembling. They can barely make out a shape lying on the other side of the lump of a body at the bottom of the stairs.

She stands up weakly and wobbles toward the voices. The woollies around her ankles trip her and she falls forward and struggles to pull them up. When she stumbles over the body laying in her path, this time she finds she can scream, and does, loud and clear. She pushes past Andy and Danny and scrambles up the stairs, half-crawling, half-running out into the air, gulping and sputtering. Andy and Danny follow.

"Are you OK, Hallie?" Danny whines.

"Hallie, what's wrong? You look awful." Andy eyes are darting from side to side. "Hallie, say something."

"Gemeumm," she says.

The boys look at each other in puzzlement. "What're you saying, Hallie?" asks Andy.

"Home," she manages to say. "Home."

"But, Hallie," Danny whines again. "You're covered with dirt and— is that blood?"

"Hallie, what the bloody hell happened down there?" asks Andy who was not usually one for cursing. "Are you OK? Is that your blood?"

"Home," she repeats and begins limping in that direction, her limbs stiff and uncooperative.

"Mommie will be so mad, Hallie, if you come back all dirty like this," says Danny beginning to cry. "You'll be in big trouble, again."

Andy is all business. "We've all been out looking for you, and everyone is worried."

"Father?" Hallie asks, swaying on her feet.

"Well," says Andy, "he wasn't home yet when we came out. He probably worked late again." All of Henry's children cover for his drinking, even to one another.

But before they can go any farther, Hallie faints. Danny and Andy half drag and half carry her the three quarters of a mile home. They leave red streaks in the snow periodically, when they shift her around.

At home, Alice is waiting anxiously at the door. She emerges in her robe, her slippers slipping on the icy front steps as she helps get Hallie into the house. They lug her into Alice and Henry's downstairs room and lay her out on the bed.

"Is she dead?" Alice asks calmly. "Is that her blood everywhere?"

Andy replies, "No, she spoke to us and even walked a little until she passed out—dunno about the blood...."

Andy tells Alice how they had found her and how all she said was "home" and "father."

Alice mumbles under her breath, as she begins to take off Hallie's clothes, "Lot of good, asking for her father." To the boys she says, "You've done what you can, now go and fix yourselves some hot chocolate—eat a cookie. I'll take over."

"But is she OK?" asks Danny, wiping his runny nose on his red flannel shirt sleeve.

"Just go and get warm or you'll die of pneumonia. Danny, you look all wet down the front—go and change those pants," Alice demands. "Get yourselves in shape to fetch the doctor if we need him."

Alice finishes undressing her and finds blood on all of her clothes right down to her woolies. She has bruises around her neck, on her arms and between her legs. But her right hand which is so bloody, when cleaned up reveals no apparent wounds. Hallie breathes steadily, not wanting to be awake yet. Alice, thinking she is still unconscious, watches her a minute before getting up to leave. Then Hallie begins to stir; she doesn't want to be left alone.

"Where, wh...Mother?" she looks around. "Your bed?"

"I don't know, Hallie. You tell me. Andy and Danny found you in some stairwell, covered with blood."

"Oh, no. Tom Nestor." Hallie thrashes about on the bed throwing off the covers and trying to get up. "Is he dead?"

"Be still now, child." Alice can barely look at her. "You've lost your mind. What's Tom got to do with this?"

Looking at her drawn, white face, Hallie knows Alice can't handle hearing the story. Hallie thinks maybe she'll never tell anyone. Out loud she says, "Don't remember."

"You'd better tell me the truth, young lady, then I'll figure what to do—your father's still not home. I told you not to go into places like that by yourself. Didn't I tell you? Why do you disobey me? I'll keep you home, that's what. From now on, you go nowhere."

Hallie stares at the wallpaper as if she'd never seen it before. What are those animals? Sheep? Wolves? Or just an abstract pattern? It seems imperative that she figure it out, and she twists herself to get a better look.

"Father," she pleads.

Alice says in her told-you-so voice, "Yes, it'd be lovely if he were here, wouldn't it, and if we were all fairy princesses, too. You'll have to make do with your shabby old ma, won't you? Tell me." Alice grabs her and starts shaking her.

Alice is hurting her and saying something then, but she may as well have been speaking in tongues, as much meaning as Hallie can glean from her. Alice continues asking questions, but at the same time her manner screams out that she does not want answers. Hallie closes her eyes on the confusion.

Maybe it will just all go away if she says nothing. But no matter how hard she tries to make herself believe that nothing has happened, the world continues to look different—the wallpaper, Alice's face, the way the kerosene light flickers. It is as if she has entered a brand new reality. Things in the room, the bureau, the way the door jamb meets the ceiling at an odd angle, the faded pink and blue dotted curtains. It is as if she's never seen them before.

She is awakened by banging on the front door. She is disoriented by her proximity to the front door. Then it comes flooding back to her.

Men's voices murmur softly but she cannot make out words. They must be the police. She tells herself not to panic, that she has done nothing wrong. She defended herself—that's all. What else can she say? What do they want to hear? Certainly not that she feels invincible, super-human, stronger than any man and worth defending to the death. That she has finally claimed her life as her own. No, not that.

Alice comes into the room and sits stiffly on the edge of the bed. "Hallie, the police is here. They say Tom is dead down there…" Her voice catches in her throat. They want to speak to you. Tell them you didn't kill no one. Please, Hallie, tell them there was someone else down there. They found your knife down there, Hallie—they got it now." She twists the bedspread as if she wishes it were Hallie's neck, or Henry's. "Oh, where is your father? Why do I always have to be alone?"

Hallie stares blankly at her mother. She is crying and that never happens. Tom is dead, and she killed him; nothing will ever be the same. Then, she thinks, I won't say a word until I figure out what would be best to say—I'll stay quiet.

"Hallie, tell them something—the police'll haul you down to jail, do you hear me? Say something."

Hallie closes her eyes, reliving the event and then a slow smile spreads across her face—that dragon can't hurt me again. Why, I am a hero. I slew the mighty foe.

Alice slaps her hard. "You can't be smiling, young lady—there's nothing in this world to smile about. You've brought such trouble into this family. How do you think my friend Mrs. Nestor feels—she's not smiling—her son…"

Alice thinks Hallie is the one who should be dead, all the trouble this is going to cause. It is just as she thought—Hallie is an unruly beast, abnormal, uncontrollable, unnatural. Now she has killed a deacon's son. They will all have to pay for this crime. Hallie will go to jail; Alice will never be able to face her friends in church again; she'll lose all of her friends; Henry will lose his job. She murmurs the Lord's prayer under her breath.

Finally, Alice says, "I'm letting the police in—tell 'em you didn't do nothing, please."

When the two police men enter the room, Hallie turns back toward the wall and begins counting the animals, the bodies, the lumps on the wall. It is imperative that she know how many there are. She must look tiny to the police in that double bed, so small they can't imagine that she has killed someone. During the questioning, she says nothing responsive and occasionally they can make out that she is counting.

They debate about taking her to jail—she is their only suspect. Then, when she continues counting, one suggests that they take her to the state hospital.

The short one with a sympathetic tone in his voice replies, "A little girl over to that place? That's worse than jail. At least there're only a few folk in jail right now. Over to the state hospital, they've got people everywhere screaming and carrying on. She'd be scared, poor little girl. Hell, I'd be scared over there."

When she shifts in the bed, they can see bruises around her neck and decide to take her to the regular hospital for the night and post a guard at the door to make sure she doesn't run away.

Alice pleads with them not to take her away, but they insist, saying, "Get her dressed and we'll be out of your way. You look like you need some rest, Mrs. Kaufmann, ma'am."

"Nothin' new," says Alice in her grayest voice. She looks at Hallie as if she is too damned much trouble, as if she wishes the boys never found her and brought her back.

I blink, losing sight of the picture. I can no longer feel my connection to the ground or to the story. It's gruesome—the whole thing. The thought of a fourteen-year-old girl going through that kind of trauma. It feels fantastic, fictional. Maybe she just made it up. I want to believe that. Slowly the realization dawns that the story is true and that I am related to it.

The wind has penetrated my head and is whirling my thoughts around. I can't trust myself to say anything.

Hallie mistakes my silence for judgment and says angrily, *"Listen, listen, listen. If I'd told you I'd been held down and raped at fourteen and left for dead, you could, would feel pity, then and commiserate with me, the poor victim. You're just like all the rest of them. Yes, yes, I've heard it all before, many, many endlessly many times before."*

The howling wind makes me feel vulnerable on this hilltop, as if I could be taken away and plopped down in any reality at all, even one where my own mother kills someone. I am shocked by her words, but I don't know what to say. She's wrong. I can't imagine being pleased at the idea of her being raped and not fighting back. She still feels she has to defend herself after so many years. Yet, I can think of nothing to say that will be true and sensitive. I say nothing, and the wind dies down.

Chapter 14—Gravitation

She snowballs down the hill from the cemetery. The stories stick to her, making her heavier and heavier. She wants to know, is compelled to listen, and yet she doesn't know if she can carry the weight without totally losing control. The closer she and Hallie become, the more pull she feels toward her and what feels like chaos, a black pit of what? Reality? All her worst nightmares? And what of worst nightmares, if that story was no dream?

October 10, 1996

I gaze at the pastoral countryside to take my mind off the pain, only to be reminded that wars and famine have decimated even this innocent-looking place time after time. How many buried in that graveyard at the top of the hill were victims of unnecessary violence, of human against human and of men against women?

Blackberries are dripping off the bushes. I need to do something normal, friendly, civilized, so I load up my bag beyond the number I alone can eat. They're sour if you yank them off before they're ready. Maybe that's what happened to Hallie.

That evening Hallie's experience haunts me. I've never known anyone who killed someone before—except maybe Lucy's ex-husband, a Vietnam vet. Hallie is right on one count: I am shocked to find that perhaps in some weird way I would have been more comfortable with Hallie having been raped than with her having killed someone. I know that's wrong.

As it is a drizzling, sleepy sort of Sunday and there is no Protestant church nearby, I walk down to the shore to conduct an improvised church service. I have the beach to myself only for a brief moment because a man comes down to gather seaweed. I wobble my way along the round, loose stones for a while but cannot put enough distance between myself and the seaweed gatherer to allow me privacy. Silently, I ask for the strength to hear Hallie's stories without flinching and give thanks for my rape-free life, which has allowed me the luxury of trusting others.

Later at the Centre working on my egg tapestry, my mind wanders. I try to think of Ralph and Lucy and Diana—anything but the most recent Hallie story. Eggs, hymens, humans—all are so fragile. One moment in time can damage the rest of a life. I wonder if there is love strong enough to counter it, a love moment that can heal that life in an instant? Maybe if Hallie were religious…?

Then it hits me—this egg is not Hallie, it's me; and there is nothing inside it. It's as if the contents had spilled out, absorbed into the black background. It's too late to change it. An empty feeling takes me by the throat—I am choking.

Coughing and sputtering in the otherwise silent room, I run to the water fountain in an adjacent room. As the choking eases up, I sit down on a small red sofa, collecting pieces of myself that seem to be floating just out of reach.

Colleen follows me and asks, "You having trouble?"

I nod. "I feel as if the air is being sucked out of me."

She sits down next to me on the couch. "Better now?" she says cocking her head sideways and examining me. "Sometimes these projects bring up unresolved questions. Can you talk a wee bit?"

I hesitate, not knowing if this young person could be capable of understanding my experience. "It's as if I let something very important seep into darkness and never claimed it. Does that make sense?"

When Colleen asks for some background, I start to tell her the same story I have always told—about how my real mother couldn't keep me, so I was adopted by generous people who treated me just like a daughter. But I stop myself, not certain that my mother couldn't have kept me and not certain that my adopted parents were all that generous. In fact, at this moment, I don't know what I believe about my life.

"I'm in transition now, I guess, and nothing I think of to say seems true, certainly not the story I've always told myself. One of the reasons I came here was to 'find myself,' see if there is something that is mine alone. Now this birth picture makes me feel like there's nothing here—inside me." My hands are layered over my heart, clutching at pieces of nothing: clothes, skin. The heart must be there somewhere, underneath it all.

Colleen adds her hand to the layers over my heart. She pauses a minute. "It's not too late to add something to the tapestry."

She links arms with me and we return to the weaving room where she shows me a new technique for adding texture and giving the tapestry a three-dimensional feeling. I use a bright red yarn to make a flaming heart inside the shell. My feelings about the tapestry and about myself begin to shift to include more dimensions, more layers within myself. The energy I felt the other day as we drew up energy from the center of the earth returns to tingle my feet.

"Would you, could you read tonight or let the wind stir you up some story?

The wind and her voice startle me. I am in my pajamas and robe, curled up in the stuffed chair enjoying a Maeve Binchy novel about an Irish girl and an English boy, something I would never read at home.

I sigh and switch back to the pain channel. "Hallie, I want you to know—I am not judging you guilty—you did what you had to do. The two stories—the one about my birth and your near-rape—seem similar in some way I don't yet understand. I'm trying to work them out in my weaving."

Then I whisper as if I am speaking to myself, "When something so soft comes in contact with something so hard... I remember in *Man of La Mancha*, Don Quixote's servant Sancho says, 'Whether the pitcher hits the rock or the rock hits the pitcher, it's going to be bad for the pitcher.'"

"Pitcher, pitcher, pitch her, pitch her into the abyss, see where she goes; she goes on," Hallie replies and then is silent.

I ask what I have been wanting to know for as long as I can remember, "Could you tell me about Charles now? Tell me about my father."

This time, when I feel a story coming on, at least I am sitting in my own place, comfortable and warm, unlike at the cemetery yesterday. I stare at the blank window and reflecting back is a face that is only vaguely familiar from pictures Lucy showed me of Charles. I can see the dimple in his chin that I passed on to my youngest son, Adam. Yes, I see a resemblance.

June 23, 1919

Charles is standing at a podium addressing a union of machinists, advising them to consider becoming socialists. Hallie is seated behind him on the stage along with another speaker on the bill. Hallie likes Charles's manner and his astute mind immediately, and she appreciates the way he handles the questions after the talk. He isn't argumentative but instead listens intently and may surprise the questioner by actually changing his viewpoint. He enjoys give and take much more than Hallie does. She is so used to arguing with her brothers and father that she's learned to battle until she drops or wins. But with this man, it isn't a battle. He sincerely wants all of the pros and cons to emerge so he can see the situation clearly.

Hallie also notices that Charles is a tall, handsome, boyish-looking man with a dimple in his chin (kissed by a fairy, his Irish mother used to say—could see things other people couldn't). Gangly but strong, he is in good physical condition. But suits look better on the average hanger in the store than they do on him. His angular bones pull the material out but then it just hangs down at odd angles.

The audience loves him and claps wildly when he finishes talking. He smiles humbly and tries to quiet them for the next speaker, Hallie Kaufmann, who will be talking about women's rights. The cheers turn quickly to boos and jeers, but Charles admonishes them to give her some respect.

Charles listens intently to Hallie's talk. Halfway through the talk, a pimply man with his hat pulled way down over his forehead yells out, "I like the way they do things in Switzerland. Every man has a sword, and when it's time for elections, he goes down to the square and votes by raising his sword into the sky." He stands up and raises his arm for emphasis. "And only the men have swords," he cries, and the men applauded furiously.

Hallie makes no comment. Then at one point, she moves to set up a slide projector and can't get the light to come on. The same man begins sniping about how women can't do anything mechanical, can't understand the twentieth century. She asks if he'd care to come up and fix it; he does—and fails to locate the problem. She asks him his name, almost flirtatiously; he replies, "Edmund." Then, loudly so all can hear, she says, "Edmund, we're going to have to take away your sword!" As the room breaks up into nervous laughter at his expense, he turns and walks out, red-faced. Hallie finally gets the machine to work and returns to the talk with no more heckling.

After the program, Charles introduces himself to Hallie. "Pleasure to make your acquaintance. Your ideas are even more radical than mine—maybe we could continue talking over coffee?"

"Sure, why not," Hallie answers. Why not? Afterward she could think of a million reasons not to have coffee with that fellow. She loves a good conversation, and if she gets sexually aroused over it, then she is not opposed to following where it leads. She tries not to box herself up with ideas of marriage or sin or all that garbage. She follows what her heart—or other body parts for that matter—tell her. And her brain is certainly one of those body parts. She loves an intelligent conversation more than just about anything.

So Hallie and Charles go down the street to Max's Cafe for coffee. At twenty-six, Hallie has already been an activist in the anti-war, suffragette and union movements. She is used to meeting people this way. Currently, she is in a rocky relationship, but they have not pledged to be faithful forever—not possible given her philosophy—and freedom tops the list.

She and Charles talk until the waitresses begin putting chairs upside-down on the tables and mopping the floor. They finally take the hint, walk out the door and begin a whole new life together.

As the image of this handsome man fades, I begin to feel all that we lost, Hallie and me.

"Water over the dear damn dam, dear," says Hallie, pleased with her poetry.

I ask, "Do you ever wonder how it would have been with just the three of us?"

"No—a wasted paste of the past, stuck together with wishes. Besides. I know, no, know, I'd have ruined the good bird Charles was—grounded him, chewed him up, blew him out, cold. You see, I couldn't stop fighting. Every little war, every wayward word, every everyday warp. If I didn't fight, I'd be lost. Once the fighting was done, I had nothing, nothing but words, drier than sand. Not recommended as a way of life, more a way of strife."

I have finished my tea and nibble tentatively on a biscuit, hypothesizing, "If you lived today, maybe you'd have gotten help, lived a different life. There's more support for independent females, and there's rape counseling. No one would expect you to deal with that alone."

"Uh-oh, therapy, you mean, don't you, you? Hallie says with a biting edge whistle in her voice. *"I'd never have sat there and let it rip. More like RIP, rest in pieces."*

"Even with a woman therapist?"

"Oh, my. Would have killed a therapista. Too much like Mother, trying to stuff me into small spaces, change me to fit the world. Did anyone ask me, did anyone, if I wanted to change? World needs to change, not me. Sit still for a therapy session, a still life? Still, so the world would have a better shot at me. Just let me be wind, a moving target."

"No...," I interject.

She interrupts me gently, *"No matter, Emma. What I had, I was not giving up, not to Charles, not to a lady therapist, not to God. Held on 'til it was ripped away, like tree ripped out at the roots by tornado. Don't see the tree running, running, running out of fear, leaves flattened to its branches, do you? I'd do it again."*

"Charles wasn't trying to take anything from you."

"Easy to see what he took. When he died it was gone, gone with the wind."

"Oh, I see what you mean. You couldn't stay on the farm with me and still make a living."

"So exactly practical of you, dear. Just be practical and you'll see it's not death nor romance that breaks things up, it's money to buy honey."

"Maybe if they'd had welfare in those days? You could have stayed on the farm with me."

"And we'd never, never have survived, Emma, my little Emma. I couldn't take care of you and write and teach and travel. I tried that. But there were times I had to puff off and leave you with people—sometimes even signed myself into an asylum for a few weeks. You passed through more homes in your first six years than maple seeds, spun by every gust of wind. Don't get idealistic, make me something I never was."

I can't win. She has a "yes, but" for every occasion. My heart is beating fast. I say sarcastically, "I get your point. You were forced to be a mother; you didn't choose it. You should never have had me."

"Be calm now, dear, not so blustery. Can't change the past. But you can do something positive for Lucy and you?

I shake my head, not able to imagine what she could do for us now. "I thought some assignment from purgatory brought you here, that you were fighting to win my soul—or yours."

Shocked, Hallie says, *"Purgatory, hell, as if either of us believes in that rot!"*

"And I don't believe in ghosts either, as a matter of fact. So what should I call you?"

She shifts gears, *"You believe in the elements, don't you—water, air, earth and fire? Well, don't you? That's what I am now—elemental. That's all, all I can tell you about who I am now. I'm not in purgatory, heaven, or hell. I'm not trying to escape. If you could stand under my umbrella for a day. Will you? Will you...?"*

Her voice becomes indistinguishable from the gusting winds. I shiver and wrap my arms around myself, Hallie's last words echoing in my mind. I think of the Bible—one story after another, and the truth in there somewhere.

Looking at my tapestry now, in the clear afternoon light, I see that even in the midst of human frailty, there is life, spirit and connection. Charles may have died before I was born, but now I know that he advocated for my birth. Hallie and I had enough breath left between us to feed the flame. It is alive. I am alive.

Lea is the first to share, as we are asked to show our tapestries and tell our birth stories. She was the first baby of her parents, immigrants to the U.S. from Mexico. They had tried for years to get pregnant and finally, when they had almost given up, Lea was conceived. Lea used primary colors in her weaving because her birth had seemed so primary to her parents—not like mine at all.

I do not have to speak in front of all these people. I could pass.

But after she has finished, Lea smiles reassuringly at me, and I regain my courage, take a deep breath, and speak dispassionately, looking at the weaving and not my classmates. "I used both black and white to represent death—the death of my father by an automobile when my mother was eight months pregnant with me and the death of my mother's dreams for her life, which were cracked open and spilt, wasted. I added the flame with Colleen's help, a flame that represents spirit alive in me. They passed on something more to me than emptiness and heartache—I don't know exactly what, but fire captures it for now."

I am surprised at how many stories have pain in them. Margaret's weaving is of a ship bouncing on fierce waves in the ocean. She was born on a ship headed from Ireland to New Zealand. Her mother died in childbirth. I feel less sorry for myself.

One of the women was an unwanted child; one, a child who could not be cared for by her parents for financial reasons. Another was lost in the shuffle of ten brothers and sisters. I find myself going out to each individual as she speaks. The variety of symbols and colors are astounding: teal seeds, blessed smiles, towering purple trees, ancient scrolls, weathered bones, multi-colored persimmons, figs, grapes.

Colleen looks off into the distance, a peaceful look on her face. "Let me tell you a story of the Dagara people in Burkina Faso, Africa. They have a ritual for when babies are born. When the baby cries out as it emerges from the birth canal, they see that as a question, 'Am I in the right place?' And the children of the village answer resoundingly so that he/she knows he/she is in the right place."

I gasp and hear others doing the same. What an affirming, life-sustaining gesture! I had only my mother's ambivalence to welcome me. No wonder I feel so unsure of myself.

Colleen continues, "Before the child is born, the Dagara people pray to the ancestors to bring them a child to help them, and the child is seen as an answer to their prayers. What naturally follow then is an attempt to make sure the child has whatever it needs to foster the gifts it has brought. Just think how different that is from what happens in our culture."

The next assignment is to design a representation of a time when we felt totally loved, understood and accepted for who we are.

Colleen walks around the room looking at the looms, taking in the collage aspect of the work as the parts sit side by side. "Love does not have to be from parents or lovers but may take a variety of forms. It doesn't have to be human love but might be a religious experience or one having to do with trees or seas, or birds or bees. Think lively and big."

At the break, I go into the gardens at the back of the building. I overhear Olivia complaining to Lea that she thought this workshop would be more political and less personal. They go off to talk to Colleen, and I sit on the grass in the sun. There is a tightness in the pit of my stomach, a familiar feeling, just thinking about arguing with Olivia and Lea. It's my if-I- disagree-they-will-not-like-me-anymore feeling—a desperate anxiety that makes me want to capitulate at all costs. I imagine I developed it early on while watching and listening to Alice and Hallie fight. That conflict was resolved by Hallie getting locked up. That "resolution" had dire consequences for all three of us: Alice, Hallie and me. It reminds me of the plate full of liver and onions that my mother made me eat the day I ran away from home. To this day, I can't face liver and onions. How am I supposed to help with anyone else's conflict when I can't stand my own? I was born into conflict—the black and white of the egg—and I've been running ever since.

I remember one weekend Lucy came home from college bursting with excitement about feminism, wanting to liberate me from being the sole person responsible for housework. Oh, she had a good argument: if both Ralph and I were both working full time, why was I still doing everything in the house? Later in the weekend I got to thinking that maybe she was right. So I confronted Ralph, and he agreed to do more. I never would have done it without Lucy. And, I'm sure I had the familiar fist in the stomach when I did it. Still, it gives me hope that conflict resolution is possible.

When class reconvenes, Rhiannon refers to Lea's and Olivia's complaints. Her figure is tiny against the backdrop of the huge shelves full of fabric and yarns, her white hair seemingly a part of the pattern of the fabric behind her. She stands firmly rooted in her belief in the methods of conflict resolution the Peace Weavers have developed over the years. She says, "There are so many intellectual ways to make these arguments that will be forgotten a week or two after the class ends, but these assignments rooted in art, in the body, have longevity."

Once again, I notice that her words are more like song than speech. As she speaks, her body makes small movements, as if her spinal cord is itself a wave. Instead of commenting directly on the feedback she has just received, she begins to tell us a story.

"Finding themselves in a land with few trees, the settlers made their shelter from the stone that had burrowed into the earth throughout the centuries. Once the stones were uprooted from their places of origin, they did not want to go together to make solid walls. In fact, some of the stones, when placed together, simply butted up against one another, some part of each stone hitting the other and the rest of the stone seeming to get as far away as possible.

"Wise people took those warring stones and moved them around, looking for the common curves that would fit them together, using the least amount of connecting mud to make the strongest container. With great patience, they got to know the various faces of each individual rock before the jigsaw puzzle came together. For some purposes, such as fencing, they used no mortar at all. This method left room for flow back and forth. In fact, sometimes the space between the stones seemed as important as the stones themselves.

"And so," sings Rhiannon, "in this room today and as we proceed," she makes a gesture that includes us and the whole of our environment, "take your stones and turn them about. Look for the places that connect you with one another. That's how we will make our bonds strong enough to weather the storms."

Chapter 15—Emptiness

Your body as an instrument has so much more resonance if it were empty.

October 12, 1996

Since the tide is all the way out, to reach the edge of the shore, I would have to walk onto rocks slippery with seaweed: yellow ribbons, spongy green goo and red leafy kale-like plants. Oil paints on rock. I settle for watching the ocean from a distance, imagining that only hours ago, this place where I sit was covered in water.

There is no wind. Breathing in the still air, I wonder if Hallie will visit tonight. Where has all the energy gone, all the howling swirls of anger and heartbreak? Today's pleasure is a seduction for tomorrow's woes—that's what Hallie might say.

But right now, in this moment, I can think of no reason for worry. Air let out of an overblown tire—what more to say, when words solidify what is not solid? I linger in stretched out time, looking at hollows, at nothing, and at the four winds, at everything. Worn-out advice hisses as it empties into the abyss.

I stay empty for a while, thinking nothing. Finally, I fill my lungs, breathing new air. There are no voices at all, not even mine. And the stillness of the water reflects a place in me that I recognize. My body carves out a warm hollow cradle in the rock and my feet hug the ground.

Tonight, Hallie does not appear. I do not read or cook or eat, but let the twilight seep into the house without turning on lights. Only stillness, emptiness, holiness. When I finally sleep, I dream of an empty vessel, a vase made up of my throat, esophagus and widening at the bottom, my stomach. I arise and bathe in fresh, clear, warm water. A baptism.

Finally feeling hungry, I eat apples Valerie brought me and fresh, fat, sun-ripened blackberries with creamy oatmeal. Rolling blackberry seeds around in my mouth, I let the texture and taste grow in me. I do not run ahead to check on the future; nor stub my toes on the past. The berries are enough.

A light movement of air brushes past me. I feel all the places my body touches itself, my arms against my side, my ankles as they cross, my lips where they met, teeth and tongue behind them. Cupping my hands over my mouth, I feel the warmth of my breath.

Softly, I run my fingers across my wrinkled, soft face, feeling each moment of my life imprinted there, without naming or changing it. The sound of birds fills my head, and still there is no wind. I gaze at the trees, the water, the hills beyond and let them merge together in dots of color. The world has become liquid; my eyes drink, my throat drinks, my ears drink.

The morning has passed by the time I break from my reverie and take notice of the clock. This I do with an uncharacteristic nonchalance, knowing I have come through an opening but with no idea to where.

The next weaving project comes to me easily once I sit in front of the loom. I will weave the dream image of the empty vase inside myself. It will be a dark blue vase the color of Crater Lake when the sun is shining. No flowers in the vase, at least to start. If I feel discouraged later with the plainness of it, I can add as I did the last time. The vase will float in water with the land across the bay visible in the background, land with steps leading down to the water.

I sketch the vase with a belly button in the widening bottom. Never have I created anything so concrete, yet so abstract all at once. It is freeing. As I begin to work, I hear the rain outside, wishing its way in. Other students trickle in, but I do not notice if anyone needs help.

After class, the weather is still wet; Colleen offers me a ride home. Though I ask her in for tea, she begs off to get home to fix dinner for her family. I am relieved that I don't have to serve anyone.

Chapter 16—Tug of War

War tugs on us in a peculiar way, creating winners and losers. To simply pull as hard as you can while the other side does the same does not engage the imagination. Where is the tug of imagination?

October 13, 1996

"Don't worry and don't think of cutting your trip short but..." Ralph says in our next call. After that mystical experience of yesterday and today, things were going too well.

"You're sick, injured, what?" I ask leaping carelessly to conclusions.

He sighs deeply. "I'm fine, but Phyllis broke her leg late Saturday night. Just one of those things."

Turns out that Saturday night they had had a bit of an argument, and Phyllis left the house abruptly. The Sunday paper (which always gets delivered late on Saturday evening) was sitting on the second step and she hit it on the way out, throwing herself down the rest of the steps and twisting her leg under her.

"I got there as quickly as I could and had to drag her to the car and lift her into the passenger's seat—you know how high those seats are in the van—and get to the hospital. Didn't know it before but Phyllis does not tolerate pain well. Anyway, she's back home now, and I set up a bed in the living room since she can't climb stairs."

I don't know what to think. Is this a message that I am needed at home? "She's not much help to you in this condition, is she?"

Ralph hesitates a moment. "Well, no, and since she can't put any weight on it, I am cooking and bringing all of her meals to her." Quickly he adds, "But so far it is working out and we are getting along fine."

I just shake my head. There go all of my careful arrangements. At least it wasn't Ralph who got hurt because then I'd have to leave for sure. Judy has already offered to help them out so I figure I will just play it by ear. I am not going home to nurse Phyllis—that would be just too much.

After the call, I return to my apartment, turn the flame on under the teakettle and stare out the window, wondering how painful a broken leg must be. Adam broke his arm one summer when he fell out of a tree. The hardest thing for him was to keep it dry. He usually swam every day in the summer. And I remember he complained about the itch that he couldn't reach to scratch. But a leg. That means immobility for a while, I'm sure.

I can only remember breaking a bone once and that was an arm, too. I must have been about five but my memories of that period before my adoption are vague. I believe it was a summer Hallie and I spent with Alice at a summer place in the country. The pain of the arm wasn't as bad as Hallie and Alice fighting.

As I turn off the fire under the teakettle, its whistle becomes Hallie's crooning.

"Remember, remember, remember, can you, the sun porch at the summer house?

"Nothing leaps to mind," I say, thinking of that broken arm.

"This is a pleasure story until Alice enters. In Alice's world, the more fun you had, the more the devil had you."

Staring now into the darkness of my teacup, first I see my face as it is now, and then that image fades into an image of me at five.

July 10, 1931

Emma is such a flower, opened-up face, blowing in the breeze, stretching her petals toward the sun, a purple morning glory. Even the sling on her left arm doesn't stop her from performing this ritual with Hallie on the sun porch on Sunday, a day free of tightness, rigidity, and duty. Their bodies are altars, the sunlight the offering. Hallie read some controversial studies showing that rickets could be cured with vitamin D from the sun. And Emma has been diagnosed with rickets. So every opportunity she has, Hallie places Emma in the sun—the more skin exposed, the better.

Hallie already feels there is a capitalist plot to keep kids inside, leave them pale and sickly so they are less rebellious about working all day on some dark, noisy assembly line. She is sure that the owning class is trying to keep workers and those in training to become workers, such as five year olds like Emma, away from the power of Mother Earth. But she knows better, knows that sunlight will make children grow, just like plants.

Alice's strict religious beliefs lead her to oppose nudity. She even bathes with two wash cloths, one to cover herself and the other to wash with. Even in the hottest of summers as that one surely was, Alice stays covered, except for her face and hands.

Sundays are sacred days even for Hallie, though she never can bring herself to go to church. Instead of identifying with the sinner, as she is supposed to, she always identifies with the sacrifice—what they offer up to be killed, mutilated or consumed. After Hallie picks Emma up at Sunday school, and while Alice is still at church, they have their own sacred time on the sun porch.

"Come on, sweet Emma," Hallie says, "time to get ourselves warmed up." She starts spinning the handle of the phonograph where she put on some ragtime tunes that are usually kept hidden in her room.

The old dilapidated porch at the summer house up at Lake Michigan has worn wooden floors, smooth from the years of bare feet pounding into it. The screening is partly covered by vining jasmine; some of the shoots reach into the room, searching for an anchor. Since the porch is on the east side of the house, the early morning sun comes there with its morning freshness.

They shove the white wicker rocking chairs and end tables back against the wall to make room. Emma knows the routine. Off come the tight Sunday school clothes—the red ruffled socks and the patent leather shoes, the white lacy dress and cotton slip and undies, too. Then, listening to the music, they dance naked in the slanted rays of the sun. Moist from the heat, pores opened up. Anything is possible.

They swoop to the jazzy tunes, joining hands in a circle, energy flowing back and forth between them. Gradually, they slow until their movements are so deliberate they can feel every muscle in their bodies as they stretch and ripple. Breathing in the delicious summer air, the scent of jasmine and newly mowed lawns, they forget themselves.

Finally, out of breath, curled up against each other, Hallie takes out the Emily Dickinson and begins reading to Emma.

The sound of the words is a song. Time slows; their hearts beat slower and slower, like cats, stretched out and dreamy.

Emma is too young to understand why she can't tell anyone about their Sundays. But she knows not to tell. She has no awareness about right or wrong, just that it feels good to be that close to her mother.

Emma wants her grandmother, Alice, to stay home and be with them out there, too, but Alice never dances or reads poetry or listens to jazz. If she sings, she sings hymns. Emma isn't sure what God would have said about the sun porch; but before "the incident," when what they are doing seems innocent and right, she feels God wants them to be happy, and they are.

Happy, yes, but not entirely free. Hallie worries that in her half-hypnotized state, she might lose track of time, and that will be the end of them. They have to be dressed and back to normal when Alice returns; the knowledge of her return hangs like the certainty of the setting sun.

Hallie thinks this must be the way powerless people feel, having to know the schedule and whims of the powerful, if they want to do anything subversive. Alice has the power in that house—it is her house. But Emma doesn't have to feel that oppression. She can rely on Hallie and be entirely free. When time runs out, Hallie helps Emma get re-dressed in her Sunday ruffles and they pretend nothing out of the ordinary had gone on. She comes into the house and starts playing with her dolls, the ones Alice gave her with the white dresses and porcelain faces, pretty and delicate.

While Emma plays, Hallie often goes outside to the picnic table under that ancient oak tree—the one with a particularly gnarly knot that looks like a scary old man. She writes, and sometimes Emma plays out there if she is quiet. When Alice stays at church all day, those are the best-stretched Sundays of all.

But this particular Sunday, Alice returns home from church early with a terrible stomachache. She wants Hallie to make her some chicken soup and she rushes out onto the porch before Hallie and Emma have a chance to do anything. She sees her daughter and granddaughter curled up naked next to one another on that porch, and it was as if the world was ending. Grabbing Emma by her good arm, Alice has the strength of Samson. She screams, "The devil—in my house! Hallie! What are you doing? A sin, a sin under God." Then she slaps them both, hard.

Hallie can't believe Alice hit Emma. She's never done that before, at least not with Hallie as a witness. When Hallie recovers a little, she sends Emma upstairs with her clothes.

From upstairs, Emma can hear loud voices. Hallie is screaming, yet she feels so tired of being angry, of fighting. At that moment, she can't remember a peaceful day in her thirty-seven years. All she wants to do is lie down and rest—be taken care of. How desperately she needs a mother. Hallie thinks she might have to die for Emma, die to give her life—why, it sounds almost Christian. But she is never going to go passively; she will have to be killed.

If only she can keep the world out of Emma's life a little longer ... If she can give Emma the gift of safety, warmth, and a love of her own body, then she will consider that she has been a great mother, a success.

The five-year-old me fades out and I am seventy again and feeling weary. My left arm is throbbing where the cast must have been. I can remember ever so vaguely the feeling in the arm—and maybe more.

"I wish I could rewrite the story; but it's all done now but for the recollection. I'm sorry, I fell backward into pain—a gain, a loss. But, you see, that's how it always went. When I had pleasure, equal or worse pain around the corner. The world would collapse if I had my pleasure without pain—like a law of nature."

As I ponder the story, my memory begins to wake up. Aloud I say, "Oh, I'm beginning to remember! I'd forgotten!"

Hallie must be smiling, *"Happy you remember! You have something I never had—clear, sunny days, no clouds, no shame...*

Sipping tea, I let my memories seep out of long-ago boarded-up windows. I have a nebulous sense of my innocence back then. Too agitated to sit still as these memories return, I pace the kitchen, glad my apartment is below Valerie and Sean so they can't hear me.

"Yes, Hallie, it's coming back—I see how it happened just that way. After Alice discovered us, I went upstairs and began doubting. Were we sinning against God? I'd gone to Sunday school, and no one had ever said anything about this particular sin. I was angry at you for not knowing. Grandmother knew. I remember thinking that if I'd had a Daddy, he would have known. I started thinking maybe my father's death was your fault, too. Maybe Daddy was taken away because you didn't know what sin was."

I sit down in the living room facing away from the window, shaken. I had pushed it to the back of my mind. At the time, I came to believe what Alice said—that we'd sinned. I see now that, while it surely was unorthodox behavior for a mother and daughter, it certainly wasn't sin. What a relief to remember something from before the now infamous picture of me in the wicker chair.

Because I'm beginning to trust Hallie, I tell her about the portrait and the birthday party, thankful that she retrieved that memory for me.

"I had begun to think you despised me from day one, always looking for a way to unload me onto someone else."

Hallie snorts. *"Hah! No, maybe when I first got pregnant and maybe after you first emerged. But after that, I would, would've done anything for you. I gave up everything to save you. Not the triumphant heroine that time."*

"What do you mean, everything?"

"Another day for that story. Maybe on the weekend I'll tell the Charlotte story, my own true love story. For now, you rest your old bones—wake up to a new day, fresh day blown in from tomorrow."

I can't sleep for thinking about those Sundays. For the first time, I can relate my life to something Hallie said. I have deep anchor feelings about it that I can't articulate, maybe it's love. I wonder if it didn't save my life, having that in my heart.

There is a storm percolating. My arm is aching where I broke it so long ago. It often hurts when there is a storm coming; I always thought it was arthritis encroaching into my bones. I listen to the rain come in waves against the windows. Even with all of the covers I feel a sudden chill and shiver uncontrollably. Outside the drops coalesce into a voice, but it's not Hallie's.

"Emma," the voice says faintly and in waves as the rain on the windows. *"It's grandmother, Alice. Company, yes? Can't wait."* Her voice sounds strained, as if it is taking all of her strength to be here talking to me. *"Stayed out ... thought she couldn't hurt you."*

She pauses and I listen only to the rain. Then, as if in concert with the streaking rain, she continues. *"Afraid you believe her ... Thought I wouldn't have to come. Now you lean toward her ... beware."*

Her staccato is so different from Hallie's breezy speech. Not now, not this. They are bringing this conflict from the dead and setting it down in my peaceful apartment. The strange thing is that it doesn't bother me, hearing another voice from the dead. "Grandmother, I don't know what you're talking about. Today has been one of the most pleasurable days I can remember."

"Always... starts with pleasure ..."

Her voice sounds spooky, so unlike Hallie's. It's cold and strangely rhythmic, like a snare drum. I shiver again as I remind myself that she is, after all, a ghost, and I should be at least a little frightened.

"Remember my message… and pray...Pray with me....: Our father…who… art… in heaven..."

Her prayer sounds like the hammering of a hammer, stopping, starting, hitting the words into me. I do not join her in this forced march of a prayer, and she finally stops.

"Stories, you want—I tell. Started after. After the summer... porch."

I have been looking forward to a good night's sleep. Sighing, I reluctantly pull myself out of bed and sit in the overstuffed chair by the window, staring into the streaked and splattered reflection of a pink ruffled dress.

September, 1931

It is the day before Emma's first day of school. Emma, Hallie and

Alice are living in Alice's small Detroit house. Alice wants Emma with her but Hallie won't leave her and Hallie has nowhere else to go. Alice bought Emma a beautiful new dress with pink ruffles and lace to wear the next day. She tries it on and is just going back upstairs to take it off when Hallie catches her. "Emma, come back down here. What is that ghastly dress you are wearing?" She and Emma have already chosen what she is to wear to school.

Hallie says, "Emma, remember how we talked about this and agreed that you would wear an outfit that gives you room to move, brown knickers and that red shirt? You wanted to climb trees and monkey bars and play sports, now that your arm has healed?"

Emma nods demurely, eyes closed, rubbing the silky material of the sleeve back and forth across her cheek.

"If you wear that dress," Hallie warns, "you'll have to sit still and act like a girl. Is that what you want?"

Emma says nothing. She wants friends, not to stand out as different for the sake of principles she doesn't understand.

But Hallie deals with children by treating them like adults. She stands up tall, towering over her young child, lecturing her on women's rights. It is quite a sight, this little girl with tears in her eyes, not understanding anything but that her mother hates the beautiful dress and will hate her if she wears it. Hallie hoists that hefty decision onto Emma's shoulders, saying, "You are 'one of us,' Emma, and women everywhere are counting on you."

Emma likes the dress and doesn't want to hurt Alice's feelings and yet, to let Hallie down is to invoke her wrath. So she starts crying, and Alice takes her onto her lap. Hallie hates it when Emma cries and Alice sympathizes with Emma. Hallie believes that tears show weakness and to be respected, a woman must remain strong. She raises Emma stricter than a hard-hearted father might raise his sons, tolerating no signs of weakness.

When it becomes clear that a fight is in the offing, Hallie sends Emma to her room, as has happened so many times before. Hallie and Alice fight it out, the same terrible battle. Hallie is trapped because she has worn out her welcome with her friends and all other relatives. There just isn't any alternative to this nightmare of the two of them raising Emma together. Alice, for her part, is sure that both she and Hallie are being punished by God because Hallie is not a good Christian woman.

After hearing Alice say that she will not stand by and watch Emma's life be ruined the way Hallie's own life was ruined, Hallie says, "And I suppose your life is a bowl of cherries full of pleasure and fun! And you want her to marry young, have five children and be a slave all of her life—get bitter and old at an early age and chase her husband out of her house, never to be seen again?" Hallie's face turns bright red, her eyes on fire. Though the fight has a ring of familiarity to it, Alice has never seen Hallie that frightening before.

Alice's head is reeling. She does what she has done so many times before to calm herself, she begins to recite the Lord's prayer. Meanwhile, her thoughts cannot be stopped. Hallie is the cause of all of her unhappiness—Hallie and her father's spoiling her. And though she knows she shouldn't bring it up, she says, "Henry spoiled you and now he's not here to undo what he did."

Hearing Henry's name invariably enrages Hallie. She moves closer to Alice, and Alice backs up until she is against the wall. Alice can see her pupils dilated and glazed. "You pushed him and pushed him to be something he wasn't." Hallie says, pushing Alice ever so slightly against the wall until she can feel the frame of the picture of Christ hanging on the wall behind her. Hallie continues, "You'd do the same thing to Emma if I let you. You've hated me since I was born, and now you hate Emma, the way you hate yourself."

Alice tries to slip out of Hallie's trap, but each time she moves, Hallie moves with her. Alice says in as calm a voice as she can muster, "I'm not the one's rigid. You—you insist Emma not marry, never have children, never trust men. What's fair about that?"

Tearing at her own clothes, Hallie goes on uncontrollably. "She's not wearing that slave rag that says kick me, beat me up, abuse me and I'll sit by passively and smile. No!"

Alice takes a deep breath and says coldly, "You will dress Emma in that new dress and you will walk with her to school or else leave my home now."

Hallie, inches from Alice's face, screams, "Keep your ways to yourself, old woman, or you won't die a natural death! I'll do anything to keep my daughter free—ANYTHING."

Just then, Danny comes around the corner whistling, "When the Moon Comes Over the Mountain." The whistling stops abruptly when he hears Hallie yelling. Danny races to protect his mother and throws Hallie aside, sending her reeling into the kitchen table, knocking the black ceramic teapot to the floor. Hallie scrambles to stay upright. She rights herself, turns her full glare on Danny, then stomps out of the room. The bond between Alice and Danny tightens against this threat. This behavior cannot be ignored. And since Hallie has killed before...

I am tired of the acrimony Alice is describing. I didn't want to hear it in the first place.

I say, "It's all past history, can't you let it rest in peace?"

Alice insists that I see her side of it. *"See my point. You grateful to me ...yes."*

I say, softly, "Thank you. Is that what you want?"

"I want," Alice says in a slightly nasal whine, *"that you remember … her … evil. Evil all ways. Don't want ... your thanks. Thanked me … already. Look ... at your life—perfect."*

I am feeling compromised here, disloyal to Hallie. I say in a surly voice, "I didn't do it for you, you know. It's what I wanted."

"Never mind why."

I am still the football in the middle between Alice and Hallie, but I have no intention of playing such a game.

I say, "I've had enough." Alice moans softly, evidently still feeling misunderstood, and I feel sorry for her.

She's getting slightly stronger, but still speaks in short sentences as if the sun might come and dry her up any minute. *"Show you—my early life,"* she says as I feel compelled to watch the drops of rain on the dark window and see a lone farmhouse on a hill.

March 29, 1881

After the church bell tolled ten times, the preacher said authoritatively, "It is time to surrender—yes, I say it is time—time to surrender to God's will." Alice trembles in her seat. If there is a time for questions and answers, Alice would like to ask if surrendering to God's will means that she has to sit back and wait for God to take control of her life. That is what she has been doing, and so far it has gotten her nowhere. Why the sermon is on that subject on the one day she has decided to take her future into her own hands and be introduced to Henry, she doesn't know. Maybe her own stubborn nature keeps her from reading the signs right, maybe...

She and her father live on a tiny farm outside of Amhurstberg, a small town in Canada. Alice picked Henry out after seeing him at the bank where he worked. The bank manager was busy when Alice and her father got there, so Henry told them to sit in a couple of straight-backed wooden chairs until he returned. Henry was strange, with his thick German accent and shyness around women.

Alice sized up his potential as a husband as she did any eligible-looking man in the area. He looked to be a decade older than her eighteen years, and judging by his accent, he hadn't been in Canada for many years. He was a tall, rather awkward man who walked about as if he had so much on his mind that he couldn't bother to make sure the ground he walked on was level, or that he didn't run into things. Alice took that to mean he was highly intelligent and likely to go far.

Alice studies the back of Henry's head as he sits several pews ahead of her and her best friend Clarissa. His dark brown hair is unevenly cut and falls carelessly on the top of his collar. She knows she can cut it better than that. She's cut her father's hair since she was small, and his looks much neater. She figures she'd be good for Henry. Purposely, she overlooks the rough edges of the shirt he is wearing and the dingy brownish-gray of the suit that has been worn for what looks like a hundred years. She knows he is poor—that goes without saying in this town. But she has hopes.

Alice isn't sure how she will break away from her father, but she knows she has to. Before Alice was born, her mother was often ill and had two stillborns; both times she almost died. Finally, Alice lived and her mother died. Frederick has no interest in remarrying and puts all of his energy, what little there is, into the farm and into raising Alice. But Alice feels confined there on that isolated farm with only a silent, grim father for company. Alice learned to read and then never went back to school. There is too much to be done on the farm, anyway. Her social life comes mostly from church attendance. She doesn't know much, but she knows that life has more to offer than that dark, vaguely menacing farm on the edge of nowhere.

After the service, just as they planned it, Clarissa introduces Henry and Alice. While it isn't love at first sight, they have a friendly conversation. Henry has mastered the structure of the English language, but he is not yet entirely comfortable speaking it. Alice likes the way her name sounds coming from Henry's foreign lips—something like All-Ease and she tries to become the name. She sets the bait in the trap by making him feel at ease, by being interested and taking the lead. She presumes that since he is smart, he will find a way to go to college and they will at least get to leave town and go someplace more interesting.

On the way home from church, Alice tells Clarissa that she has taken her life into her own hands. She looks down in the snow and sees a spring beauty pushing its way up to the sun. She points out the tiny white flower hardly visible against the melting snow and says, "That flower is me—out of place but getting warmer. I can see my future just like I know spring is on its way. It's all so sure now."

"And that was the beginning?" I ask her.

She tells me that before long she and Henry were planning their wedding and researching colleges in Detroit. He wanted to get an engineering degree. She would put him through college and then they would be on the road to a new life.

After they were married and living in Detroit, Henry was about to start college when Alice got pregnant and started having babies. If he could have controlled his appetites—Alice always thought—but that was too much to ask. No, he had to get a job almost immediately, a job that took everything out of him, until he was so tired that he couldn't consider college. Alice was almost constantly pregnant in subsequent years.She miscarried three times; two infants died—one, Ronald, died of flu in the epidemic of 1890 and Michele, her only other girl died of some mysterious illness at age six months—Michele was the one who could have been what Alice wanted and needed in a girl. When Michele died, Hallie was about six.

"Enough ... tonight ... Emma

I am weary of stories, but I tell Alice, "I'm glad to know something about your life—I need some context, at least that's what my weaving instructors say."

I yawn widely, feeling all of my seventy years now, needing to sleep. "Maybe we'll talk again sometime. Could you and Hallie come together sometime?"

"Storm and a half. You ... ready?"

"Well, what if you tried listening for a change?"

"Hallie ... listen? Pfffft! Miracles."

As the rain fades, I marvel at how I could stay up so late—not going to the pub but just sitting in my own place letting the party come to me. How full my social life has become. But then I wonder, do dead people count as a social life?

Chapter 17—Long Division

Fence after fence on the soggy landscape dividing and dividing. What is this obsession with divisions? Maybe to break the wind, or as a hindrance to erosion? Or maybe it is just a place to put the rocks when roads were built and areas cleared for farming or for a house. Then again, perhaps fences are simply for show, to make humans believe in divisions, such as the one between life and death.

October 14, 1996

Until now I'd imagined the division between life and death was impenetrable. What is dead is gone, buried, forgotten. This leaching of death into life is disconcerting. I want to build a wall around my conversations with Hallie and Alice not only to keep them to myself but also to keep them from contaminating my beliefs. I have no intention of trying to make the conversations stop, even if I could. But I'd like to build a few containing walls and suspend making sense of it all until some other time.

Walking to class, I ponder Alice's appearance, this interruption of my flow. When she came pounding in on the rain, I didn't want to hear her. I have only just begun to feel connected to Hallie, and Alice shows up to contradict her. I never thought Hallie was evil *per se*—hard to get along with, yes. Argumentative, yes. And I have thought perhaps she was crazy—I'm reserving judgment on that for now. But evil?

Alice's voice is harsh compared to Hallie's, and I am having a hard time generating sympathy for her. The way she describes their fights, the two of them were in utter deadlock. Maybe I'll get a chance to mediate if they both show up at the same time. Ground rules. There will definitely have to be ground rules, I think, as I dread the possibility of being stuck in the middle of this melee. Where's Lucy, the mediator, when I need her?

As much as I would like to keep these conversations to myself, divided from the rest of my life, I'm also feeliong compelled to talk to somebody about what is going on. I can't talk to Valerie and Sean because they don't know me well enough. I can't tell Ralph because he'll surely think I'm losing my mind, and he'll put himself on the next plane. Besides, he's got enough on his mind with Phyllis' broken leg. Maybe Diana would listen, but she is so unpredictable. What about Lucy? Well, I'll tell her, but only after she gets here. It's easier to explain to people who have the magic of this place working on them. I toy with the idea of telling Margaret—I had a good feeling about her right from the start. We agreed yesterday to meet for soup at the little cafe at noon today, so maybe …?

Margaret is in good spirits. "I've been weaving all morning and even though it's damp in this country, my arthritis is manageable—at least so far."

Margaret does most of the talking at lunch. She expounds on her birth story. The story that was told to her was that her mother was on a ship from Ireland to New Zealand when Margaret was born. Margaret's mother took ill on the journey and never made it to New Zealand; someone on the ship took care of Margaret for the rest of the journey and took her to the authorities once they landed. She has no idea what happened to her father. Margaret was never adopted, instead living her life in an orphanage with a hundred other unadoptables.

"I don't even know my parents' names," she says, tearing up, "though there was a time I tried every avenue to find out. Dead ends all."

I say to her, thinking that my experiences might actually help her, "Maybe, if you listen on some of these windy and rainy nights, they will speak to you."

She says, "What? Speak from the dead, you mean? Right, and I suppose I could hire a psychic, too. To think, I hadn't considered that ..."

But seeing Margaret's discomfort, I say, "I'm sorry—really sorry—about—your parents and your childhood. I didn't mean it as a joke. I'm actually serious." All of a sudden, I feel lucky that I at least know who my ancestors are, even if I don't know much about them. I even appreciate knowing about Alice.

She examines me, puzzled, "You don't seem the sort to believe in something like that." Noticing the waitress coming, she jumps at the chance to change the subject, "Oh, here comes our potato leek soup—their specialty. If potatoes don't ground you here and now, nothing will."

I look at the ghostly white of the soup; I know I could still back out now. But I continue, looking directly at Margaret. "Can I trust you?" I lose my appetite as I consider telling her, and I wipe my sweaty hands on my napkin.

She nods, "Of course."

I go on, "It's unlike me to believe in voices from the dead but... can I tell you something in strictest confidence? You won't report me anywhere as about to lose my mind, will you?"

Her eyebrows lift in surprise, disappearing behind her thick white bangs and she answers, "I'm not the type to run out and report anyone to the authorities. I've been locked up myself, first in an orphanage, then in a loony bin. Don't imagine I'll ever be the cause of someone else going in—not in a million—but that's a story for later—let's hear yours."

I look at her quizzically, wanting to hear that story, especially if it means not having to finish what I just started. But I take a drink of water and tell her about the voices.

Margaret doesn't know whether to take me seriously. "You mean you can make out what they say? And it's not just your name or anything—like, Eeeeeemmmmmaaaa," she says, making haunted sounds and grinning.

I do not laugh, but look at her intently, wondering if I trusted the right person. "Nothing like that, actually. I can hear them well, though they speak a little strangely. They tell me their stories—that's mainly what they've done so far. One was about my birth, the one I described the other day in class. I didn't know any of that before I came here."

She considers the implications of this news. "Don't you think it's just a voice in your head that you didn't know was there?"

As I butter my bread lightly, I explain, "I don't know where the voices are, but if they are in my head, I don't see how I am learning things that no one has ever told me. Some of it I'm sure I can confirm with my daughter Lucy when she gets here because she's done research; some of it can be confirmed by going through old newspapers."

"So you suppose, then, that if I listened really hard to the wind and rain, I might hear my relatives?" Margaret pushes her bangs out of her eyes and stares at me intently, serious now.

I shrug. "Who knows? This country is magical. If nothing else, I'm convinced of that. Back home I don't believe in magic. I'm quite a realist, honestly. I'm religious, yes, but not superstitious."

Margaret again looks puzzled and I realize how little we really know each other. "I'm sorry, but I find it hard to tell the difference—then again, I'm a dyed in the wool—New Zealand wool—atheist. To me all religion is superstition. Oh, I don't object to mysticism. Part of the world will always remain mysterious—a part for which science can never break the code."

I nod, wondering what my scientist son Mick would think of that. I'll bet he believes it can all be figured out. Maybe he could tell me how it was possible that ghosts were talking to me? For a fleeting second I consider telling him, then I know I've lost all my good judgment. I'll quit with one person knowing—for the time being, that will have to do.

In class, Rhiannon tells us a story about conflict: "Two brothers were riding bicycles through town. One was much smaller and could not pedal as fast as the other. While the younger one pedaled and pedaled, his face red and streaked with tears, the older one did not turn around to notice. Their mother came out and saw the younger one just as he was giving up, and she said, 'Oh, honey, it's OK that you did not win the race—winning isn't everything.' And the little boy said, 'But Mama, I wasn't racing to win. I just wanted us to be together!'

"The intentions we attribute to people's behavior," says Rhiannon, "may simply be projections of how we view the world and have little to do with actual motivations. Remember this in conflict resolution. Actions may be taken for reasons that are entirely beyond your scope of knowledge."

To me, the moral of the story is that listening to the stories of my relatives' lives is important ... and that my assumptions might be completely faulty.

When I get back to the apartment, I find a letter under the door from Lucy saying that she is going to make it after all. She is due to arrive at Shannon on October 26th. That way, she will have a week with me. She asks if I can check with Valerie about renting her place for another few weeks so that she can stay and work on her book.

Exhilarated by the prospect of Lucy's arrival, I arrange it with Valerie who is happy to rent to Lucy especially once she finds out that she is a writer. She says, "Maybe she'll put me in the book, yes!" Her eyes glow with delight as she thinks of a writer living in the apartment. "Thanks a million," I say, and she replies, "It'll be grand to meet your daughter."

Valerie's last word is uttered on the inhale. I have heard other women here speak that same way. It sounds peculiar, as though one doesn't want to waste the time it takes to inhale between words and so the speech comes out on both the inhale and exhale. This way you can take back some of what you say and keep it for yourself. I might try it.

As I finish up my letter writing, memories flood me. I particularly remember a summer when I was about ten and I visited my uncle Hank's cabin on Lake Michigan. Hank was Hallie's brother and was one of the more honest of that bunch. He spoke in a down-home way and had been accused of being blunt and crass. The rest of the family seemed to alternate between pitying me and spoiling me, treating me like a wounded bird. They made me feel uneasy and weak, as if my fix were only temporary, like my skates at home. When one of the wheels came off, I fixed it with a rubber band, but I couldn't skate with abandon, always worried the wheel would fly off.

I had never been heard a good account of how I came to be living in Ohio without my real mother. No one seemed to want to talk about it.

This particular day at Lake Michigan, I remember it was late morning and it grew hot as we clung to the shade of the tree. When I asked Hank what had happened, he wanted to know how much I knew. I told him that before I was adopted, I would be dropped off at somebody's house, an uncle maybe and Hallie would pick me up later. But for four years now, she hadn't returned. Mother—the one in Ohio who made me call her that—told me Hallie was crazy and didn't want me and that she had left me with Grandmother Alice who was too old to take care of me.

I sometimes fantasized that I had been like the Lindbergh baby, stolen away and not killed but maybe sold for a million dollars. I created scenario after scenario of how my real parents were going to rescue me.

I asked Hank if we could find my mother and bring her home. "She didn't give up on me just because I wore dresses or cried too much—or was that it?" I asked.

He looked me in the eyes. "No, honey, it's more complicated than that. Hallie needed a lot of breaks from being a mother. And what's more, sometimes she needed to do research for her writing. And then there was our mother Alice who couldn't stand most of Hallie's friends and wouldn't allow them in the house. So Hallie, from time to time, went to see her friends elsewhere. And a couple of times, she signed herself into the hospital for a rest."

"Was she sick?" I asked.

"Well, sort of," Hank answered, "but it wasn't physical. I'd say she was sick in spirit. You remember how mad she'd get, mostly at your grandma? She wanted to take you and raise you to be a strong and powerful woman, but she wasn't fit to do it. She had been so heartbroken when your daddy died and you not even born yet. Too much to handle—no way to support herself with a baby and all..."

Unable to sit still any longer, I climbed off of his lap and began making a pile of small stones at his feet. He explained that Grandmother Alice couldn't stand to see Emma raised by Hallie.

"So," Hank said, "in a way, they both wanted you so much that they fought for you. Neither of them won, so your mother in Ohio got you."

This I did not understand. My friends had the same mothers from the time they were born, whether or not they were good mothers. I didn't see how it was possible to be taken away from a mother who wanted me. To me, mothers were the most powerful people on earth. I pondered this as I built a small fort with the stones I had gathered, putting a particularly sharp stone at the top to make the tower.

When Hank told me my mother was a radical, I was puzzled. "My daddy says radicals are tearing the country apart. They want violence and upset so Russia can come in and take over. Is she a Red?"

Hank explained that Hallie called herself a socialist, which meant that she wanted the people to own their own factories, get paid better and have more rights. "She is for the people." He turned and stared out over the water for a moment as if he could almost see Hallie's envisioned world glimmering in the near distance.

"She is even more radical than that," Hank reported. "She believes in women's rights—not just the right to vote, which she played a part in winning—but she also wants women and men to be equal in all ways."

Hank continued, "They put her in Mannington, the loony bin. She's not coming out, not this time." Hank had been to visit Hallie a few weeks before and found her withdrawn and strange. She did seem at that point to be as crazy as everyone had said. The way the doctors talked, she was seriously ill and they had no cure. They had told him that she was getting worse, not better.

I begged Hank to get Hallie out. But he said, "There's not a thing we can do, deary."

Before Hank and I left, I kicked down the fort, sending the stones flying towards the water. I cried for a long time after that talk—it didn't seem right that my mother was locked up, especially since she wasn't a criminal or anything, but just had funny ideas. I had funny ideas, too—ones that were different from my parents in Ohio. Now I knew to keep those ideas to myself.

I feel a draft and realize that Hallie has entered the room. I say to her, "There are a few things you need to know about what was happening with me while you were locked up."

"Tell me, I am empty of daughter. Fill me."

"At first I was angry about what had happened to you," I say, pacing the room, "but as time went on, Alice and the Parkers convinced me that you really were crazy and if I took after you, I'd be locked up, too. Mrs. Parker even took me to Mannington when I was ten. You and that place scared me to death! My aunts and uncles and adopted parents in Ohio were there for me, taking care of me day after day. And where were you? You had deserted me—couldn't keep your mouth shut, had to make trouble. I heard it over and over. After a while, I was just as angry at you as the rest of them were. I believed it was your fault for never conforming.

"You personified for me all that was wicked and evil in the world. I remember once when they took me to see you, I wouldn't let you touch me. I clung to Alice's dark navy velour skirt, worried I could catch what you had. You were some crazy lady in a nut house. After that first meeting, you didn't even know who I was.

"I had two mothers and no mother at all. I felt duty towards my adopted mother, not real love. Toward you, I felt aversion. I craved normalcy, run-of-the-mill happiness. When I left home, I found ways to put myself through college, to be self-reliant. I made friends, close friends. I was giving and caring. Everyone liked me. I made friends where you had made enemies. Since I had no brothers and sisters, I made friends as close to family as I could. I am still in contact with some of them.

"If I had a child and no husband, I would have a place to go. I would keep her with me always. I could type. I could make others feel good. I had skills that would keep me safe. You could have done that, too, but you didn't want to. You wanted your own way all the damned time."

I am shocked by my feelings. I had never said these things to anyone before, nor had they occurred to me. My throat is terribly dry all of a sudden, and I feel hot.

Hallie asks quietly, *"Are you just going to go on and on and on doing this that you describe until you die?"*

I don't know what she means and instead of replying, I ask, "Did you know that Alice visited me last night?"

"No, no, no, I didn't. I wondered, wondered, wondered if she'd emerge here in your life and time. What does the old girl, the dreary old girl, want?"

"She never thought I'd give you the time of day. So, when we started to connect, she got scared and rushed in here, telling me horror stories about how you tried to murder her."

"I was forced, forced to give you up—never wanted that. Gave you up to save you. Had I selfishly clung, Alice would have won, would have raised you. Part of me never gave you up. That's the sweetest part that survived all these rugged, dusty years, the part that loves you. Couldn't let go 'til someone, somewhere saw the injustice. Lucy did. In my ghostly toes, I know she will tell it."

By now, tears are running down my face.

"Please, please, please, don't feel sorry for me or for yourself. It is so, so, so long ago, like another lifetime. Think of it as a past life. Don't fret so, Emma. It's just a story, passed on from generation to generation. The Charlotte story will tell soon but Alice might come out then—got some powerful hate of Charlotte.

I gather myself together and take a few deep breaths. "Before you disappear, can I ask one more thing? Lucy is coming here. Maybe you could talk to her, too?"

"I don't know if she could hear me, steer me, as you do. You couldn't, 'til telling time came."

I want a witness, want to know these stories are real and not a strange figment of an over-active imagination. As Mick my scientist son would say, it needs to be replicated.

"You rustle up rest now—you need it ..." She fades away into the distance, leaving me to worry about my sanity. Perhaps Hallie seems so sane because I'm losing my own sanity.

I come into the cafe to meet Margaret, shaking my umbrella and wiping my feet. Margaret is anxious to know if the voices returned last night. I simply nod. Then I ask her if she heard anything last night.

"Just a lot of moaning and whimpering in the wind. Nothing I could make out. I felt a little silly, though," she replies, laughing at herself.

"But let's hear your story, the one about being committed to a mental institution.

She shakes her head disgustedly. "It happened ... oh, about forty years ago. I was married at the time, and my husband thought I was not taking care of the children properly."

I interrupt her. "You know my own mother was institutionalized for a similar thing, perhaps, but she didn't get out for thirty-seven years."

Margaret shook her head sadly, her eyes bright. "Well, I was only in two months, enough time to straighten me out, at least on the surface. Underneath, I was steaming. First chance I got, I was gone."

"You left your husband?"

"Let's just say that he gave me the ground I needed for a divorce, and I dug it. Luckily, he must not have cared that much about Jay and Audrey; he never fought for custody."

Because they were Catholics, Margaret is sure that if she had stayed with Bill, many more children would have been born. She had to leave the church to get out of the marriage.

"I took a civil divorce and before they could excommunicate me, I quit. Lucky for me, too, since I turned out to be gay. Found myself a good woman and settled down on a huge farm and never looked back."

I take this information in stride. "I've never known any homosexuals but have always been for gay rights in the abstract—well, for a long time, anyway. When Lucy attended the national meeting of our church, she came back and told Ralph and me that not only did the church need to include gays and lesbians, but she argued that they should be ordained as ministers. We argued with her for a while and then began to see the wisdom of her stand. Our national church is one of the few Protestant ones that ordain gay ministers.

Margaret raises her eyebrows. "I didn't know any of them allowed it." She nods her head approvingly, "It's surprising."

Then out of the blue, I ask something that has been on my mind lately. "Margaret, do you think your life has a purpose?

Margaret laughs. "You don't fool around, do you? People have been trying to figure that out for thousands of years."

"Alice has gotten me in this frame of mind with her division of the world into good and evil and her incessant need to be reassured that her long-suffering life was for a reason.

Instead of answering, Margaret throws it back on me. "What do you think?"

I say, "Frankly, I always thought my purpose was to have children, be a mom. But I'm now wondering if that could be all?"

She shifts around in her chair, uncomfortable. "Can I be frank?"

I nod.

Then, using her hands for emphasis, she says "I don't think you should put off to the next generation the question of the meaning of life. If you are just here as a work horse to bring in the next crop of wheat, then why give you a brain or a soul for that matter. And why interest you in these matters beyond the family.

"OK, so let's say I've got something else to pass on or leave here, aside from my kids. What would it be?"

"You're at this workshop, aren't you? Learning about peace? As long as people have been asking the meaning of life, they have been sending their children off to war—the meaning can't be all about producing more fodder, now can it?"

Chapter 18—A Normal Life

Normalcy is a measure held over your heads to keep you from being who you are. It has always been an ideal fiction, representing a null and dull group.

October 15, 1996

For the new assignment, I am paired with Kathleen, a twenty-five-year-old Irish woman. Both of us will tell a story from our lives that epitomizes our way of being in the world. Tomorrow we will begin a weaving to represent the story the other person just told us. The instructor emphasizes that the exercise is designed to teach listening and empathy.

I don't know who I am just now, so I decide to stick with who I have been. And that is not very glamorous. I have always thought that I lived a perfectly normal life, certainly not inspiration for good fiction.

No story pops to mind right away so I concentrate on the current weaving. This vase is giving me trouble because the top of it looks like lips slightly parted—it is vaguely sexual. I can't seem to change it and, besides, I'm beginning to like it. It looks as if the vase were embedded in me.

As the afternoon wears on, I become more desperate, searching my memories for something to tell Kathleen that characterizes my life. For now, I feel separate from that fought-over five-year-old that Hallie and Alice told me about. What I can remember about my life is that it was very normal. Normal—like anyone else's. Boring, really. Then a scene pops into my head from when I was a student at Heidelberg College, just a little younger than Kathleen. This is the story I tell Kathleen:

> "It was 1946, just after the war, and the world was slowly starting to get back to normal. I was older than most freshmen because I'd had to work for a couple years after high school to save money for college.
>
> I knew I wanted more than my MRS degree. I wanted to be able to fend for myself, make a living if I needed to. Studying both music and social work, I followed both my dream and reality.
>
> My best friend Peggy and I studied together. Other girls found us boring because we didn't seek out parties or dates. Statistics bored me, but if I fell asleep or stopped paying attention, I would be lost the rest of the semester.

"Miss Parker," Mr. Patina, the statistics professor asked me one day, "can you explain what a normal curve is and how to ascertain one's place on it?"

I stuttered, unable to answer on the spur of the moment. I glanced over at Peggy who was drawing the curve for me. I said, "Um, the curve, the curve shows us that when a population is studied, ah, there is a pattern...the majority has a certain amount of a particular quality—not too much and not too little but then a minority of people have quite a lot of it or only a little bit—they are out at the ends of the curve."

"And how would you place yourself on that curve?" he asked.

"I would say I'm right in the middle, not too smart or too dumb, not too crazy or too, uh, what would it be? Boring, maybe? I make a point of being normal." The classroom broke up in laughter.

"Not where you personally fall on the curve, Miss Parker," he said sternly, trying to regain the control of the room, "but, rather, the technique used for placing someone there."

Mortified, I stuttered out some kind of answer. I felt exposed. And what had I meant that I made a point of being normal? Wasn't I just who I was?

I never lived it down. Peggy kept referring to it: "How are you today, Miss Normal?" or "Tell me, what would a normal person do in this situation?" She even suggested that I write a Miss Normal advice column for the school newspaper."

Kathleen chuckles. "Oh, I can relate to that all right—not wanting to be different or call attention to yourself. And yet, that's just what you did, isn't it—in the classroom, I mean?"

Then Kathleen, very self-consciously, tells me her story:

"I was the oldest of ten children. There was much pressure on me to baby-sit. Usually, I did, until one day I had had enough of those screaming brothers and sisters, and ran off into the middle of Connemara to where there were no people. I climbed to the top of a very tall hill, one where you think the top is but as you reach that, you find that another higher peak and you have to keep climbing.

Frustration and anger fueled me to keep going. When I calmed down, I was lost. All I could see for miles were stone fences, cows, grass and stony fields. Since the sky was overcast, I couldn't even make out where the sun was.

Once on the way back down, I slipped and fell and passed out for a while. When I came to, I was cold and damp and it was dark. My foot hurt fiercely. I took cover for the night near a stone fence and some shrubbery but couldn't sleep with my body shivering, my foot throbbing and my conscience telling her how stupid I was. In the daylight, I could see that the foot was off at right angles to the rest of the leg and must be broken.

It rained on and off so I was soaked through. I fashioned a crutch out of a branch. Every time I came to a fence, I had to figure out how to get over it. Sometimes I just took it apart and went on.

I hallucinated houses that turned out to be big rocks. A car turned out to be a sheep. Just as it started getting dark again, a light came on in a nearby cabin. The residents took me in, gave me dry clothes and food and called me mam to come and get me."

"I learned my lesson, though. I haven't gone off the road since—least ways not very far, that's for truth. It's the straight and narrow for me. Now I've three kids and another on the way—no running away for me."

I look at her young face and wonder how many more she will have and how much longer that face will look young. One impulse to escape that way of life is deemed irresponsible. How quickly we judge and dismiss our impulses! I wonder if I'll look back on this Ireland trip that way, as an impulse run amok.

I walk home feeling the heavy damp air; it's almost as if the air itself is weighed down with all of these stories. Perhaps dreams and reality, imagination and myth all offer a piece of the truth, if only one has the time to hear them.

Chapter 19—The Straight and Narrow?

Logic tends to be straight and narrow. In fact, if you want to figure out a problem in logic, the way to do it is to replace all concrete information with variables like P and Q. That way, it can be purely mathematical, pure form. Bring any real data into the mix and you might get curves, and we all know about curves—they make us forget all about logic.

October 16, 1996

Maybe Kathleen's weaving will be about being fruitful and multiplying instead of running away to live your own selfish dreams. Oh, Hallie is going to love this weaving!

At lunch Margaret tells me about her life in rural New Zealand, where she and Stella, her much younger lover, raise sheep and shear them for wool. She is interested in what this course can teach her about weaving in wool because, though she already has a market for scarves, she wants to branch out into tapestry.

"Does Stella weave, too?" I ask.

"Ha!" Margaret says rolling her eyes. "She wouldn't be caught dead doing such indoor work—got to be outside or she goes stir crazy. We've got the chores pretty much split up. She does the outdoor stuff, except for the vegetable garden which I do, and I do the inside stuff—cooking, cleaning and weaving. But she makes breakfast, since she gets up earlier than I do. Works out."

Lowering my voice, I ask, "Do you ever get any trouble for being lesbians?

Margaret takes note of my discomfort with a look, but goes on. "We did at first, but now we're just an old fixture. We might even be on the tour." She feigns speaking into a microphone. "'Now to your left is the old homestead of two lesbians arrived in 1965.'"

"We haven't had trouble in years. When we finally came out, so many people were friends of ours, they just adjusted to it. Some of the religious ones were bothersome for a while, but, luckily, we weren't teaching school or the like which would have been a harder sell."

"Thought I'd let you know that both Hallie and Alice might come out tonight so you could get ready. I know today is beautiful, but tonight and tomorrow—look out!"

"Damn!" Margaret hits her fist on the table. "You would have to spoil my weekend. I've got a tour scheduled tomorrow to the Aran Islands. Couldn't you have waited?"

That evening, after dinner, I sit down in the living room with hot chocolate and a book to read, hoping that Hallie will appear.

Then, before I hear any words, I feel a breeze making the hair on my arms stand up. *"You're anxious to hear today, are you, lassie?"* Hallie asks mimicking the Irish accent. *"And just what's the topic to be today, if you don't mind me askin'?"*

I play straight to her clown, "It's the weekend. You promised a Charlotte story on the weekend."

"Oh, but the weather is so fine, so far, so fine. Are you sure you want me to whisk into what most certainly will lure the rain?"

"I worked late tonight so I don't have to go in tomorrow. I'm free to stay curled up here until Sunday, when I should go in again."

"Now, can you promise not to be shocked, blocked, locked and run out of here with your ears burning, turning and burning?"

I tingle with anxiety and anticipation. "I make no such promises."

"Charlotte, Charlotte. Where are you now? When it was good, it was very, very good and when it was bad, oh, oh my ... We'll think about that later, later for the traitor. I'm not so sure you're ready, but you asked, you did ask. Even after all these years, I get teary, sometimes mad—what we had, what we lost; what we had, and what got scattered needlessly into the wind, hmm, the wind." Her voice trails off for a moment, as if she is considering that maybe now that she rides the wind, she could actually find Charlotte. She continues, *"Ran after the pieces for a while ... but sometime you have to stop running; time runs out on you, too."*

I am getting used to staring at the window and focusing and seeing a story emerge. Now I see two women dressed in knickers, standing on a porch, legs apart, with their arms linked, thumbs hooked into their pockets, and big confident smiles on their faces.

June, 1908

"Did you see that bride's face? Oh what she doesn't know ..." says Charlotte, as she and Hallie put away their photographic equipment and head to Helena's house where they have a darkroom set up. Hallie and Charlotte are the photographers for a gushingly romantic wedding. Hallie and her paternal grandmother are living in a little house on the east side of Chicago that Helena's husband David had left her when he died a few years before. Luckily, Helena is away at a conference because she is threatened by Charlotte and disapproves of their friendship. Char makes everyone, including Hallie, uncomfortable by the way she dismisses gender roles completely.

When Hallie first moved to Chicago after the rape/murder trial, she knew no one but Helena who was often at meetings and demonstrations trying to win women the right to vote. Hallie started going to the meetings, partly because she was lonely and partly because she believed in the cause. When she met Charlotte, Hallie was working on a mailer at the little office of the Chicago chapter of the National American Women Suffrage Association.

Hallie had never seen anyone like Charlotte, a woman, yet acting so much like a man—such strength and confidence. Charlotte was volunteering for the Association for the summer between her sophomore and junior years in college. She was about three years older than Hallie.

Charlotte seemed comfortable with herself, in her body. And Hallie did take notice of what she could sense about Charlotte's body under her loose, white cotton blouse and fit-to-a-tee knickers. Her comfort made Hallie uncomfortable. She sweated and stuttered as she introduced herself. Charlotte sauntered up to Hallie, grabbed her hand and shook it. Hallie had never had anyone shake her hand like that before. She felt like a grown-up, maybe even like a man. Hallie could feel the sweat prickling under her arms and worried that it would start to show any minute. The room felt too small for the both of them to be in it at the same time.

"Charlotte," she said. "The name is Charlotte but my good friends call me Char or sometimes even Charlie—good to meet ya. I'm down to pick up some leaflets to hand out 'round Palmer Park. They're having an ice cream social—lots of folks. Are they ready?"

Are the folks at the ice cream social ready for you, thought Hallie. I doubt it.

"Oh, the leaflets, you mean," Hallie said out loud. "No, they're not ready. In fact, I was just starting to work on them." Char insisted on staying to help. When she saw that the leaflets were all words, she offered to fancy them up by adding one of her drawings. She took out her satchel and leafed through the pictures. She found one of a woman holding a baby and delivering a speech.

"This always gets them where it hurts," she said.

Hallie felt so naive and stupid next to her. She wished she were older, more sophisticated. She had the strangest urge to comb her hair—most likely she had not combed it all day, and at that moment she couldn't remember if she had combed it after waking up that morning. Her hair tended to have a will of its own, wispy and taking off. All of a sudden, she was embarrassed by how she looked. Yes, Charlotte had an immediate effect, but at that moment Hallie hadn't a clue as to why. She just felt thrown—good, but off balance.

Char must have liked Hallie, too, because she started spending time with her, working the same hours she did. For the longest time Hallie didn't get over being nervous around Char, but she longed for her company. Part of her desire was to have a friend, a real friend, that she could confide in completely. She'd been so lonely. It'd never been any different, but at least at home in Michigan, she had had her brothers to talk to.

Hallie latched onto Char so tightly that Char started to feel suffocated. When Charlotte went back to Albion College in the fall, she may even have been glad to get away from Hallie's clinging and, yes, her jealousy. Hallie had tried not to let her know, but each time Char talked to anyone else, Hallie felt cheated, betrayed. Through the first semester of her last year of high school, Hallie wrote to Charlotte practically every day but she got so few letters in return, she began to feel silly. Char was in all kinds of activities at college and had better things to do with her time than write to Hallie.

When Char ran out of money, she quit school and came back to Chicago to work for a while. This time Hallie was more grown up. Since Charlotte and Hallie both needed income, they decided to go into business together. At first Hallie planned to work in the business just for the summer before school started at nearby Ipsalanti College. But she ended up working with Char whenever she could.

Going into business was risky, but they were young and didn't know any better. They set up a photography studio and called it CharKauf studio—part of Charlotte's first name and part of Hallie's last (without the 'man'—Char never liked the man part).

Hallie and Char were young and full of gamble and plunged right into the business. Char was the photographer at first, and she taught Hallie. Hallie was the public relations person because Char threatened the public even more than Hallie did. She was pretty, well-spoken and could pass for genteel. And she was still wearing women's clothes for the most part. Char wore only men's shirts and knickers—never any make-up. Most people considered her homely and masculine.

Hallie offers their services to anyone who in any remote way may have wanted a picture taken. When people announce engagements, she calls on them and asks if they need a photographer for the wedding.

Hallie and Char do the whole thing tongue-in-cheek, exaggerated in style, almost satirical; but no one ever notices. The customers just see tradition and glowingly romantic pictures and like them. Hallie and Char laugh all the way to the darkroom at the ignorance of the couple, particularly the woman. They have to laugh or they most surely will cry to see these bright young bright women sell themselves into slavery—their view of marriage in those days.

As partners, they are together almost all the time. That day, they observe a particularly romantic wedding, laughing at the foolishness; yet at the same time, they gaze at each other the way the bride and groom do. Hallie doesn't understand the giddy feeling. She knows she wants to marry Char, but she also knows that isn't possible.

When they return to the house this particular day, they are alone. The moon is full, shining across the roofs of the tenements and into the living room where they plop down to get off their feet after standing the whole day. They don't even bother to light the lamp as they fall onto the couch. Moonlight is enough.

Char and Hallie sit facing each other, leaning on the wooden arms of the old red crushed velvet couch, their feet overlapping in the middle. The moonlight on Char's face and body make Hallie lightheaded; Char is so beautiful. Maybe she isn't to most people, but to Hallie, she is perfect. She has strength and toughness, yet she is a woman. Her shirt, a man's shirt, does not fit her well and in her relaxed state, falls off a bit at the shoulder. Hallie fixates on that shoulder, its vulnerability and yet its strength.

Her shoulder becomes the moon and she sees how close she is to it. She moves to kiss it, to touch it. And Char acts as though she's been waiting for Hallie to notice her this way for months. She sighs, a sigh of relief. It is a sigh that lets Hallie relax her boundaries. Hallie tastes Char's shoulder, swirling her tongue around the soft flesh. And that place where the shoulder meets the neck, the dire curve of it.

Hallie lingers there, not knowing what to do next, just wanting to savor the feelings and keep at bay the terror of what all this means. After a while, Char moves Hallie on top of her so that the lengths of their bodies are touching, and they begin to move and rub against each other. They sit up again, then turn and gaze into each other's eyes, igniting the space between them, and begin slowly to unbutton each other's clothes. The clothes feel so bulky, a barrier forced on them. Hallie gets Char's shirt loose and she has nothing on underneath; she is so free, unbound by convention and Hallie loves her, then. She plunges her hands into the heat beneath Char's clothing; she has never felt anything like it before. Char's skin is luminous. Where Hallie touches, Char responds, moving toward her hands.

"I need you naked," Char says as she begins taking off Hallie's clothes. Hallie thinks she needs them naked together and Char has the same thought, as they get up and hurriedly remove the remaining barriers and lie back down, sliding against one another. Hallie has never even imagined such pleasure, such warmth beyond heat to sweat to liquid to steam. They explore each other, each curve and crevice, each dimple and swelling. Their mouths, their hands, the pores of their skin exploring each other for the first time. Where they touch, they feel the current of passion creating wetness along the lengths of their bodies. They slide into each other inexorably, down into the tingly, electric place of no return. Hallie's nipple under Char's arm, Char's tongue, oh, her tongue, tasting, lingering, repeating, lapping, spreading, sucking, drinking. Hallie's breathing is growing short and quick; she wants to resist and can't. The inevitability in that moment, the certainty of abandon and release, the rush of waters gathering momentum a few short feet before the falls. One moment of pause, not hesitation but a relished certainty, hanging mid-air, knowing that the fall, the rush is coming. Pulsing, pulsing, lingering and going on. She will never be the same. She knows this; she wants this.

Hallie speaks as though this happened only moments ago. Her voice loses its breathiness and she sounds almost human. For a moment my living room seems alive with the wind. I have been there, too, in the telling of it.

She hadn't intended such detail but the memory was so fresh— *"No, no, no, "* Hallie reminds herself. *"It's far, so far away now. Gone forever and ever and ever. My life, my loves, my desires.*

I am shocked by her passion and her frankness; but the way she spoke of it was so heartfelt that I couldn't help but be drawn into the sensual passion of this first love. The rain fills the silence as it begins to come down in torrents, striking the window and seeping through the tiniest opening with its rage.

"Alice is here," I say quietly to Hallie. "Can you feel it?"

"I knew it, knew it would bring her. My pleasure, all pleasure, punctuated, punctured by Alice."

The room grows considerably colder as the rain pulses and seeps in at the windowsills. Emma hears Alice's high pitched, rushing voice, *"No shame ... I taught ... you don't learn. To speak ... like that ... in front of family ... and*

God. Emma ... Emma ... you have died ... of shame?"

I respond, still a little dazed, "I'm here; I'll live."

"Emma, don't listen," says Alice. *"Between Hallie...and me."*

"I'm not a child anymore, Alice," I say.

"Hallie...never in control...of self. Ut-ter-ly selfish...and weak, god...less, no morals. Need decency...to regret it. Like the sun porch. She...tried...to take you...Emma ...down the same path—make you like women...too much.

Hallie sighs; this sigh signals pain, *"Emma, this business, ancient business, too tiring even for the wind. I'm leaving you two to conspire. Emma, I'll be back—back because there's so much, so much more to say. You aren't upset too, too much. If you want me back..."* With a huge gust of wind, Hallie leaves Alice and Emma alone.

Alice settles into a steady downpour. She says I should've stayed home and tended my own garden instead of coming here, that my search is for nothing; my answers are all at home with my husband.

But I feel there is something missing, something I need to find out. There are hollows that need filling out. What happened to the women in my family that it got so bad that I had to be bartered away like cattle?

Alice rants on, now she is saying that Hallie's life is not a grand event that marks the century like the coming of Christ. She's a fluke, an error, an outpouring of sin. *She told you yes of muuuurder she committed? I supported her evil...then so she...didn't rot...in jail."*

"You'll wear pink ruffles and keep your mouth shut," the only attorney in town they could afford says to Hallie on the eve of her trial.

The prosecuting attorney is Mike Honey, and he is running for State Attorney General. He reads the public, mainly the male public, who are, after all the voters, and decides to have a trial. Lots of women are unhappy with Hallie as well. Anti-suffrage crusaders of all genders use her case to justify their views that women in power would annihilate men. They accuse her of being irrational, a man-hater and a man-killer. They try to make it look as if all feminists are men killers at heart and raise the specter of what women will do if they get the vote.

There is so much furor about the death of the boy and the philosophical and political ramifications that most people simply forget the pain Hallie has endured. She does not remind them because she, too, would rather push those feelings aside and concentrate on what she still sees as an heroic outcome.

Alice has always been afraid of scandal, and she feels that this case is unjust. She testifies under oath that she had taught Hallie never to allow a boy to touch her and that Hallie is a good girl and always does what she is told.

Alice's good friend, the mother of the deceased boy, testifies that Alice told her many times that Hallie is a hellion who never obeys. The judge finally rules it self-defense, but he also rules that Hallie has to leave the county. He says this is for her protection because there are those out there who want to see her punished for what she has done.

The trial garners so much publicity that any friends Hallie may have had are now nowhere in sight. The cartoonists have a field day with the whole situation. She is treated as a pariah—avoided in the street. By the time she moves to Chicago, much of the furor has died down and most of the people there don't connect her to the controversy. Helena's friends in the women's movement are supportive. To them she is a hero.

Alice has been dead set against Hallie moving to Chicago, thinking it is her responsibility to deal with Hallie—until after the trial—and then, well, it is the judge's order. Alice doesn't think she can go to hell for something a judge orders her to do.

Alice's voice drops one spooky octave. She says, *"See how…she got to…Chi ca go, city of sin? Can't leave...the devil out. In me--I passed him... to Hallie. Can't tell her...the truth."*

I ask her what she did that was so terrible. Be ambitious? Try to be a good mother and raise her kids, get rid of a no-good husband—what? And she tells me ominously that I have no idea the magnitude of her sins—that she has never told a soul.

"If you've held onto something this long and not told anyone, it is probably poisoning you."

She responds quietly, *"Poison, yes! But if it poisoned...just me, wouldn't care. Me, I deserve it—but...you?"*

Outside, the rain falls softly now like tears. It is quiet without wind. I peer out into the darkness and can see no light, not a star or moon. Clouds muffle the sky.

"Alice, are you still there?" I ask after a while. "You know, you must tell; it may be the only way we can piece together the past." As an afterthought, I say under my breath, "and move toward the future."

But she has disappeared, leaving behind a steady stillness.

Chapter 20—Listening into Change

Can you let go of your story for just one day? Throw it into the wind and see if you can hear a different way to share your life.

October 17, 1996

My legs are stiff from my having slept all night on the so-called comfortable chair in the living room. As I unfold myself and step onto the floor, my foot twists into a horrible cramp and sends me sprawling.

The storm has picked up again and is raging; but I am in no mood for stories. I go into the bedroom, draw the curtains, crawl in under the down comforter and go back to sleep. When I awaken around noon, I can't say whether Alice's appearance was a dream or just part of my wild imagination.

Starving, I fix myself a brunch of French toast with blackberry syrup and ponder over what went on last night. I wonder how the pieces of these tragic stories of Alice and Hallie fit together. I have an unsettled feeling, similar to one I get at a certain point in the middle of a large jigsaw puzzle when I feel that it's either going to fall into place suddenly, or I'll give up and throw it all back in the box. I'm beyond color and into shape. The big difference, here, is what's at stake. If I were a gambling person, I'd say that my life is on the line. I'm not the person I thought I was—but then who is this person in my skin?

Alice is right. I have a good life to go back to; what do I really want to change? If only I could control the changes—take on only what I want and leave the rest to the dead. I'm afraid of what Alice will tell me, afraid of what my ancestors did to one another, what the poison is she talks about.

I pick up my sticky plate and lick off what's left of the blackberries. I wonder about the all-or-nothingness of rules and of beliefs. Couldn't we determine them on a case-by-case basis, decide whether they fit the circumstances?

These ghost stories are getting to me. My head is weighed down with a density of unfinished stories and suspended beliefs. Again, I have the urge to scrap it all, put it back in its box, tape it shut and store it away up in the hall closet with all the other someday projects.

For the first time since I came to Ireland, I turn on the TV. As the wind and rain whip about outside, I mindlessly watch an interview with an Irish doctor about arthritis, a common disease in this damp country. I make a few notes of suggestions that may help Margaret. Then I watch some sit coms brought over from the US and a couple of comedy shows from Great Britain. Nothing remarkable, but they allow me to escape my thoughts for a while.

Sunday, as I approach the Crafts Centre, I see what looks like litter on the Centre's side of the road. It reminds me of houses the morning after Halloween. First, I think—it was kids, probably, they're the same everywhere with their pranks. Then, as I get closer, I realize that I have sold the kids short. The "trash" is seaweed. My mind goes wild at the thought that the ocean had been up over the road at some point in the night. If the ocean can do that, can encroach this far into the land, into the man-made arena, then where are the boundaries that I always thought so firm? I can't believe the ocean did that. What about my own ocean inside? We were getting so close and now this big trust-breaker. It feels sneaky or criminal or fraudulent. I can hardly picture the waves up this far, but there is no other explanation for the Centre's yard being littered with globs of seaweed. What's to stop it from doing it again, right now, for instance? I stare suspiciously at the now-benign-looking waves, searching for clues of lawlessness and malice.

Margaret is not at the Centre when I get there, but has left a note saying, "Thanks a lot for your cooperation yesterday! We had to postpone the trip until Sunday. You'll see I got a lot of work done yesterday in spite of the storm. Hope you got what you wanted."

I stare at the drawing that I do not want to weave. I have sketched out a straight and narrow path leading to a large tree with orange fruit. Yellow light surrounds the top of the tree like a halo. Then to the sides of the tree are red paths, curved and dangerous, and all leading down to flames at the bottom of the piece. I pencil in a title, "The Straight and Narrow Way to Fruitful Life."

I can't shake the image of the ocean rearing up and encroaching on the civilized side of the road. Especially after that, the idea that a life could be so starkly good-versus-evil as depicted in this sketch makes no sense at all.

How do the terms "straight" and "narrow" fit into the stories from the other night? Hallie certainly had not "gone straight," whereas Alice seemed to stay narrow. Alice, heading up the straight and narrow, and Hallie, down the curved and dangerous, had broadsided each other. Neither was happy; neither got what she wanted.

The weaving makes it look like the devil is awaiting just off the path. Alice might look at it that way, the way Kathleen does. But it's simplistic. Straight and narrow, curved and wicked—no, it can't be that simple. Kathleen is only twenty-five. She has a lot to learn.

I keep trying to make the flames look bad and evil, but instead they appear warm and inviting. It occurs to me that maybe I should have found a church to attend today, instead of working on Sunday. These stories, the ocean, my life right now: I'm sure if I talked to a pastor about it, I'd have been talked out of the whole thing. It's not possible that these things are happening. For now, I'll just keep weaving.

On Monday, Margaret comes breezing into lunch and sits down breathlessly across from me. "You've got to go to the Aran Islands. Mystical is what they are. Almost glad your storm made us change our trip to Sunday. The music seeping out from under the doors of the small wooden church up on the hill—unearthly. Residents made it through one more storm and the music swelled with gratitude and praise. I cannot even imagine being on that vulnerable island through that kind of storm."

I'd like to go, but right now I am hardly looking for entertainment. Aloud, I say, "Maybe I'll go when Lucy is here; right now, I'm kind of busy. And I'm starving. I got to the Centre so early I didn't get breakfast."

We take a minute to order our lunches. Food is a great comfort to me in this time of upheaval, the one thing that stays steady while all else swirls. I like a simple potato soup on a windy day.

"Judging from the inclement weather," Margaret interrupts my thoughts, "I take it your voices arrived again?"

I nod. "But they deserted me late Friday night. Then I got a little of the empty nest syndrome—too much time to think."

Margaret is curious about the stories, so I summarize them.

"Are you going to document it?" Margaret asks.

I nod and smile, feeling happy that she understands and is not giving me a hard time. "I'm taking notes, but writing is Lucy's department. Besides, this story embarrasses me. And, of course, as we expected, Alice interrupted with a story of her own. She hasn't told it all yet, though—just gave me a sneak preview...full of evil and damnation."

I watch the clouds swirl just outside the cafe. I thought today would be sunny and bright. Nothing, nothing, here, save the soup, is reliable. I take a sip of the creamy, white, comforting, slightly salty soup and sigh, wishing it were all that easy.

Margaret examines me closely. Is she picking up signs of insanity? All she says is, "Well, remember, if you feel like talking, I'm available." She points east. "I just go off to my little bungalow in Galway every night and read a book or watch the telly. Nothing compared to what you do here in An Spideal...makes me think of spies, a deal with the spies."

"Or it could be spi as in spider and mean a spider's web," I add. "Fits with a weaving workshop. Reminds me: wait 'til you see my latest weaving. You'll just die, especially being the atheist and feminist that you are. It's about the devil and women's duty to be fruitful...a little much even for me."

Margaret scowls. "Are you kidding? What'd you go and do that for?"

I shrug my shoulders innocently. "Don't shoot me, I'm just the messenger from good little Catholic Kathleen."

Margaret shakes her head. "Maybe you took the assignment too literally. Olivia's story was about racism and exclusion and I wove something very abstract."

"Well, Kathleen's story *was* literal. If you'd heard it, you would have come to the same conclusion. She's young—still thinks in terms of good and evil, right and wrong."

"That's religion for you, isn't it? I'd think you'd agree with her."

I snap back, "No, people have such wrong-headed notions about religion. They think all Protestants are holy rollers of some sort. In my experience, church-goers have the same spectrum of people as any other group, from the kindest, most considerate people to the most judgmental.

"Is heaven and hell open to interpretation, then?" Margaret asks.

Shaking my head, I say, "Heaven and Hell is not where it's at and don't even talk about the devil. We're more liberal."

"Still," she remarks, and I hear sarcasm in her tone, "God is a man, and the birth was still virgin, right?" I feel unnecessarily defensive. I drink the last sip of soup and try not to get angry.

"We say God, he or she, in our statement of faith now. But, me—I still see Him as a him. I'm not so conceited as to think that he has to look like me physically. He really has no physicality except through Jesus Christ."

Margaret crosses her arms over her chest. "You're not that far from Kathleen, if you ask me. But once again, it's class time, so move your rear, missy." Margaret gets up stiffly and limps a little toward the door. I wonder if the weather is exacerbating her arthritis.

Kathleen loves the weaving I did of her story, says she will hang it on her wall immediately. I feel a little sick to my stomach, as though I encouraged her.

I am surprised by the eerie weaving Kathleen presents me. She took normal, bell-shaped curves of all sizes and combined them into an ocean of waves. In the landscape a figure that I presume to be me is lying down passively allowing the waves to wash over her. The weird thing is that the figure is pregnant with a bell-shaped curve forming the swollen belly. She seems to have fit my young college-age self into normal curves.

At first glance, I am repulsed by this passive pregnant woman. I am dizzy, reminded of the feeling I had at my birthday party when I saw the picture of the Dealer and the Dealt. I stare at Kathleen, and her face fades, and my face at her age stares back at me. I try to remember why I decided to have kids. I know it was expected of me—the normal woman. It wasn't a choice, but it wasn't a burden either. Oh, Lucy is not going to like this weaving—Lucy, who as far as I know, has decided not to have children. Nor would Hallie like it, I imagine.

When I snap out of my reverie, I notice that Kathleen is looking at me expectantly. I praise her efforts and technique. "I like the way the figure fits right into the landscape at the edge of the sea—that part is lovely." I would like the weaving, if I could just get over my odd aversion to the pregnant woman.

The instructors ask us to talk over with the whole group what these weavings evoke. I voice my concerns, "I'm worried that since I don't agree with the point of view that I put in the weaving, I am selling myself out—giving that point of view tacit approval. I tried not to judge it, just listen and weave back, but I can't help thinking I am betraying my own feelings."

Others have similar feelings; and as we discuss the ideas, the point of the exercise becomes clearer. Lea says, "At some stage in every conflict—if it's to be resolved—someone has to just listen and mirror back what the other person has said, so she knows she's been heard."

Victoria adds, "It's not so much about agreement as about listening. Nelson Mandela says we've got to hear each other first before we can reach reconciliation."

"But what about, if you feel something is really wrong, really detrimental to the world, maybe even evil?" asks Margaret. "Then you can't just parrot it back, can you? What if it were Hitler?"

Colleen, taking Margaret's comment seriously, thinks for a minute and then talks about what it means to listen and what it means to condone evil. She asks us, "Did you notice that there were things in the other's weaving that were accurate, yet made you uncomfortable? A mirror is sometimes exactly what we need."

I think about my response to the weaving and wonder what is being reflected back to me. What is it I need to change? I can't change being a mother, nor would I want to. But something isn't quite right.

Lea tells a story about by a man who went to Germany to make a documentary about the rise of the right wing there. The filmmaker followed a Neo-Nazi around and filmed him. He didn't question the man's views or hit him up with inconsistencies; he merely filmed and taped his actions and speeches. And the subject went through a metamorphosis. By the end, he was working on the other side. The act of someone listening to him, witnessing, made him see himself differently; he saw the mistakes he'd been making.

"Excellent," says Rhiannon. "That's exactly the theory. Think about it in terms of your own weavings." She continues, "The next assignment will be a woven dialogue with one other person in the class on an issue about which you disagree."

I am teamed up with Pilar from Costa Rica. Our instruction is to find something about which we disagree, to agree to use that topic and then go off by ourselves and consider how our views might be represented in a weaving. We are to sketch out a drawing of it, in color. We will have until the end of the week to weave our part of the argument. Then we will exchange seats and looms and add the other point of view to the weaving already in progress. That way, we will both begin a dialogue and contribute to a dialogue already in progress.

Rhiannon emphasizes that this project can be tricky technically and that the instructors will be available for consultation. "Remember, you can use some of the smaller looms to weave add-on's—we also have paints that go directly on the weft for your responses. But, for now, just concentrate on beginning the volley, on the serve."

Chapter 21— Dialogues

Dialogue used to be a noun until it was made into a verb and now everyone dialogues. Go ahead and leave it a verb but expand it to mean communication with or without a common language and make sure the definition includes more about listening than talking.

October 19, 1996

At first, Pilar and I are shy with each other, avoiding topics we disagree on. She is from Tortuguerro, Costa Rica. She says that the only way to get there is by boat, through rivers and canals or by ocean. "It's where the sea turtles come to lay their eggs every year." Because the turtles are so predictable, they are easy prey for poachers. Even after the thirty or so years it takes for a female to mature, she comes back to the same shore on which she was born to lay her eggs. Now, all too often it means that the shore on which she was born is also the shore on which she dies. Though she doesn't know it, she is making the ultimate sacrifice in order to reproduce.

The government of Costa Rica has taken measures to protect the sea turtles, but poachers still find ways to get to them. And it is in the tradition of the people to kill a certain number of returning turtles for their own subsistence—not to make huge amounts of money on the international market.

Worried that we are running out of time, I ask Pilar if she thinks that we could argue about the turtles. But, no, we are both on the same side of the issue.

"Maybe we could do something in the area of reproduction, though," I say. And then, since it has been on my mind lately, I ask her if she is Catholic. She responds that she was raised Catholic and still attends church, but that she disagrees with some of what the church hierarchy hands down—for instance, she is pro-birth control and abortion.

Since we agree on those issues, I dig a little deeper and even though I have told myself not to bring up the topic, I say, "I think it's disgraceful to have Mary be at the center of church doctrine where the Catholics put her. She should be seen as instrumental but not key. I'll bet you disagree with that."

"Ah, Dios mio!" Pilar pales. "Mary is the saving grace. Without her, I don't believe any of it."

"Good, then. That can be our disagreement. It's on the theme of Catholic and Protestant, apropos for this country, don't you think?"

She's a little hesitant, wondering if we can handle it, but finally agrees to try. I stay for a while and sketch out a pattern. I think of the Trinity—no Mary in that. The Trinity would be a good solid place to begin, especially here in Ireland. A three leaf clover seems trite and what would Mary be—the stem? I sketch and re-sketch. I think of ice, water and steam to represent the three of the holy trinity, with Mary as the freezer unit, but—I smile to myself—that seems mechanistic and, well, cold.

Finally, when I am just about ready to quit, an image comes of Mary as a virginal white basin resting in brown mud of earth. The translucent blue water inside the basin is Jesus Christ. The gray rain of God comes down from the sky and through it blows the warm red wind of the Holy Spirit. Simple and natural. Mary has little power over the content of the basin, but is instrumental in keeping the precious liquid from dispersing.

So many colors will make it more difficult to weave, but I keep it small. I wonder, offhandedly, what Pilar will come up with as her argument. I feel my competitive juices flowing.

It seems right to picture the water as Christ. After all, bodies are made up of at least sixty percent water—or something like that. So the water, the physical representation of God, fits well. And, of course, I muse, the rain falls from the heavens where God is, and the Holy Spirit provides divine guidance as the wind. Yes, this tapestry will be the best yet.

When I get home, I call Hallie. The room has a becalmed feeling, as if we are at sea with no wind at all. It takes a while for her to get there. The energy reminds me of dreams where I need to go somewhere but my legs are frozen or unbelievably slow. When she finally arrives, she asks tentatively, *"How are you, how are you, daughter, after storytelling and yelling?"*

"Don't worry about me, I can take care of myself. I've not lived to be seventy without learning a few tricks."

"I need, need to explain more...more about where I was while you were growing into a young woman, getting married, having little ones of your own."

I focus on the dark window and see a huge medieval-looking building with a tattered sign that reads: Mannington State Psychiatric Hospital.

September 3, 1931

Eddy, a large paunchy man working night shift in the kitchen, often came into her room at about 4:00 in the morning and forced himself on her. Usually, as he pinned her to her bed, she learned to vacate her body. Eddy, eddy, eddy, she thought, as she spun like the wind in the far corner of the room—a current that blows against the main current—that's what she was. She was being punished for spinning backward into sexual pleasure in a world that reserved that right for men. What Eddy did to her was the opposite of all that she had ever loved about sex. After that, she never knew sexual pleasure again. Sex was all forced, male and horrible. For months, she was weak and unable to fight back; she began to hate herself as never before.

But this particular night, Eddy tries entering her from behind as Tom Nestor had tried in the stairwell that day, and she flashes back to that time she thought was gone. The whole thing, her whole wasted life—the attempted rape and now this slob—all this enrage her. Suddenly, instead of hating herself, an heroic anger toward him rises in her, much like the one she felt in the stairwell that day so long ago, rising up through her body. She might kill him.

His violence has nothing to do with sex; he is the dragon, preying on someone smaller than himself. He expects Hallie to be the usual weak woman whom he had been raping for some time; he is not prepared for her resistance. In an instant, she becomes the all-powerful dragon-slayer again. She squirms out from under him and uses all of her might to kick, bite, bruise and batter Eddy both in places that show and in places that don't. He has to leave, bloody and bruised in the middle of his shift. After that, Eddy and the others leave her alone; she isn't worth the trouble. And maybe they are a little afraid of her—she is crazy.

But the specter of eddy, haunts her, won't let her go; she knows to some it seems crazy but eddy is key, and she is obsessed with it. Like a drain spiraling backward the day of an earthquake. She has always swirled the opposite way from the currents of the day. Maybe she is the embodiment of a great change that is to come to the world, a great shaking up.

After Alice and Danny committed Hallie to Mannington, and Charlotte had deserted her, Hallie spent interminable days, weeks, years in that place, sitting in a room with a yellowing linoleum floor, trying to avoid yellowing staff and patients. For a long while, she hoped that Char would come charging in on a white stallion and rescue her but when she finally realized that she would never see Char again, a part of her—probably the best part—died.

Finally, Hallie gave up on being rescued—by Charlotte, Danny, or her father who had disappeared from their lives a few years earlier.

The day after Hallie sent Eddy fleeing, a beautiful young woman, with shining strands of straight hair that covered her back, down to the soft curves of her bottom, floats in like a mermaid on the tide. She is carrying a book so lovingly, as if it were a newborn baby. She is a Christian Scientist come to help Hallie find God. At first, Hallie wants to shove her out of the room with all her strength. Plenty of people had tried to help her find the Lord. But when this woman mentions the name of their great leader and writer, it turns out to be a woman and her name—that is what was amazing—Mary Baker Eddy. "Eddy!" she cries, reaching for the book *Science and Health,* which the woman gives her as a gift.

Hallie is never religious in her heart of hearts but sees how she can use religion to survive. The Christian Scientists are kind to her and take her out of the institution to church on Sundays. And they fight to keep her from having to take the drugs that were all the rage in the hospitals, psychotropic drugs that can turn people black-and-blue and make their tongues swell so that they just sit and drool, forgetting who they are.

To survive, Hallie does many shameful things. She becomes patriotic and wears only red, white and blue—no socialist ideas are ever heard aloud from her mouth again. She is Hallie Gildebecker, not Hallie Kaufmann here. She never used Charles' name in her real life, but she takes it on here, and she can be anyone they want her to be. Her days, her years, her body, her thoughts, even her excrement aren't her own. They are some other person's, some other tragic hero's, Mrs. Gildebecker who is a Christian Scientist patriot hearing voices.

Of course, they give her the dripping water treatment when that is the fad and electric shock treatment when it comes into fashion. It is small wonder then that when she hears voices warning her about her impending death from the combination of electricity and water, these are not crazy thoughts. Both water and electricity have taken on new and terrifying meanings to her. She writes poetry and destroys it all in the same sweep of the pen, wanting to give them no more ammunition with which to punish her. She memorizes a poem and makes into a song that she sings under her breath when she needs courage. She never shares the words with anyone.

Electricity

Streaking everywhere
Zapping, zapping
See it, see it
Round the corner,
Seeping from clocks,

through walls
See it, see it.

Let me sing my song
Of sixpence
Sing it, sing it
Pockets full of slips
Put in drawer cracks
(Proof you opened My drawer).
Sing it, sing it.

Open me up?
You may try
Try it, try it
See the bits of flesh
placed in the cracks of my soul
At least I'll know
Try it, try it.

I'm staying closed now
Break only into song of sixpence
Break it, break it
Break a rule; it breaks
you back.
Break it, break it.

Unplug the clock
Unplug me
Kill me, kill me
Tear the umbilical cord
from my body
Let the world bleed away
Kill it, kill it.

The one thing that she can keep track of is the moon. She feels that the moon will be full and shine through her window on her special days, like her birthday. The moon revolves around her, her most reliable friend, giving her an account of her days and months in a way nothing and no one else can. Cloudy nights she stares out the window and waits and waits for a glimmer, a light behind the gloom. And on moonless nights, she often panics, loses her grounding. Those are her most violent nights and the ones most liable to get her locked up in a padded cell. She is the opposite of most lunatics: she goes crazy not at the full moon, but when it goes away.

I return to the living room, remembering how in the sixties, there was a new philosophy of mental illness. Many people were released from mental institutions and ended up on the streets. After they dumped Hallie out of Mannington, Danny and Claudia moved her into an apartment in Detroit. My children and I came to visit now and then. The kids would glance around the strange room, shifting their weight from one foot to the other and craning their heads to hear her almost unintelligible speech. She didn't let on that she knew who we were. To her, we didn't exist. She needed to keep it that way or she'd be back in Mannington. She did so much in secret—used to slip me money hidden in the folds of the *Christian Science Monitor.* Her happiness had to be a secret. She had learned the hard way that pleasure led directly to pain. She was like one of those mice in an experiment—if you shock them every time they do a certain thing, they stop doing it forever.

"Enough horror for one night, for any night--I'll slide off now into that darkness lingering just beyond this pale, drained place.

"Good night, mother," I say, calling her 'mother' for the first time ever. Saying it makes tears spring to my eyes; I brush them away. No use crying over split milk, I say to myself. An image leaps into my mind: a breast slashed open, milk spilling all over the floor of that murky, medieval institution. I stay with the image until it becomes an ocean of milk, flooding the place like a tidal wave, taking it down.

Chapter 22— Lopsided argument

The easiest way to have a lopsided argument is to put God on your side. Any god who takes sides is questionable at best. Evil stems from disconnection, the very thing God would be creating if s/he took one person's side over another's.

October 21, 1996

I am anxious for the argument to begin; it has become increasingly important for me to win. Even though I know winning is not the point of this exercise; I want reassurance that my views are right. My weaving is deliberately minimalist, leaving plenty of room for a reply, but the lines are strong, elemental and are not, in my opinion, open for debate.

I try to rid myself of the images of Hallie in that hellhole of an institution, but they flood my mind occasionally anyway. I will be in the middle of weaving and get an image of Hallie in Mannington. I see her chanting that poem as she sits rocking in a dark and dreary corner. I can't imagine what she must have gone through living there for thirty-seven years. Over that long a period, I'm sure much happened; but from the outside looking in, it seems as if nothing at all happened, as if she contributed nothing, did nothing for all those years.

As I weave the red rain into the piece, I think of this vibrant and alive woman who had been slowly bled dry of her sanity and her intelligence. Regret fills me, brings a dull ache to my head. I know there was little I could have done for her, but I feel guilty that I didn't hold onto the childish determination to get her out of there. She was so thoroughly abandoned. And to think I thought I was the one abandoned by her. By the time I was old enough to have been of some help to her, she had become very strange—talking to herself, denying knowing me, talking about electricity. I couldn't imagine her living outside an institution, nor could I imagine my taking her in and helping her. I used to be sad about her mental illness and her wasted brilliance. Now I see the real tragedy was how misunderstood she was; if she'd just had some allies to stand up for her, get her out of that place, she might have lived the life she was born to live.

I pull myself back into the present where something can be done; I weave my emotions into this work. Hallie had tried the Christian Science route—maybe just as a ruse to get out of being medicated—but I wonder if she didn't get some spiritual strength from it. I wish she'd had something to believe in, something akin to this Trinity to hold onto.

I go home by way of the beach, and the woman swimmer is there again, allowing the water to tease her in. I can't help but smile when I see her. There is something about her that gives me courage. I imagine that she is someone who leaps into the fray and lives her life without qualification or excuse. I think, if I were just a bit younger, I might make a date and join her one day.

Keeping my thoughts on positive things, I cut up carrots, leeks, celery, onions and garlic to make lentil soup for dinner. Just as I cut into the leek, splitting it down the middle, the knife slips and I nick my left index finger. As quickly as the knife slips through the flesh, the image of the slashed breast enters my consciousness once again. I put my finger under cold water, watching the blood and water mix until my finger goes numb and stops bleeding.

Thoughts and images flash through my mind randomly. I simply can't stop thinking about Hallie's incarceration. It seems as useful as trying to punish the ocean for overflowing its boundaries. Because this they could do, whoever "they" were; Hallie "they" could control, at least physically—a woman who did not have the power of a whole ocean or even of her whole gender to back her. After all, her so-called "sisters" made things worse; Alice played a key role in impounding her there, and Charlotte never helped her.

While the soup is simmering, I long for resolution, for a way to make sense of it all. The thoughts follow me into the living room where I squirm to find a comfortable position in my favorite chair. No position seems right.

I empty my mind so that Alice or Hallie will have room to enter. It is Hallie who finally blows in and asks me if I am comfortable here without "what's-his-name."

"Ralph," I say. "Is it so hard to remember?"

"Ralphphphph," Hallie says as if now that she got it started, she can't stop. Then she asks what kind of relationship we have.

I shrug, knowing it will be hard to explain to her. "Sometimes I think my goal in life is to make sure Ralph lives as long as I do. He's seemingly unconcerned about his health, living with gusto and not feeling the constraints of a 'healthy diet.' His philosophy is that while we are on this earth, we only have today, and should make the most of it. He has a fearlessness I admire, laughing in the face of danger. I have enough fear for both of us."

"Why did you come, my little girl? Do you find what you are looking for? Is it here?"

I'm not sure I'm happy with this intrusion into my life. I'd much rather just listen to her stories than justify my own. I say, "I came to figure out who I am without Ralph." Is this true, I wonder to myself. Maybe if I keep talking, it will become clearer.

"I've always been a behind-the-scenes person, making sure the props are there when the actors reach for them." I look around the room at Valerie's painting, the rug woven by an unknown person, props that I had nothing to do with arranging. Someone else is the prop person here and I am somehow on stage?

I continue, "Maybe I wanted to see what my own play looks like—and I'm getting more than I bargained for with you and Alice making surprise entrances and . . ."

Hallie interrupts me, *"Who's writing the script? Not a ghostwriter, now, is it?"*

I chuckle at her joke but question on a deeper level whether I have any idea. "At home, Ralph and I both write it—I have my concerns and he his. He wasn't pleased about my coming here by myself, though—felt I was deserting him."

"Are you changing, rearranging here?"

The question brings me back into present time. "I haven't had much time to think—I'm not sure..." The closest I can come to an explanation is my weavings. "Have you seen any of my weavings?"

"Did you want me to peek to spy them?"

I explain the current assignment.

"You take up for the minority, then, the poor Protestants, saying Mary deserves nothing. About that I am right, or am I not?"

I tell her my thinking on the subject and end by saying, "She didn't contribute anything but her body, but none of this will mean anything to you since you're a non-believer."

She replies, *"It means a lot—my body went, too, to some cause, though I don't know which. Mary gave no consent either, perhaps. It's a loss I still feel when I speak of Charlotte...and when I know lentil soup is cooking and me, I can't smell it."*

I check the soup, scoop some into a bowl, sit down at the kitchen table and dunk in a piece of Irish soda bread, letting its edges dissolve and get soft enough to imbibe without chewing.

Suddenly the hairs on the back of my neck rise up in unison and I know that Hallie has joined me in the kitchen. She asks, *"Do you think Mary was born solely to bear and raise Jesus?"*

I shrug and then reply, "What better reason could there be?"

"Oh, daughter, what you don't know about women, wisdom and will."

My next undunked bite of bread sticks to the roof of my mouth. I remember Kathleen's "normal curve" weaving; I just want to be left alone.

"Then, maybe I can't see why you've come here, to Ireland. If your life isn't about you, but about your family, then why aren't you there with Ralphphphph now?"

With that, the room becomes still; Hallie has flown away again. I bravely try one more bite of soup and find that it is ice-cold.

I watch the almost-full moon as it creeps across the sky, like a slow searchlight, seeking. When I can't see it from one chair, I move to another. Hallie received such succor from the moon while in Mannington. I bow my head just slightly in acknowledgment of that friendship. Somehow, here by the sea, the moon plays a critical role, pulling on the water in my own body. If I could grow quiet enough, maybe I would feel the tug of the tides right now.

The next morning, the rain is relentless, with no hope of a letup; I decide not to go up early to the Centre, but to stay until the last moment and then dash up to class. So, after a leisurely breakfast, I do my laundry and while I wait for it to finish, I sit curled up in the living room, watching the clouds swirl and the rain plummet. As might be expected, Alice appears again. She wants me to know still more about her life; I know she said there was something big, something that is poisoning us all. I wonder if she'll ever tell it to me. I wonder when she will be ready.

It's as if she has been hovering, just waiting for an opportunity to make herself known.

"Few things...to clear up...with you...yes. Not yet...not yet...do you...get it. I... good mother...too many...bad times."

I look to the window and see the reflection of a large church with crutches lining the walls.

May 23, 1917

The healing energy in the church is palpable. Crutches and canes of those who no longer need them cover the walls of the church. The stained glass window behind the altar depicts Jesus healing a leper. A great white light shows through Jesus and penetrates the leper. The services always start at sunset when the sun shines through that scene, making it come alive. An electrical excitement sweeps through the congregation as the organist plays and the people hold hands along long pews, swaying and humming.

Rev. Marcus is a solid and tall man of about forty, with thick dark hair that curls around his face like a dark halo. His marbled blue eyes send out a fire to all who dare look directly at them. It is said that if you look into his eyes, he can immediately see all you have done, sins and good deeds alike—all is revealed.

On the advice of a friend, Alice and Danny have come to Zion City for healing for fourteen-year-old Danny. A few weeks earlier when Alice was napping on the chaise lounge in the living room of her little rented house in Detroit, Danny came home from school and found her moaning and thrashing. She was having her recurring dream again: the location varied from her childhood home to the forest. She runs into something hanging in front of her—could be a low slung doorway or a low limb of a tree—and she falls flat. Then a mostly black, very hairy, spider with a green florescent underbelly, four beady black marble eyes, two big and two small, walks over her, looking into her eyes with all four of its eyes. She wants to kill the spider or at least run away but never has the strength to move; she allows it to do as it pleases and though it does not seem to hurt her, it sucks something out of her. Sometimes one of her children tries to help her, telling her not to lose Christ. But always at the end she is alone.

When Danny leaned down to gently touch her shoulder, she was so startled that her arms flew up to protect herself and she smacked him full in the face, knocking his glasses into his face and shattering them. A piece of glass penetrated his left eye; blood gushed enormously.

The prognosis for the eye was not good. It seemed that the glass had lodged itself in such a position that to operate would cause blindness—not to operate, too, was likely to cause blindness in that eye. They did nothing but wait.

Alice's husband Henry had been gone for almost ten years and though Danny was still young, Alice had been relying on him as the man of the house since the last of his brothers left home a few years before. Alice felt as if her rock of Gibraltar was suddenly vulnerable and that made her vulnerable as well.

Danny rested a lot, trying to recover and during this time, Alice went to pieces. She disappeared for hours and returned as distraught as ever. She constantly mumbled prayers and flagellated herself to pay penance and take away Danny's suffering. One day Danny had to stop her from clawing at her own eyes, as if to pull them out. She blamed herself for Danny's injury, believing her own sins had caused it. Alice was crumbling before Danny's one good eye and the more he tried to console her, the more distraught she became.

Several weeks after the accident, Mabel, an old friend of Alice's, overheard her fervent prayers and told her of a place called Zion City. The way Mabel described it, the place was like a heaven on earth—large maples and oaks lined the wide streets, which all led to the hub of the town, a large and grand cathedral. The minister, Rev. Marcus, had the power in his large, sinewy hands to heal the wounded and the ill who were willing to confess their sins and make amends. Mabel herself had gone there when her arthritis had gotten so bad she could barely walk, and Rev. Marcus had healed her to the point where she no longer even used a cane. She claimed that all believers who went there with a pure heart came away healed.

For the first time since the accident, Alice was decisive. She arranged to take Danny to the service that very week. As soon as Danny and Alice got off the train, Alice felt a great cleansing wash over her. She felt drawn to the place immediately. The residents of Zion City gave all of their worldly goods to the community upon their arrival, and they took care of one another, a large religious commune. The residents all dressed the same, in black and white clothing that covered everything but their hands and their faces. They were allowed no adornments. Everyone there believed in the same God, a healing God, a God of true believers. She felt entirely at home.

Alice, upon entering the church, kneels in the aisle and puts her head on the floor. She stays prostrate until Danny gently lifts her up and leads her to a seat in a pew near the front of the sanctuary. Danny is uncomfortable with the whole affair; he is not sure what he believes in yet. Alice's God has always seemed so unlovable, even cruel. Sometimes Danny blames Him for their troubles. But his mother is the only adult he can rely on and this is what she wants—he is not going to ruin it for her.

There is a service every night of the week except Saturday, and every night people are healed. Since Zion City is on the train line between Chicago and Detroit, sick and injured people from both those metropolitan areas come here to be healed.

At one point in the service, after the fiery prayers and several scripture readings, Rev. Marcus asks that all those who want to be healed come forward and receive the blessing. Alice prompts Danny to go up and he shyly walks forward with several other people. Because of the patch on his eye, he walks off center, teetering ever so slightly. Rev. Marcus leans over each person and asks quietly what they need. He then places his hand on them and asks that the community pull together and, through their minister, channel the healing energy to this person. When it is Danny's turn, he whispers to Rev. Marcus about the glass in his eye. Rev. Marcus audaciously pulls off the bandage and Danny feels the pain of his eyebrow hair being pulled out with the adhesive. He almost screams. While the whole congregation prays with him, he cups his hand over Danny's eye. Alice prays so fervently she forgets to breathe and faints dead away and has to be removed from the sanctuary.

After the service is over, Danny, who has previously not been able to see at all with that eye, is certain that he can now see some light. Because of it, all the people he sees in Zion City have halos just like the Rev. Marcus. He cannot see shapes with the eye, but the fact that he sees light gives Alice hope.

When my focus shifts to my surroundings, I find I am staring at a spider that has set up its web between the window and the wall.

Alice explains that when they returned to Detroit, she began making arrangements for the two of them to move to Zion City and join the community there. If Danny could go to church every night and receive the blessing from Rev. Marcus, he could complete the healing. However, to become a member of the community in Zion City, one had to have money to buy in; Alice and Danny were practically destitute. Right about that same time, Helena, Alice's mother-in-law, was diagnosed with breast cancer and needed someone to take care of her. Though Hallie offered to help, Helena knew that Hallie needed to begin her own life. Helena also knew that Hallie was unlikely to be a good nurse for Helena. Even though Alice had never been able to tolerate Helena, she decided to take on Helena's care as part of her penance. She felt sure that Rev. Marcus would see the good of that in her eyes next time she saw him. They arranged to sell Helena's house in Chicago and use the proceeds to buy into Zion City.

Those years in Zion City were Alice's happiest—she went to church every night and lived a life of austerity and penance. She tried to totally commit herself to Christ as her Lord and Savior. Helena and she got along better than they had ever hoped. The spider nightmare went away; Danny regained his eyesight, and he hardly noticed any problem in the eye, except for an occasional swelling that continued the rest of his life. Alice was on the road to redemption. I almost feel glad for her, and then she continues talking.

"How bad...to be a man...maybe worse...than to be woman. War...pressures of economics...strong all the time. My sons: One died young...oldest a raging drunk...

beat his wives; another a womanizer...didn't care who...he hurt; and my baby...Danny... could not believe...in God. Except for Andy...all successful...made money...married...had children. But none happy. What went wrong? Did...spider...take away...happiness?"

I'll have to ask Lucy what she thinks of that recurring spider dream. Alice infuses it with some kind of meaning that I don't understand.

I try to connect with her by saying, "I've thought about you a lot over the years. One of the voices in my head has always been yours from when I was so little and we stayed with you. It's a religious voice talking about Christ. That makes sense now that I have heard your dream. You relate to Christ, don't you, as the primary figure?"

"Andy...told me not...to lose Christ—then he did. Mind poisoned...in war--killed himself...with gas. Never confirmed—didn't want...to know. See, he sacrificed... his life for...my sins—I keep him...always near...my heart."

I can't tell if she is talking about Andy's or Christ's sacrifice. She was always such a devoted Christian, and yet her faith doesn't give her comfort. Her God is a judge who is constantly striking the gavel and roaring, "guilty as charged!"

I think of Hallie's opposition to religion and Alice's over-indulgence in it and I wonder: where is the love?

Chapter 23—The Flip Side

Picture yourself all hunkered down behind the plate, catcher's outfit protecting you from everything. Now throw all that equipment away—you won't catch the drift that way. In fact, it's more likely to come up from behind you anyway, where you are just human flesh.

October 21, 1996

Later, in class, Pilar and I exchange seats so that we are each in front of the other's weaving. We are instructed to add a few notes orally—in case the weaving is not totally self-explanatory—but the comments are to be kept to a minimum.

Pilar's weaving takes my breath away, because on first glance I don't think about what it means. It is lovely, showing the earth's green hills at the bottom with a sunrise in the corner. Then, way up in the sky, she has depicted an empty cloth cradle held up by doves at its three corners, one at the foot and two at the head. The cloth is a burnt orange color with small yellowish circles on it, and there is a blanket in it that is light green with darker green squares and a white pillow. There are clouds around the cradle, but the sky is primarily blue. Pilar shrugs her tiny shoulders and says, "Without Mary, all we have is an empty cradle that never reaches the ground."

I will think about that later; for now, I explain my tapestry. As soon as Pilar sees it, I can tell she has an idea for how to respond. She has a glint in her eyes that makes me nervous.

I stare at Pilar's weaving for a long time. It is artistically fine. The cloth for the cradle and the blanket are lovingly depicted. Thoughts about the empty cradle and the obsession with filling cradles with more and more babies run through my mind. Making motherhood divine as the Catholics do through Mary seems to me to lead directly to the ideas that sex is only for procreation and every pregnancy must come to term.

What does an empty cradle mean, anyway? Christ would never have been born and people would be worshipping an empty cradle? Meantime, there would have been no physical manifestation of God on earth. And we need him—his birth and his death. But I never denied that Mary was needed, just that she should be worshipped.

I concentrate hard on the image, when it comes to me. I will make the cradle into a cross; it will be the cross that is empty, and this is where our thoughts should be, on the resurrection, not on the birth—on God, not on Mary. After all, the most remarkable thing about Christ is not that he was born, but that he died and rose from the dead. On my work pad, I sketch a cross panel that uses the same stitch as the cradle which lies almost horizontally from side to side. The empty cradle will become the empty cross, the Protestant cross. I am pleased with my cleverness as I count the small threads to crack the code of the fabric and the blanket. The blanket, it turns out, can be used to indicate that there has been a body there—this bed has been lain in—and now the body is gone. The cross will be beautiful as it is lifted into the clouds by the doves of peace, as the green hills below shine with sunlight.

My image matches perfectly what Pilar has drawn but, instead of being horizontal, it is vertical; and the wide part is at the bottom and the narrow part at the top. It looks like a flying cross and if one looks a little longer, it also looks like a flying star, a four-pointed star. Excitedly, I set up my loom to weave the crosspiece so that I can add it to what Pilar has done. The artistry and precision have already been mapped out for me by Pilar, obviously a master at her craft. I can learn a lot about weaving just by figuring out how Pilar set up her loom.

I have to ask Colleen for help several times because I can't quite understand how Pilar managed to get the textures she did.

A new instructor, Maeve, lectures on anger while we work. She speaks humorlessly, as if she has had much anger directed at her at some time in her life.

My thoughts wander. I have never understood people who cannot keep their anger in check. Anger isn't my problem. More difficult for me to control are hurt feelings; the tears insist their way into my eyes even when I will them away. I don't like being forced by my own body to show my vulnerability that way. Maybe with some people it's like that with anger—they don't have a choice about it.

Even when Ralph was seeing Jenny, I don't recall feeling anger. I felt uncontrollable hurt and sadness accompanied by tears. As a child, I witnessed the explosive scenes between Alice and Hallie, and I realize now that they scared me thoroughly. Then there was the time where I ran away from home after being forced to eat liver and onions and Mrs. Parker threatened to send me to Mannington if it happened again. I learned to control my anger.

Near the end of the day, I notice that Pilar is still working on her side of the argument. It is a taking long time, and I see that it has grown much larger. I restrain the desire to peek. Tomorrow will be soon enough.

That evening, I begin my moon watch early, glancing out the window every few minutes, anxiously trying to catch a glimpse of the rising moon. Finally, I see a lighted area behind a cloud and I know it is there. I stare at the clouds making fantastic progress across the light and then revealing the almost full moon. I can see the light and the changing clouds reflected on the water. Reassured by the presence of this light, I surmise that that must have been exactly what Hallie felt all those nights so many years ago. The moonlight hypnotizes me, and I think of Hallie so strongly that finally she is present with me and begins to speak.

"The full moon puts me in the mood for love. Oh, I had some—one or two—juicy sweet times before they put me away. Don't cry for me, darling."

I am still looking intently at the moon when I see reflected back at me in the window a strikingly handsome, medium-sized man, smiling seductively under his slightly cocked derby hat.

January 7, 1919

Hallie brings the photographs from Donald Miller's recent wedding to Isabelle Gettier, a rich socialite, into his real estate office. Out of sheer politeness, she asks Donald how he enjoyed his honeymoon. The question must come at a particularly weak moment, because he confesses to Hallie that he did not marry Isabelle out of love, that his marriage is a sham and that he doesn't know how he is going to live with it. He says, "The honeymoon was a fiasco. Isabelle turns out to be a prude, maybe she's even frigid."

He paces around the office, a caged man. Hallie, feeling sorry for anyone in a cage, starts to walk with him and she reaches over and takes his limp hand to comfort him. As soon as she touches his hand, he seems to come back to life. He takes her other hand and they begin to waltz across the room and back. His mood is definitely improving. Donald lives his life following his irrepressible impulses or hunches, and so far they have served him well.

When he kisses Hallie there in the office, she feels her own impulsive side leap to the fore, and she responds in kind. Her body takes over in her rush to stabilize herself. She pushs him backward onto his desk and unbuttons his fly. Images of Isabelle's repulsion toward him are pushed out of existence by Hallie's enthusiasm.

Before the appointment is over, Donald is out of his doldrums, and Hallie and he have made plans to go to Florida to check out some real estate. She assures him that there are ways to stay married and still have a little fun. Getting out of town without his wife seems appealing indeed. He tells his wife he has to go to Florida on business, and he and Hallie get on a train headed for Miami.

They have a glorious time investigating land, which turns out to be near a small town west of Miami. They don't stay long. The first thing they notice about the site was how many mosquitoes there are; and that if you walk onto it, you start to sink. Instead of looking further there, they head to a resort farther south and spend time walking on the beach, drinking martinis and dancing.

When they find a particularly private beach, the rough water doesn't stop Hallie from taking off her clothes and running headlong into the waves. Donald follows suit, and soon they are swimming and stroking each other, swimming and stroking. They come to a cove where there is a log half out of the water. They make love right there, Hallie draped over the log. Donald has his back to the water and a series of breakers begin crashing into the tree, washing over them and then sucking them toward the sea. Hallie feels the sea begin to take her, pulling her toward it and then into Donald, then like a wave, she crashes back against the tree over and over, sucking and crashing, molded and pulled—swept up—Donald a kind of toy tossed between Hallie and the sea.

When they return to the hotel in Miami, a telegram from Isabelle informs Donald that his father has died and he rushes back.

All would have been well, because his wife trusts him, but at the cemetery after his father's funeral, in the pouring sleet, his grief overwhelms him. He gets another one of his impulses, this time to confess everything to his wife. And he does it in a very public way, kneeling in the cold slush between her and the open hole in the ground with the casket hovering over it, begging her forgiveness. Maybe it was all the talk of the afterlife that got to him, and the closeness of heaven or hell.

The scandal may as well have made the papers, it becomes such general knowledge. Hallie's family is told and, of course, Alice is mortified. But those are wild days, right after the war, when things are starting to loosen up sexually. Hallie is just the right age and attitude to take advantage of it.

She is laughing when I find myself back in this room. The moon has disappeared behind some clouds and it seems I am losing my way again. I stretch out my legs to find a hard floor of reality to touch. I walk out of the room and toward my bedroom.

A heap of clothing on the bed is waiting to be folded. I feel a tightness in my chest. Hallie was a Jenny-type, luring poor unsuspecting folks like Ralph or Donald Miller into her trap, messing with them and then letting them go back to their shaken lives and shaken wives. I take a long-sleeved shirt and shake out the wrinkles; the sharp snapping sound is strangely satisfying.

I have never let my impulses lead me that far astray. A rational person should just say no, no matter how attractive the temptation. I wonder again if genes mean anything at all. I mean, the casual way she ruined other people's lives... I can see why so many people despised her. I'd really like to punch her.

Nothing more frustrating, though, than trying to punch a ghost, I think. Then I have to laugh. My impulses are perhaps not as under control as they used to be. I collect myself and return to the living room, not knowing if she is still there.

Pacing the floor, I say out loud in case she is still there, "I really don't understand you. Just when I think you maybe weren't crazy but misunderstood, you go off and launch into one of these awful stories. You do it just to shock me, don't you?"

"I am trying, and trying to tell truth, not lull you into some sense of my virtuousness and victimhood." She makes those words sound almost dirty, drawing them out as if they were sliding slime. *"Neither virtuous nor victim, I. I had my own plan on my own planet."*

I close my eyes and sit down, feeling suddenly dizzy. For her, words like *virtue* and *victim* were filthy, and words like *freedom, lust,* and *sexuality* were elevated to a high status. It was disorienting. "What, for heavens sake, was your agenda, then?" I ask.

"To live a life for myself, for me alone. To be a self-made woman. Is that too much for a world run by men to handle, those same hands that at times can handle so much so well?" She chortles.

"I live for myself," I say.

"I know only know what I see. Judgment not mine. Many religious people live lives for God—his will, not theirs be done. Am I wrong, headlong wrong, in this?"

I sigh, wishing we could agree on this but knowing we never will. I say, "If that's what you mean, then, yes, I have tried to live a life doing God's will."

"I did not try to unfly, to do god's will. Not god's, Emma's, Charles' nor Charlotte's, but my own."

Again I jump up and start pacing. I just can't sit still for this. Then I tell her, "I see why everyone said you were selfish. You are. Selfish, selfish, selfish! You think only of yourself. What about Donald's wife. How do you think she felt? You never even considered other people's feelings!"

"Guilty." Before I can respond, I feel the room go vacant, and I know that she is gone. I'm sorry I was so hard on her. As I sit here and feel my elevated blood pressure, I know that I am overreacting to her story that took place so many years ago. I am finally mad at Ralph over his whatever-it-was with Jenny. After all I had given him, done for him, sacrificed for him … It was so insulting! Maybe I'll punch him. The thought of it is certainly more satisfying than the thought of punching Hallie.

Chapter 24—Upside Down

Do you know that when you are upside down, you lose your sense of direction and even left and right fail to make sense? Maybe you should turn your leaders upside down and ask them some important questions about the directions you are headed.

October 22, 1996

I wake feeling as if I'm in the middle of a battle. I worry what people, especially the Catholics in the class, will think of me.

I shower and put on special clothes: heavy black cotton pants and a turquoise turtleneck with one of my own woven vests from home. The weather is just gorgeous and though there are a few clouds, they all look harmless enough. The wind has died down considerably.

Today Margaret has other plans so I eat my lunch alone, worrying about this afternoon. What will I say? How could this possibly resolve anything? But in some ways I am excited to have a forum to air my views. Where is that woman inside me who promised herself not to bring up the subject of the Virgin Mary?

Not quite able to finish my lunch, I pay the bill and wander over to class a little early. Pilar is still working, her small wiry figure stretched over the loom. She is so intent on the weaving that she doesn't even notice me. I walk over to my work and smile at it glowingly. It really is a beautiful piece; the pattern of the cloth in the cradle/cross mesmerizing.

As the rest of the class meanders in, I can feel a tension in the air. So it is not just me who is intimidated by confrontation. There is nervous laughter and talk of anything but what we are doing here today. Colleen asks Pilar if she needs more time, but she says no, she is just finishing up. Before we exchange weavings, see what our partners have done and get a chance to talk a little, Colleen requests that we discuss one additional question: Is it possible that the person who originated the idea for the argument secretly wanted to be convinced of the validity of the other side? Colleen says, "It doesn't always hold true, but I'd ask that you keep an open mind."

My first reaction to her question is that, no, I did not want to be convinced I was wrong. But I have a feeling that my reaction is small, controlled, and somehow frozen into an odd shape, like an icicle after a thaw and a quick re-freezing. I feel as if I cannot take a deep breath or everything will shift and shatter. My hands are icy.

"Now, go outside or stay here and exchange your weavings and talk about them." Colleen continues. "We will meet back here in one hour for more discussion."

Since Pilar's work is still on the loom, we stay inside while others go outside. We wait until everyone clears out, and then I bring my weaving over to where she is and pull up a chair next to her loom so that I can see the image.

I gasp. My beautiful rain into water through the Holy Spirit has been turned on its head: the mud in which the basin sat has become the brown spread legs of a woman obviously in labor. It looks now as if she is birthing something white, through water and into the air and the spirit. It is beautifully done; I can hardly recognize my part of it in the bottom half—it is so transformed. It is completely upside down. The imagery remains basically the same, but the woman has become central, huge, the key figure in the scene. Now, what I had meant to be the breath of the holy spirit looks like the woman's blood.

Finally, Pilar asks in her gentle voice, "Can I take this one home with me?" she asks, pointing to the woman giving birth that she has just been working on. "It pleases me."

I am a bit startled by the request, but I am also relieved. "Oh," I say, "of course, no problem—you certainly worked hard on remaking it. It bothers me, anyway..." Then, trying to change the subject, I say with forced cheerfulness. "I love the one you started. The fabric you created for the cradle is just perfect—it has many lovely little worlds on it. "

Pilar fidgets uncomfortably and goes back to my first comment. She says, "I didn't try to "remake" yours ... honestly, but, women, we are central—without us, no birth, no Christ. No me, no you, no humanity."

I cannot get over the upsidedownness of the thing. It looks more like a creation myth than a comment on the Virgin Mary—and not just that, but with a woman as creator.

I reply, "So we agree that women are vital to continuing the human race, right?" Pilar nods tentatively, waiting for the other shoe to drop. "But where I differ with you is that I believe women, including Mary, are just human—not divine. They're earth and blood and mud, exactly what needs to be transcended to reach God. They are not deserving of such a glorified role—I mean with statues and paintings and pilgrimages. It's all too much."

Now Pilar looks me right in the eyes. She is small but fierce. "You don't have a high opinion of yourself, do you?"

I look away, taken aback by her directness, my insides suddenly feel hollow, empty. "I'm not speaking personally; I'm talking about the role of women in the world." My words seem contrived even to me. Is this what I really believe now or what I have always believed in the past? As fast as I run here, I can't seem to stay up-to-date.

"And yet," Pilar says, squints up at the glare of the empty ceiling, "you make a cradle into an empty cross. What happens to the love you saw in my weaving? Reminds me of the countries near me in Central America where the women have boys as— what do you call it—when they are conceived just to be killed in war?"

I answer, unsure how what she is saying relates to my weaving, "Cannon fodder?"

She nods, excitedly, "Yes, cannon fodder. The cradle turns into a cross, a sacrifice. Love turns into something terrible and violent."

"No, that's not at all what I meant—not sacrificing boys in war, but the empty cross, the fact that Christ has risen, he conquered death, the epitome of *self*-sacrifice."

Pilar is listening very attentively. "It's what soldiers are told, too, when they march to war. I wonder what Mary would have said if she were ever given a voice? It might be the voice of women everywhere—those of us who want another way, a way of love."

I am confused by her words because I see Jesus' act of self-sacrifice as one of love. I don't want to say more until I can think about it.

"Well," says Pilar, looking at her watch, "we will not solve this now, no? It grows late." She pauses and then continues, "About Colleen's last question, you must answer. Did you secretly want me to convince you?"

I don't look directly at Pilar and instead let my eyes roam from weaving to weaving along the wall. Ever since I came to Ireland, the Virgin Mary crops up at the strangest times. Why is that?

I hesitate to respond. I want to be sure I am telling the truth, "Well, in a way, I do want women to have more power in the church. Maybe *I* want to have more power. I just can't figure out how—not in my own life—not yet, anyway."

A smile spreads over Pilar's face. She looks as though she is proud of me. I am not sure what I have said to change things. She just says, "Gracias, muchas gracias." Then we hug and look at each other with a new sense of having met. There is not time for her to answer that question about whether she wanted to be convinced by Emma.

I still feel terribly unsettled. As I stare again at that larger-than-life woman who seems to be life itself, I wish we had not spoken. An energy stirs throughout my body, a memory runs through me of the first time Ralph and I made love. Prior to our marriage, Ralph told me countless times how much he loved me. But it was the physical act of making love that manifested a truth beyond the words. When he cradled my foot—the one with an embarrassing corn on the side that makes it look deformed—when he kissed the corn, the defect itself, I knew that his love of me transcended even who I thought I was to something he could see about me that was buried so deep even I had forgotten about it. His gentle touch, his knowing my fears without my speaking them, made me whole. After my carefully guarded world had been witnessed and entered by another, I truly felt love.

When everyone returns, Maeve looks around the room at the variety of faces, some flushed, some puzzled, some angry, and says very seriously in a low tone, "How was it for you?"

I smile to myself and blush, especially after what I had just been thinking about.

Olivia, relaxed and leaning way back in her chair says, "I think I need a cigarette. It was that good."

The first pair to talk, Lea and Bett, had disagreed about vegetarianism. Bett's weaving depicted happy pigs rolling in mud in an Irish bog with plenty of fresh air. They had smiles on their faces—that is, until her partner had finished the weaving by painting on top of the weaving, a bloody knife slicing into one of their throats. Bett shows the work to everyone, and it is true that anger and hostility stared back. It is not a lovely weaving at all.

Each woman talks a little about how it felt to work on the weavings. Lea, who represents the vegetarian point of view, says she had trouble painting in the bloody knife. She felt as though she were actually slicing the pigs' throats. She says she wanted to believe the pigs were happy, and maybe they were, but surely not at the point at which she depicted them.

Bett in turn is shocked at what Lea did to her weaving, making it bloody and evil-looking. At first, she just wants the weaving destroyed; it upsets her too much. She has never known anyone who didn't eat meat, and she can hardly imagine life without it.

Colleen asks Bett, "Do you think maybe you understand some of the feelings that Lea has when she thinks of people eating meat?"

"If you'd be meaning outright horror, aye, I do."

Others in the discussion confirm that the first reaction to the final weaving was often negative. "It is difficult to see our values and our hard work contradicted," Colleen says, "and yet taking a closer look, there is a place where the two views met. In every weaving, the second weaver used the work of the first as a springboard to let her views be known. No one wove something totally separate, parallel. Somehow, it is that engagement, that makes understanding, and perhaps even resolution, possible."

Victoria, who is always articulate in her comments, talks about her difficulty in putting into words what happened. "It has something to do with power, I think. The images grew so much more powerful after we both worked on them. They are more filled out, more complete. Not that we agree now, but we certainly understand each other better."

My image seemed narrow and weak, powerless, in comparison to the way it looks now that Pilar has added her viewpoint. But then, if I look closely, I can see how careful she was to leave my image standing, even while she expanded what I had done by so much. It makes me more expansive myself, in my gut somewhere. I feel a release of something, a deep relaxation, as if I have been holding something at bay forever that I can now release.

"Both of our images say more than words can," I add to the discussion. "When I look at the weaving on my lap, I feel something stirring, something I can't pin down about the colors in the fabric that Pilar created. There is love in it, somehow."

"Feelings ... " Pilar begins. Her eyes tear up as she points to the weaving in my lap. "That one makes me feel sad, sad about empty cradles and empty crosses, the innocence of babies in a world full of war." I hold up the weaving to show it to the class. I can feel the sadness but I don't believe I made something that somehow justifies war.

Maeve notices that Pilar and I have each taken for ourselves the second piece we worked on. "At least for the remainder of the course, I suggest you take home your original piece with the addition and display it prominently somewhere so you will encounter it several times a day. Then, at the end of the class you can fight over who gets to keep what."

Pilar works on disengaging the work from the loom, adding the finishing touches so that I can take it.

I venture across the street to sit and watch the water before I return home. Threatening clouds are visible to the west over the Aran Islands. The bay changes colors as often as the clouds, as it mixes with the variations in the light. One minute it has a gray, listless look and the next, a lively shivery blue.

Today I don't see the woman in the green bathing suit; still, I think of her. Suddenly, a particularly dark cloud begins to creep over the sun and I hurry toward the path. At the last minute, I leave the weaving at the

Centre, lest the rains ruin it.

When the rain catches up with me, I am at a particularly barren place on the road. Pulling my coat around me, I walk as fast as I can. Though I had been dreading the day the rain caught up with me, I find it exhilarating and, luckily, not too cold. The released feeling is still with me.

Soon after, I am curled up in my favorite chair, and a dampness presages Alice's appearance. It feels like a cool steam room in here. I sense a hesitance, as if only her big toe has actually entered the room. I simply wait, without judgment or impatience. Finally, she lets me know that she is ready to tell whatever she has been holding back. She says she wants to tell it with Hallie here, and we each remain quiet for a while, summoning Hallie in our own ways. While we wait, Alice says very softly, almost to herself, "S*hould have told Hallie long ago. Told her... in every way—except tell her. Could... never... do... that.*"

We listen intently and finally hear the rustle of leaves and uneven bursts of air going by the window. After a period of silence and a building of wind, the voice begins to come through.

"Here I am here, Alice, to listen, hear, here." Silence again but for the gentle whistle of the breeze.

After some false starts and soft whimperings, Alice begins.

May, 1872

Alice loves her father and would do anything for him. He knows this and asks much of her. One evening when she is nine years old, still without a hint of breasts, he invites her to his bedroom. He has a strange look in his eyes, as if he isn't really seeing her but something just beyond her. Then, when he focuses on her and smiles tenderly; she relaxes. Slowly and clumsily, he winds Alice's hair up into a bun. The cracked fingernail on his thumb catches in her hair, pulling out several strands; Alice winces. Frederick is so gentle, though, apologizing for pulling her hair. He pins the hair up so that only a few untended wisps remain free. She looks much older that way.

Because Alice's mother, Susan, died in childbirth, she was known to Alice only through the stories other people told her. People said that Alice bore an uncanny resemblance to her. Susan had been the social one in her marriage to Frederick, participating in church activities and the life of the rural farming community. People loved her for her zest for life; she lived in the joy of creation and relationship.

After pinning up Alice's hair, Frederick takes Susan's wedding ring that he keeps in a golden box on the bureau and slips it on Alice's thin ring finger. Alice twirls it around, warming up the inner surface that is so cold and letting the flicker of the kerosene lamp reflect in its outer surface. Then he asks her to take off her clothes, and as she does, he pulls out of the closet Susan's long white cotton nightgown decorated with just a touch of embroidery at the sleeves and the neckline that has remained untouched for nine years.

Susan had a knack for thinking up ways to make life better. For instance, when she learned that during the long winters many home bound people were getting drunk just to pass the time, she started a storytelling evening once a week in the winter months. If some couldn't get out by themselves, Susan would organize neighbors to pick them up.

Susan became so interested in the stories of old that she began to gather them together; soon she was the town historian. To have someone care about what had happened to people in their lives made the people themselves begin to care. And the younger people started asking the older ones to tell the stories so that they could learn. Even people who lived farthest from town found ways to get into town on Wednesday evenings for the potluck supper and story sharing.

A number of spin-off groups began as well: the quilters devised quilts to tell the stories, and a few talented painters took the stories and made them into brightly colored murals on the town hall and school building. Whatever Susan had, it gave her the ability to find creativity in even the dullest individuals.

These traditions lasted long after Susan died, but Alice never participated in any of them because her father, devastated by Susan's death, forbade her to go. From the time that Susan went to her grave on the sloping hillside overlooking the town, Alice and Frederick lived an isolated life on the farm. Attending church was the one ritual Frederick and Alice participated in faithfully. Frederick's religious views never seemed to comfort him, though; they seemed like more of a punishment. He never stopped blaming himself for Susan's death.

The nightgown smells musty. When Frederick shakes it, dust flies to the corners of the room. As Alice puts it on and buttons the many little buttons that hold it together, her fingers fumble with the unfamiliar task.

Then he lifts Alice to Susan's side of the tall bed, her feet dangling down the sides, unable to reach the floor, to make contact, to run. Only then, with utmost care not to pull her hair, does he unpin the bun and let her thin hair fall over her face. She leaves it there, a cocoon to keep her safe. When he pushes her back until she is lying across the bed, lifts her nightgown and begins to touch her, Alice follows the dust to the corners of the room so that when what he does hurts more than anything she has ever experienced, she's not really there in the bed where her mother died.

This ritual is repeated many times after that first night. At first, he does things that would have gotten her pregnant, except that she hadn't started her menses yet. After her periods start, he does other things. They attend church services and hear the preacher rail against the sins of the flesh, and all the time they both know they are sinning. The preacher says it is females who lure men into doing things that they shouldn't do; Alice knows that must be what she has done. She never once says "no" to him; never once tells a soul.

Alice is conflicted; she wants to make her father smile, but she does not want to do the things he wants her to do in his bedroom. She tries to be a wife to him in the kitchen, making him dinners and keeping the hearth fires burning, thinking perhaps if she does all that well enough, he won't need to perform the after-dark ritual.

She knows he loves her because just before he starts, before he pulls up her nightgown, he smiles at her in the moonlight and tells her how beautiful she is. She lives for that fleeting look. After he finishes, there are no smiles; he turns away from her in disgust as if she has done something terrible to him. Once again she takes on his sins, consumes them, makes them a part of her. Is there no way, she wonders, to have the smile without the sin?

When the story is over, shocked silence fills the room. The tear-streaked window comes back into focus and the atmosphere in the room feels soiled, contaminated somehow, as if we all participated in those despicable events. I listen closely, and it sounds as if Hallie might be wailing far, far away.

Alice finally says what might be, *"See...see? Forgive... me, forgive... me, forgive... me, forgive... me,"* but it is so faint it could be coming from over the ocean.

I can't stand to hear her ask for forgiveness. I say, "It's not your fault. Don't you see that even now? You were a child. It wasn't your sin."

Then Hallie begins to speak in a wispy thin voice. *"I see a new, old story. Men, power, tower together making misery."* I can barely recognize her voice, the bass has gone out of it. *"You tried to stop the wheel of evil as it rolled crushingly along on its way toward me? Fearing for your only, so lonely daughter?*

"Yesssss, but I...I...started...it.....rolling," Alice says in a high pitched voice as if she has just turned into steam.

"I'm listening now, ma, I'm listening now," says Hallie softly.

It's poison all right, and I can feel it churning in my stomach. This story brings the missing puzzle piece. Now I can see why Alice got so upset when she saw Hallie and Emma on the sun porch together, why she assumed it was a sin. And why she had reacted so strongly to Hallie's defending herself in the stairwell. Hallie's affairs upset Alice so much because she saw them as an extension of the sinfulness that Alice felt she carried on her shoulders and had passed onto Hallie.

"ONE... MORE... THING," says Alice, wearily gulping between each word. *"A confession... to make..amend....mend."*

I let the story unfold before me, afraid. I am surprised to see that it is my first day of school, and Hallie is walking with me to the school. I am wearing knickers and a practical, boyish shirt.

September 1931

Emma has no idea what is happening at home as she sits at her desk, twirling her newly sharpened pencil, looking at the other children sitting near her and at her teacher, Mrs. Dunbar, a young woman barely out of school herself. It is Emma's first day of school, the day after the fight between Hallie and Alice over what Emma would wear to school.

Emma's absence makes it much easier for the men to take Hallie off screaming to Mannington. Both Alice and Danny sincerely think that the best thing for Hallie is to lock her up for a while and hope she comes to her senses. But they also want to make sure Emma is taken away from Hallie and cared for properly by Alice.

Alice knows that if Charlotte finds out that Hallie is locked up, she will fight to get her out and also fight for Emma. Hallie has maintained a relationship with Charlotte for years and, in fact, was in a relationship with her even while married to Charles. Hallie thought Charlotte understood that and could handle it, too, but gradually, Charlotte came to believe that Hallie loved Charles more than her.

After Hallie got pregnant, her relationship with Charlotte was never the same. During the pregnancy, Charlotte couldn't bear to look at her; once Hallie had Emma, Char blamed that baby for everything. Emma was the evidence that Char had been wronged. Even after Charles' death, Charlotte couldn't let it go.

Alice knows that she has to do something—Hallie's evil streak is taking her over: after all, Hallie is still seeing Charlotte; she is raising Emma with her depraved sense of what is "female," and she has no morals.

Alice knows that whenever Hallie gets out, she will resume the relationship with Char unless she, Alice, intervenes to stop it. If that relationship continues, Alice is certain Hallie will be damned for all time. Hallie will never find another husband. What other man in his right mind will put up with Hallie's keeping Charlotte on the side?

When Charlotte shows up at their house a few hours after the men have taken Hallie away, only Alice is at home to give her answers. No witnesses can report later to Hallie what happened.

What Charlotte sees when she arrives is a distraught-looking Alice. The last two days have been murderous—the big fight with Hallie over what Emma was to wear to school, not sleeping the night before, the visit to the lawyer, and then watching them take Hallie away. These events are certainly enough to make anyone distraught.

Alice feels nothing but distaste for Charlotte and though she knows it will forever change Hallie's life, she begins her dissimulation. "Hallie said to tell you good-bye for her," Alice says to Charlotte. "She couldn't bear to say good-bye in person, but she feels she has to raise Emma without meddling from...from either of us." Alice puts on a good act, weeping into her handkerchief. " Said you couldn't come with her because of your bad feelings towards Emma. And me...well, we both know she don't care much for me. I tried to stop her, but I am old and weak..."

Before Alice can finish her sentence, Charlotte blurts out, "Where… has… she… gone?" She stops after each word, as if she can barely get the next one out of her mouth. Her face drains of blood like a ghost's, threateningly close to Alice's face, as if she'd just as soon choke her to death as listen to this news.

Alice says, backing slowly away from her, "California's all she'd say, Charlotte. Don't know. Said she wasn't about to tell no one where she was." Alice cries real tears as she thinks about the truth of Emma's being adopted by someone else, maybe far away. "Maybe we never see Emma again?"

Charlotte pushes past Alice and barrels up the stairs to Hallie's room. Alice has already packed up Hallie's things, and it certainly appears that she has moved out. Charlotte lies down on Hallie's bed clutching her stomach and moaning. Hallie had threatened to do this very thing many times before, but Charlotte cannot believe she actually followed through with it. An hour later, barely able to control her movements, Charlotte picks her way back down the stairs, past Alice. She walks like a marionette, as if someone else is controlling her movements.

When Emma returns home from school that momentous first day,

Alice tells her mother has been taken to Mannington "for a rest," but Alice never speaks of what happened that day with Charlotte. Alice never hears from Charlotte again. The staff at Mannington is given strict instructions that any letters Hallie writes to Charlotte are part of her illness and should never be mailed. Alice doesn't expect Hallie to stay in Mannington for long. She expects her to be cured and released and to marry and live a normal life. But Hallie never gets normal; she just seems to get worse. It is out of Alice's hands and in the hands of the experts who convince Alice that Hallie is psychotic.

I hear a sharp outtake of breath like a gust of wind and no more words. Hallie and Alice go screaming and steaming off to the bay and make a sharp right to the sea.

Now I know what dead quiet really means. I wonder if they are gone for good. Drops of rain slide slowly, tortuously, down the window, a silent movie. I remain still, though inside I am whirling with this new information. I knew Alice had been holding something back, but I would never have guessed that she had held onto this into her death. How different Hallie's life might have been if she hadn't had to think all those years that the love of her life had betrayed her, not to mention the fact that maybe Charlotte could have managed to get her released from Mannington. That betrayal feels as real to me as if it had been staged against me.

How did Alice live with herself after that cold-blooded betrayal of her own daughter? She must have rationalized it, believing it was for Hallie's own good. Good, what did Alice know about good? No wonder she stayed bitter, and nothing was ever good enough. She never managed to purge herself of the poison that had been given to her by her father. It has poisoned us all. My very blood feels tainted as it moves through me.

I want them to come back and speak to Lucy; I need another witness.

The next morning, I am in a state of half-sleep, dozing and awakening, when the wind picks up and the rain begins to splatter against the window. I think drowsily, oh, maybe they're both here. "Are you there?" I ask softly.

Hallie speaks first. *"I am blowing you kisses goodbye, must blow away now."*

She startles me with that statement and I am suddenly wide-awake. I tell her she doesn't have to go. "Don't worry," I say, "it'll be safe with

Lucy, too. She's bringing her computer along to work on the book based on our lives—it's called *Strands.* She'll make sure I don't forget anything."

"We'll see if our tongues are tied around her—can make no promise. Alice and I have been mother/ daughter talking."

"Is Alice here, too?"

"I'm here. Can't stay-forecast dry...cold. Wanted...goodbye in case. You carry... stories. And Lucy."

"Yes," says Hallie. *"Tell her if the truth won't work, make up, take up, something that does. Details don't matter—get the big Truth in the right light, fair?"*

I am alarmed by that. "How will she know what the big Truth is? I don't."

"Emma," says Hallie gently, *"leave this work for the next generation to generate. Leave figuring, theory, myth. Take what is yours."* Her voice begins to fade away and I can barely hear that last part. I want to hug each of them, make it all OK, but how can I hug the wind or the rain?

I run to the window and hug myself, begging silently, "Please, don't leave. I was just getting used to having a mother and grandmother around. Come and chat with me at home, maybe in the garden or in church or somewhere?"

Hallie can't seem to resist taking a parting shot, *"I'll not be caught dead in church, ha, ha—but we'll see, agree, about gardens."*

"Listen for rain pounding on church roof," says Alice.

I am bereft, as if family members are suddenly dying. I shake my head a little, reminding myself that they have been dead for years. I say urgently, "I know you've got so much more to tell—when?" I find myself talking in staccato ghost talk myself.

But the only answer is the wind eddying, a drip or two of rain and a moving on. I sit in my pajamas by the window for a while longer, but the voices do not return. I didn't say goodbye—not really. Then I remember the stories of Hallie teaching poetry to her niece and about Alice meeting Henry, and I think, no, they are present still.

PART FOUR

TANGLES

Tangle: To bring together into a mass of confusedly interlaced or intertwisted strands. To attempt to pull them apart only makes the tangle tighter and less likely to untangle. Only patience and pushing the strands back toward the knot will loosen them.

Chapter 25—Melting: Emma

Puzzle pieces float just out of Emma's reach, threatening to add up to a looming iceberg. It is as if she is suffering from amnesia, except that she has never known the pieces lost beneath the surface. The pieces she so relentlessly seeks do not add up to her identity. They are not static like pieces of a jigsaw puzzle but three-dimensional, combining and recombining into strange forms as they melt and then re-freeze. Her identity is not hers to claim; it is an amalgamation of the past and the present and not just her past, but the past of relatives on other planes.

October 23, 1996

When Rhiannon steps forward to introduce the final project, I'm not worried about knowing what I will weave. What I need to know will occur to me. However, if someone asked me just now what I have faith in, I'd have a hard time describing it. One thing has certainly changed in these last days: I know that if I need them, my ancestors will be here for me. Even thinking that is so strange. It sounds almost African or something else foreign to me. I have always imagined that once people are dead, they are completely gone from the living.

Today we are starting our tapestries that express our wishes for the world. We have today, the weekend and Monday to get a good start on the image. Each subsequent day through Friday, we will move one seat to the left and begin a dialogue with whatever appears on the loom in front of us.

"Don't put the same thing in every piece," says Rhiannon. "This should be a true dialogue, so respond to whatever is in front of you. Since you'll only have one day to add, you may not be able to put in a whole thought. Just offer an image or a color that comes to you."

As an example, she shows us a weaving of a spiral completed in a previous class. With animation, she describes how each weaver stayed with the original image of the spiral but added a texture that was entirely her own. "Let your imaginations range, pay attention to warm and cold, soft and hard, dark and light, thick and thin, shiny and dull, tight and loose, light and heavy. All these qualities bring meaning."

Sketching out a cartoon, I can't concentrate. Alice's story is the story of so many women. Today it would be easier to think of what's wrong with the world, than what might make it right. Images of shifting sands and constant change come to me. Instead of sketching exactly what I will weave, I start with a foundation of sand. Not long ago, I used the biblical parable of not building one's home on a foundation of sand for a talk I gave to Church Women United. It stirred up little controversy; after all, who wouldn't build on rock? But what if such a thing is not possible? Perhaps all we have to build on is constantly shifting sand; experiences come and go and wear away even the rocks into more sand. So, over time, even what once felt solid turns out to be transient, too.

Preoccupied with Lucy's arrival, I mention to Margaret that I need to go to Galway to purchase a few things. Margaret says quickly, "Let me drive you, and you can stay overnight at my place and take the bus back in the morning.

When Margaret and I leave the Centre, I take my woman-giving-birth weaving with me and forget to drop it off at home when we stop by for my things. Margaret notices the weaving and asks to look at it more closely. The overhead light in the car is reminiscent of the glare of a delivery room, making the images look graphic and unsettling.

"It's downright provocative," Margaret says. "A woman with her legs spread—my, my, my."

In mild disgust, I respond, "Well, it's not about sex, you know—it's a woman giving birth."

Margaret laughs, "No, no, nothing to do with sex."

"You and Hallie," I say with irritation, "—always bringing sex into it. You know, for some of us, sex was not the first priority. I met Ralph in my junior year of college, and he was my first and only sexual experience, and that was enough for me. I'm fortunate not to have gotten tangled up in it before I was married. All I missed was the trouble."

I have always kept that part of my life under close control. I go along with Ralph when he wants sex, but I am rarely the one to initiate it. When I was young, I remember comments made by various people who knew Hallie, comments about how her sexual feelings ran her life. I vowed that those feelings would never have that much power in my life. I enjoy sex, but it does not control me. I have never became obsessed by it.

Margaret slows the car down. "It's not just sex but sensuality." She sighs and looks out her window where the sun is beginning to set. "Being overwhelmed by the pleasures of the senses—the beauty of this place called earth, the beauty of the body. Just letting go. Look at that ocean, would you just look!" Margaret exclaims, as we pass particularly close to a rocky beach. "Have you ever felt that," she motions with her head toward the view, "in your womb, or in every cell of your body—the engulfing beauty of a place?"

I turn in my seat as the orange moments of the sunset spread over the watery horizon. Taking a deep breath, I say, "Now that you mention it..." I turn back to sit upright in the seat. "I had an extraordinary experience the first week I was here ..." I pause, looking once more at the spectacular sunset and trying to put into words the feeling I had of being empty. The sunset is decadent, revealing the all-stops-out wonder of this planet. How could I justify holding back now? Margaret's face reflects the innocence of youth, unjaded, not yet hurt and cynical. I see I can confide in her and she will understand.

Still, I choose my words carefully. "I got excited just by breathing and looking out the window at the ocean. It did seem somewhat sexual in that butter-melting feeling in my womb. There was yearning coupled with peace. I didn't eat dinner or turn on the lights. I just sat there breathing in total stillness."

Margaret pulls the car over to the side of the road, excited. She says fervently, "In the name of the goddess, *that* was a ..." Margaret seems to be fighting for just the right words, too. "... an embodied religious experience, an experience of female divinity!"

Taking the tapestry with her, she leaps out of the car as if she is twenty again, opens my door, motioning for me to follow, and we pick our way across the rocks down to the unfamiliar ocean edge. As Margaret speaks, her eyes reflect the orange of the sun; she looks possessed and utterly enchanted. With those orange eyes, I feel that Margaret can see right through me. And, for an instant, I see myself as Margaret sees me: a person in my own right, an individual and not part of a couple. Me with no crutches, no excuses. I wonder if there is a Zion City room of the soul somewhere, lined with the anachronistic crutches that are no longer needed. And I wonder if my crutches are on the wall for good or just temporarily, until I return home.

Suddenly, I feel very confused. I say, trying to catch up with myself, "But divinity is sexless. I've never heard of female divinity."

I step unsteadily onto the uneven rocks, reaching out to Margaret to steady myself. Margaret, too, is unsteady, and we hold each other up. There is a current in our touch as the orange spreads everywhere. I feel mortal and weak; yet, at the same time, I am as ageless and timeless as the rocks that roll about in the surf forever, a contradiction I cannot grasp.

"Look at this," Margaret says, spreading the tapestry out onto a flat dry rock and pointing to the woman. "Looks alive, doesn't she?"

I can see her undulating, giving birth, almost hear her cries. Margaret goes to the edge of the sea and splashes water on her face. Time is moving beyond twilight now, into the darkness, and our silhouettes dance in the darkening. The orange is molten lava sizzling and then merging into water on the horizon.

Margaret yells in the direction of the sea, "Maybe we have to discover it—or unearth it; yes, it's buried here." She points to her heart. "But instead of looking inside, we insist on looking up at some god in the sky. Where is he now?" She gestures to the sun that has disappeared from the sky.

I stumble again, having to look down constantly to get my bearings. I shiver, thinking about the set sun, still able to make out the vague outlines of the tapestry. "Makes me feel dizzy," I yell back at Margaret, "as if I don't know which way is up." Just as I say those words, a rock that is perched beside the tapestry draws my attention. I pick it up and another shiver goes up my spine. It is a sensuous naked body, all curved and smoother than any rock I have ever touched. It seems almost as though it is covered in ginger-colored skin. I envy its close relation to the sea. It has been licked by a million waves, rolled over, handled roughly and endlessly caressed. Suddenly, wanting utter fidelity and exclusivity, I put it in my pocket without showing Margaret.

Margaret goes on, "I'm not talking just about sex. It's bigger than sex; maybe it's life itself. Listen to the relentlessness of it that we ignore most of the time. Wave after wave after wave, inevitable yet unpredictable. The breath, the pulse. And smell it!" Margaret throws her head back and takes a deep breath that looks as if it reaches through her whole body. "This is the smell of passion—it's exactly it. It's the smell and taste of us, of our fluids as they pulse through us. We are this ocean and she is us. Feel the spray on your face. 'Remember,' she is saying, 'we're not separate.' Look how that lusty one hit the rocks with total abandon. Trust yourself; trust it all."

Margaret's joy is contagious. I felt it, too—for a few moments—and then just as quickly as it came, it abandons me and is replaced by uneasiness. If only I could get my bearings again. Funny thing is, I can't remember when I lost them.

As we walk back to the car, my hand finds the curves of the rock, and I stroke it over and over. The rock seems so familiar; it is as if I have a place just like it inside myself. As I touch it, that place within me quickens. It is somewhere right beneath my belly button. That is one bearing I can be sure of. I'll start there and hope the rest will follow.

The next day Margaret drops me off in Galway. The streets are jammed with people—travelers, shoppers, beggars, musicians. I take my time to look around at the variety of shops and people. Galway seems festive, as if something exciting is about to happen. Finally, I wander into a small entranceway and find that downstairs is a huge area with a health food store that sells bulk food: nuts and rice, and products like peanut butter with no added salt or sugar. I choose items, pay, load up my backpack, then make my way to the bus station.

On the bus to Spiddal, I tell the driver that I want to go one mile shy of Spiddal, to the high school; he grunts and asks for four pounds. He seems uninterested in me, and I just know he will not alert me when it is time to get off; during the entire journey, I strain to see if I can notice any landmarks signaling that we are close. As I watch the countryside go by, listening to the Irish-speaking voices, I wonder about the unpredictability of life, of how I had set everything up for Ralph and then Phyllis broke her leg.

Studying my transparent reflection in the bus window, I look the same as always. But if I think of who I am, of how I define myself now, all I can picture are the fleeting scenes outside the window, scenes that go through my reflection as we speed along. These stone houses, rocky beaches, waves, weeds reddening with fall, dogs barking at the bus, a young girl's wave all move through my image of myself, not attaching themselves but changing me anyway. Background and foreground switch places: where I had seen myself as the thin image in the bus window—the narrow, wrinkled face, adorned with steel rimmed glasses—my focus now shifts to include both me and all that is going past me and through me.

At one point, an old woman at the back of the bus yells out something and flies down the aisle. The bus driver evidently understands and stops on cue. She gets off waving. A little later, a woman on the road with a baby carriage flags down the bus, and the driver stops and helps her put the carriage into the luggage compartment. She hauls the baby up the stairs, looking for a place to sit.

I wonder what women do when they have four or five kids and need to take the bus. It's one thing to haul one baby and quite another when there are many more. .

Finally I see a landmark I recognize, the high school. I jump up and start down the aisle, lurching from side to side. Thanking the driver, I exit. I hope that he will be more helpful with Lucy. He seems to act as if he has no idea where the high school is, though he passes it each day.

On Sunday, I am still having difficulty coming up with images. Frustrated, I take my sketch pad across the street to the beach. Each time I visit the beach, I see a unique arrangement of rocks brought in or taken out by the latest high tide. Today a river runs perpendicular to the beach and blocks me from walking the whole distance. I sit down and let the rhythm of the water speak to me. Ocean air, so fresh it doesn't yet know the difference between right and wrong, washes over me. The assignment rolls around in my head—an image of what I want the world to be. An obvious image is a dove, but obvious isn't good enough.

Just as I begin to jot down a few notes, a wave washes over my shoe, startling me. I scramble back away from the waves, astonished at how much I misjudged the reach of the sea. When I find another flat rock conservatively well back from the waves and my breathing returns to normal, I ponder how that happened. Then I watch the waves for at least fifteen minutes, and none of even approach that point where I was sitting. It seems a very personal and purposeful nudge.

One of the instructors said yesterday that life is made up of a series of exchanges. The ocean gave me a wet foot, now what will I give back? I watch while the ocean and the beach exchange rocks, little creatures and seaweed. Didn't my son Adam tell me that the tidal strand is one of the most richly diverse ecosystems? All these lives, some in the water, some on land and some in between, intricately connected and balanced, a microcosm of a world I would like to live in.

I sketch what I see and then run back to the Centre to set up the loom. Weaving two strands at once works well to get across the fuzziness and unevenness of the sand. As I stand back a little, it truly looks like sand. The sand is both on the beach and under the water, the rocks are both in and out of the water, and the shells and seaweed are between the rocks and lichen on the rock. Finally, the water is overlaid unevenly over the shoreline. I will use the same method to portray the quality of fuzziness and change, even for the rocks.

I work steadily until after dark. Most of the rest of the class pass by at one time or another during the day, but I barely notice. How different the walk is at night. The starkness of the region stands out. Feels like the moon.

The looms have been rearranged into a circle so that we can all see one another. There are no more formal lectures, and throughout the week we weave while talking quietly. Someone speaks, drawing a response of some sort, a nod or a yeah. The space feels sacred, almost like a church, but instead of a preacher, the sermon is formed and passed from busy hand to busy hand around the circle, the rhythm a subdued well-wishing to the present moment.

Long silences are the norm, though some of the most interesting exchanges of the month are happening. We speak of politics, community organizing, the environment, women's issues, family. The only rule is keep weaving, keep up the rhythm of the loom. Even our thoughts seemed shared while we breath in the same air and work together. Sometimes two people say something at once, and even those perhaps unintelligible remarks are left to stand. We work in parallel lines, yet, those lines do connect somewhere, just beyond.

On Monday at four o'clock, Colleen stands up and announces that we have one hour to complete this portion of the weaving. At five, when she calls time, no one makes a move to leave. She promises that it can only get better once the exchange has begun. "Move to the next seat in a moon-wise direction." Seeing confusion, she clarifies, laughingly, "It's actually counterclockwise, if you face north—rising in the east and setting in the west."

After we settle in, she says, "Now take a few deep breaths and look at what is on the loom, absorb it and place it squarely within your soul. Make a sketch if you need to, but memorize the colors, the images, the patterns; think of it before you go to sleep tonight. And perhaps a dream will come. From now on, work on these projects only while everyone is present. If you have other projects still outstanding, a few extra looms will be available, and the doors will remain open."

The image on the loom in front of me is that of a tree whose roots go through the earth and become the roots of a tree on the opposite side of the globe. The trees are a combination of green and orange, and the globe is a marbled green, blue and brown.

I am so absorbed in the weaving that I almost forget about Lucy's arrival. Realizing that she is due any moment, my stomach lurches with anticipation, and I head for home.

Luckily, she is not there when I arrive, and I sit in the living room, enjoying my last moments of solitude. As dusk claims the light in the room, try as I might to look elsewhere, my eyes are inexorably drawn to the tapestry that I hung in the living room on the blank wall next to the big window. This perspective of the world is so different from mine—this woman giving birth to the Holy Trinity. Imagine a woman that powerful and creative!

I now regret using Mary as the subject for the weaving. I should have chosen something which, if "lost," would have meant only a minor shift in the way I live my life. But this one involves my very religion, and my religion is my core. Before I came to Ireland, I would have told anyone who wanted to listen, that religion (and Ralph, of course) form the rock-solid piece of my identity, the sun around which I rotate. Now it seems there is no rock-solid center, and the orbits are stretched beyond knowing. Don't worry, I tell myself, I'm not going to do anything drastic; I'm just re-thinking a few things. I reach over and pick up the rock I found on the beach with Margaret. Its strength is reassuring.

When the air brakes of a bus sound, I run outside and across the street to see Lucy pushing up the lid to the luggage compartment. I look at her, startled, as if I have never seen her before. She is a large woman, big boned with broad shoulders—a strong-looking thirty-seven years old. At that moment, with her backpack slung over her shoulder, Lucy looks robust, as if she could have just stepped out of an epic Russian proletarian movie, as if she could walk right out into the fields and begin a day's long labor or take up a rifle and defend her revolution. Her long auburn curls are braided and wound around on the top of her head. She smiles wearily at me. I now see Lucy not so much as my daughter but as a grown woman in her own right, and I suddenly feel as if I know the bus driver who just dropped her off better than I know her.

Chapter 26—The Witness: Lucy

Few mothers and daughters know the savory details that shape each other's lives. There is so much posturing, protection and saving face on each side of the generational divide. Even when mothers and daughters are still alive, as with Lucy and Emma, this divide can seem insurmountable. What Lucy shares with her mother is meant to make her look good in her mother's eyes. And Emma? Well, we know that Emma didn't know much about her past until a few weeks ago. She kept up a front of sanity, well-being and cheerfulness for her kids. It's not that these things aren't true; they just aren't the whole truth.

October 26, 1996

My first glimpse of my mother tells me she has changed. She looks at ease, as if she is at home here. I could use some of that feeling of homeness myself. Even my home in Berkeley did not feel like home when I left there. Memories, heartbreak, regret, an abortion that Terry accompanied me to. How thoughtful that was, but it only made me miss her more in the end. I don't believe there is any way we can stay friends—it is just too hard. The only normal thing around my apartment was my cat Mancha. And now that I have abandoned him for this trip, he also may turn on me.

Who is this woman who claims to be my mother? Do we have any kind of relationship other than biological and historical? We have never spent any substantial time together, just the two of us. Even when I was interviewing her for my book, Dad would insinuate himself into the middle of it saying that Mom's memory was bad and that he remembered more about her past than she did. And darned if he wasn't sometimes right. Mom's memory for detail was practically non-existent; whether it was a deliberate letting go or a faulty memory, who could say? And when I was with them both together, she would stay in the background and let him tell the stories.

I don't know if I will tell Mom what I have just been through. The abortion was just three weeks ago. I knew I couldn't wait until after the trip to decide what to do because my mother would have tried to talk me out of it. I also couldn't postpone the decision because I want to be free to stay in Ireland for a while and write my novel. If I stayed too long, the window of opportunity would have slammed shut, my future smashed between sill and sash. Ireland, after all, is no place to seek out an abortion.

So I acted fast, maybe faster than I would have liked. It was the only time I have had to make that choice. Usually I am so careful.

If I tell my mother, she will be disappointed and perhaps even angry. She will want to counsel me, and I don't want that. I am tired of people projecting their feelings onto me. When I told friends about the upcoming abortion, the most common thing I heard was, "Oh, you must feel awful, poor thing." Well, the truth is, I didn't feel awful about the abortion; what I felt awful about was everyone's assumption about how I *should* feel. In truth, I was thankful that abortions are legal and I was scared about having surgery—that was a first for me. I worried about pain and anesthesia. The fetus was made up of cells that never bonded with one another, let alone with me; afterwards my primary feeling was one of relief that the surgery went gone off without a hitch, that those cells would never coalesce into an unwanted life.

Mom waves to the bus driver as if they are old friends and then grabs my duffel bag, while I pick up the other miscellaneous bags. The strap of my computer bag feels as if it has grown there across my chest. We make our way awkwardly across the street, behind the house and down into the apartment below.

"A paradise, just as you described!" I say casting my eyes about the place and gazing longingly out the kitchen window, so peaceful and orderly—everything my life has not been for a long time. I feel oddly adrift, outside the currents of my life.

I awaken from a nap to the surprising aromas of curry and ginger. Mom usually sticks to salt and pepper and maybe oregano. When I am cooking at her house and look for more exotic spices, she tells me they are at the back of the spice drawer. Then I find that the spice drawer sticks terribly and I have to really work to get to the spices, only to find that they have never even been opened.

As I enter the kitchen, I say, "My stomach's growling, so whatever the clock says, I say it's time to eat."

I sit down at the square table set for two with a couple of roses from the garden in a bottle in the middle.

Mom tells me about Brigid, the old woman she met on the plane. "I don't know if I dreamed Saint Brigid or if she was there and not assigned officially to the seat next to me. Maybe she was a stowaway."

I sigh, disappointed that my trip is starting out ordinary. "Nothing so exciting as that, no." Too bad, I think, I could use a sign that I'm on the right track. I don't understand why I got pregnant, why I am here in Ireland with my mother, what the bigger picture is. It seems distant from where I was headed before.

Mom continues, "She told me I would meet relatives in Connemara who are not on this plane—and about halfway into this stay, I finally got her meaning." She chuckles to herself and I don't know what she is referring to, though there were mysterious references in her letters.

I say, "You mentioned something in your letter about stories from your past? What's that all about?"

Mom shakes her head and says, "No, first tell me how Dad is."

I study my mother's face for clues. She has a tendency to hide her feelings under a cloak of casualness. I remember, growing up, that when she was most upset, Mom would whistle a cheery tune—so contradictory and confusing, especially to a kid. Anyway, I am relieved that she wants to talk about Dad. This is more like the mother I know.

"You just talked to him a few days ago, didn't you?" I ask.

"I did, but he'd never tell me if anything was wrong." Mom says. "How's Phyllis?"

I laugh loudly. It feels reassuring to laugh. "She's making the most of the situation. You should see Dad scurry around to get things for her. What a trip—so to speak!"

Over the years I've resented the time and energy Dad spent on Phyllis. I always feel sorry for her, but there is an underlying jealousy as well. It is almost as if Dad knows it and uses Phyllis against the rest of us. Frankly, while it amuses me to see Dad playing the nurturer to Phyllis, part of me longs to be the object of his care.

"But he seemed OK to you?" Mom asks, fishing for something that I can't quite read. I stare at her wondering it she has gained weight or gotten taller or something.

I slurp down soup. "This tastes great—I'd like the recipe. No, I think Dad's jealous you asked me to come and not him." Mom nods nonchalantly "I played up the fact that I'm writing this book, but still, he's not happy without you—you must know that."

Mom shrugs. "And are he and Phyllis getting along all right?"

I stretch my tired shoulders up towards my neck and then let them relax. "So it seems. Until the accident, she was living upstairs in my room. You know, her things were everywhere, and I had to make do with the boys' room. I wonder if she plans to stay there longterm. But she's the same old Phyllis. Nothing to report that I noticed. House is still standing.

Dad is still standing—that is, when he's not napping from being exhausted with the cooking, cleaning and waiting on Phyllis."

"Hmm," says Mom, "and to think I tried to save him from all of that ..." She pauses for a moment. "I'll make it all up to him somehow. Right now, I've got other things to worry about."

I can't imagine what she has to worry about, if not her family. But she lowers her voice, as if she is afraid of being overheard, and continues, "What I have to tell you will sound strange, but maybe once you've been in Ireland a while, it'll get easier. In a magical place like this, you just have to suspend your beliefs—something to do with all the wind and rain. Maybe you'll see after dinner."

But I am exhausted and can only think of bed. "After dinner, I want to crash, if you don't mind. My brain is all fuzzy, and there are gaping spaces between every cell in my body."

I am already up doing yoga the next morning as Mom tiptoes past my room and continues into the kitchen. As I interrupt her thoughts, she looks sad, almost bereft. Then she sees me and quickly shifts gears, brightening up.

"You got coffee?" I ask. "It's so dark and quiet here. I woke up just once, tried to look around, couldn't see anything and went back to sleep."

After breakfast, my mother leads me into the living room to see one of her weavings.

I sit and look up, noticing the weaving of the woman giving birth. "Whoa, Mom, did you weave this?" As I draw near it, I can feel its power. We are both quiet for a moment, listening to her message. Mom says nothing. But I am troubled by what it depicts: a woman giving birth. Just what I need to see, day after day, right now.

After my mother shows me the Crafts Centre, we cross the street to the beach. Looking out over the water, she says, "It's as if we're at the edge here, so far west. If the earth just hiccupped, we'd be over the edge. Our lives are out of our control, really. Look how close the edge of the world is. And who among us can control a hiccup?"

I don't know who this woman is. Has she been possessed? She has always been in control. Me, no, but mother, yes! Is she finally giving that up? That would be a good thing; after all, she has always been a control freak. But it's so out of character for my mother that I feel a foreboding in my bones.

Chapter 27—Storing Stories: Emma

After we die, what happens to our stories? Perhaps they form a golden spiral around the planet that can be brought to the living again and again through the wind and the rain. "That's the story of my life," you say, as if your stories are etched in stone. But if wind and rain could can reach out to Emma from the past and help her build a whole new sand castle of a life, surely we must recognize that our life stories have more in common with water and air than with stone. A swirling golden spiral of stories stored in the atmosphere around us.

October 27, 1996

This morning the strangest thing happens while I am making breakfast. Nothing. The weather is cold and dry, just as Alice predicted before she took off. The ocean looks flat and listless, almost dead.

As I fill the tea kettle, out of the corner of my eye, I keep seeing something at the window, but as soon as I look, I find nothing—less than nothing—a total stillness, a minus, where not even the normal seems to be happening: no grass rippling, no nonchalant swaying of leaves or branches twitching. It is eerie to be drawn to inactivity with such anticipation. Usually it is the bird flying or the branches scratching on the windows or Valerie putting clothes up on the line or even the sun passing under a dark cloud that draws my attention.

Never have I seen the water so tame. I think of dead, stagnant water but quickly remind myself of the cycles of time, the tides and the moon. Maybe it is time itself that passes by my window calling me. Time is like the tides—it does not stay in the past, present or future but mixes all three. The sands of time. I picture the hourglass dripping its sand through the thin piece of glass, but that image does not work because time does not only go one way. Better to picture the sand on the beach. And the tides... death is really only one of the phases of an ever-moving flux and flow.

Before Lucy came, I was anxious to have another witness, but I feel too shy to talk about the voices. They feel precious and young, as if a harsh word may injure them irretrievably. I avoid talking about anything of substance until I get my bearings around her. She looks different somehow, and sad. I realize with a start that I have no idea what her life has been like since she got her divorce from Kent. She doesn't tell me much.

Later in the day I leave Lucy to explore Spiddal while I return to the workshop. My thoughts about yesterday's class can't be put into words. I compare it to the spices in last night's soup. Voices arise out of the class, staying separate and distinct yet mingled with other voices. Nothing jarring or confrontational. Just talk, just ideas and feelings that are whole—no need to decide on a winner or a loser, no need to find out which is best.

I refresh my memory with the image on the loom, the shape of a tree, roots reaching through the earth. No dream image came to me about it and, now as I ponder, I decide to extend the branches of the trees until they come around to meet in the middle, forming a circle around the globe. I think whimsically, perhaps Hallie and Alice live inside that extra circle. I sketch golden rain and wind in the space, a tribute to Hallie and Alice. After a while, the rain looks to me like tombstones falling through the air.

Maybe I'm getting a little weird, but that doesn't stop me. When I stand back and look again, the rain reminds me of the tablets of the Ten Commandments. Later still, as I continue to weave, the objects shift from stone into a softer shape: lemon drops. Then, I begin at first to hum and then to sing very softly a song I used to sing with my kids, a meaningless ditty that they loved to sing over and over: *If all the raindrops were lemon drops and lollipops...I'd stand outside with my mouth open wide...*

I sing it repeatedly like a chant, and others join in when they get the words. Soon everyone is weaving to the lemon drop song. I feel about age six innocent, newly fascinated with the world.

When it is time to leave, one by one we go outside, where it has begun to rain. We turn our mouths skyward and sing and sing ourselves into a circle.

My plan at dinner is to get Lucy talking about her life, but I run into a stone wall. She answers with "yes" or "no" and does not elaborate. After dinner we go into the living room, and I try again by asking about her novel, *Strands*. Now she is animated and even chatty. She jumps up to get pictures she has brought with her. She lays them out on the coffee table, and I am swept back into the ghosts' stories. There is a picture of Charles looking so handsome with the dimple in his chin. I say, "Look at my father! I so wish I had gotten the chance to know him."

Lucy looks at me. "I know. What would your life, and mine for that matter, have been like if he had been in it?"

When she shows me Hallie and Charlotte on a front porch, the one I saw in one of the ghost stories, I blurt out, "Do you believe in ghosts?"

Lucy looks puzzled, "Well, I haven't seen any that I know of, but I wouldn't rule it out either. I just don't have any evidence."

"Well," I say tentatively, "I think I have some evidence for you, if you care to hear about it." I point at Hallie in the picture. "She, she came to talk to me." I rush on before Lucy can respond. I look at the fireplace behind her, the painting, the window—anywhere but directly into Lucy's eyes, and I begin to explain step by step how Hallie's voice came to me first through the boarded-up fireplace. When I finally look, Lucy's face is ashen, and she looks as if she is about to flee. I stop talking and go over to her and grab her hands.

I speak softly, trying to reassure her. "I know it's overwhelming to hear this. I can't imagine what I'd be thinking if I were in your shoes. Can you just trust me and not worry too much about the 'how'"?

Lucy takes a deep breath that sounds like one I would take in the middle of sobbing. It is ragged, like a series of short breaths within one breath. "OK," I say. "You stay right here and just keep breathing. I am getting us some blackberry cobbler. Just take a minute to breathe. There is no rush."

In the kitchen, I find I am shaking. This was much harder than I thought. Instead of bolting her cobbler as she usually would, Lucy eats it slowly and mechanically, almost like a robot. She says nothing but sits looking haunted. Well, I think, I'm the one who's haunted, and I went through it alone. After I take the dishes into the kitchen and return, she says, "OK, go ahead and tell me."

I start to tell her about the first story, but she doesn't seem to be listening.

"Lucy?" I say to get her wandering attention.

"Yeah, Mom, I'm listening. I'm just having a hard time grasping the changes in you." Lucy looks directly at me as if trying to see if I have lost my mind. I understand it must be hard for her to hear me talk so strangely. Well, think how hard it was for me to hear ghosts talking!

Suddenly irritated by Lucy's hesitance, I say, "Well, for heaven's sake, stop trying to grasp it. It's just what is. Take it or leave it."

"Why are you so mad at me?" Lucy asks.

I am impatient. Maybe because I'm used to being alone; maybe because I don't feel like explaining myself; or maybe because I can't.

"Just take my word for it for now, OK?" I say. "If you need to call the Center for Paranormal behavior and test the premises for ghosts or, better still, call the men in white coats, go ahead." I cross my wrists in front of me, pretending to be handcuffed.

Finally feeling contrite about my outburst, I continue gingerly, "Just listen to the stories and tell me what you think. That will be enough."

Remembering one of the last conversations I had with them, I say, "Lucy, they know about you and your project, and Hallie especially is grateful to you for doing it. Hallie even said that's why she could finally let go and die—that she knew you would tell the story."

Lucy's eyes light up as she hears this and then she says softly, "I didn't think she understood who I was and what I was doing. She showed so few signs of understanding… She did have some memory of the long distant past, but even that came out in dream sequences and images rather than linear stories. I knew I would be interpreting, not reporting."

"Yes, exactly," I say. "And she gave her OK for that, too. As she left the last time, she said you should make up what you don't know."

Lucy visibly relaxes, maybe because she was starting to see her relation to these stories. Then she quizzes me about what the voices sounded like and if I could summon them up at will.

I answer as honestly as I can, leaving the content of the stories for later. "Anyway," I continue matter-of-factly, "I've got the topics all written down and can tell you all the stories they told me. And, who knows, if I botch them up, one of them may be back to set it straight."

Lucy is sitting in my customary chair, the one facing the window and the wall hanging. I sit across from her with my feet curled up under me. I begin to tell the stories in whatever order they come back to me. Sometimes Lucy interrupts with burning questions that take us off the track or lead to another story. I tell as many details as I can remember.

Lucy listens intently to the story of the attempted rape. By the end, she is sitting with her head in her hands. She looks up bleakly. "I'm surprised that that story never came to light in my research. I can't imagine how horrible that must have been. I thought her move to Chicago to live with Helena was simply because she'd turned into such a pain at home... I had no idea what she'd been through."

I cock my head to the side, seeing it happen before my eyes again. "If you heard her tell it, you'd believe it," I say. "The strange thing was how proud she was of it. I think Alice resented Hallie's strength. It was as if Hallie were channeling the anger of women over the centuries who had been abused by men. It seemed a much older anger than fourteen years." I pause, thinking about that skinny little girl."

We muse about how she had been in such a vulnerable position, both in the stairwell and in the courts, but in both cases in a way she had triumphed.

"I'm going to have a glass of wine," announces Lucy, jumping out of her chair. "Do you want one?"

I nod absent-mindedly, unable to return from the stories too quickly. When Lucy brings in two glasses of red wine, I imagine that the wine is the color of that boy's blood. I roll the liquid around, looking into it as I might a crystal ball. "How do you live your life after that? A taste for blood, isn't that what people used to say?"

Lucy sets her wine down and paces the room excitedly. I cannot see any signs of the doubts she had a few hours ago. The stories seem to have won her over. Lucy says, "Detroit must have been abuzz with it. I imagine the men were terrified about what women might do once they started fighting back. And that's a good question even for today. What would happen if women started fighting back? And, what's more, why don't we?"

I recognize the militant Lucy as a Lucy I saw a lot of when she was growing up and learning of injustices. "Maybe we still don't see what they are doing to us," I reply, thinking of Alice's story of incest that I haven't yet digested or told Lucy.

"Yeah, and we still think it's our fault," says Lucy as she plops into her seat and takes a gulp of wine. "Incest, rape, brutality against women. Still it goes on without an uproar. Not so long ago, there was that incident in which a woman cut off her husband's penis. Now, she meant business. Not often you hear about a case like that."

I explain that Hallie's act was hailed as a victory by small groups of feminists, but quietly, because it threatened to besmirch all of feminism. Feminists had already been accused of being castrators and such. They did not need the Hallie Kaufmann story thrown in their faces when they defended the rights of women.

I shrug my shoulders, feeling the weight of the world there and, after a moment continue, "When Hallie was fourteen, she thought she should be treated like a hero, like the men in the books she'd been reading—a far cry from what really happened."

Lucy adds, "Men could go out, find the enemy, kill him and then be glorified for it. But here comes Hallie, having done the same thing, and people are appalled. It was a mythic act in some ways, but it brought shame instead of glory because she was a girl."

"From what I can gather," I say, "she was perpetually headed for disaster from the time she was a child. High drama followed her wherever she went."

Lucy's eyes are shining. "She was courageous, even a heroine."

In spite of myself, I dread hearing her say that. It brings up my fears built up over many years that Lucy or any of my children might follow in Hallie's footsteps. No matter how I try to shake it, the idea that Hallie's genes are in me and in my children is never far from my consciousness. "Well, I don't know about heroine. She had a miserable life, and we certainly wouldn't want to live like that, would we?"

I sigh, realizing I am avoiding telling Lucy Alice's secret. I brace myself, sip some wine, and retell the story about Alice's father and her nightly visits to his room and how she had kept it a secret long past her death.

Lucy's eyes have grown dull again as I finish the story. She looks depressed. We talk softly about the ramifications of that cruelty and wonder how many families have a similar secret.

"What was it like for her to hide that her whole life?" I shake my head in disgust.

We are both quiet for a minute, wondering if there is anything in our lives that we have deliberately kept a secret. Then Lucy says, "When Hallie's reaction was to fight back, Alice was beside herself in fear—fear that she should have stood up for herself against her father as well. If Alice believed Hallie was mentally ill, she could affirm her own sanity for keeping quiet."

Rain is pounding on the window now and it occurs to me that Alice might come back if we are wrong about this. I listen for her, but hearing nothing, say, "We're all like that, don't you think? We see others' lives as critiques of our own?

Lucy considers that idea for a moment, then says, "Yeah, it was almost as if Alice suffered her abuse as the price you pay for being a woman when men are in charge. And when Hallie chose a different path, she broke a code that women participated in and lived by. Creepy."

I think for a moment about my own life, my own need to do things the "right" way and how that parallels Alice's life. Alice tried to make up for her "sin" and I, her granddaughter, had conformed so that I wouldn't be abandoned. We both lived our lives at a distance from the here and now—the present leveraged to the past and the future, keeping one step ahead of the fear and one step behind the happiness.

My thoughts return to earlier that day in the workshop, when I stepped into the present and let myself go, not worrying about where I came from or where I was going. I was open and alive to the energy in the room and in myself. That small taste of freedom gives me some notion of what Hallie wanted to protect, some notion of what is possible to have and to lose.

"Tell another one," demands Lucy as she drains her wine glass.

But I am tired and go off to bed, promising the rest of the stories the next night.

The next day I leave Lucy to record the stories while I go to class. Yesterday class broke up before we moved to the next loom, so the image of two people, one brown, one white, shaking hands is a surprise. Because the people have no legs or feet, I set out to make footing for them—rocks with waters rushing around them. As I sketch, I remember the time Ralph was fitted for his first prosthesis when he was in his mid-forties. The doctors put off the amputation as long as possible because it was such a major and irreversible operation. They were so sure that he would be depressed by the loss of a foot that they delayed and delayed, adding years of suffering to his life. Maybe if they had gotten to know him, they would have realized that his desire to end the pain was greater than his desire to hold onto the part that ailed him. Once he had recovered from the operation and had his prosthetic foot, he was pain-free and so much happier, insisting that we take long walks and make up for lost time.

I remember the exact date that he was walking comfortably again because it was the first day of spring, 1966. That spring was the most vivid I can ever recall. Because of our twice daily walks around the neighborhood, I knew exactly which trees and flowers were budding, and which birds had returned from their Southern sojourn. Ralph's new foot helped us both step out into life again, after a long winter of darkness and pain.

I am again drawing that place between ocean and shore. I think about firm rock foundations with room for water between the rocks to make an exchange. We often focus so much on the solidity of our footing that we forget to leave room for the exchange. Make it solid, we think, and we will be invincible. But such solidity is only an illusion, not reflected in nature with its atoms swarming with empty space.

I have woven the ocean so many times now that it is almost second nature to pick out what colors and textures look best and how to get that wave effect. I like the water a steely blue with whitecaps. The ocean usually looks that way just after a storm, before the waves have settled into flatness. Feet are hard to draw, and these end up looking more like rocks with toes. It occurs to me that such an image is not bad—the people are then part of the landscape instead of separate from it.

Suddenly, I wonder what Ralph will think of this person I am becoming. Only a short time ago, I myself would have been embarrassed by a drawing of feet that didn't look like real feet. Ralph might even laugh at this rendition; it is so far from perfection. And yet, at this moment, it looks OK to me—so much more than literal feet on rocks. I realize with some dismay that my vision itself has shifted. For so many years, wherever we went, I have always known what Ralph would focus on, what would interest him; and I planned our trips accordingly. I thought we were close enough almost to read each other's minds. Will I lose the ability to see what Ralph sees? I can still picture it, but it is fading fast.

I can imagine that Ralph and I would have judged that the ratty and unkempt ruins of barns and sheds should be torn down as eyesores. Now I look with fondness at walls that stand crumbling, gradually returning to the landscape from which they came. Berries, grass and perhaps a tree grow up through the floor of the ruin and through what used to be a thatched roof. The ruins are simply embraced by the modern farm in whatever capacity, maybe as storage for old machinery or just to act as a windbreak. People here don't seem to view them as messy looking rubbish and have no need to tear them down.

"Yes, that may be true in some parts of our fine land," says my classmate Bett, "but in other parts it's 'tear it down and put up something useful!' I've even seen people take down perfectly good stone fences, I have, and replace them with ugly metal things—sticking out like sore thumbs with shiny nail polish right in the middle of the landscape."

I am taken aback, realizing my thoughts have been spoken out loud—either that or Bett was reading my mind.

Sarah continues in her proper British accent, "More like the middle finger, wouldn't you say?"

Delighted by the joke, others join in the conversation and the soft talk continues almost as if people are talking to their weavings, audible only if one listens hard enough.

Hypnotic sounds fill the air—sheds opening and shutting, shuttles moving through looms, back and forth, and muffled murmurs as we beat the weft sections into place.

Chapter 28—Projective Geometry: Lucy

Over-simplifying Euclidean geometry renders it irrelevant from the perspective of one who wants to see connections, since there is, in reality, no such thing as a point standing free. We are all intersections of lines, coming from somewhere, going somewhere. The past connected to the present and the future. Measurements of angles abstractly dangling in space strip us of movement, stop the flow, take the rug from beneath our journey.

We each see the world from our own little relative perspectives. The only way we connect is to project our perspective onto the world and allow others to do the same.

October 28, 1996

"It started out as the story of Hallie's life but has ended up being the story of mother/daughter relationships through the generations," I tell Colleen about my book project. Colleen and my mother came racing in the door a few minutes ago, dripping wet. Colleen offered to bring my mother home so she wouldn't get so wet and Mom invited her in for tea.

While Mom is in the kitchen preparing the tea, Colleen asked me about the novel my mother mentioned I was writing. It doesn't take much for me to get excited about it. I tell her, "When I first started interviewing Hallie for the book, maybe ten years ago now, she spoke in dream images. I wrote them down to decipher later. I imagine that she spoke that way because she'd had to keep her views a secret or get into trouble in the mental institution."

Colleen looks surprised. "Why would her views be trouble?"

I laugh saying, "Well, she was a radical and a feminist, and I'm sure she didn't get rewarded for espousing those views. Quite the opposite."

Colleen asks, "Do you remember any stories she told you?"

I think a moment, and remember one of my favorite Hallie stories. "One day I was helping her put a white bobby pin into her hair when she looked at me intently and said, 'Tell me, why do they keep giving me white bobby pins. My hair isn't white!' I looked at her pure white hair and asked her how old she was. Hallie replied, 'Why, I'm fifty-six.' I was shocked to hear that answer and asked how that could be when her daughter was sistey three. She looked me straight in the eye and replied in a firm voice, 'I only count the years I was in control of my life.' That was the most lucid thing I'd heard her say. She didn't inbclude the thirty-seven years she spent in Mannington Psychiatric Hospital!"

"I don't blame her," says Colleen, shaking her head in amazement. "Your grandmother was how old when she died?"

Mom walks in with the tea and answers before I can. "Ninety-nine, just about a month shy of one hundred. She was living in a nursing home near me. A fighter all right."

"She learned various ways to cope while she was there." I add. "She picked up some very peculiar habits. I have a lot of her scribblings from there, and much of it talks about the moon."

"That's interesting," says Colleen, leaning in toward me. "I am just finishing a book about ancient spirituality from the Siberian region of Russia where my ancestors are from. The spirituality is based on a worship of the elements. Or, not exactly worship, but a kind of acknowledgment that the elements of earth, air, water, fire—and they include a fifth one, space—are not just 'out there,' but are within us. In that cosmology, they believe that we should breathe in the moonlight and swallow it—that the moon's energy gives us the ability to flow freely. What was the term they used? Oh, effortless illumination. Yes, that was it."

Her comments send my mind into all sorts of places. Didn't Mom say that Hallie's ghost considered herself elemental? "Do you have a reference for this cosmology I could find somewhere?" I ask Colleen.

"I'll do you one better. I have a book on it in my car. I'll lend it to you if you want. I'm sorry to have to rush off, but I've got to go home before my kids get into a panic over my not being there." She puts on her brown, tattered coat, takes a deep breath and pushes her way into the weather with me running behind her to get the book.

When I return and settle back into the cozy living room, Mom says, "Colleen is about your age, I'd guess, Lucy, and she's got at least five kids. Can you imagine your life with five kids?"

I am appalled by that, especially considering how bright she is and how little time she must have to do anything but raise kids. I'll bet the reason she had the book in the car is that she grabs time out on the road whenever she can to read. I respond, "Absolutely not, not even with one kid."

"You've decided not to have any, then?" My mother asks, trying to sound casual. But I cringe visibly. Here it is, this territory into which we have not ventured for some time—like a restaurant where you got food poisoning on the last visit.

Usually when my mother and I get together, she finds a way to bring up the topic of my having children by hinting about clocks ticking or some such thing. I am relieved that it hasn't come up sooner, but now when she does mention it, I double over with a sudden pain in my abdomen.

My mother says, "Are you OK?"

"Just some gas pain, I guess," I answer. I don't want to fight over whether I am going to have children or not, not here when there are so many positive things happening. I bend over, looking at the zigzag pattern on the throw rug under my feet. I feel as if I constantly zigzag through a mine field with my mother, when it comes to this issue. The older I get, the harder it is to miss the mines.

Mom seems to want to have the last word. "I just hope you won't be lonely in your old age—or that you wake up one day when it's too late and regret your choice."

I sit up and establish eye contact with her. Then I say with as much certainty as I can muster, "I'm not planning to regret it." I hate this part of the discussion because there was no way to argue it. How could either of us look into the future and see one way or the other?

Emma mumbles almost under her breath, "I'm sure when you meet the right guy and get married, you'll change your mind."

I turn bright red, biting my tongue and trying hard not to lose it. So many damned assumptions!

My mother sees my fury. "I just can't imagine my life without you kids," she says, trying to establish eye contact with me. "I want to make sure you know how what you mean to me."

Finally, I look at her, tears welling up in my eyes, "I know, Mom, really I do."

Suddenly I have to get out of here. I say, "I'm going to take a short walk—don't worry, I'll try to stay dry. I'll be right back and we can fix dinner, OK?"

I walk up near the schoolyard across the street from the house. The wind has died down some, and it is just sprinkling a little. I pull my coat around my shoulders and brave what feels like nothing compared to the storm that was brewing where I came from. I try to get control of myself, not wanting to blurt out anything and ruin this trip or the relationship my mother and I are developing. If we could only learn about stories of the past and not have to deal with what is currently going on, I'd be much happier.

As the wind gusts, I feel my defensiveness rearing up again. I see a man walk by and think, no one runs up to him and tells him his clock is ticking. His wife is probably up at the house cooking dinner and trying to keep their eight kids from driving her totally bonkers. And he probably takes the long way home and stops in at the pub while he's at it.

Whenever I get into the argument about choosing not to have kids, difficult, strong feelings come up. Others, even my mother, assume, as they do for every woman of child-bearing years, that I want to have a child. They often pity me or assure me that there is still time. Abortion rights advocates talk about the rights of women to choose *when* to have children, but they rarely talk of the right to choose *whether* to have children at all.

One time, when I was about thirty, I was on a boat in the San Diego harbor during a court investigator's conference. The warm haze settled on the water with the sun in the blue above it, and time had slowed down. My friend and co-worker, Amy, who had mothered two boys, asked me if I planned to have children. Before I thought about it at all, I answered, "Oh, I've already done that." It was a strange thing to say, and yet it was how I felt. I have always made friends with people who are older than I am. My ex-husband Kent was eight years my senior and most all of my friends are at least that much older. In fact, I have always felt at home with folks my parents' age. Maybe that has something to do with the quick answer I gave—that I relate to many who have already had children. Or, I thought, maybe it was an answer from a previous life—not that I believe in reincarnation—but again, I'm not ruling it out—that or ghosts either.

As I consider the forces that acted on Alice, Hallie and Mom, I am convinced that they were not personal and couldn't possibly be changed by a single person. They were societal, a set-up causing a chain of action and reaction throughout the generations.

These ghost stories have brought up all sorts of unresolved issues for me. I wonder about my own purpose here on earth. Is it something other than reproduction? Might there not be an instinct just as strong as the maternal one that is aimed at something else, something creative and generative, but not reproductive? That instinct is what motivates me to create my books. I am prepared to believe in the maternal instinct even though I've never felt it, so why can't those who don't feel the creative instinct admit to its possibility?

The rain picks up again and though I've got nothing figured out, I go back.

We put aside our differences in the kitchen, working together on a vegetable stir fry. Mom comments on how I measure the water for the rice with my knuckle, just as she does. It seems to comfort her. The kitchen window steams up, and the raging storm outside disappears, except for the sound of wind.

Later, as we sip our after-dinner almond tea in the living room, Mom begins the story of Charlotte in the office of the women's suffragette movement and ends it with Hallie thinking that Char had deserted her and then Alice's confession of her complicity in that deceit.

At the end of the story, I feel as if my heart has been broken by Charlotte as well. Tears are streaming from my eyes, as I consider the waste of Hallie's precious life. To have your mother betray you so heartlessly…

I am so absorbed by the stories that I don't even question where they are coming from. They seem to flow as naturally as the blood in my veins. I don't want them to stop flowing until I've heard the whole depth and range of these stories I was evidently starving for.

Mom goes on, "Alice had been saved by marrying Henry and getting away from her father. And she wanted Hallie to see that her only protection, too, would be marriage—securing a protector, signing on as a team so she wouldn't have to suffer at the hands of just any man. She thought of marriage as the only way to be safe ... no room for Charlotte."

I can see what Alice was thinking. "Alice could only believe that for you to thrive, Mom, you needed to be raised by someone other than Hallie. I see now that she was trying to protect you!"

We look at each other, realizing the enormity of the mistakes and misperceptions that happen every day in this world of flawed humans.

Mom breaks the silence, saying, "What Hallie did wrong was to love the 'wrong' person. All this hysteria over that. Alice put homosexuality in the same depravity camp as incest and thought she was saving Hallie and me from a fate worse than death."

I look at my mother, perplexed and say, "You look weird. What's wrong?"

Emma makes a face. "I'm not sure how to ask you this—or if I really want to know the answer—but here goes. Are you a lesbian? Is that why you decided not to have kids?"

I look at Emma's face and see there an old innocence but also a willingness to know her daughter. I hesitate, and then say softly, "I am bisexual. Does that shock you?"

She slowly shakes her head. "Shocked after this month of surprises? No, not really." She pauses. "But I've been wondering about something else, too." Then, looking away from me and as offhanded as she can manage, she asks, "you don't think it's necessary for everyone to be bisexual, do you?"

I can't help but laugh loudly and across my mother's face flickers a look I interpret as a worry about disturbing Valerie and Sean, the landlords upstairs. I can see it come, and I see her let it go, knowing that this discussion that is too important to censor. I appreciate that and let down my guard.

I say, considerably quieted down, "I wish people would follow their hearts, you know? And not limit themselves to loving a certain type of person—the kind they were taught it was okay to love." I never knew if I would tell my mother these very personal things. "I was in love with a woman recently who broke my heart." My eyes fill with tears; I still can't talk about it without those damn tears.

Mom comes over, kneels beside me and puts her head on my thigh.

I continue, "Even though there is so much pain, I'm glad she came along. She taught me how to love women; and in some strange way, that taught me I could love myself."

I stroke Mom's hair gently and she says, her voice muffled by her position, "I wish I had learned that lesson at your age."

Now I am thinking out loud. "Whether I'm in love with a woman or not, I can always be in love with myself, the one partner that never leaves. Maybe I'll be the only one who doesn't leave me."

At some other moment in our relationship Mom might have said, "now honey, don't wallow in self-pity." But for now she is silent, maybe thinking of Ralph and how lucky they had been to have each other.

I tell Emma about Terry and the intense joy and intense pain she caused. I explain that I can't even consider another relationship at this point and don't know whether it would be with a man or a woman.

"Why is it that we have to legislate who to love?" I ask, feeling the magnitude of thirty-seven years. "If Hallie could have lived with the person she loved, all of this might be moot. Why was there no place for her but that horrible institution?"

My mother gets to her feet slowly, her joints cracking, and goes to turn on more lights as the intruding darkness has begun to feel uncomfortable. Then she settles again in the chair by the fireplace and looks again at the upside-down weaving. "At times, when Hallie spoke of Mannington, I would get this feeling that I should have done something to get her out of there. I had swallowed the story that she was crazy without much critical thought. I had the whole thing upside down as I'm beginning to think I have done with a lot of things."

My heart goes out to her. "But, Mom, you were just a kid when it all started. You had no way of knowing what the real situation was."

She says quickly, "Yeah, I've told myself that, but at some point

I did grow up. By then, the thought of her in that place just scared me. I distanced myself from her as much as I could. I didn't see her as a fellow woman, one who may have been wronged. It's not until this trip that I have been able to see the context of her life, learn who she was and develop a modicum of understanding of her."

"Hold on a sec, I have some letters with me that she wrote in the institution," I say as I run to my room to retrieve them. As I kneel on the floor by the coffee table and spread them out, I say, "I have letters she wrote that I presume never got mailed—letters to the local newspapers pleading her case, informing them that her daughter had been taken away, that she had done nothing wrong. See, look at this one. They seem to be drafts, but the actual letters probably ended up in the same place as her letters to Charlotte—the garbage heap at Mannington. That's exactly where Hallie ended up as well..." I pause, thinking about how many people who don't conform, or in the alternative, conform themselves into oblivion, and end up in that garbage heap.

I look up at my mother's face as she tries to decipher one of the letters. It is strong and surprisingly serene. I say, "You know I visited Mannington as part of my research when I was in Detroit interviewing Danny last year—remember?"

"You went there?" Mom's face drains of color.

I run my fingers through my unruly hair and look away from her. "It was traumatic, so I didn't think you'd want to hear about it. Do you now?"

Emma shakes her head back and forth slowly, "Listen, by now, if I didn't want to know about what happened I'd have had to go deaf, and even then I think those ghosts would've signed their stories for me. Don't feel you need to spare me."

Yes, I feel her strength and decide it is time to quit sparing her the truth. "Well, the place is still standing—old medieval-looking place. Do you know there were three thousand people in there at one time when Hallie was there? Only a small portion of it is now being used as an outpatient clinic, and the rest is boarded up. The screens that go all the way to the ceiling on the porches were still intact. I pried off a board on a ground floor window and went in. I swear I could still hear screaming. But I thought if she could be there as long as she was, I could stand one moment of it."

Mom gets up and stares out the dark window at the rain as it puddles and pools its way down the window. "I was there a couple of times, you know, once when I was about ten."

"That place must have been mighty scary for a ten-year-old."

Mom nods, still staring out the window into nothing.

Again I look at her, wondering if I should go on. "Do you really want to hear this?" I ask as she turns around to face me, a resigned look on her face.

"Yes," she says, "Yes, it is time I heard it."

"Well, this part is actually fascinating. I interviewed Alan David, Hallie's attorney and Charles's good friend. I had found his name on some of the legal papers she had in her stuff. I called ahead and made the appointment but I'm sure he wasn't clear who I was. Mr. David was ninety-five years old and had only just stopped going to his office in downtown Detroit the year before. He was still practicing law from his home. His mind was very alert, but this blast from the past would have been a bit much for anyone. He stood there and stared at me for the longest time until it sank in that I was the granddaughter of his good friend who had died seventy years before. I had the same problem thinking about him as my grandfather's best friend. He had lost track of Hallie soon after Charles' death and never saw their baby.

"I wanted him to tell me honestly the Hallie he had known but he was too polite to say a bad word about her. Just said they had differences and he ended up getting off of the case against the truck company in the wrongful death suit. I'm sure she treated him wickedly, more as an enemy than a friend. Too much of a gentleman to say so, even after all of these years. But you could see he remembered Charles very well and had a great fondness for him."

Mom sighs wistfully, "I sure wish he had stuck around long enough for me to get to know him instead of just listen to stories about how great he was."

Mom continues, "Look, I'm starting to feel me age, can't keep my eyes open any longer." She heads down the hallway, calling back to me, "You're the one who's got to keep a distance on this story. Remember, you're the writer."

After she leaves, I switch chairs and sit looking at the Woman Giving Birth weaving and reflect back on the stories. I don't know if I believe any of this ghost-talking is true, but hearing these things from my mother gives me answers I have been seeking—why I came to Ireland, maybe even why I got pregnant. I feel an intense energy run through me. This time I do not feel too small to contain it. This time I feel myself expanding to meet it.

It's a metaphor, this birth thing—a metaphor that we have wrongly taken literally. It's about a life force that can create a new world.

I get up from the chair, straighten myself up tall and go to bed, hoping that voices from the dead will not include the voice of the fetus I aborted. That is one voice I could do without. Ridiculous, I tell myself, there weren't enough cells strung together to make a voice. Any voice I hear will be my own.

My room feels slightly chilly, and I am thankful I brought along my silk long underwear for nighttime. As I get ready for bed, I consider my mother and her amazing changes. If the stories weren't so powerful and seemingly true, I would think she had completely lost her mind.

Yesterday, unnoticed by the group, I was a witness to my mother leading the group of weavers out of the workshop and into the rain singing the Lemon Drop song. I came back early because of the rain and was huddled in a doorway across the courtyard from the group. When they finally broke up and went their separate ways, I saw that Emma was crying, smiling and laughing all at the same time. Her face was almost unrecognizable; her wrinkles gone, the stresses in her face, gone. This, though very strange, does not look like mental illness to me.

I pick up the book Colleen brought over. "We are all made of stardust from the original Big Bang. All that exists, ever existed and will exist in this universe is made of those same elements." I stare out at the stars, wondering where Hallie and Alice are now.

I can't sleep with the weight of the stories immobilizing me. The idea of Mannington as a garbage heap for humans reminds me of a bleak poem I wrote when I first started writing *Strands*, a poem about my paternal grandmother Marie. Marie bore six children and all but one of them, Ralph, died before she did. Before I wrote that poem, I had given little thought to my paternal grandmother and was not conscious that she was so sad; but somewhere inside me, I knew all too well.

I go to the computer and find *The Crow* and print it out on the portable printer I brought with me. There it is, I think—those last lines: "From atop the garbage can reeking of dead women."

I wonder how many women end up in the garbage? It isn't so much about motherhood per se, as the position we put mothers into—no support or help, no status or recognition. I wonder about the stories no one bothered to ask Grandmother Marie about, the ones stored in the back rooms of the person she had once been.

I sit at the computer in a state of not knowing, staring out the window, the only light a glow from the computer. Assumptions and judgments I made about motives, deceit, betrayal in my family are all held in abeyance now. They can no longer thrive in this place of uncertainty as story behind story reveals itself. In that eerie, shadow-casting light, I imagine I can see the invisible outside—as if it has come alive. I listen carefully for the sounds of the invisible, thinking that perhaps Hallie or Alice will visit me tonight. I am as receptive as a sea cave, taking whatever flows in and enveloping it with appreciation.

Though I do not hear Hallie or Alice, I do hear something, perhaps it is the elements themselves, urging me to write. The words pour out onto the screen. This is not just a story of Alice, Hallie, and Emma; it is the story of women. I don't question what is coming out. I simply type until my eyes can no longer focus on the screen.

Chapter 29—Dream Mail: Emma

Dream mail comes to us every night, and many of us rip up those night letters without ever reading them. Lucy had come to see them as vital messengers. The women in Lucy's weekly dream group knew one another's psyches on a level deeper than any other friendships. There is no place to hide in a dream group. Lucy was so used to "working" on dreams, she felt fluent in dream language—a mix of emotions, words, puns, images and story. One of the "rules" in her dream group was to say honestly what images or thoughts a dream evoked, not just in the dreamer but in the others as well, censoring nothing. In a mysterious way, the group drew on a larger consciousness, one that the dreamer alone could not access.

October 29, 1996

"Looks as if you slept in that hair, Lucy," I say smiling, as Lucy stumbles into the kitchen.

Lucy feels her head and pats it a bit where it is sticking up. "I'll brush it in a minute..." Her voice trails off.

"Mom," Lucy says, "I had a dream—I just remembered it."

As I reach out and smooth Lucy's wild hair, I wish I could take back all my comments last night about her having kids. I knew it would upset her, but I just can't seem to stop myself from bringing it up. I remember stroking Lucy's hair like this when she woke up in the middle of the night with a terror dream, something that happened regularly until she hit puberty. "Tell me about it, sweetie," I say, picturing sitting on the side of little Lucy's bed as Lucy tightly hugged her Raggedy Anne doll.

I'm in an auditorium sitting next to Mary Eunice, a woman with long dark shiny hair. Someone had shot this woman through the heart. Surely she is dead, I think, but a man comes over and gives her a bottle of Irish whiskey saying it will stop the bleeding. The woman drinks it and then I help her to the library, which is where she wants to write two letters: one to her father and the other to her daughter. I offer to write the one to her daughter if she will dictate it. She agrees, and the letters are written and ready to send. Later I go into the hospital and Mary Eunice is there. When I ask how she is, a nurse answers, "She had extensive damage to her heart and surrounding tissue." She begins to cry and says, "She won't live to be one hundred and ten."

"It's really weird but I just keep thinking of the Virgin Mary."

I jump at the strangeness of this remark. I put down my jellied toast, which is inches from my mouth, and ask, "Why on earth would you say that?"

"I don't know. It's something to do with the straight dark hair—that's the way she's often pictured—and then her name: Mary. And then Eunice which reminds me of 'eunuch.' Mary Eunuch (virgin). I don't know. Somehow that's what comes to mind.

"And then yesterday we talked about Hallie almost making it to 100. And the drink from Ireland kept her alive long enough to write her letters... One to her father (could that be God?), and one to her daughter? Who would the Virgin Mary's daughter be? We sure never heard of her!"

I shake my head, marveling, "I haven't even told you what's gone on around that subject since I got here. And yet you dream of her. Remember the tapestry that you liked so much, the one in the other room? When you're done with your coffee, I'll tell you the story."

Lucy quickly gulps the rest of her coffee. "Oh, I'm done. Tell it."

We move into the living room where we can see the hanging, and I explain the tapestry's origin, Pilar's and my disagreement, and our subsequent dialogue.

Lucy looks astonished. "Sure took guts, I mean, to argue with a Catholic over the Virgin Mary. Where are you getting all of this chutzpah?"

I just laugh, "Oh, and now you're going to bring the Jews into it. Next it'll be the Muslims!"

"Yeah, all the patriarchal ones. They can all share the blame." Lucy goes into the kitchen to get more coffee and when she returns says, "Speaking of patriarchy—have you told Dad any of this? The weaving stuff or the stories from the dead?"

I roll my eyes. "Not yet, it's hard to explain long distance. And I haven't sorted it out myself."

Looking out the window, Lucy notices the islands and asks me what they are.

"That's the Aran Islands. Margaret says we must find time to visit there."

At lunch, I talk to Margaret about what's been on my mind: Lucy's choice not to have kids. Margaret advises me not to pressure her. But what I want is for Margaret to help me find a way to change Lucy's mind. "I feel as if now that I've gotten my history and my stories straight, I to want to see the thing continue—see how it all turns out."

"I understand the feeling," says Margaret excitedly pulling her soda bread into little pieces. "It's like reading a novel only to find out the final pages have been ripped out and you're left without an ending. I certainly feel that way about wanting to see my grandkids grow up." She stirs her soup, looking pensive. She continues, "But then, I guess whenever we pass on, there will always be unfinished pages."

"Well, luckily, I already have some grandkids to watch grow up," I say, but there is something compelling to me about my daughter having kids. I want to see what they will be like—how Lucy will be as a mother. It's hard to talk to Lucy now because I am speaking my truth much easier than I used to; it isn't always what she wants to hear.

Margaret is quiet for a minute and then says, "It's hard to speak the truth in the present when you know so little of your past. There's a part of me that thinks I'm a fraud when I act as if I know anything, even in the weaving class. It's something to do with the erasure that occurred at the very beginning of my life. I wish I could fill it in with something the way you have." Margaret rests her right elbow on the table, looking dejected.

I reach over and take Margaret's left hand and then say, "It's never too late, you know. I mean you're only a few years older than me."

Suddenly, I feel as if I am going to pass out. Margaret says, "Damned if you don't look as if you've seen a ghost! You're pale as a sheep."

I sit there for a moment thinking about that phrase, "looks like you've seen a ghost." I hadn't seen them, but I had heard them clear as day and it took me this long to realize that those ghosts were *my* family.

I speak almost to myself saying reverently "Sometimes the stories seem to be just stories, from a movie or a novel. " I nod my head repeatedly. "But these visitors from the dead weren't strangers. They <u>belong</u> to me."

Margaret looks across the table at me sympathetically, then whispers, "I asked my mother to sing. She begins, and my grandmother joins her." Margaret pauses. "Did you ever hear that? It's the first two lines of one of my favorite poems by a poet named Lee Young Lee."

I repeat the lines to myself and make them my own. "Maybe that's what's happening. Lucy's writing the book, so she asked me to sing; I began, and my mother and her mother joined us."

When I return home after class, anxious to talk with Lucy about my conversation with Margaret, I am surprised to find Lucy gone and no note. Thinking I might find a clue as to Lucy's whereabouts in her room, I begin searching there.

As is her habit, Lucy, even in such a short time, has taken up all the space in the room, clothes draped over every chair, papers scattered in piles here and there. I have never been a fastidious person, but I keep my house reasonably clean and tidy, no matter how busy I am. I hoped Lucy would outgrow her cluttering tendencies, but looking around the room now, I see that has not happened, at least not yet.

Though Lucy and I have been getting along fairly well this trip, with the exception of the baby issue, I feel as though Lucy is holding something back. Glancing furtively around the room, I look for clues. Without thinking, I pick up a piece of paper at the top of one of Lucy's piles. It is the poem entitled "The Crow" that Lucy printed out the night before. I am immediately drawn into it. I read:

THE CROW
for Grandmother Marie

The birds won't stop screeching
Remember, remember

I remember Marie

I don't like being told to remember. What I forget, I forget for a reason. I hate to go back and dredge up dank days gone by, especially when others expect so many things from me in the present. Now, though, the poem forces me to recall my mother-in-law. Marie lived for her children—wanted their lives to be perfect. After Ralph and his sister left home, Marie stayed involved in their lives and expected regular visits. Still, the "empty nest" must have been hard on her, and I often wondered what kept her going. I know I spent years proving myself worthy of Marie's only living son. I read on:

The black crow at her house
After her death,
Refusing to leave, knowing, knowing
Staring into my bedroom
Mocking my attempts at sleep

This reminds me of a bird I saw at the beach. Maybe it looked directly at me as I imagined. I remember that Lucy went to her grandmother's house after she died and stayed there cleaning up the place and readying it for renters. Had she really encountered the crow, imagined, like me, that it singled her out? I rarely read poetry. How is one to know if it is true or not? At least with fiction, one assumes the prose is made-up and with nonfiction, that it is as true as it can be. But is poetry like fiction or nonfiction? Is the "I" the poet or some made-up entity?

Love killed her
turned her against herself
Unable to squeeze another drop
Of help, of worrying

Old, futile, fragile inability
To do more.

"Old, futile, fragile inability to do more." I read the line over several times. Ancient, I think, maybe even going back to Mary and before. She couldn't save her son and she couldn't save the world, and yet the impetus to try was there. And it isn't an inability to do more for herself—it is always in regard to others, to her children. We are never even told what became of Mary after Jesus died, what it must have been like for her to see her son killed in such a horrific manner.

That "inability" is in a lot of mothers I know—limited, human women asked to be everyday superhumans, to protect their offspring against all odds. It has never been fair.

The screen porch screams
Of nostalgia, depression
and aphasia

The screen porch, which is now mine and Ralph's, is where we take our meals in the summertime, amid the trees, a little paradise into which ever-present ultra-soprano mosquitoes could not intrude. I remember helping Marie carry the meals out there, as I often do now. I can still taste the real maple syrup they dripped over their pancakes, no matter how limited their income. Grandpa loved his maple syrup, and Grandma knew that no imitation syrup would do.

In the morning I am afraid
I take off her leeches, one more time

Discard them down the sink.

Leeches, what is she talking about, leeches? The kids acquired some actual leeches when they played in the river that burbled along at the bottom of the steep hill on which the porch was perched. But Marie never played, never explored the woods or the river. No, she's not talking literally.

The crow is still there
Its caw makes me lurch

She who gave her arms and legs
Her womb, her blood
Her turkey dinners

Drooping apron barely
able to cover loose breasts

She cannot speak as the crow
Cannot be remembered

I cannot remember her.

With her false teeth
and false selflessness

And yet you do, Lucy, you do remember her. The turkey dinners, the apron, the false teeth. The clean house. I look around Lucy's room with a new appreciation. Lucy does not fit into one dimension, sliding neatly into any old box. She overflows them. But what of Marie? I don't know what she wanted or loved, other than her husband and children. She served. Was there ever anything else?

She gave all of us her life
"I give you my purple heart.
Take a bite, take the whole plum.
Stuff it in your mouth.
Slurp the last juices running down your chin.

Do you want it now?"

Too much squeezing of entrails
The last iron breath of a strong woman
Who would do nothing for herself.

Crow makes me murderous
Witnessing the crucifixion
Doing nothing but gawking
From atop the garbage can
Reeking of dead women.

The intensity of the last stanzas shocks me, especially the part of about the crucifixion. I never thought about anyone being crucified but Jesus. Now Lucy is using it to describe her grandmother and all women? I shake my head to banish that vile image from my mind. But in spite of myself, I picture the hill on which Jesus was crucified, fleetingly imagining that it was formed by the haphazard layering of the bodies of women sacrificed for the cause.

If she feels like this, it's no wonder she doesn't want to be a mother.

Chapter 30—Science: Lucy

When did you become so "scientific" that you ruled out mystery and synchronicity as only for the gullible? Have you ever noticed how someone will come into your life just at the right moment to teach you something you need to know? Even when it feels like a negative experience, it can turn out to be, in retrospect, a sound lesson from the universe. Or maybe the Grandmothers?

October 29, 1996

While Emma lunches with Margaret, I work again on the "story." It has some of the features that I learned about through Emma and the ghosts, but it is universal, more like a myth that explains the origin of gender dynamics. I haven't dared question what is happening or where it is coming from for fear it will disappear. I just keep writing.

The story is becoming uncomfortable for me because a new character has shown up. Luz's life resembles my own. I am a bit frightened about what might happen, as if the writing is a kind of prediction of my own future. I'm not certain that I want to see into my future.

I walk up to Spiddal to pick up a few things for dinner. The sky transforms itself each moment, as fluid as a river but without the banks to limit it. As usual, a view of the ocean and the sky puts my troubles in perspective, shrinking them into more manageable packages.

About a block before the grocery store, I pass by the taxi office and notice a woman of about sixty, sitting in a rocking chair with her feet up on the window sill reading a book called *Blue Highways: A Journey into America* by William Least Heat Moon. The woman is evidently killing time, waiting for the next call. A wind chime made of small dancing spirals of what looks like coral catches my eye. I poke my head in the door to ask the woman where she got it.

She shrugs her shoulders and cocks her head. "It's the owner's," she says. "I just work here. I'm Connie." She flashes me a mischievous smile and motions for me to come in and talk.

She seems anything but conventional with her short curly gray hair almost completely covered by a baseball cap worn backwards.

As we are talking, the woman hands me a glass of Guinness beer, raises her own glass of tomato juice, and says, "To Ireland, land of the Bloody Virgin Mary."

I raise my eyebrows thinking that she must have heard my mother's and my conversation. I raise my glass, just as the last foam separates from the pure brown below.

"You got a problem with the Virgin Mary or is it Ireland you want to insult?" I ask.

"I'd say it's virgins in general, starting with the original one. And that reminds me, I always thought original sin was a good thing—the more original the better. How 'bout you?"

"I'm all for originality," I say, unsure of where this was going.

"What are you, some kind of artist?" the woman asks, squinting as if she could see my creativity if her eyes were just good enough.

"A writer, yeah," I reply smiling. "How'd you guess?"

"I guess you'd be famous then, huh?" Connie asks, sitting up straighter in her rocking chair.

"I would be, but if you don't know me then maybe not," I respond in a flirting tone. This woman is really attractive in a rebellious way. Of course, I have always been attracted to rebellion, especially rebellion against gender roles.

"What do you write, romance novels? I'm likely to have missed your stuff, then."

"Well, romance in a very broad sense."

"I don't get it."

"Well, romance in the sense of love of life—yes that's it, a romance with life. How'd you like to get in a romance with life itself?"

"Tell me how and I'm there," she says looking excited as if such a thing had never occurred to her before.

I straighten up to look authoritative. "Okay, you tell me a problem in your life, and I'll tell you how to romance it."

Connie glances up at the ceiling for a moment and then begins, "I've got six brothers living within spitting distance of this town. My mother's ill and I'm the one who takes care of her. My sibs all have more pressing matters, supposedly. My kids are grown and gone, and no sooner had they left when my parents started to fall ill. First me dad—he died about three years ago—and now me mam. My brothers figured since I had no kids around, looked as if I had nothing better to do than take care of her. It's OK but depressing, since we never did get along. And it's my nature to be a traveler, a nomad, but do you think I ever get the chance? Love to go to America and ride the blue highways—that is, if those least traveled roads are still there. Yeah, I get about as far away as Galway and back on a good day. And that's more traveling than at my last job. No, I'm grounded and have been since I was born. Don't tell me I have to romance my mam. I won't do it!"

"No, no, it's not like that. Now tell me something you like."

"All right. I like swimming in the ocean by myself when no one else dares to go in—did that today."

I am impressed. It makes me shiver just to think of it. I am improvising, "Now picture yourself swimming there and get the feeling of it strong within you. Go home with that energy surrounding you, and anytime you see or think of one of your brothers or deal with your mother, imagine the spaciousness of swimming in the ocean."

"That really works?"

"I have no idea, I just made it up. But it might..." We both laugh. "I have a penchant for dispensing advice that seems to come out of nowhere. But I have learned to trust it; I have seen it work out more times than not. In fact, if I have a strong urge to say something to someone and don't, that omission bothers me far more than any negative reactions I might receive by going ahead and speaking. Still, I have to be careful, especially when people tell me their dreams. I will often get a very strong urge to jump in and say something that crosses some uncharted boundaries."

Suddenly serious, Connie stares out the window at the ocean and then points to the huge boulders lining the road rocks and exclaims, "See those rocks? That storm we had last weekend brought them up onto the road. She just picked them up and bounced them right down."

I gasp. "Did they shut the road down?"

"No, not this time. There was still a way to get through. One year the water came up like that—took a car with it on the way back. Nobody knew it 'til they found the car and driver washed up down the beach a ways." She takes a deep breath and sighs. "But not this year, not yet, anyway."

Connie lives just up the street, and when her replacement comes into the office and she is off-duty, she invites me to come up to her house for another Guinness. I accept. We munch on tortilla chips and salsa while I tell Connie about California and all the places I have visited around the world. Connie eats the stories for dinner but her hunger only grows larger.

PART FIVE

SELVEDGE

Selvedge: A woven edge on a fabric made of the strands of the fabric and designed to keep it from fraying.

Chapter 31—Every Being was Once our Mother

Women who become mothers have as little in common as any other group of people. They are the selfish and selfless; the humorous and humorless; the young and middle-aged; the fat and thin; the happy and sad; the chosen and forced; not to mention all those in between, a cacophony of warring values, motivations, goals, ideals, thrown off-stage into the orchestra pit of life.

Why, then, do you think you know what a mother is, what she should do, what is good enough? Did these women lay down their instruments when they became instruments of delivery, or maybe they are still blowing away and you just can't hear them, huddled together below your line of vision, sound-blocked, your attention focused on the man-made production on stage. Or perhaps your ears have been trained through the centuries to be deaf to the sounds of women? Listen hard. Can you hear the high shrill whines of mothers calling for the cessation of violence or for food for the children? Or is it just the wind?

October 29, 1996

Around 7:00 Lucy ran breathlessly into the kitchen with Connie at her heels. When Lucy was through with her second beer, it had suddenly occurred to her that Emma may be worried that she had been gone so long. Connie offered to drive Lucy home in her salt-eaten blue pickup truck.

But Emma wasn't worried. She was sitting at the small writing desk in the living room, munching on mixed roasted nuts and writing a letter to Ralph. Each time she wrote to Ralph, she dropped hints about what had been going on with her, but she censored more than she wrote. She ended up throwing away drafts and sending letters that skimmed the surface.

Emma heard Lucy enter and twirled around in her chair just in time to see traipsing into her own living room an almost mythical creature, a fish out of water—the woman in the green bathing suit.

Lucy introduced Connie to Emma who was tongue-tied. How does one greet a character out of a fairy tale?

Emma said, "Please sit down," and she indicated the empty chair next to the fireplace, Emma's customary spot.

Connie sat down and glanced at the weaving of the woman giving birth across the room. Suddenly uncomfortable, she looked away and toward Emma, who had sat back down in the swivel chair to her right and said, "Oh, I know you—I met you on the beach one day. You didn't want to swim."

Emma said, hedging, " I wanted to, I just didn't have your nerve."

Lucy sat in the rocking chair by the window and continued the conversation she and Connie had been having about Copper Canyon in Mexico. Lucy knew Emma and Ralph had taken that trip a few years before. Emma, though at first reticent, was soon excited, describing their experiences: the gorges they could see from the train, the hairpin turns the train took and the Tarahumara Indians. "We started the trip on the Day of the Dead and saw pilgrimages of people all dressed up walking to the cemeteries carrying flowers and gifts." Emma paused. "Are you Catholic?" she asked Connie.

Connie laughed, "Might as well ask if the Pope is. You don't find much else around here."

Emma, feeling playful, grabbed a red candle out of its holder and held it up to Connie's mouth, interviewer style, saying, "So tell me, as a Catholic, what do you think of the Virgin Mary. Was she merely a vessel without divinity or was she divine in her own right?"

Emma's voice carried an undercurrent. On the surface, she was just being funny but not far beneath was a real desire for an answer. Connie looked perplexed and felt as if all of a sudden she were on the hot seat. "I can't answer that as a Catholic but only as Constance O'Riley, who happens to be Catholic."

Emma backed off and sat down, sighing deeply. "Good enough, then—it's all I could hope for."

"OK, then, personally speaking, I'd say she was always divine."

"If that's so," Lucy added, "then couldn't you say that we all have that divinity, not just Mary—that she represents the divinity in us all?"

Connie shrugged. "Can't say I think all that much about the Virgin Mary." She paused, her eyes following her hands as they slowly smoothed nonexistent wrinkles in her jeans. "But, now that you mention it, I was thinking about her the other day, thinking that it was a lucky thing abortion wasn't an option for Mary because she would have been a prime candidate—what with all the speculation about the father and her marital status at the time of conception."

Ordinarily Connie wouldn't have brought up the subject of abortion when she didn't know her companions' opinions, but this seemed a safe way to do it. After all, who would be pro-choice in the case of Mary?

But she realized her mistake when Emma continued the conversation. "I suppose, being the good Catholic that you are, you oppose abortion..." said Emma.

Connie sidestepped the question. "I certainly wouldn't have wanted Mary to have one—I mean, would you? I can't say as I see two sides to that issue. Kill Jesus; don't kill Jesus. Which one sounds right to you?"

At the mention of the word "abortion," Lucy's face paled. The subject had come up so suddenly, without warning—lightening without thunder, a police car with no siren, sneaking up. Powerless to change the subject in this seemingly cosmic play, she mumbled that she was cold, went into the bedroom to get her sweater and stayed there for a few minutes, breathing deeply. When she returned, Emma was holding up the argument for choice. "I say, if you don't like abortion, don't have one."

Connie's face looked blotchy and full of righteousness; Emma seemed to be enjoying the fight.

"That's easy for you to say, but I bet you've never had one," said Connie. "How do you know you could do it? It's easy to talk about women in general, but have you ever even known anyone who had one?"

Lucy threw herself down on the couch and, in the slight pause between the two sides, between the in breath and the out breath, one wave and the next, she quietly said, "She does know someone—you both do." Lucy went from cold to hot in less than five seconds. She could feel a blush extending beyond her face to her whole body. She felt exposed, inside out in the middle of a searing spotlight.

The room, noisy with argument a minute ago, had suddenly gone stone dead. The wind gusted behind the fireplace, sounding like God breathing. Connie froze, not knowing what to say. She felt as if she were being watched.

Emma looked stricken as she put two and two together and came up with minus one. All their theoretical arguments had melted down to Lucy who was lying on the couch, confessing it to them.

Both Connie and Emma would rather have stayed in the abstract, giving their hypothetical arguments. When it came to her own daughter, Emma felt only deep disappointment, the wasted possibility of a grandchild. Connie liked to think that no one she admired would ever do such a thing—or maybe more to the point, admit to it.

Lucy turned to face the back of the couch so she could think. She couldn't understand why it was so hard to admit to this action, which she believed in without qualification. This was why abortion rights aren't carved in stone, she thought. Women are still ashamed of it.

At that moment, her own body was ashamed of it. Gradually Lucy regained her resolve, turned to face them, and sat up. Before either of the others could recover, Lucy went on. "I'm sorry. I didn't mean for it to come out like that." She paused, running her fingers through her hair, resisting the urge to pull it out handful by handful. "You know what, though? Why should it seem shameful? It's not illegal or immoral but I'm helping to make it that way if I treat it as top secret, all hush-hush." She sat up straight, thinking how the right-wing ideologues win when women continue to feel shame, regret and disappointment about abortion.

Connie fidgeted, listening to the wind in the fireplace and wondering what her priest would say about her being friends with someone like Lucy, someone who not only had had an abortion, but did it without remorse. Debate was one thing; confession another.

Finally, Connie broke the silence, hesitantly. "Are you saying you don't regret it?"

Lucy wasn't sure she wanted to discuss it now that she had lobbed it into the room, especially in front of such a hostile audience. But she responded, "Right, I don't."

Emma walked over to the window and stared at the growing darkness, wondering what Hallie and Alice would have to say. It wasn't hard to imagine. Hallie would applaud; Alice would be outraged. And what about her own thoughts, she who had always been a supporter of a woman's right to choose? So many thoughts. She felt like an airport at Thanksgiving, going every which way. Emma knew that this decision was not about timing, about family planning, but about never having children at all, ever. It felt so final—no space there for an accidental, serendipitous life to worm its way into her heart. The image from Lucy's poem, a garbage can reeking of dead women, came to her mind. Was the choice between a garbage can of dead women or one of dead fetuses? What kind of choice was that?

She silently asked Lucy, you have so much to give to a child. How can you end it all here? It's so unresolved, don't you see? Why did Alice and Hallie go through all that they did?

Aloud she said, "About the father? Are you in love with him?

Lucy's bitter laugh sounded more like a cry. "It was some primal thing in a waterfall. I hardly know the man, though he wishes we would at least date. I just can't do it at the moment with my heart so broken."

Emma said gently, "Were you ever going to tell me?"

Lucy walked over to the window and stood beside Emma. Her

voice was muffled, as if she needed most of her breath for something other than talking. "I planned to, yes." She paused for a moment. "But I didn't want to blurt it out like that."

"We could have managed together. You wouldn't have to be alone," Emma said, taking Lucy's hand.

Lucy pulled away and sat back down on the couch. "I want to do more than just manage. I decided not to sacrifice myself for some uncertain future." Her shame had turned to anger, and it showed in her red face and bright eyes. "What if we all stopped convincing ourselves that managing is good enough, quit adjusting and took some power over our lives? What would happen then?"

Connie's eyes flashed with recognition. She closed her eyes for a moment to re-orient her spinning mind. Then she said, with her voice shaking, "'Tis what I have done... manage." She looked suddenly very old, the lines in her face etched there by a thousand things she'd done from duty and dried out from all the unexplored dreams. "I've been able to manage for nigh on sixty years... and I'm still moaning and groaning. My whole life is about moaning and groaning."

Connie looked thoughtful. Her breathing began to even out as she walked over to the bowl of mixed nuts on the coffee table, knelt down and, taking her time, deliberately picked out seven cashews. In silence, she was performing some kind of ritual. She rolled them around in her hands and then ate them slowly, one by one while she thought about curled fetuses, smiles and frowns, duty and fulfillment, dolphins diving—about half-circles and half-lives, her life.

Finally, she said, looking down at the ground, head bowed, "I feel as if you two have fast-forwarded me somewhere I have resisted going, couldn't face." She got up and stood in the middle of the room looking back and forth between them. "It's not so much about abortion as about making a bold choice, taking some initiative, not just letting life happen and sitting there and taking it. I'm sixty bloody years old. Why am I sitting around in a taxi office? I'm done waiting. Hold on, have you got a match?

Emma went into the kitchen, retrieved a box of matches and handed them to Connie. She lit the two tea candles that rested in rock holders on the coffee table. "I say, let's bring it into the light, take it full circle—anything but go on making do!"

Emma and Connie had completely switched positions.

Lucy sighed, kneeled next to Connie in front of what had become a small altar and said, "You, at least, swim in the cold ocean all by yourself—bravely staying alive. That's what I want to do—change a pattern of fear that we repeat over and over again generation after generation. Emma knelt down with the others, and they formed a half-circle in front of the altar. They took a deep breath together, feeling the rise of their shoulders and the rise of the others, seeing the flames flicker.

Then Lucy said prayerfully, "All we have is now. Isn't that enough?"

They stayed a silent tableau for several minutes and then Emma, unable to stay in this position for too long, broke the circle and got up and returned to her chair.

The conversation had reminded Emma of Lucy's poem, and she said, breaking the silence, "Lucy, I have something to confess as well. I read your poem about your grandmother. It seems that might have some bearing here."

"Oh, yes, something about the ancestors' stories made me print that out last night. I'm relieved you read it. I've not shared it with anyone else yet."

"Would you read it for us, Lucy?" Connie asked as she resumed her chair by the fireplace. "I'd love to hear it."

While Lucy went to get the poem, Emma said softly to Connie, "I'm not sure what is happening here, but I feel like whatever it is, is working itself out. None of us need apologize for who we are."

"Non-apology accepted!" said Connie. "I know what to do now. It's just like Lucy told me earlier—I have to see myself swimming in the ocean as I'm doing everything. Life is about swimming in the ocean, feeling the aliveness and smarting of the endless cold water here and now!

Lucy returned and handed the poem to Emma, who switched on the lamp on the desk and read it out loud. When Emma came to the part about "the last iron breath of a strong woman who would do nothing for herself," Lucy began to cry—that part always got to her. Lucy's crying made the other two cry as well. Emma had never been able to see Lucy cry without starting herself.

Who could say what they were each crying about? Their tears were not just for themselves, but for all of their women ancestors who carried burdens beyond imagining. For such was the responsibility of being the carrier of life—the power to endlessly replicate and the power to stop.

Live and let live was a great motto, but who could figure out when to do which? Sometimes just living means something dies. And sometimes letting live strangles you.

Chapter 32—Desire

Prior to belonging must come longing—longing being one's own deepest internal desires; and belonging implying more of an external or social thing, belonging to some group. Maybe longing comes from long ago, something you are born with. For so long, Emma had lived her life making sure she belonged somewhere—with the Parkers, in her church, in her community, in her marriage. For her the two things—longing and belonging—had become merged. She longed only to belong. Lately, though, she was experiencing something outside of belonging that seemed to fall more into a prior category: a primordial longing. Her desires were now arising from an entirely different source.

October 30, 1996

Emma awoke the next morning from a dream in which a horse had fallen into a well, only it wasn't totally immersed and she could still see it. She had tried in vain to figure out how to help the horse. Then a woman beside her simply reached out a hand and helped it up.

In the long shadows of early morning, Emma and Lucy walked up one of the roads that wound into the hills, where the only form of life seemed to be cows. They watched for a while as a large light-brown calf sucked on its mother's teat.

Rain began to pelt them and they sheltered in the doorway of an old abandoned shed. After the rain stopped, they ran into a fellow walker who said, "Beautiful day, isn't it?" They nodded, puzzled, wondering how it could be considered a beautiful day after the downpour they had just encountered. "Beautiful moment is more like it," Emma said after the man had gone. "With weather this changeable, how can a person judge the whole day, based on a moment in time?"

"Or judge a whole life from a few bad episodes?" added Lucy, thinking of the stories Emma had told her.

After Emma left for her last class, Lucy felt brave enough to finish the story she had started. Perhaps it had to do with telling Emma about the abortion, but she felt stronger, more sure of herself. She turned on her computer and closed her eyes, listening to the drip, drip, drip of the slow rain outside. After a while, she read over what she had already written, and then the words began to flow again. When she finished the piece, she let it be unknown how she might use it. It read like a myth, outside of time. She set it on the table near the window. Feeling a little stiff, she stretched her back and suddenly noticed that the papers were fluttering about. They didn't blow off the table, but seemed merely to be ruffled gently, almost stroked by the wind.

Lucy halfway expected to see a grade on them, but instead she saw the vaguest outline of a full circle, not quite perfect, maybe more of an ellipse, that looked like a cross between a burn and a water spot from an egg-shaped glass. She looked out the window and bowed to whatever teachers were out there... or in here for that matter, she thought, as she concentrated on her breath.

At lunch, that day, knowing that they might not have many more chances, Emma and Margaret exchanged addresses and telephone numbers and vowed to visit each other one day. Emma told her to bring Stella, too—that she'd love the Midwest.

Margaret asked skeptically, "Could your husband deal with the two of us, though?"

Emma responded without thinking, "Oh, sure, he'd be fine—he's very adjustable." She hesitated and then continued, "Of course. To be honest, I don't even know what he's going to think of me when I return. I feel very different. Know what I mean?"

Watching Emma slurp her soup, Margaret said, "The only thing that hasn't changed about you is that you still order the same potato leek soup." She laughed.

Emma replied, "I know. It's as if the inside and the outside are coordinated; I don't censor ideas, they just come out. The other day in class I was talking out loud when I thought I was thinking to myself. I'm going to shock a lot of people if I keep that up. " She paused, then added tentatively, "I wish I knew what happened to me here. What if it disappears?"

Margaret corrected her. "You mean if *you* disappear again, right? The 'you' that's been in hiding, the 'you' who's afraid of being abandoned—so afraid that she'll barter her whole self away to avoid it?" Emma nodded, and Margaret said with assurance, "That 'you' is always there."

Emma wondered how changed she was. And suddenly, without thinking, she blurted out, "Do you think after all this figuring I'm going to have to become a lesbian and leave Ralph?"

"Good God!" exclaimed Margaret loudly, looking around to see who might have been within earshot. "Where the holy hell did you get that idea—from Lucy?"

Emma didn't seem to care who heard her, "Not directly. But she told me she is a bisexual, and she keeps talking about women's passion. Anyway, last night I dreamed that a horse fell into a well and a woman beside me helped it out while I stood not knowing what to do. I think it's a dream about desire. Horses represent sexual feelings, don't they?"

Margaret cocked her head, her bangs bouncing a little with the motion, and replied, "I don't know that much about dreams. It matters what the dreamer thinks, though."

Emma folded her arms across her breasts, as if she had it all figured out. "I think it means that I have a hidden desire, and I need another woman's help to get it out of the unconscious."

Margaret raised her eyebrows, considering it. "Could be, but ... it doesn't follow that you're a lesbian. The woman who helped you could be anyone—Lucy or me or one of the other people in the class. It might even be your mother. And if it does have to do with sexual feelings, it could be about your own sexuality."

Emma put down her spoon and looked Margaret directly in the eyes. "I don't want to stand apart anymore—do you know what I mean?"

Margaret looked puzzled so Emma continued. "I want to live without worrying about what others will think. I want a combination of dealer and dealt. I've proven over and over that I can play whatever hand is dealt. I'm great at that, but from now on, I want a hand in the dealing, too. Open to surprise, showing my tail feathers as I go. Being myself. Getting rid of the middle man."

Margaret was not following. "Who is this middle man?"

"I don't know, it's not like I've thought of it before this moment. I guess it's the voice in my head that's always judging, telling me what's appropriate and what's not, the one who censors me before I can even be me. I want directness."

Emma reached over and took Margaret's hand. "So when I do this, I am not thinking about what you or the rest of the restaurant thinks of me, but I am present to touching you and to how I feel—which happens to be an unqualified fondness, gratitude and happiness that I had a chance to know you."

Margaret's eyes are intense and sparkling. "I think this has something to do with the twilight when we were at the beach with the Birthing Woman! I don't know how you're doing it, but you seem to be living what we felt there."

Emma's thoughts were everywhere at once, back in the 1800s with Alice and Hallie and now and into the future. She began speaking in a kind of stream of consciousness. "How is arousal possible with so many lines drawn of don't go here, don't go there? Arousal like what we felt that evening on the beach. I felt it, then became afraid and stopped myself. What am I afraid of? Life without the middle man? I'll take it. I'm leaving the middle man right here in this restaurant."

Emma looked down at her hands, turning her wedding ring around and around. "If you want to know the truth, I've been wanting to be with Ralph." Then she blushed and stuttered out, "You know, sexually?"

Margaret nodded knowingly. "I'm homesick myself—for Stella. I know it's been hard on her, too."

Emma sighed. "It's as if I'm more awake. Every time I look at that Birthing Woman weaving, I think that life is about openness."

"I hate to say this but it keeps pushing at me to say so you take it or leave it." Margaret takes a deep drink of water. "Maybe God is the middle man. Like I said on the beach, we humans are embodied divinity."

Emma gulped. Could God have been in the way all this time? She hardly thought that could be. "It's a radical idea, but I'll surely take it home and live with it for a while."

Margaret relaxed visibly and smiled. That controversial statement had not been easy to make because it could have ruined everything. She was heartened that Emma took it for what it was, an idea that may or may not have validity.

"It's been a miraculous trip for you, Emma, and I hope to heaven you find you're more in touch with yourself sexually and otherwise when you return. And I have been going through a few changes of my own—as I see it, I've been riding the coattails of your journey."

Emma said, "You've done some fine weavings as well." Knowing that Margaret wasn't leaving until Monday, Emma said, "You could continue to come along on the journey if you want. Lucy and I plan to go to the Aran Islands tomorrow. My cousin Diana is coming, too. In fact, come for dinner and stay overnight, so we can leave first thing in the morning. Yes, we're having a dinner-party sleep over!"

Margaret said she'd love to come and then added, laughing, "Monastery ruins—that ought to put the horse right back into the well."

Chapter 33—Make Believe

Fiction often tells you more than "just the facts, ma'am"; and make-believe can be a path to finding one's truth. Humans make believe every day that you are the same today as you were yesterday and that your dream trips don't take you to real places, so they don't count to the writers of non-fiction who are penning your autobiographies. Try substituting "make believe" for believe in your everyday life. I make believe in God. I make believe that the sun will rise tomorrow and that I can predict and control my life. If you make your own beliefs, maybe you could try making believe that you are not in control of your universe and also that all will be as it should be. How's that for fiction?

October 30, 1996

Before the party planned for the end of class, Pilar and Emma pulled two chairs over into the corner of the damp, slightly chilly, and soon-to-be-abandoned workshop area, placing their two weavings on the floor in front of them to decide their future homes.

Pilar sighed, equivocating, and Emma said, "If I took this one," she pointed with her toe to the woman giving birth, "I'd shock my husband, Ralph, right out of his Lazy Boy."

Picking up the tapestry and running her hands over it, Pilar said, "Maybe knocking Ralph out of his chair is just what you need, yes?"

Then she picked up the other weaving. Staring at it she said, "This empty cross feels like the end—yes, the end of suffering—not what the cross represents, I suppose." She pondered it a moment. "Or is it? Gives me the feeling that the green hills are enough." She sighed and then continued, "Well. now, the more I look at it—no wait, it's looking at me, yes—it looks like a flying turtle—you can see it? I like that. Its name is Soaring Turtle."

Suddenly alarmed, Emma cried out, "No! That would mean that both tapestries turned out non-Christian."

"This one," Pilar said calmly, as she lifted up the weaving of the woman giving birth, "is very religious—it's a creation myth and, after all, the Christian Trinity is still born."

Pilar took her seriously, shaking her head decisively and handing the weaving to Emma. "Look at it! It prioritizes the Mother but it's a psalm. Both of these are."

Emma fidgeted with tying a tight finishing knot on a loose end in the piece and got a strange look in her eyes. It was a familiar feeling from not that long ago in her life. Yes, now she remembered. It was after the birthday party. "It reminds me of when my kids took a photograph of me for my seventieth birthday. We hung it up high in the living room. But there was no comparable picture of Ralph. It felt unbalanced, unfair."

"Perhaps, well...you just could not see the weight on the other side. When something is very powerful, it doesn't need a picture, yes? Maybe your children, they tried to balance what is already out of balance—that's what I tried to weave."

When she pictured the living room now, Emma could still see Ralph tipped out of his chair. Something was shifting; she just wasn't sure what it was.

"Then for all those reasons, you have her—Birthing Woman." Pilar said as she reached over and patted the tapestry gently as if it were itself a baby. Then she leaned over and took Emma's puzzled face into her wiry, warm hands and, looking softly into her eyes, said, "Te amas, Emma. Love yourself, that's enough."

This gesture touched Emma so deeply that before she could stop herself, she was sobbing. It felt catastrophic like an earthquake or a volcano erupting, and she had just as much warning and just as much recourse. Pilar hugged her and let her cry. These were not her usual casual tears. This grief came from a place in her so young there were no words, so interior that every cell in her shook, until she felt she would disintegrate, collapse in on herself.

The rest of the class heard her and at first were at a loss. After her sobs began to subside, they formed a circle with Pilar and Emma as a part of it and hummed in harmonious tones, at first very softly. When Emma let go of Pilar, she was uncertain how long she had been sobbing. As she looked around, she felt as if she were in a womb surrounded by nurturance and peacefulness. Her body had never felt so relaxed. She tentatively joined in the humming, shifting notes, the sound of spirits merging and separating, merging and separating. Her sounds were coming from some deeper register, lower, she felt, than her soprano voice had ever sung before. When the sounds finally died into silence, the circle moved in closer and arms were flung over shoulders and around waists and the circle was complete. Emma, breaking the circle, remembered a gesture of gratitude she had seen Lucy perform. She put her palms together in front of her and began making eye contact with every person in the circle, bowing her head to them. The gesture spread around the circle.

The feeling of peace and relief stayed with Emma.

When Colleen asked them to find the last tapestry they had started and claim it, Emma saw that the subsequent weavers had followed her lead on her weaving, staying within the space between ocean and land, incorporating lovely, animated details that vibrated with life. Alone, she never could have woven anything quite like this with its changes in texture and color. She wouldn't have imagined it could look like this. But it was whole and perfect. Everyone began milling about looking at all the other weavings and remembering how it was when they worked on it. It was like birthing a child, being separated from it and then years later, seeing how that child turned out.

It was clear from everyone's reluctance to leave the party that this little band of former-strangers had woven themselves together inextricably. As impending darkness etched itself into their realities, they began one by one to leave the Centre.

Emma made her way to the beach and sat on her favorite rock, now well-uncovered since the tide was out. Connie was just getting out of the water not too far from where Emma sat. They laughed to see each other so soon and ran to each other and hugged like old friends. Emma got a wet streak up the front of her, but that was as close to the water as she was going to get that day. Emma, on a whim, invited Connie to come to dinner, and to stay over and go to the Aran Islands the next day. Connie shook her head and said, "It's starting already. My life is no longer predictable! I'll go home and change and be right over. Can I bring anything?"

Emma shrugged. "I don't even know what we are having so if it's not too much trouble, bring some bread."

After Connie left, Emma sat in stillness for a few more minutes, knowing that she had invited people for dinner without a clue what she would feed them.

Emma brought herself back to the present moment in which the sun was setting and the moon rising. The clouds could not be spoken of in one breath. They were at once a fierce and threatening dark gray and a benign white, fringed with a pinkish-orange glow as they mingled their way across her line of vision. She looked west, toward the Aran Islands, dipping her foot in the waters of return, and wondered what Ralph and Phyllis were doing right then, if they thought of her. Hard to believe her sinking sun was their afternoon sun. It didn't seem possible one sun could be in so many places at once.

Chapter 34—Madness

What is madness? Was Hallie mad as so many asserted? Is it mad to follow your heart, to desire something you are not supposed to want? The normal curve that Emma had been so fond of had a context, a location in space. Isn't it possible that the entire curve is in the territory of madness and that what is normal for humans in the twentieth and twenty first centuries is the maddest thing of all?

October 30, 1996

Delicious aromas greeted Emma as she entered the apartment. Lucy had prepared an elegant meal to celebrate her graduation. Every burner on the stove, as well as the oven, were on, dirty dishes scattered everywhere. Acorn squash was baking, and Lucy was whipping a sauce using tofu and sun-dried tomatoes. There was wild rice and, of course, Irish potatoes. Lucy had splurged on two bottles of French wine to accompany the meal. Her face was sweating and oily from the heat.

Emma broke it to her gently that she had invited two more people to dinner, saying she'd pitch in so they could stretch everything to accommodate the extra mouths.

"Have a seat in the living room for now, Mom. Ill bring you a glass of our finest French wine and some fried zucchini swirls. You know me, I always cook way more than we need, so we will probably be fine. Maybe the guests are bringing a little something?"

Bringing in the wine, Lucy added, "Consider it a reward for your outright bravery in the face of talking ghosts. And, of course, for finishing your weavings."

Emma still had a hard time receiving, especially from her daughter. "You must have spent a lot of writing time making this feast."

Emma sat in the rocking chair near the window, and Lucy dragged over a footstool for her to put up her feet on.

"There rest yourself," she said. "I only started cooking after I finished an interesting piece and documented the stories, too. I'll have plenty of time to do the serious writing when you are gone."

Emma said, "Feels good to put my feet up. I'm relieved that class is over, but also sad. I've gotten quite comfortable with these folk. Like yesterday, the strangest thing happened, and it just seemed normal to me. The first hour went by in silence, and then a humming started. Most of the time, there was no easily discernible melody, but once in a while someone took center stage and a melody and harmony emerged. At one point, the humming became the repetitive chant-like song of "She changes everything she touches and everything she touches changes. Over and over we chanted: change and touch, touch and change."

Taking a sip of wine and visibly relaxing, Emma said, "Maybe touching something does change it?"

Lucy nodded pensively. "Even history seems to keep changing—at least my idea of it. The more I know about Hallie and Alice, the more the past and present seem to change."

Until recently, Lucy didn't imagine that Emma's stories mattered. Everything around her, in school, on TV and even in fairy tales told her mothers were important to keep their children fed and clothed—but their stories? No, for a long while she didn't even wonder if Emma had stories.

Emma sniffed the air. "Is that squash burning?"

Lucy dashed into the kitchen, saying over her shoulder, "Doing too many things at once…"

Emma followed Lucy into the kitchen. "Oh, by the way," said Lucy, "I talked to Valerie's husband today, Sean. Is that his name? He offered to take us to the ferry since otherwise we'd be going into Galway, only to turn around and come right back by here."

Emma went upstairs to arrange details with Sean and Valerie, asking if he could accommodate five of them. Sean said it would be a squeeze, but they could do it. Emma remembered to ask what she had wanted to know for along time: "What does 'Spiddal' mean in English?"

Valerie smiled, remembering the conversation with her cousin Padraig to line up Emma's stay with her. She remembered that Emma had used the Irish name for the town. "Oh, it is a word that changed over time, that An Spiddeal. This place used to have a hospital—in Irish 'Ospideal.' Somehow the O was dropped and it became Spiddeal or Spiddal. We have no hospital anymore, as you can see."

"It is a place, then, of healing," said Emma, speaking the last part on the in-breath, keeping some of the healing for herself.

When she returned to her apartment, candles were burning and the electric lights were low. "Just to make it special," said Lucy, glowing with heat and pride.

"The squash is gorgeous, as the Irish would say," Emma said.

Lucy said, laughing, "You'll be talking like a regular Irishwoman soon. They won't know how to take you back home."

Emma frowned. "I'm not thinking of back home yet, if you don't mind. I don't want to waste a minute of my time here with you worrying about 'back there.'"

Emma nodded her head west toward the Aran Islands. "Speaking of predicting the future, they say the ferries go in most all kinds of weather, but not gale force winds... I can't tell you how many times since I've been here, there have been warnings for gale force winds. I thought maybe it was just Alice, letting it all come out!" She refilled her wineglass and reclined a little in her chair.

Lucy listened to Emma while she began the clean-up of the kitchen and put on some more rice.

Emma was feeling proud of herself for having done as well as she did through all of this strangeness here in Ireland. She slid off her shoes and wiggled her toes sensuously. "I think this all started with seeing Diana." she said loudly, so Lucy could hear her. "She loosened me up, made me feel young again, as if we were adolescent sisters. That reminds me—she should be getting here soon. She was leaving Dublin around four. We should wait dinner on her. Well, actually I don't know when the rest of the crowd is getting here either. Good thing you made appetizers."

Before long, both Connie and Margaret arrived with their hands full of 'little things' to make the meal stretch. Connie just happened to have made Irish soda bread the day before and Margaret stopped at the little store to pick up cheese and crackers and two bottles of wine. Lucy ushered them into the living room and brought in a tray of appetizers and the cheese.

"This should keep you busy for a while, and here are wine glasses for you, too." Connie, usually strictly a beer drinker, decided to go with the flow and drink wine.

A little leery of the sounds coming from behind the fireplace and still thrown by the woman-giving-birth weaving, Connie sat on the couch this time. By eight o'clock, Diana had still not arrived, so they decided to go ahead with dinner. They filled up their plates in the kitchen and came out to living room to eat. Both Connie and Margaret sat on the couch, and it was intriguing to watch them interact. Margaret was a creature Connie was unaccustomed to—an out lesbian and agnostic. And yet, they seemed quite compatible. Connie was pumping Margaret on what New Zealand was like, and before long Margaret was telling the tale as she knew it of her first journey on a ship from Ireland to New Zealand.

"You never had a chance to know who your parents were, then?" asked Connie.

Margaret replied, "No, never could never find out a thing and was raised in an orphanage. Could have been my mother was crazy, too, to get onboard such a ship so far along in her pregnancy ..."

"Crazy or desperate, I'd guess," said Connie. "If she got pregnant outside of marriage, her choices were few, especially if she wanted to keep you, and it seems she did."

Margaret continued, "It's always been a bit disorienting to have absolutely no family anywhere that I know of. You know, you have to be circumspect about what you do. No one is obligated, as it were, to ride to your defense if you get yourself into trouble."

Connie nodded her head, but said. "Yes, but on the flip side, you don't have to spend your life riding to everyone else's defense like I have. Family's got its pros and cons, and so much depends on your role in it—taker or receiver."

"Dealer or dealt," said Emma wistfully, dovetailing on Connie's remark. "For my seventieth birthday, my kids put together two photographs of me posed in wicker chair: one picture was at age six, the other, age seventy. There was something about seeing them juxtaposed that made me wonder what happened to that six-year-old? She seemed to have dealt me a hand that I have played ever since. From those cards, I created a self based on fear and security. She was the 'dealer' and that made me—ever since then—the dealt. I am just now getting around to undoing that deal and uncovering the original cards I came in with.

"And have you done that?" Connie asked.

Emma laughed. "That and a whole lot more than I bargained for, but I'm sure we'll get into that tonight or tomorrow. I will tell my story to you all, but I want to wait for Diana to get here."

Just as they finished eating the varied and colorful food that Lucy had prepared, Diana knocked at the door and then burst in, stumbled through the kitchen and before realizing that there was a crowd in the other room, said, "Hey, where are you, ladies?" She glanced around at the darkness and finally made out that there were candles in the living room and that Emma and Lucy and two others were there. She acted as if she came on people sitting in candlelight all of the time. "Is the electricity out? I brought my torch."

Lucy and Emma scrambled to turn on the lights for her and help her with her things. She continued, "Oh, man, this place is hard to find in the dark. I know I've been here before, but for some asinine reason, I thought it was closer to Spiddal. I've been up and down this road like a nut."

Diana had been fighting with herself all the way to Spiddal. Last time with Emma, old wounds had been opened, not to mention new ones inflicted. This time it wouldn't just be Emma, but another member of the family, and she second-guessed suspiciously where the weekend might go.

They made quick introductions and apologized for surprising her with extra people. "But," Emma said, "I just couldn't stop myself from inviting them. And I know we'll all get along splendidly."

Diana was a little taken aback by the crowd, but realized that now she could hide more easily. They pulled out the swivel desk chair for her to sit on. Since the chair was on wheels, she had to be careful how she sat in it so that it did not take off flying. Once she got herself stabilized, she looked back and forth among them, noticing that they seemed melted at the edges and flushed; she was fleetingly reminded of how people look after they've had good sex. She also noticed the almost empty wine bottle on the coffee table. Her impulse was to want a piece of whatever it was that they had.

"Wine or tea or orange juice?" Emma asked Diana. Diana, surprised that Emma offered her wine, agreed to a small glass of wine and a plate of "whatever it is that smells so good." When they were all settled again, Diana looked at Emma and said, "What happened to you, Lady? You look like you've been put through the wringer and had all the kinks ironed out. Why, you're ten years younger than when I last saw you. If weaving can do that to a person, I'm buying a loom tomorrow!"

Lucy turned the electric lights back off. The candlelit room set a mood of mystery. With only the candles to light the living room, they could see the stars outside.

Emma took another sip of wine and said, "It's a long story, but now that you're here, I can tell it. Before I do, though …" She shook her head a little as if to clear it. "I've got to show you all something that I've been keeping to myself until this moment but feel compelled to share."

She took out the rock she had found on the beach near Galway and whispered, "Look, isn't it sensuous? I've heard of what they call mamillia, spots on the ocean floor, shaped like breasts and so smooth, but I've never heard of a portable stone that had similar qualities—not the breast but the whole torso. Look at those curves, the way the veins mark the surface. It has a soft ridge like a back—what they would call Arainn or Aran, like the islands we're going to visit. And there is something about the ginger color... I found it on a beach near Galway."

Lucy reached out for it, and Emma gently and a little reluctantly handed it to her. Its cool smoothness on her hands reminded Lucy of the feel of her own body. As she rubbed the rock, its coolness warmed up.

Lucy smiled slyly, coveting the rock but knowing she couldn't ask

Emma for it. "Can you find one for me?"

"Don't know if I'll ever find another one, certainly not one this good." Emma had already decided that even if she had to throw out the keys to her own house, she would take this rock home with her. Fact was, perhaps anywhere the rock was, *was* home.

As they passed the rock around the room reverently, Emma kept a watchful eye on it. She wasn't sure she wanted to share it, but she had felt generous—at least momentarily. Each woman sighed when she received it and passed it on only reluctantly. When it returned to Emma, she took the rock and it seemed to curl like a kitten in her lap.

Then Emma said contritely, "Even if you asked me very nicely for it, I wouldn't give it up. I'll will it to you, Lucy, but while I'm alive, it's mine. Feels to me," she continued timidly, "like my own self without all the rough edges. Funny how something so solid could give me the feeling of liquids, of water, but that's how it was shaped surely, by the constant stroking of waves. And I have to say, since none of you has, that it feels sexual to me." She took one more sip of wine and said, "In fact, gals, I get aroused when I stroke it. Is that too strange?"

Lucy quickly said, "I felt it, too, I didn't want to embarrass you. But..."

Margaret said, "Did you find this when we were at the beach?"

Emma nodded somewhat guiltily, since she hadn't shared it at the time.

Margaret continued, "Just to catch up the rest of you, we experienced some kind of mystical moment of the divine feminine, at least that's what I would say. The boundaries between human and ocean and sky melted, and we were part of some kind of birthing. That's what it felt like. Maybe it was our own birth or re-birth—I don't know. And She has something to do with it." She pointed at the weaving of the birthing woman on the wall.

Connie's feelings about the birthing woman were similar to Emma's initial reaction: shock and disorientation. She didn't quite know what this creature stood for, but she was obviously giving birth to something. And she appeared to be as powerful as anything could get.

Emma said, "I had such strange feelings that evening on the beach. I was scared, as if I had lost my bearings. But when I touched the rock, I felt everything was going to be OK. I wanted to keep it to myself for a while. As if there were a spell on it that I could break if I showed anyone. Its presence still makes me feel vulnerable and strong at the same time."

Lucy asked, "Is it male or female?"

Emma rolled her eyes at Lucy, ever the philosopher, making terms more precise. Emma hesitated, not knowing how much she wanted to share of her intimate life with this crowd. But she looked around and saw the faces of women who had been through so much and so much of it had never been spoken about, and she decided to speak.

"Let me back up a minute before I answer that. I have a confession to make that is quite revealing.. I rub this rock it on my skin and get feelings I haven't had in a very long time, if ever. It is extremely powerful . . . or else I am. Maybe it has nothing to do with the rock, except that it provides a passageway, a method for me to reconnect with my sexual power, reconnect with creation."

Margaret smiled. She had been hoping Emma would get here eventually. She said, "You know that rock was dealt to you and you took it, and then you became the dealer, took the initiative."

Emma blushed at the compliment but not at the fact that she could experience sexual power—or any power for that matter. "In some mysterious way," she said, "it seems to be helping me stand in my own truth."

Emma jumped up and began to walk in circles around the room. "I feel like I gave Ralph my sexuality—just gave it to him to hold onto and use as he wanted. I don't even think he required that, but I volunteered! Well, with you all as my witnesses, I am taking it back."

She walked around the circle looking each woman in the eyes. "I can have these feelings with or without him." She paused for a moment, looking at the startled faces around her. "Oh, I'll still share it with him when I want to, I guess. So to answer your question, Lucy, I would say the rock is neither male nor female—or maybe both. The best of both worlds."

Margaret, always a stickler for detail asked, "Which two worlds, male and female, or earth and sea?"

Emma thought for a moment. "I was actually thinking of spirit and body. The one side is totally smooth, no blemishes and the other side has pockmarks, flaws—it's more human. And, let's see, it rests easily on three sides," Emma said placing the rock three different ways on the table.

Diana, always the movie buff said, "Three faces...Three faces of Eve—wasn't that a movie about madness?"

Lucy put her palm on her forehead, thinking. "Ever wonder what connects women's desire with madness? There is a connection, I think, especially since knowing more about my grandmother's life. We go mad if we know what we want and can't have it. Or maybe if we pursue our desire, people think us mad? Women and desire; women and madness."

Diana laughed, "I relate to Hallie on this one. We were both determined to unwrap our desires—not keep them in a sealed container, put them up on a shelf for a more appropriate day. Hallie refused to let anyone tell her what pleasure was, or what her body was. Charles never had any illusions about 'possessing' Hallie. And look where we both ended up—her in that damned Mannington and me teetering on the edge my whole life long. A kind of mad if you do, mad if you don't scenario. Acceptance of what we're supposed to be—now that is certain madness, isn't it? And yet just the opposite will get you locked up for sure! Almost did me."

"Me, too," said Margaret. "In fact, I *was* locked up, luckily only for a few days. But it gave me time to think, and I decided I needed a divorce from my husband and the Catholic Church. Then to come out as a lesbian to boot! Now, is that crazy, I ask you?

They all laughed, not a carefree, delighted laugh, but a sharp- edged laugh at of the closeness of such things to every woman's daily life.

Connie squirmed a bit at the mention of the Catholic Church and lesbianism, but she said nothing. These women were all manifestations so far from her normal encounters that she was struggling just to keep up with the conversation. She knew it would take some time to process all of this. And things were barely getting started.

"Speaking of things that could get you locked up," said Emma, "there are a few things Lucy and I have to tell you about what has gone on here since I came."

Connie, unable to contain herself, blurted out, "You mean there's more?"

Margaret reached over and put a reassuring arm around Connie. "Hang in there … I only know part of this story but even that is mind-blowing. My advice? Just listen without judgment."

While Emma went to get her tapestries, Lucy brought out a piece of rosemary she had pinched off a very healthy rosemary plant in Valerie's garden. After Emma had laid out the tapestries around the living room floor in chronological order, Lucy said, "Before we go further, I want us to make an offering and say thank you to the ancestors. All of our ancestors were kind enough to at least give us our starts, even if they may have disappeared soon afterward." She looked at Margaret and winked. "Would it be going too far for any of you if we went out into the yard and thanked the elements, the ancestors and the directions and burned this rosemary as an offering in remembrance of them?"

The others looked at one another warily. Lucy added reassuringly, "I don't think it will be against anyone's religion or lack thereof to do this. It's about gratitude. And I learned about burning rosemary from one of the people I work with, Mattie, an eighty-year-old woman who would have been so pleased to join us in this discussion tonight. Any objections?"

No one spoke, and they filed outside to participate to the extent they felt comfortable. Lucy led the ritual, burning the rosemary in an ashtray and wafting smoke onto each woman in the circle. Connie likened it to incense and felt more comfortable.

Using the new information she had learned from Colleen's book on Siberian spirituality, Lucy had them all face east, the direction of earth, and thank the east and all beings in the east, the direction of peacemaking. Then they turned north to the direction of air, green, prosperity, health and well-being; then west, the direction of fire, red, enchantment and magic; then south, acknowledging water, dark blue, the direction of the internal warrior that fights negative emotions; then to space itself, white light of the moon, the place of unconditional love, of no limitations, of the rainbow, which includes all of the other elements. After they thanked the ancestors and the elements, they meandered back inside, ready to hear the stories.

Lucy put on the tea kettle and those who wanted tea got some, and then they returned to the living room.

After they were settled, Emma said, "Now that class is over, I just wanted to have a look at all of the weavings and share them with you." Then she added a bit shyly, "Maybe you'd like to hear their stories now, and while we are at it we can catch Diana up on some of the family stories as well."

It helped Emma to have Lucy and Margaret as backup as she began to explain the voices that came in on the wind and the rain. She did not tell every story, and Lucy jumped in with some when Emma faltered.

At first, Diana thought, oh no, more madness in the family! Maybe Emma did have Hallie's genes after all. But with both Lucy and Emma in apparent agreement over the voices, and Margaret who seemed so grounded and sensible going right along with these stories as fact, Diana's more rational side was out-voted. Besides, she was too tired to reason with them. She suspended her judgment, at least for that moment.

Connie did as Margaret had suggested and just listened without judgment.

Emma took her time explaining each weaving, beginning with the tentative name of each one. The first one, Break of Birth, was the broken eggshell with the flame inside. As she spoke, the depth of what Emma had experienced dawned on Lucy. No wonder Emma appeared so changed.

The next one was The Clean and Empty Vessel, the vase on water. Emma explained that it had come through a dream image with those words attached. Remembering the dream image, Emma said, "It had something to do with my being clean and empty so that I could hear the voices. I had to clear out old voices to make way for the new ones—not exactly new, but different. The lips at the top represent speaking, perhaps?"

Connie said, "You mean what you are doing now—telling us?"

Emma nodded, "Maybe so, though I think this is just the beginning."

Diana was intrigued. The stories, the weavings—everything so carefully orchestrated. But by whom? She asked herself, by whom? Diana's interest was drawn to the next piece, Kathleen's weaving of the pregnant woman as part of a wavy seascape. Emma had titled it "Normal Illusions." Emma reiterated the story she had told Kathleen that had prompted this weaving. Emma's story seemed to Diana in keeping with the Emma she used to know, the one she had always thought of as so utterly, unalterably normal. But she could see by looking at Emma that she had changed.

As Emma and Lucy filled the others in on Hallie's and Alice's stories, Diana felt turned around and turned around again, until she was dizzy from the turning. The stories rang so true; she couldn't imagine who else could have known save Hallie and Alice themselves. Obviously, Emma's world view wasn't the only one that was shifting. She seemed to be pulling all of those around her into a vortex of suspended beliefs.

And still they wanted more. As if guided by a conductor, all five sets of eyes moved from Normal Illusions toward the woman birthing.

Emma smiled, "I guess we should call it Mother of God. Maybe I'll come around to seeing it that way. Lightening hasn't struck yet. I'll put a question mark after the title, at least until I'm sure."

Diana was struck by this apparent reversal in Emma's feelings about religion. But when Emma explained the assignment and how both Pilar's and her weavings had been transformed, Diana followed the logic. Emma finished by telling them what had happened earlier that day with Pilar. "I was not in control—it was sobbing me—that's what it felt like."

Lucy looked alarmed, "I'm surprised you didn't mention it earlier. Are you OK?"

"That's the strange part. After it was over, I felt so much better than I ever have, as if a dam burst, letting the water flow freely, as it was meant to flow.

In the weaving, a woman's water had just broken and she was giving birth to the elements themselves. There was no actual baby, but instead the elements of earth, air, fire, water, and—if the Siberian philosophy were true—the space that surrounds it all. The woman was life force itself. The Big Birth instead of the Big Bang. Lucy thought of reading the myth that she had been writing these last few days, but she didn't want to take away from Emma's night. It *was* her night, after all. Lucy's thoughts were churning from the stimulation. From women's sexual power, to the voices of women past and present, to the future of womanhood itself. Oh, this was fodder for her next three books.

Diana felt herself swept away by the power of Emma's journey. Her discarded doubts became like the many shavings beneath a sculptor's feet. "Maybe it's not the world that has to change—maybe it's us, each one of us." Diana looked at Emma lovingly. "You did it—I don't know if it was the weaving class, these ghosts, or just your being away from home..."

Emma focused on her last weaving with an intensity that put her into a near trance. Emma explained that it was called "Tidal Exchange," since it was about the exchange between land and sea. But she also meant it to refer to the exchange she had made with others in the class—the collaborative effort that they had just finished.

Emma spoke very softly, and Diana and Lucy strained to hear her. "Funny, how I feel this one is more me than any of the others, though it is the one that four other people worked on." She reached in her pocket for the rock and stroked it as she struggled to speak a truth that she herself hadn't known. Thinking not just about the class but about her visits with her ancestors, she said quietly, "With each exchange, I feel more myself."

Words gave way to image. Long past midnight Emma and Lucy showed Diana, Margaret and Connie the way to their beds. Maybe three bedrooms with five beds had been just the right number after all.

After the guests were settled, Emma and Lucy stood for a moment at the living room window, the boarded-up old fireplace at their backs, as they watched the moon set over land and sea. Swallowing the moonlight, both Lucy and Emma were more spacious than they had ever imagined. They did not end at this skin, at this lifetime, on this finite island of time. Their lineage did not end with Lucy. Finally, they could feel where their strands joined with so many others in earth's tapestry: with the stories of the ancestors, the rocks and the oceans and tides, the animals, the creative energies of this world, and elemental time itself.

For more information about the author and the author's ideas about what happened to these characters, please see the web site: www.ArtBetweenUs.org where you will find an afterward (that includes the myth Lucy wrote) and an epilogue.

On that website you can also find information about Art Between Us, Inc, a non-profit organization dedicated to teaching and making collaborative art similar to that of the Peace Weavers in this book.

The sequel to *Strands*, called *Between Here and Hereafter* will be coming out in the not-too-distant future.

Made in the USA
Charleston, SC
19 December 2009